BLIND EYE

BLIND EYE

JOHN MORGAN WILSON

ST. MARTIN'S MINOTAUR
NEW YORK

Every character in this novel is purely fictional and any resemblance to a real person, living or dead, is strictly coincidental. Likewise, a number of churches or parishes, as well as their names and locations, are used for fictional purposes and are not meant to duplicate or suggest any from real life. Though inspired by real-life events, *Blind Eye* is a work of fiction throughout.

www.minotaurbooks.com

Library of Congress Cataloging-in-Publication Data

Wilson, John M., 1945-
    Blind eye / John Morgan Wilson.—1st ed.
        p.   cm.
    ISBN 0-312-30919-8
    1. Justice, Benjamin (Fictitious character)—Fiction.   2. Journalists—
Crimes against—Fiction.   3. Los Angeles (Calif.)—Fiction.
    4. HIV-positive men—Fiction.   5. Gay men—Fiction.   I. Title.

PS3573.I456974B58 2003
813'.54—dc21

                                                            2003046828

First Edition: October 2003

10   9   8   7   6   5   4   3   2   1

for Pietro

who keeps the home and heart fires burning

ACKNOWLEDGMENTS

As with all novels, many people make contributions, directly and indirectly, in addition to the author. In the case of *Blind Eye*, my editor at St. Martin's Press, Keith Kahla, deserves special praise for his exceptional wisdom and insight, and the gentle and effective way he conveyed it during the revision process. I must also single out my longtime agent, Alice Martell, for showing me the way to St. Martin's; my friend, fellow writer Larry Kase, for the many times he's helped with research; my fellow members at Sisters in Crime (www.sistersincrime.org) and Mystery Writers of America (www.mysterywriters.org) for their support, in so many ways; to the Lambda Literary Foundation (www.lambdalit.org), for its support and promotion of literature that may not fit conveniently into certain mainstream categories or onto some commercial bookshelves; and to the many librarians and booksellers who have supported the Benjamin Justice novels through the years. I also wish to acknowledge two valuable resource books: *Los Angeles: An Architectural Guide*, by David Gebhard and Robert Milton Winter; and *Los Angeles A to Z: An Encyclopedia of the City and County*, by Leonard Pitt and Dale Pitt.

BLIND EYE

ONE

I began my search for Fr. Stuart Blackley in the cool of October when I'd just turned forty-five.

The reassuring brightness and warmth of summer were gone. The slanting light and crisp colors of early autumn were starting to fade. It was that time of year when the shadows deepen early, dusk falls suddenly, and—if your mind is conflicted—an unsettling chill creeps into your life like an unwelcome visitor moving in.

My mind was often in conflict, so that was nothing new. But thinking about Father Blackley after so many years was stirring uneasy feelings I hadn't anticipated, which made getting through the day that much harder. The walls felt close, the short days oppressive, the loss of light threatening, all for no good reason. I might be walking down the street and see a shriveled leaf floating in the gutter, or hear a child wail, or glimpse a hummingbird sucking furiously for fuel at a sugary feeder and shudder without explanation. I felt something coming after me, but I couldn't flee; the weight on me was too great, yet I didn't know what the weight was, or why it was there, or what it represented. At times, I felt so crushed, so compacted, I was afraid I'd stop breathing. Tears were always near the surface, which wasn't like me. I was smart enough to know it had something to do with Father Blackley, which made finding him all the more important.

In my mind, I saw him as I last remembered him, beckoning to me from his rectory door while I eagerly responded, thrilled by a mix of excitement and fear, shame and desire.

"Benjamin," he'd whispered, glancing furtively about while laying a hand on my downy neck. "Come in, why don't you? We need to talk. Be quick!"

He'd been in his early forties then, a decent looking man of average height and build, with a kindly smile, mild amber eyes behind black-rimmed spectacles, and brown hair neatly clipped and always carefully combed; his dress that day had been a full-length black cassock and a cleric's comfort collar, his customary uniform. I'd just turned fourteen, my body changing fast, feeling strangely possessed by a wild and independent energy beyond my comprehension or control. I was growing up, Father Blackley had pointed out; his feelings for me were different now, though he assured me we could still be friends. The important thing, he'd added, was that we keep our special friendship to ourselves. He'd stroked my blond head fondly, his voice warm and reassuring, as he told me how much he trusted me to keep our secret. Still, I'd glimpsed a trace of fear in his manner, as faint and fleeting as the shadow of a flighty wren; his eyes, in particular, had betrayed him. We'd knelt and prayed, the two of us alone, as always. He'd just come from showering and I could smell his spicy aftershave, which I'd always found intoxicating. It was the last time we'd commune with God together, but without the affection and touching and other feverish activity that had always preceded our prayers. Since my first time alone with him, when I was twelve, Father Blackley had made me feel special. I'd loved him profoundly. But suddenly, not two years later, as I'd turned fourteen, he was finished with me.

Now, after three decades, I wasn't sure just what I'd do when I found him. Confront him, certainly—but how? Would I be content with a confession, and the details I needed for the autobiography I was writing, recounting my troubled and complicated life? Would I demand to know if I'd been the only boy, or if

2

there'd been others? Or would I be tempted to put my hands around his wrinkled throat and strangle the life out of him, drawing once again on the combustible rage that had shaped so much of my behavior for so many years in ways I was only beginning to understand?

I had no idea where my search would lead me. I only knew that I needed to find Father Blackley and ask him some questions. I'd been a reporter once, a good one. When I want to find someone to ask him questions, I usually do.

"Here's to your search for the errant priest." Alexandra Templeton raised her flute of non-alcoholic champagne, as we sat on the front porch of the little house on Norma Place. "To your quest, Justice. May it end successfully."

"And what about you?" My blue eyes sought out the deep brown in hers. "You deserve a toast, Alex."

"Your turn then."

"No, you pick. Toast yourself. Something really important."

"Why?" She smiled mischievously. "Because you can't think of anything?"

I shrugged, more with affection than carelessness. "So I'll know." I laughed a little. "So I won't get it wrong."

"OK." She lifted her glass once more. "To my engagement to the wisest, most courageous and affectionate man I've ever been blessed to know."

"I thought that was me."

She smiled again, letting her lively eyes do the laughing, while she touched her crystal flute to mine, making the rims chime.

At thirty-two, Alexandra Templeton was still the most gorgeous female creature I'd ever encountered, with a willowy figure, lustrous ebony skin, and flawless facial features worthy of an African princess. She might have been a movie actress or a supermodel but she'd chosen a career as an investigative reporter instead; inspired, in part, by articles of mine she'd read while still in college. We were drawn together by a mysterious force, two odd pieces locked in an improbable mosaic, although we couldn't have been much different, physically and otherwise. I was as blond and fair as she was dark, as slack and paunchy as she was toned and erect, happily going bald and careless about my clothes, while she was the fashion plate with the ever-changing coiffure. In life, I was alone again, with a contract to write a book that seemed like a gift from God to someone who hadn't held down a decent job in more than a decade. Given my unpredictable mental state, I had serious concerns that I might fail to deliver the manuscript as promised. My health was a constant question mark, monitored by blood tests and dependent on pharmaceuticals for stability. Templeton, on the other hand, radiated energy and well-being, and never took a pill. While my career was a shambles, her reputation as a reporter for the biggest newspaper on the West Coast was vaunted and unblemished. Most of all, she seemed deeply and truly happy, with an impending marriage that would probably mean motherhood as well.

That is, if the union lasted. To me, that seemed problematic. Templeton's one deficiency of character in the eight years I'd known her had been her questionable choice in men, and I wasn't sure she'd learned her lessons yet. Her fiancé, Joe Soto, was a charismatic and uncompromising columnist for the *Los Angeles Times,* unafraid to tackle the most sensitive issues, which made him damned attractive. I liked the guy, a lot. But he'd also been married a couple of times before, and was known to strut among the ladies like a rooster. Joe also had a longtime love affair with the bottle—we'd shared more than a few drinks after work before I'd self-destructed as a journalist—and he could turn angry and combative faster than you could say Wild Turkey.

Templeton knew all that, of course. Joe had changed, she'd told me. Like me, he'd been off the sauce for a couple of years now. Pushing fifty, he was finally settled in his own skin, ready to appreciate life without alcohol as a social lubricant, an antidote to insecurity, or an anesthetic for the pain. At least that was how Templeton saw him. I hoped she was right, although it was none of my business at any rate. My business consisted of taking my pills, paying my bills, and somehow getting through another day. Beyond that, I wanted as little involvement as possible with other people's lives.

"So where's the ring?" I asked.

She shook her head. "No can do. The *Times* has a policy against married employees. For now, we're keeping the romance hush-hush."

"Except for me?"

"I wouldn't keep the truth from you, Justice. We've been through too much together. When the time comes, Joe and I will solve the work problem. Meanwhile, his family knows, along with our closest friends. Just not anyone at the paper."

"I'm happy for you, Templeton, I really am." I sipped the harmless bubbly, worked up a smile. "I wish the two of you nothing but joy, prosperity and lots of beautiful brown babies."

"One or two will suffice, thanks, and not for a few more years." She reached over as we sat in the swing, taking my hand. "He's a fine man, Justice. He makes me feel good about myself. Treats me like a real person, an equal. Makes me laugh. That's not so bad."

"Let's get down to essentials. Is he good in the sack, or not?"

She showed me a dreamy smile. "In a word, *primo*."

"Details, please."

"Passionate, uninhibited, unselfish." She held up a cautionary finger. "That's as far as I go. No graphic details."

I winked. "Far enough to make me jealous."

Nearby, on a corner of the porch, one of the cats stirred. Templeton looked away for a moment, watching it stretch like a yogi. When she glanced back, her face was more thoughtful.

"And what about you, Justice? How are you holding up these days?"

"I'm healthy, all things considered. I have some money in the bank, from the advance on the book. That's quite a change. No one special in my life, now that it's over between Oree and me."

"Acting the recluse again?"

"It suits me, now that Oree's gone."

Templeton had introduced me to Oree Joffrien four years ago, hoping we might hit it off, which we had. He'd been a professor of anthropology at UCLA then, a tall, handsome black man with a deep intelligence, infinite patience and an open, accepting heart. I'd loved him in a serious way, which may have been the problem. Loving someone means having something to lose. Loneliness often seemed preferable to more loss, a different kind of pain, but bearable.

"You must miss him," Templeton said.

"I'm doing OK."

"You sure?"

I nodded. "I need to put my life back together in my own way, standing on my own two feet. Oree was too good, too strong. I was leaning on him too much. I hated the idea that he was paying the bills." I shrugged, trying hard to sell it. "Besides, he deserves someone better."

She slapped at me, without touching. "Stop that!"

"It's the truth, all the same. I did him a favor, breaking up."

"He cared bunches about you."

"Helped me get my book deal, before he moved to Europe. I'll always owe him that."

"This autobiography could be very good for you, Justice." She studied me keenly, from an angle. "It could help you figure some things out, put some issues in the past. And finally start over, for real this time."

I laughed carelessly. "Somehow, my name on a book cover doesn't jibe with how I see myself. After all, I live in a one-room apartment over a garage, behind an old house in West Hollywood. Except for a restored '65 Mustang, I own nothing of value. For the last couple of years, I've laid low, keeping my nose out of places it doesn't belong."

She raised her eyebrows, smiling. "No easy feat for you."

"As for my name—we both know what's happened to that, don't we?"

"Benjamin Justice." She spoke it crisply, as if trying it out. "I think it's a fine name to go on a book."

"You're turning into a cheerleader again, Templeton. I'm starting to get the sugar blues."

"This book is a very big deal in your life, Benjamin. Go on, admit it."

I shrugged. "It's something to do, a way to keep the bills paid."

"And Father Blackley is part of that something." She sought out my eyes, making me look at her. "Finding him is awfully important to you, isn't it?"

Out on the street, dusk was smothering the last of the light. A mother passed, humming as she pushed a baby stroller, looking incredibly content. Across Norma Place, two men walked their dog, holding hands, laughing easily. They all seemed so grown up, so comfortable with themselves, so normal.

My gaze swung slowly back to Alexandra Templeton. She was my closest friend in the world. Still, there were things I couldn't share with her, things I couldn't explain. I sensed the wind come up, chilling the air, shivering the leaves. Streetlights flickered on, but darkness was all around. I could feel it, closing in like plague, like grief, like a memory that causes you to tremble but you can't shake.

Fr. Stuart Blackley. I could feel his hands on me even now.

"I'd like to ask him some questions," I said.

TWO

That autumn, as I began my search for Fr. Stuart Blackley, the sex scandal involving priests of the Roman Catholic Church continued unabated. In the preceding couple of years, hundreds of priests in the U.S. had resigned after being accused of child molestation and dozens more had gone to jail. Tens of millions of dollars had been paid out to settle liability claims, possibly much more that wasn't being revealed. Virtually every U.S. diocese had been caught up in the scandal, made all the worse because so many bishops had known for decades about the abuse. More than just known—they'd carefully covered it up and dodged the law, continuing to employ many of the abusers, some of whom were high-ranking clergy themselves.

No one really knew how many more priests were guilty of molesting or raping young boys and girls, although the authorities were aware of some who'd fled the United States to avoid investigation or arrest, sometimes with the encouragement and assistance of the Church. Because of legal delays and the ongoing subterfuge of the Church, the statute of limitations had run out on hundreds of cases that would never be tried. Together, the Archdiocese of Los Angeles and the Diocese of Orange serving Orange County were faced with so many lawsuits between them—more than three hundred—that a judge was considering combining their cases into a single trial, to ensure that all victims would be fairly compensated before the liability coverage was depleted. The notion that significant numbers of ordained priests had used their positions of religious authority to prey on vulnerable children was no longer in doubt or dispute. What remained for speculation was only how many victims were still uncounted, how many molesters had escaped exposure or prosecution, and whether top officials of the Church who had engineered the massive cover-up would ever face punishment themselves.

I didn't really give a damn about that. The larger world and its problems were not my concern anymore. I simply wanted to find Father Blackley, ask my questions, write my book, collect the rest of my advance and be done with it.

I began looking in the most likely place, as trained reporters tend to do—even those like me who have been drummed from the trade. That meant my hometown of Buffalo in upstate New York, where Father Blackley had been the pastor at the parish my family had attended throughout my childhood. When I phoned the office of the governing diocese, I figured that locating my old priest would be a relatively easy matter. I was wrong.

When the administrator at the other end was silent for a moment, I realized that using my legal name had probably been a mistake. When I'd killed my father at the age of seventeen— emptying his .38 Detective's Special into him—I'd been known as Benjamin Osborn, son of Buffalo homicide detective Benjamin Osborn, a boy who'd inherited his father's brashness, volatile temper, and taste for alcohol. Soon after my father's death was ruled a justifiable homicide, I'd fled the city, running from my past and hoping for a fresh start. My first step had been to legally change my last name to my mother's maiden name, Justice. Now, not quite thirty years later, the name Benjamin Justice was tainted as well—the reporter who'd been famously ruined by a Pulitzer scandal, never again to be trusted or believed. That kind of notoriety had helped get me a hundred-and-fifty-thousand-dollar advance to write my autobiography. But the name could also put people on guard, as it was doing now.

"I'm not asking you to put me in direct contact with Father Blackley," I told the church administrator. "A post office box would do, or an e-mail address. I merely want to write to him, in the hope that he writes back."

"And what does this concern?"

"That would be between me and Father Blackley."

She asked me to hold the line a moment. In fact, she was away for nearly ten minutes. When she returned, her manner was terse. "Father Blackley is no longer with the diocese. He left us twenty-seven years ago, back in 1976."

"He renounced his vows?"

"He was reassigned. I'm afraid that's all I can say."

"Surely you can tell me where."

"We don't discuss confidential personnel matters, Mr. Justice."

"You know who I am, don't you? You recognized the name."

She hesitated a moment. "I'm familiar with your background, yes. From old news accounts. Since leaving journalism, you've gotten yourself involved in some high profile murder investigations. Not always invited or welcome."

"Then you have a pretty good idea how I work."

"You're known to be rather determined, as I recall. Also, a bit reckless."

"Lady, I can be as tenacious as a pit bull, when I get my teeth into something."

"Really, Mr. Justice, I—"

"If you won't help me, I'll be on the next plane for Buffalo and on your doorstep in the morning. Is that how you want this to go?"

In the silence that followed, I could almost hear the seconds ticking by. Finally, sounding piqued, the woman said, "You might try the Los Angeles archdiocese."

My gut tightened. "Father Blackley's here, in L.A.?"

"I'm afraid I've already told you more than I should. Good luck, Mr. Justice."

There was a click as she hung up.

For several minutes, I sat stock still in the two-room apartment I'd rented for years from my elderly landlords, Maurice and Fred.

The Norma Triangle where we lived was situated at the west end of West Hollywood, nearly on the border of Beverly Hills. It was a leafy neighborhood of small, quaint houses, once middle-class but now pricey, an enclave of quiet in a city more famous for its exuberant nightlife. Named for the angling street that provided its triangular shape, the Norma Triangle was far enough between the bustling club scenes of the Sunset Strip and Santa Monica Boulevard to seem like a world removed, although each was only a few blocks away, north and south. In the Triangle, it usually took a wailing siren to disturb the hush, and there were no sirens to be heard at the moment. The insistent sound now was of my own anxious breathing.

Father Blackley, here in Los Angeles. Closer than I'd ever imagined.

I took a deep breath, trying to understand why that felt so unsettling. Twenty-seven years since he'd left Buffalo, she'd said. Father Blackley would be an old man now, in his early seventies if my math was right. Without recognizing him, I might have passed him on the street, driven by a church where he was conducting Mass, glimpsed him in his vestments during ceremonies on some holy day. Surely, with all the attention I'd drawn, all the media coverage of my various exploits, he must have been aware that I was here as well. Within reach of him, and he within reach of me. Was it possible he'd never noticed, never made the connection to my altered name, never seen the face of the boy in the face of the man? And, if he had, had it bothered him, given him a moment's pause, caused him to feel anything at all?

I had to know.

I found myself shaking so badly my teeth rattled. I realized then that pursuing Father Blackley might not be the best course, given my health issues, my fragile mental state, and my need for a calm and stable life. Letting this Father Blackley business go, writing around the holes and blanks, would have been the wiser choice.

The problem was I had to know. Not knowing was unacceptable.

Next morning, I placed a notebook and pen on the kitchen table and dragged the phone over from beside the bed. Down in the rear yard, Fred mowed the lawn while Maurice picked dead blossoms off the honeysuckle vine. It was something they'd done together one morning each week, weather permitting, for nearly fifty years, since buying the little house on Norma Place as a couple in the 1950s. Maurice looked up, waving extravagantly from his slender wrist. Then he mimed drinking from a cup, pointing toward the house and inviting me down for coffee. I showed him my notebook and pen, we each shrugged, and I got down to work.

My first call was to the headquarters of the Roman Catholic Archdiocese of Los Angeles, whose over four million parishioners made it the largest diocese in the country. An automated answering system offered me the option of a staff directory. When I accessed it, I failed to find Fr. Stuart Blackley among the names.

I returned to the original menu and started over, this time working my way through the options to the public affairs department. I informed a low-level administrator that I was seeking the whereabouts of Fr. Stuart Blackley, who had once been assigned to the Los Angeles archdiocese. The official asked me to repeat Father Blackley's name, which I did. He then suggested I put my request in writing, along with my reasons for seeking contact with Father Blackley, and send it through the mail. I complied, although the reasons I gave were vague and less than forthright.

Not quite a week later, a letter arrived from the office of Bishop Anthony Finatti, on his official pastoral region letterhead.

Dear Mr. Justice:

I am responding to your request for information about Fr. Stuart Blackley, a priest who was assigned to a number of parishes within the Los Angeles archdiocese over a period of roughly seventeen years, beginning in 1976.

Sadly, Father Blackley died in a hiking accident in 1992. You will find his remains interred in a small plot reserved for priests located behind the Church of the Blessed Sacrament in the city of Whittier in east Los Angeles County, the last parish where Father Blackley presided in his service to our Lord.

I hope you find this information helpful. May God be with you each and every day.

Sincerely,
The Most Reverand

Anthony Finatti

Regional Bishop, St. Agnes Pastoral Region
The Roman Catholic Archdiocese of Los Angeles

So, Father Blackley was dead.

I turned to the nearest wall in my apartment, leaning my head against it, fighting the urge to vomit. I began perspiring but at the same time felt cold, almost icy. Panic hovered, triggered by a sudden feeling of emptiness—as if a gaping hole had just opened inside me that I knew I'd never fill. I went to the bathroom, bent over the grubby sink, splashed water on my face. In the mirror, my eyes looked so troubled that I turned quickly away, back into my room. For many years, the small room had felt cozy and comforting, a Spartan but necessary refuge. Now, it seemed frightfully small, like a prisoner's cell. I sat on the edge of my unmade bed, staring at the hardwood floor, trying to get my bearings.

Father Blackley, gone.

There had to be another way to bring him back, I thought; a way to fill in the blanks, at least some of them. A diary, perhaps, or personal letters, or a psychiatrist's file, even if I had to steal it. Some way to answer the persistent questions. Why he'd chosen me. Whether I'd played some role in the seduction, even at the age of twelve. If I'd been his first, and his last. Countless questions, many still unformed, but that haunted me just the same.

Back in the eighties, I'd written plenty of investigative pieces without ever interviewing the primary subject, the target of my inquiry. Dogged reporters did it all the time. When you encountered an obstacle, you used it for inspiration, redoubling your efforts. You went to secondary and inside sources, people with a reason to get the truth out, or just an ax to grind: ex-wives, fired employees, disgruntled relatives, righteous whistleblowers, or some low-level person with a trace of sympathy who might open a file drawer for you, if only for a minute.

Sometimes, I reminded myself, you deliberately sought out people of good conscience, who had the information you needed or could point you to it, and you worked on them until they caved. That's when I remembered Sister Catherine Timothy.

"Benjamin? Is that really you?"

I recognized the voice of Sister Catherine Timothy as if time had stood still. The tone was still warm and effusive, the cadence energetic.

"It's me, Sister, calling from Los Angeles."

"The switchboard announced you as Benjamin Osborn. Have you changed your name back?"

"Only long enough to get through, Sister. How are you? It's been a while."

"More than thirty years, hasn't it?"

"I was fourteen when I stopped attending Sunday Mass." I did the math. "Yes, just over thirty years."

"I've followed the news of you in the press. My goodness, what a life you've led. I sent letters, tried to keep track of you, but I never heard back."

"I'm sorry about that, Sister. I was never much at staying in touch, after what happened."

"Things have been hard for you, haven't they?"

"I caused a lot of it myself."

"You went through a terrible ordeal, Benjamin, at such a tender age. My goodness, seventeen. What your father did to your little sister—"

"And what I did to him, with his own gun."

"You acted in defense of Elizabeth Jane, everyone knew that. She was just a child. I don't know anyone who holds it against you. I imagine God forgave you a long time ago, if you even needed forgiving at all."

I laughed a little. "You haven't changed much, Sister. You're just as kind and compassionate as you always were. I'll bet your smile can still melt butter."

"I'm an old woman now, Benjamin. Old and wrinkled and ugly as a goat. But my heart's in the same place. I'm still close to our Lord and Savior. I still pray for you, you know. You were always in my prayers."

"I'm not sure they've helped."

"You sound troubled, Benjamin." She paused, but I was silent. "There must be a reason you've called me after all this time."

"I need your help, Sister."

"In what way, dear?"

"I have some questions about Father Blackley."

She paused, while I imagined the curious cock of her head. "Father Stuart Blackley?"

"Yes."

"He left the parish, an awfully long time ago. Reassigned to Los Angeles, out your way."

"Yes, I knew that much."

"He died some time back. Must be a good ten years now. Bishop Finatti of the Los Angeles archdiocese was kind enough to notify us. If it's information on Father Blackley you need, you might try the Bishop. He and Stuart Blackley were lifelong friends, from childhood."

"That I hadn't known."

"They grew up together, right here in Buffalo. So if anyone can help, I'm sure it's Bishop Finatti."

"People out here tend not to talk to me, given my reputation."

"Why such an interest in Father Blackley, Benjamin?"

"I'm writing my autobiography. There are a few holes I need to fill in. Things about Father Blackley he can't tell me now."

"Your autobiography—isn't that wonderful! When's it coming out? I'll be sure to buy a copy."

"I'm just now planning it, Sister, pulling the research together."

"Of course—books take a while to write, don't they? Things about Father Blackley, you said. What exactly do you need to know?"

"I'm not sure, Sister, to be perfectly honest."

"You are troubled, Benjamin. I can hear it in your voice. What's happened?"

"Tell me what you can about him. Anything at all."

"Goodness, I haven't thought about Stuart Blackley in longer than I can remember. I was new to the parish when he was here. I didn't know him terribly well. He was a nice man, outgoing, active. Good with children, I remember that much."

"Not so good as you might think."

"How's that, dear?"

I took a deep breath. "When I was twelve, Father Blackley took a special interest in me."

"He took an interest in many of the boys, Benjamin. Girls, too, as I recall. Especially children who were having trouble at home."

"Kids like me who were looking for a father figure, an adult male to be close to, to trust."

"Exactly."

"Kids who would do almost anything to feel affection from a man. Even if it meant letting Father Blackley do whatever he wanted with us."

I heard a quick intake of breath at the other end. "Benjamin, what are you saying?"

"I think you know what I'm saying, Sister."

"Oh my Lord." Over the phone, I heard the rustle of garments and assumed she was making the sign of the cross. "Why didn't you come to me, Benjamin, all those years ago? If not me, someone else?"

"For all kinds of reasons, some you wouldn't understand. Besides, no one talked about those things then, did they? No one really wanted to hear it, Sister. Better to sweep it under the rug, for the sake of appearances. The way my mother would have preferred it, when she learned that my father was messing with Elizabeth Jane."

"God bless their souls," Sister Catherine Timothy said. "They both died, didn't they, while you were still a young man?"

"It didn't help that I ran away, after what I'd done, leaving them on their own. In some ways, I've been running ever since."

"If only you'd come to me, long before things got so bad. I would have listened, Benjamin. I surely would have." Her voice quavered. "This is extremely distressing, hearing this. Your revelations about Father Blackley, I mean. It comes as a complete shock." She sounded near tears. "How could we not have seen?"

"These kind of men are good at hiding things, Sister. Especially when the Church offers cover. You must know that by now, with everything that's come out."

"It's been so troubling, Benjamin. The lies, the deception, while so many children suffered." Her voice grew sharp. "Damn them all, for what they've done."

"You're still different, Sister. You're not like the others."

"How do you mean, dear?"

"The truth is important to you, first and foremost. You always taught me that."

"I'm not without my flaws, Benjamin. I'm not infallible. No one is."

"But your heart's with God. You said so."

"Yes, I did, didn't I?"

I adopted a tougher tone, almost accusatory. "Actions speak louder than words, Sister."

A long moment passed before she spoke again. When she did, her voice was firm, resolute. "What is it you need? If I can help, I will."

"Any details about Father Blackley and his private activities that you can give me, any way you can get them. There must be files, old records, things like that."

"Of course, they'd be confidential."

"Of course."

"Toward what purpose, Benjamin?"

"You know the old saying—the story's in the details. I'd like to flesh Father Blackley out as much as possible, give him some dimension in my book."

"You always were an inquisitive boy, weren't you? So many questions, so little patience." I heard a deep intake of breath, a slow exhalation. "I'm so sorry about what happened to you, Benjamin. So terribly sorry."

"Just help me, Sister, if you can. That's what I need now."

"You need to find your way back to the Church, Benjamin. We're still here for you, you know. For every Father Blackley, there are many good priests who never touched a child improperly."

"Right now, Father Blackley is the only priest who interests me."

"Yes, of course. I understand."

Sister Catherine Timothy suggested we have no more contact with each other, at least not for some time. Just before she hung up, she promised to continue praying for me.

Down in the yard, on the lawn, one of the cats stalked a lizard. One paw at a time, placed delicately in front of the other, inching closer. I could just make out the narrow whip of the reptile's tail rising above the blades of grass, which were almost ready for another mowing by Fred. Forward with a paw, then stop. Another paw, stop. Back to the other paw, stop. Suddenly, the cat froze, all alertness and stealth. Silently, almost imperceptibly, it bunched its shoulder muscles for the kill.

At that moment—why that moment I have no idea—a thought struck me that had been lost to me in the chaos of my feelings when I'd first read Bishop Finatti's letter informing me that Father Blackley was dead. Looking back, it seemed odd to me that it took a letter on my part to such a high official—and a note from the bishop in return—to elicit the simple fact that a priest had met an accidental death ten years before. Couldn't something so routine have been handled over the phone, by a low level administrator, when I'd first called? What was so different about Fr. Stuart Blackley that required Bishop Anthony Finatti to intercede?

The cat pounced. The lizard scrambled, but too late. I watched it wriggle frantically, its tail in the teeth of the predator. A life-and-death struggle, or so it seemed. Then the tail broke and the lizard darted for the safety of Maurice's rock garden. The cat leaped and whirled, trying to reclaim the lizard as it slithered away. But it was gone, safe among the rocks to grow a new tail and live another life.

The cat sniffed around for a minute before giving up. Then it turned back toward the house, reptilian tail proudly in mouth, while I continued to ponder why one deceased priest out of thousands might warrant such special treatment.

THREE

Several days after my conversation with Sister Catherine Timothy, a bulky envelope arrived postmarked Buffalo, but with no return address. I opened it to find a bundle of photocopied documents, several inches thick. I also discovered a small, simple crucifix carved of dark wood, attached to amber beads, just like the rosary Sister Catherine Timothy had always carried with her.

I was spreading the contents of the package on my kitchen table when Alexandra Templeton tapped on my screen door. She was dressed for serious work, making a statement in a sharply cut suit and heels, her long hair braided and woven neatly into an elaborate bun that added to her already formidable dignity. On one arm hung a Louis Vuitton handbag that must have set her back a couple of thousand dollars, unless it was yet another gift from her wealthy father, a corporate attorney who doted outlandishly on his only child. Templeton wasn't just one of the most accomplished reporters in the city, she was easily the best dressed.

"I was passing through," she explained, "on my way to an interview with the Beverly Hills D.A. I thought I'd drag you from seclusion for some lunch. Hungry?"

"Preoccupied."

"A man has to eat." She glanced at the big table, covered now with photocopied papers. "What's all this?"

"I'm about to find out. Interested?"

She glanced at the postmark on the envelope. "Buffalo— Father Blackley?"

"Looks that way."

"Where's the phone book?" She found it before I could answer, and began pressing buttons on her cell phone. "I'll order Chinese, have it delivered."

Over the next half hour, we examined dozens of documents related to several claims of child sexual abuse against Fr. Stuart Blackley, from the years when he'd served with the Buffalo diocese.

The papers included angry, anxious or distraught letters from parents; more formal letters on official letterhead exchanged between lawyers, and legal contracts settling secret lawsuits for sizable sums of money and stamped CONFIDENTIAL. In each settlement, the parents had agreed to a permanent gag order, promising never to speak publicly about their claims. Among the papers were also copies of letters from the bishop to parents, suggesting that by taking their complaints to the police they might subject their children to humiliation in the courts and in the press. He urged them to let the Church handle the matter privately, and they'd apparently complied. In the same letters, the bishop assured them that Father Blackley had been reassigned far from Buffalo, where he was undergoing counseling that was certain to help him find his way back to God and avoid the temptations placed in his path by the devil.

"Here's a letter from Monsignor Anthony Finatti in 1976," Templeton said, showing it to me. "Promising the bishop in Buffalo that he'd keep Father Blackley under his personal supervision here in Los Angeles."

"They were childhood pals," I said, "according to my source in Buffalo."

"Finatti's certainly risen through the ranks since then. Right up near the top, as Cardinal Doyle's right hand man. Doesn't hurt that he's got a law degree, especially now, with so many lawsuits being filed against the archdiocese."

From the documents, it appeared that Father Blackley had been caught in six molestation cases, four involving boys, two involving girls, all in the age range of ten to thirteen. Sister Catherine Timothy had blacked out the names, addresses and phone numbers of the victims, but had taken the trouble to type a brief physical description of each. The boys had all been blond and blue-eyed, and solidly built for their age, as I had been; the girls, slight and dark, and on the younger end of the age spectrum. At one time, a pile of evidence like this would have been shocking. Now, with all that had come out in the press, it seemed almost mundane.

"Isn't it unusual," Templeton asked, "a pedophile attracted to both genders? I thought they tended to follow patterns, one or the other."

"Generally, but not always." From my experience as a reporter, I knew that child molesters were sometimes attracted to both males and females, though the age group and physical type tended to be consistent within the gender. Male victims had predominated in the priest sex scandal, nationwide as well as locally. It was something certain Church officials were emphasizing, as if homosexuality alone accounted for the problem. Although a closer look revealed a different picture. Only last year, for the *Los Angeles Times,* Templeton had compiled a list of nearly three dozen priests within the Los Angeles archdiocese who were under investigation or prosecution for child sexual abuse, or were already serving jail time. Slightly more than two thirds of the cases involved boys, the rest girls, some of whom had been impregnated. In at least one case, the offending priest had secretly paid for a teenager's abortion. Even with the statute of limitations expired in many cases, the L.A. district attorney had vowed to keep digging, looking for something he could prosecute.

Looking back, it occurred to me that I'd never seen Father

Blackley's name or face in Templeton's gallery of molesters. Had he been there, I surely would have noticed.

"You're right," Templeton said, when I brought it up. "My report included priests who'd abused children going back twenty years. The ones we knew about, anyway. Father Blackley wasn't among the bunch."

"Maybe he learned his lesson back in Buffalo." I worked hard to put resolve in my voice. "Maybe he was one of those rare molesters for whom therapy was successful. Or maybe they kept him away from kids."

Templeton's eyes landed on mine, but only briefly. "Sure, that could explain it."

Our food arrived, Templeton paid, and we got busy with our chopsticks. As we ate, she asked me what I intended to do about Father Blackley.

I shrugged. "See if I can pry loose anything more from the L.A. archdiocese."

"You know they won't cooperate with you, Justice. First, because of who you are. Second, because the archdiocese has put the personnel files of priests off limits, except for the past ten years. And they only turned those over because the D.A. put so much pressure on Cardinal Doyle, threatening him with a subpoena. Even then, Doyle's refusing to give up any records of private communications between priests and bishops, which covers a lot of ground." She cocked her head quizzically. "Didn't you say Father Blackley died eleven years ago?"

"According to Bishop Finatti's letter."

"There you are. He's outside that ten-year period. They'll brush you away like a fly." Templeton dipped a slice of mu shu pork in sauce, then held it poised in mid-air, like a thought. "When you get stonewalled, give me a call. I have something in mind that might stir things up."

That afternoon, I trotted down the stairs to the house and asked Maurice if I might use his PC again to write another letter.

He was fussing about the kitchen, baking a peach pie, dressed in lavender shorts, a pink tank top, and rubber sandals with a yellow plastic daisy at each toe. His long hair, silky and white, was pulled back into a ponytail and fastened with a paisley scarf. The accessories were the usual—rings festooned along the rim of one ear, jangling bracelets on the narrow wrists, and showy rings on the bony fingers. Not many men in their seventies could wear such an outfit and make it work, but Maurice was one of them.

"Writing another letter, are we?" He slid his baking dish into the oven, closed the door, and checked the settings on his dials. "I'd say you're about ready for a PC of your own, now that you have this big book to write. You're quite the busy boy these days."

"I'm sorry to have to ask again, Maurice."

"Not at all!" He waved a hand from the end of his flexible wrist. "Use it any time you want. It's just that we're thinking of upgrading to a new model. Aren't we, Fred?"

Fred looked up from the kitchen table, where he sat reading the sports page, unshaven in boxer shorts, scratching the hairy patch on his big stomach. He growled in agreement, went back to his football scores.

"So you might as well have our old one," Maurice went on, "which isn't all that outdated, truth be told. We'll call it a birthday gift."

"My birthday was last month. You gave me a gift then."

"Oh, stop quibbling! You're getting the computer and that's that. Now go write your letter and get your business taken care of." He paused, looking at me aslant. "Who's it to, by the way—if you don't mind my asking."

"Private, Maurice."

"Of course. None of my business." Again, the pause and sly look. "If you'd like me to look it over for typos, I have a pretty sharp eye, even at my advanced age."

I was on my way out of the room. "Thanks just the same, Maurice, but I'll use Spell Check."

"Spell Check, of course. Very handy, if you don't become too dependent on it. It's so good to see you back at work, Benjamin. This book is just what you need. I can't tell you how pleased we are for you."

"Save me a slice of that pie, will you?"

"If Fred doesn't eat the whole thing first!"

Fred grumped from the table, without looking up. Maurice gave me a wink. I turned down the hallway toward the den, where the PC and keyboard awaited.

Within the hour, I'd typed and printed out a letter to Bishop Anthony Finatti. In it, I explained who I was, mentioning my former "relationship" with Father Blackley and the autobiography I was writing, and requested an examination of his personnel records, dating back to the time he'd joined the L.A. archdiocese in 1976.

Not quite a week later, I received Bishop Finatti's response.

Dear Mr. Justice:

This letter is in reply to your request to inspect the personnel records of Fr. Stuart Blackley, a former priest with our archdiocese, who died in 1992.

It is the policy of the archdiocese and Cardinal Kendall Doyle that all personnel records be kept confidential, as a matter of personal privacy, even when the subject in question is deceased.

We have made available limited personnel files on a select number of priests going back ten years because of criminal investigations being conducted by the office of the Los Angeles district attorney. This was done for the sake of the victims, whose welfare we always place first.

However, since we have seen no evidence supporting the claims regarding Father Blackley made in your letter, and because he has not been named in any official police inquiry, I am afraid we cannot grant your request.

Respectfully,
The Most Reverand

Anthony Finatti

Regional Bishop, St. Agnes Pastoral Region
The Roman Catholic Archdiocese of Los Angeles

I called Templeton downtown at the *L.A. Times*. She was out covering a child kidnapping in Orange County—yet another young girl abducted—so I left a message. Templeton got back to me late that night, as I was taking a handful of meds and getting ready for bed.

"They found the girl's body," Templeton said. "She'd been raped before she died." Templeton sounded down, the way a lot of reporters do who work a violent crime story that ends badly, particularly one that involves kids. "They caught the guy who abducted and raped her, though. At least there's that. So why'd you call?"

"I got a reply from Bishop Finatti." I read her the brief letter, preparing myself for what was coming.

"Told you so," she said, right on cue.

"Last week, you said you had a plan if they stonewalled. Let's hear it."

"You mean you haven't guessed?"

"Come on, Alex. It's almost midnight. I'm bushed."

"Joe Soto," Templeton said.

FOUR

"Here's what we do." A rapscallion grin cracked Joe Soto's well-lined face. "I'll write a column about this Father Blackley. Lay the story on the table, challenge the bastards to respond. That should pry the lid open."

Soto, Templeton and I lounged on the wide veranda at the rear of the house Joe owned in Silverlake, as the pale light leeched from the gray-blue sky. The house was a simple stucco box, undistinguished in style, easy to miss from the street. But its two stories angled down a steep hillside, allowing for a private patio and garden and a clear view across a cascade of tiled roofs to the oblong reservoir below. Around the reservoir perimeter, joggers circled alone or with dogs in the late afternoon. It was one of those rare enclaves in L.A. where you could buy yourself a little piece of pastoral quiet if you had the money, even if the trees were non-native, the water they thrived on was diverted and the lake was fake. Within the L.A. city limits, that passes for a close relationship with nature.

"How will you handle my name?" I glanced across at Joe, who huddled with Templeton, rubbing the back of her hand reverently as if polishing fine stone. "Given my former affiliation with the *Times,* it might prove awkward."

Joe Soto was a ruggedly handsome man, with wavy gray hair

streaked darkly, thick shoulders and chest, and intense brown eyes set nicely in his tawny face. His nose was broken, in an attractive way; he'd done some prizefighting before getting drafted and sent to Vietnam, one of the poor kids who couldn't buy his way out of the war with a college deferment or family connections, like the sons of the men who waged it from behind their desks in Washington did. While in 'Nam, he'd picked up a Bronze Star and a Purple Heart, along with the G.I. bill, which had paid his way through journalism school when he'd come back with his medals and his wounds.

"I'll treat you the same as other victims I've written about, when they request it. I'll keep you anonymous."

"It doesn't bother you, associating with me on this?"

"The Pulitzer business?" Joe shrugged. "You screwed up. So what? It's got nothing to do with being diddled by a priest when you were a kid. If you didn't have the documents from Buffalo to back you up, I'd have second thoughts."

"I appreciate it, Joe."

"I appreciate the new angle on the priest story. It's a way to get after Cardinal Doyle again. Especially now, when he's trying to focus as much attention as possible on his new cathedral. He'd like nothing better than for all of us to forget how many child abusers he's protected over the years."

At Templeton's urging, I'd shown Joe the cache of documents sent to me by Sister Catherine Timothy, while keeping her name out of it. With each new page he'd grown more animated, his eyes keen for the details. As a staff columnist for the *L.A. Times,* he'd been outspoken on the subject of priestly sexual abuse years before it had erupted into a national scandal, well ahead of the more timid pack. He'd made some phone calls to Buffalo, causing an uproar but finally confirming that the diocese had settled several claims against Father Blackley involving sexual abuse, back in the seventies.

"While Joe's putting his column together," Templeton said, "I'll be writing a follow-up on the D.A.'s attempts to force the archdiocese to hand over more files. He's threatening subpoenas again, maybe a Grand Jury. He wants files beyond ten years, on any priest who's been named or suspected in a sex crime. Off the record, he figures there's at least a hundred or more, in L.A. alone, each with an unknown number of victims. He also wants all records of communications between bishops and accused priests. The archdiocese lawyers are fighting it on constitutional grounds, citing freedom of religion."

"Not surprising," I said. "What was the number of accused priests in Boston? Four hundred?"

"Something like that." She glanced at Joe with affection. "Not a bad one-two punch, my news piece and your column."

"Not bad at all." He leaned over and gave her a kiss. "If anything can put a burr under Kendall Doyle's saddle, this should do it."

"Unless Lindsay finds a way to throttle us," Templeton said. She caught my curious look. "Lindsay St. John, the new editorial manager at the *LAT*. Publisher's niece, strictly on management's side."

"What the hell's an 'editorial manager'?"

"They created the job just for her," Templeton said. "Liaison between the advertising and editorial sides of the paper. At least that's how they're peddling it."

"What's her background?"

Templeton made a sour face. "Corporate PR, including some work for Enron. Edited a woman's magazine once, the homemaker variety, and a couple of travel and dining rags. No hard news experience."

I grimaced. "It sounds like editorial and advertising are getting cozier all the time."

"And Lindsay St. John personifies the trend," Templeton said. "Wants to make the pages more advertiser-friendly, and avoid stepping on the wrong toes."

"Spine of a jellyfish," Joe said, spitting it out. "She's determined to tear down the traditional wall between business and editorial."

"She's been especially protective of the archdiocese and Cardinal Doyle," Templeton added.

"What accounts for that?"

She reached over and tapped me on the noggin. "Think. What does the *Times* own a whole lot of downtown?"

I smiled, remembering. "Property."

"Bingo," Joe said. "The new cathedral's vital to downtown redevelopment. St. Agnes." He spoke the name with mocking reverence. "The Cardinal's rather costly vanity project." I'd read plenty in the *Times* about the new cathedral, although the articles tended to downplay its two-hundred-million-dollar price tag. "I've never known the *Times* to assign so many puff pieces on one subject," Joe went on. "Meanwhile, St. John's trying to muzzle our coverage of the child abuse mess. She wants more 'balance'—at least that's the way she puts it." Joe put an arm around Templeton, drawing her closer. "But we just go with the facts and ignore Lindsay St. John, don't we, baby?"

She smiled proudly. "We do our best."

They kissed again, longer than before. Then Joe bounded to his feet, rubbing his hands together like he was trying to create sparks. "Let's go, kids. I got a column to put together. Let's see if we can turn over some rocks."

Templeton took a deep breath. "Oh, boy—here we go again. I can just see the memos flying from Lindsay St. John."

"Get ready for the ride, baby." Joe grinned broadly. "This is when it starts to get fun."

In the kitchen, Templeton set about grinding beans and brewing fresh coffee. While she got the java going, Joe led me down a short hallway and into a room that he used as an office. He closed the door behind us and pulled open the drawer of a file cabinet, extracting a file. "Alex doesn't know about this yet." He handed over a sheaf of papers. "It's the outline for a book I plan to write, after I give notice at the paper."

"You're quitting?"

"Retiring, come summer. Alex and I can't be married and both work at the *LAT*. Personnel rules don't allow it. I've got my twenty years in, pension's secure. Alex has her whole career ahead of her. If somebody has to go, it should be me."

"You're quite a guy, Joe."

"Bullshit." He flashed the grin again. "Truth is I'm tired of filing four columns a week. Hell of a grind, after all these years." Joe pointed to the document in my hands. "Besides, I want to write a book. Take a look at this proposal."

I glanced at the title on the cover page: *Monster in the Shadows: The True Story of Pablo Zuniga, the Fearsome Assassin Known as the Mutilator*. After the cover page came an introduction and chapter-by-chapter outline for a nonfiction book, double-spaced, running to sixty-four pages.

Joe watched me for a response. "You know about this guy?"

I looked up. "Pablo Zuniga? Vaguely. Assassin for hire, wasn't he? Linked to various drug cartels and governments south of the border years ago, back when I was paying attention to this kind of stuff."

Joe moved closer, lowered his voice. "He's here in L.A. I'm sure of it. Hiding out, mixing with the immigrant population. I've got good sources, learned a few things. Some pretty explosive stuff, especially his cozy relationship with the Catholic Church."

I raised my eyebrows. "You don't say."

He gave me a knowing look. "Take the outline home, let me know what you think." He poked me in the chest. "For your eyes only."

"What about Alex?"

"Pablo Zuniga's been credited with close to fifty contract hits, and he enjoys hurting people. They don't call him *el Mutilador* for nothing. I don't want her to worry, not just yet."

"She'll have to know at some point."

"I'll tell her after the wedding." Joe flicked off the light, slipped an arm around my shoulders, led me back down the hallway. "Weddings—now there's a truly scary subject." His laugh rumbled. "If I can live through another wedding, writing about Pablo Zuniga will be a piece of cake."

In the living room, Templeton had torched a few logs, which crackled and spit in the fireplace. I found a comfortable section of the sofa for sitting, while Joe poured two cups of coffee for us and pulled a chair closer. The living room was decorated simply but dramatically, with evocative, black-and-white photos by Alvarez Bravo set off by the more colorful contemporary paintings of Carlos Almaraz and Patssi Valdez. Joe's numerous journalism awards were nowhere to be seen; he still kept them boxed in a corner of his cluttered office downtown, under a stack of old editions of *La Opinion*.

Templeton bundled up and excused herself for a hike around the hills. For the next hour and a half, Joe prodded me through my story. His style was sensitive but probing, with insightful questions less capable reporters might have overlooked. When we were done, I felt wrung out but glad to be putting the Father Blackley matter into Joe Soto's capable hands.

The dusk was deep as I pecked Templeton goodnight, thanked Joe for his support, and turned up the pebbled path toward the street. When I glanced back, they were framed in the doorway, locking lips as if it was forever.

I hunkered down with my hands in my pockets and kept moving. I wanted to feel good about things: their wedding plans, Joe's column helping me out, the book he was so eager to write when he retired. But I couldn't. All I felt was morose, immersed in a perplexing sadness, when I should have been nothing but pleased. Maybe it was the prospect of writing my own book, I thought, and the responsibility and commitment that came with it. Maybe it was all this Father Blackley stuff, getting stirred up after so many years. Maybe it was a lot of things I'd tried not to think about for a long time, including the lingering death of my lover Jacques from AIDS back in 1990. That was something

I'd tried to put behind me years ago, but apparently hadn't, given how often I found him in my thoughts lately. Not bright, happy memories of a wonderful man I'd loved fiercely, the way it should be, but darker reveries of night sweats and decaying flesh, of fevers and physical agony and that special kind of fear when death is so close you can feel it in the room. I'd tried to push away all the ghastly memories, to ignore them, but it wasn't working anymore.

I zipped my jacket, turned up my collar. The warmth from the day was gone, along with the light. I climbed flagstone steps to the street, wondering how I'd fill the hours tonight until sleep came. My autobiography, I reminded myself—I could work on the book. At least I had that.

FIVE

The morning Joe Soto's column on Fr. Stuart Blackley was set to appear in the *Los Angeles Times*, I woke abruptly at seven.

I lay in bed for half an hour, trying to get a fix on things, trying to figure out how important Joe's column was to me. More important than I wanted to admit, I knew that much. I was grateful for his help, but it felt strange, being an anonymous source for someone else's reporting and commentary. Strange and disquieting, because it reminded me how far I'd fallen from my lofty perch as an investigative reporter, reduced to begging for some coverage—for a *voice*—in another journalist's space on the page. How valuable and precious those inches of newsprint, I realized, when they're taken from you forever.

I got up, swallowed the capsule from my HIV regimen that required an empty stomach, and cleaned up enough to look respectable. Then I headed down to Tribal Grounds on Santa Monica Boulevard, where I ordered a whole grain muffin and a cup of dark roast before finding a window seat and opening the paper. Funny, spending my money in Tribal Grounds, which had once been owned by an ex-priest defrocked for fondling altar boys. In the old days, I hadn't given it much thought; the coffee was good, it was convenient, so I'd spent my money there, exchanging mindless pleasantries with the owner. *Let he who is without sin cast the first stone.* I was hardly a saint, so I'd handed over my money and dropped my change in the tip jar, ignoring his past transgressions. That was before I'd cut a deal to write my autobiography and jotted down the personal events that had most influenced the direction my life had taken. Templeton had suggested it as a way to help me remember important turning points, as a structural device and research tool for the book. My introduction to sex by Father Blackley at age twelve had gone on the list, up near the top. For months afterward, I hadn't been able to set foot in Tribal Grounds; the mere thought of it had sickened me. Then the ex-priest who owned the place had died. The little corner coffee bar with the rainbow flag above the door was now in the hands of three cheerful lesbians who served the same rich coffee and even better muffins. So I was back, reading the *L.A. Times* several mornings a week at my favorite window table.

The front page this morning was dominated by a spectacular feature on St. Agnes Cathedral, extolling it as an architectural achievement of monumental proportions—a "cathedral for the ages"—even though its official opening was six months off. The article, accompanied on page one by a color photograph capturing the cathedral's sweep and grandeur, jumped inside, where it continued as a massive spread covering two full pages of text, floor plans and more color photographs. Despite the extensive coverage, the price tag—two hundred million dollars—was mentioned only once, buried in a small sidebar on an inside page. Missing altogether was mention of the millions taxpayers were coughing up for a special off-ramp from the Harbor Freeway, the main thoroughfare through downtown, being constructed exclusively for cathedral traffic. That was a story Joe Soto had broken in his column a few months earlier, one of many that had stripped away layers of the archdiocese's formidable public relations campaign. The *Times* spread also included a sidebar explaining how Cardinal Kendall Doyle had chosen the cathedral's name: It was in tribute to his younger sister, Agnes, who'd died from polio as a child, and who was herself named after St. Agnes, the patron saint and protector of girls.

Templeton's much shorter news article ran on page one of the California section, under a three-column, two-deck headline:

D.A. Presses L.A. Archdiocese
for Files on Priest Misconduct

It was a straightforward news piece, neatly assembled and neutral in tone, detailing the most recent attempt of the district attorney to force the archdiocese to turn over personnel files on any suspect priests, regardless of how far back the claims of victims extended. It also mentioned the Church's latest legal maneuver to protect communications between bishops and priests as confidential and sacrosanct, even though Cardinal Doyle had once promised "full and unlimited cooperation so that all the facts might be aired." Templeton had given the church ample opportunity to respond, but Bishop Anthony Finatti had offered only a prepared statement:

> *The archdiocese has provided the proper authorities, including the district attorney, with all relevant files on priests suspected of criminal misconduct going back a full ten years. To open our files further to such scrutiny would violate the privacy not just of priests who have undergone counseling and come to terms with their behavioral problems but also of victims who have put certain unfortunate incidents behind them and moved on with their lives. We feel bound by our word to honor their requests to keep these matters confidential. To open these files now would cause unnecessary pain for the victims, who are always our first concern. It would also pose a serious threat to the fundamental Constitutional guarantee of freedom of religion and its time-honored protection of all communications between bishops and priests.*

As Templeton reported, this latter position was being taken throughout the country by a number of bishops who were hiring the best constitutional lawyers they could find. So far, their claim of immunity from civil authority had fared poorly in court, most notably in Boston, where a court-ordered release of documents by the archdiocese there had triggered the scandal that was still making headlines today, more than two years later.

I read Templeton's article again, then skimmed the colorful spread on the new cathedral, looking at the pretty pictures, gaping at the numbers that measured how high, how wide, how big. But I knew I was procrastinating.

Finally, I took a deep breath and turned to Joe's column on page three of the California section.

Joe Soto at Large

Simple question, dear readers: Why are Cardinal Kendall Doyle and his underlings at the Los Angeles archdiocese keeping the lid on details about a deceased priest named Fr. Stuart Blackley?

Frankly, I didn't even know Father Blackley existed until a reader of this newspaper contacted me recently. College-educated guy, mid-forties, who claims the priest engaged him sexually more than three decades ago back in Buffalo, starting when he was twelve.

Now, you might write this guy off as a flake, a crackpot, or maybe somebody looking to cash in on a quick settlement with the Church. After all, he never told his parents about what was going on. Never contacted the police. Never informed a school counselor or even a buddy. The sex went on for nearly two years, and the kid kept going back for more. Or so he tells me. Back to Father Blackley's bed, he says, letting the priest do things with him that he never knew people did with each other before then. Remember, this kid was only twelve. It was a long time ago, before MTV, *Queer as Folk,* and those homoerotic Abercrombie & Fitch ads.

If any of it ever happened at all. There's no proof, so the guy could be making it up. He's had some troubles in life—alcohol, violence, a serious problem at one point with telling the truth. So maybe he is just a jerk, looking to take advantage of the Church.

Except there's more. He's produced confidential legal documents from the Buffalo diocese that indicate he wasn't the only kid being used sexually by Father Blackley back then. There were at least six other victims—four boys, two girls—all under the age of fourteen. These are just the ones we know about—I confirmed every one.

Starting in 1976, the Buffalo diocese covertly began settling their claims, paying several million bucks to buy their silence. Remember, that's how the Church works. It's been secretly settling claims like this for decades, all across the country. Hiding the truth, obstructing justice, and reassigning its pedophile priests to other parishes. Sending them back out to do God's work—and find God knows how many innocent kids to seduce and exploit all over again. Better an abused kid than a defrocked priest, right?

Nineteen seventy-six by the way, was a pivotal year for Father Blackley. That was when he came out here to Lotus Land, reassigned to the L.A. archdiocese, where his good buddy, Anthony Finatti, was sitting at the right hand of Cardinal Kendall Doyle.

Father Blackley died in a hiking mishap in 1992, so he's not around to answer any questions. My correspondent wants to know what Father Blackley was up to during those sixteen years in between. The archdiocese won't tell him. In their released statements, they insist that the victims are always their first priority. Well, here's a victim who needs answers to get some closure, and all he's getting is the runaround.

What's the archdiocese hiding? That's the question in my craw. I suspect that Father Blackley figures in another stinking mess that Cardinal Kendall Doyle would like to see go away, especially with his new cathedral, St. Agnes, set to open next year.

Maybe I'm wrong. Maybe Bishop Finatti helped straighten out his boyhood friend, turned him into a living saint. So prove me wrong, Bishop. Open the files and show us what you've got. I'm sure the D.A. would like to have a peek as well.

You might as well come clean now, Bishop. Because as long as I'm around, I'll keep digging until I get to the bottom of this dirty little saga. That's a promise—to you, to the victim, and to the residents of this city, who deserve the truth.

I read Joe's column a second time, admiring its punch and brevity while wincing a bit at the overkill. No question, he liked to showboat, to make himself part of the story. But his passion and honesty were undeniable. Like some of the best crusading columnists, he gnashed his teeth when he wrote; he talked directly to his readers, who knew exactly where he stood. It was the kind of writing I'd never had the courage to attempt as a journalist, revealing something about myself instead of hiding behind facts and other people's words, the way most reporters do.

I got a refill, finished my muffin, washed it down with the last of my coffee, and sat staring out at Santa Monica Boulevard as Boys Town came to life. Wondering what came next, now that Joe Soto had let the cat out of the bag.

Joe called at midafternoon to tell me that he was already getting phone calls and e-mails in response to the column, many from Catholics whom Father Blackley had once served as a pastor. Joe invited me to join him and Templeton for dinner to celebrate, but I begged off. I'd just switched to a new cocktail of HIV meds and was reeling a bit from the side effects.

Joe, who knew about my HIV status but little of my treatment, was persistent. "It's your story more than mine, Ben. You're sure you're not up to a quick bite? It's on me."

"Another time, Joe, when I'm feeling better."

"Sorry to hear you're under the weather."

"Nice job on the column, by the way. If it doesn't shake some information loose, I don't know what will."

"You read my book proposal yet, the one on Pablo Zuniga?"

"I'll get to it soon."

"We'll talk tomorrow?"

"Sure Joe, tomorrow."

SIX

Tomorrow came sooner than I expected—at half past midnight, with a screaming phone that shocked me from a restless sleep. I wasn't accustomed to getting phone calls so late—I didn't have that many friends, and no blood relations that I knew of—and the shrillness jolted me into a moment's panic. I grabbed the receiver on the second ring, trying to shake off sleep.

It was Alexandra Templeton. She was sobbing.

I listened to her for nearly a minute, trying to make sense of what she was trying to tell me. I'd never heard Templeton lose control like that.

"Calm down, Alex. Tell me what happened."

The sobs diminished, coming out of her like hiccups. She told me that she and Joe had gone to Pietro's on Third Street for dinner, taking separate cars. Afterward, they'd stepped out to the sidewalk to say goodnight. They'd kissed, and Joe had held her for a moment, telling her how much she meant to him and what a lucky guy he was, getting another chance like this. Then he'd parted, throwing a final kiss, looked both ways, and crossed the street toward his Austin Healey. That's when a Jeep Grand Cherokee, light gray with tinted windows, had come out of nowhere, tires squealing, the unseen driver accelerating. The heavy vehicle had struck Joe head on, propelling him like a soccer ball after a good strike, then ran him over, while Templeton watched in horror. The driver had sped away, never slowing, disappearing around a corner, while she dialed 911 as she ran to Joe's side.

I sat up, my legs over the edge of the bed. "How's Joe? How's he doing?"

Templeton lost it again, heaving up a tidal wave of sobs. Finally, she sputtered out a few words. "Joe's gone, Benjamin."

"Where? To which hospital?"

"Don't you get it?" She was shrieking now. "Joe's gone—he's dead."

Pietro's was an Italian place on a section of Third Street that thrived on refugees from trendy La Brea Avenue and the hip-hop circus that popular Melrose Avenue had become. Joe had loved the little restaurant because the food was good and reasonably priced and he could usually get a window table; it reminded him of New York, he'd said, where you could find an endless number of cafés like that tucked here and there all across the city, both sides of the river, charming but unpretentious the way a good little restaurant should be, with hospitable chatter and rich aromas wafting from the kitchen. At first it hadn't been quite showy or tasteful enough for Templeton—she liked her dinners out to be more elegant—but she'd grown more relaxed with Joe over time, and she'd come to appreciate Pietro's almost as much as he did. They'd become regulars, a pair of lovebirds whom the roly-poly owner greeted like family, wiping his hands on his sauce-splattered apron and dispensing hugs each time they came in. One evening, after taking in a play not far away in the Equity-waiver district, Joe had proposed to Templeton at their favorite window table. For Templeton, that had pretty much sealed the deal. Pietro's had assumed a special place in her heart, she'd told me, and having dinner with Joe anywhere else had never quite meant as much.

Now he lay dead in the street out front, while Pietro and his employees stared bleakly out the windows. In between, on the sidewalk, Templeton stood facing a cop in a suit. I approached them at a measured clip, tucking in my shirt and steeling myself to play a role I didn't want for one second.

I glanced across Third, where a crime scene unit had strung yellow tape, since the hit-and-run made Joe's death a felony homicide. His body lay in the westbound lane, a big lump under a white blanket. Because of the hour, most of the businesses along the street were closed. A few bystanders gawked from the sidewalk while passing drivers slowed for a look and a uniform waved them on their way.

The detective with Templeton asked questions and jotted notes, looking equal parts sympathetic and frustrated. She appeared to be close to shock, her lips moving slowly, not quite all there. As I came up, he handed her his card. I introduced myself, he asked if I could drive her home, and I said I would. When he was gone, I embraced her. It was like holding a mannequin, stiff and lifeless. I asked if she'd gotten a good look at the driver, which was a cold way to start but the best I could come up with. She shook her head, drew away from me, stared out at the street. Two attendants were loading Joe's body on to a stretcher for a trip to the morgue.

"Everything changes so fast." She sounded distant, numb. "One moment he's here, and the next—"

She wept quietly, her face in her hands. I went to her, held her again, but didn't know quite what to say. Finally, I asked if there was someone she wanted to call.

"I did. I called you." She explained that her best girlfriend was out of the country, and that she'd never told her parents about Joe, so calling them would be pointless. They wouldn't have approved of her relationship, she said, let alone plans for marriage with someone outside her race. She'd been putting off telling them, knowing how they'd react. Templeton was rambling, the way some people do to fend off the onslaught of grief just a little longer. "It would have been easier if I'd had to tell them I was gay. They wouldn't have been thrilled, but they would have accepted it better." She laughed bitterly. "They're very lib-

47

eral, you know. Except when it comes to interracial dating and marriage. Race mixing—isn't that what the bigots use to call it?"

"I'm sure their reasons are different. Your parents, I mean."

She separated abruptly from me. "Their reasons don't mean crap. It's my life."

"OK, take it easy."

She hugged herself, her chin trembling. "Sure, take it easy, why not?"

"You'll need to tell them at some point, that's all I'm saying. You can't pretend this never happened."

"God, I wish I could." She watched the coroner's van pull away from the curb, making a U-turn and passing close to us before disappearing in the direction of downtown. Her tears came again and she turned back to me, burying her face against my shoulder. "I feel so alone. I've never felt so alone."

"I'm here, Alex." I wrapped my arms around her, drawing her closer. "I'm here."

But I wasn't really there. Not in the way Templeton needed me. She didn't know that yet, but I did.

I left my old Mustang on Third to pick up later, and drove her home in her new Thunderbird, a recent birthday present from her father. On the way, she said something that suddenly cast the night's events in a whole new light.

"The way the driver came at Joe, accelerating, then speeding off like he did. It almost looked deliberate."

"It happened awfully fast. Your perceptions can't be too clear."

"He sped up, Justice. I'm sure of it."

"You're assuming it's a man."

Templeton looked over as I drove, while I kept my eyes on the road. "Whoever it was," she said, "it looked deliberate. That's what I'm saying."

"It was a shock, Alex. Your impressions are bound to be muddled."

"You're saying I didn't see what I saw?"

"It's been a long night. We can talk about it later."

"I told the detective the same thing. That it looked intentional."

"Good. He can pursue it then."

She cried for awhile and I paid attention to my driving until we reached her condominium a few blocks from the beach in Santa Monica. It was an upper story place in a swank high-rise with an ocean view, with towering palms all around—another gift from her rich old man, who'd paid cash for it when the market was low, then watched it triple in value. For the next few hours, Templeton and I sat on the white Berber carpet with our backs against the eggshell leather couch, sipping herbal tea and listening to our favorite jazz cuts. Miles, Dizzy, Oscar Peterson, a favorite Nina Simone CD that I'd given Templeton two years ago, on her thirtieth birthday. I kept my arm around her and let her talk, about whatever came into her head. From time to time, she wept; once or twice, she got up and left the room to be alone. A lot of what she talked about had to do with growing up and becoming her own person, finally confronting life, with all its randomness and risk. For all her smarts and social skills, all her accomplishments as a journalist, her fine background and lofty education, Templeton had never faced this kind of loss before. I had, more than once, and as I sat listening to her, I was already retreating into a protective shell, separating from her pain and need. Her grief was too raw, too intimate, too saturated with fury and frustration. Her helplessness frightened me, so I withdrew.

Besides, if someone had murdered Joe Soto, as Templeton seemed to be suggesting, I didn't want to be involved. Murder investigations inevitably lead one into a dark and forbidding place, filled with terrible secrets and populated with monsters that often lie dormant behind the most innocuous smiles before emerging to commit their horror. If you venture deeply enough into that world, willing to see in the darkness, you can learn things about yourself that might not be so easy to live with when you come back out.

I'd been there, too many times. I didn't want to go back.

SEVEN

After calling Templeton the next afternoon to ask how she was holding up, I never called again, at least not with the intention of reaching her.

I spent the next several days hiding out in my apartment, with the shades drawn, hoping she didn't appear on my stairwell landing. If my phone rang, I let the machine take it. If I called back and Templeton picked up, which happened twice, I hung up without a word. When I caught her out, I left messages on her voice mail apologizing for missing her, explaining that I'd been feeling ill and keeping the phone off the hook. Two of her messages informed me that there were no leads in the investigation into Joe Soto's death. Each time she left another message, her voice sounded stronger, or at least tougher, with an edge that became increasingly ugly.

I spent the rest of my time organizing material for the autobiography I hoped to start writing by the end of the year—cataloguing articles I'd written, marking old notes for rereading, jotting down ideas for chapters and sections, or areas to be researched. There was a lot to do. It wasn't that hard convincing myself how important it was, putting the book ahead of helping Templeton get through what must have been the most difficult period of her life.

On Monday morning she showed up at my door. Her beauty was blunted now by sadness and self-neglect—no makeup, hair braids left dangling and unattended, clothes chosen without much care. Redness rimmed her eyes; her look was sullen and spent.

"I know what's going on," she said.

"Do you?"

She nodded. "I've known you too long and too well, Benjamin. I'm going to ask just one favor."

"OK."

"Joe's memorial is set for tomorrow, at a little church on the eastside, where he grew up. It would be nice if you'd go with me."

"Sure, I can do that."

"It's at three. I'll pick you up at two. I don't want to be late."

"Two o'clock then."

"I'd appreciate it if you'd wear some decent clothes. You need money?"

"No, I'll cover it."

She turned away, leaving me to stew in my guilt. I started to say something, but caught myself. I let her go in silence, feeling like the coward I was but also relieved to be off the hook.

The memorial Mass was to be held in La Iglesia de la Virgen de la Caridad—the Church of the Virgin of Charity—a mile or two east of the Los Angeles River in Boyle Heights. Templeton drove.

We passed through the downtown business district within the shadow of the ten-story *Los Angeles Times* building at First and Spring. Minutes later, we were crossing an antiquated concrete bridge festooned with decorative lampposts that had probably been used as a backdrop in every L.A. film noir ever made. Below us, the river was encased in cement, like a corpse with rigor mortis. Weeds and other vegetation struggled up where they could find a crack, a reminder of what civilization had done to a region that had once been an unpolluted paradise where Indian tribes had roamed for thousands of years before the first Europeans had arrived. After that we were cruising through a neighborhood of taco stands, shabby dance clubs, and auto wrecking yards. At the turn of the century, Boyle Heights had been a pleasant streetcar suburb of artisans and white-collar workers comfortably ensconced in quaint houses with pretty gardens, built around picturesque parks. Now, miles of elevated freeways decimated the district, leaving it impoverished, neglected and choking with smog. Still, there was life here—roughly a hundred thousand people, almost all Hispanic—crowded into faded houses and crumbling apartment buildings, where families and working people struggled to survive the cancer of drugs and gangs. As we passed along the boulevard, vendors hugged the curbs, the music of *corrido* mixed with *norteño* from the radios, and colorful murals competed with gang graffiti for wall space.

Templeton made a couple of turns in her T-Bird, following a street guide. We quickly found ourselves surrounded by pre–World War II houses with small yards, their vintage charm marred by burglar bars on most of the windows. Every so often, a muscular guard dog charged its fence, snarling as we rolled by. Vehicles lined the long block, parked bumper to bumper, so we knew the church must be close.

"There it is, just ahead on the right." Templeton's voice was subdued, as if she might be speaking to herself. "Joe told me it was small. He was right."

For the service, Templeton had worn a long-sleeved black dress with matching shawl, hat, and gloves, looking stately but also strained and older. The previous afternoon, I'd purchased my first new suit in fifteen years, selecting deep gray, with a darker tie and silk handkerchief for the pocket, telling the sales guy I wanted a style that would last, since I only wore suits to funerals. I'd even spent twenty bucks on a trim for what was left of my darkening blond hair, and shaved away my customary stubble. Ordinarily, Templeton would have beamed at my appearance, and showered me with compliments. Today, she'd barely glanced at me as I'd climbed into the car.

Up ahead, mourners crowded the sidewalk in front of the little church. "Looks like Joe's getting quite a sendoff," I said.

"He had a lot of friends." Templeton sounded far away, deep inside herself. "A lot of admirers."

"You doing OK?"

"I'm doing fine, Justice." Her voice turned sharp, punishing. "Don't worry about me."

By chance, a pickup was pulling away from the curb. She slipped into the vacated space, parallel parking with cool precision. A minute later, we were approaching The Church of the Virgin of Charity. I noticed the graffiti diminish, as the taggers ended their spray-painted messages just as the church property began.

La Iglesia de la Virgen de la Caridad was small and unimpressive by most standards, discounting the history resonating from its whitewashed walls.

The main structure dated to 1856, according to a bronze plaque near the arched entrance, which also declared the site an official historical landmark. The rectangular building was a simple, gable-roofed adobe, Mission Spanish in style, its upper portion rising to a *campanario,* where three bells hung in arched openings, with a plain wooden cross at the apex. As we entered with a stream of mourners, the musty odor of ancient wood and adobe was pungent. Just inside the door, I reflexively made the sign of the cross and knelt to one knee. At that moment, a powerful sensation swept through me, what felt like pent-up memories and feelings suddenly being unleashed. They came without warning, like the rush of bats out of a secret place at sundown, a startling flutter of webbed wings that was frightening and wonderful at the same time. A moment after that, as I regained my equilibrium, a priest draped in a dark Mass cassock and white collar appeared before me like a vision, coming slowly into focus.

He introduced himself as Fr. Ismael Aragon, glancing at me only briefly before turning to Templeton and expressing his sympathy about the passing of Joe Soto. The priest was a beautiful man, in his early thirties if my guess was right. He wore his thick black hair on the longish side, letting it tumble above impossibly large brown eyes capable of causing hearts to beat a little faster. His lips were full and deeply colored, his skin a radiant bronze, his handsome features youthful and unlined.

"Joe grew up only a block or two from here. This was his family's church." Father Aragon's voice was deep and strong, yet its thrust was gentle. "I visited the house yesterday, to get a better sense of his past. There's a nice family living there now, three generations, originally from Guatemala."

Father Aragon glanced my way and caught me admiring his profile. Our eyes locked momentarily, he smiled awkwardly, and quickly returned his attention to Templeton. He told her that he'd reserved a place for her, in one of the pews near the front. When he glanced in my direction a second time, he managed to avoid my eyes entirely.

"Your friend is welcome to join you, of course." He cast his eyes toward the entrance and beyond, where the crowd was growing, spilling into the street. I recognized a few faces from my old days at the *L.A. Times*. "I never expected this many people," Father Aragon said. "Joe left specific instructions to hold the service here, or we might have found a larger space to better accommodate so many."

Templeton cocked her head curiously. "Joe left instructions regarding his death?"

"He started coming to church last year. He sensed he might not live a long life. We talked privately several times."

Her curiosity gave way to hurt. "He never mentioned anything like that to me."

"Joe was finding his way back to the Church, Alexandra, after many years away. Perhaps he wasn't comfortable yet discussing it with you. He told me that if anything happened, he wanted cremation and a simple memorial service. He also sought advice about his impending marriage. He was trying to work through some issues."

"What kind of issues?"

"He loved you very much, Alexandra." Father Aragon placed a hand on her arm; his fingers were long and delicate, the back of his hand burnished with fine, dark hair. "Joe's conflicts had nothing to do with you, but with the fact that you're Baptist and he's Catholic."

"And what did you tell him?"

"That God blesses every union that's based in love, even if the Church doesn't."

"*Every* union?" I asked.

Hesitantly, Father Aragon's eyes met mine. "That's what I believe. It's a liberal interpretation, I know."

"And counter to Church doctrine." I put out my hand. "Benjamin Justice. We haven't been introduced."

"Yes, I recognized your face." His voice had lost its feeling, as if he'd slipped into a neutral gear. "From some of the news accounts years ago."

He attempted to withdraw his hand, but I didn't let go. "Perhaps I'll start attending Sunday Mass, Father." I smiled wickedly, pinning him with my eyes. "Who knows? We might become friends."

"We welcome everyone here." His pleasantness was forced now, almost pained in its self-consciousness. He extracted his hand and caught the attention of an usher.

"Jorge—this is Miss Templeton. Front row right, please, on the aisle." Then, smiling gently, to Templeton: "We'll speak after the service."

The usher led us to our seats, close to the altar and pulpit. He was a light-skinned Hispanic kid in his late teens, with tattoos on his forearms and neck, and what looked like a knife scar across his unshaven chin. All around us, other young men of a similar age and appearance served in various capacities, looking awkward in their ill-fitting suits but trying hard to carry out their duties properly. Most were grown, but a few were young enough to be altar boys.

"Father Aragon works with gangs," Templeton said, when we were seated. "Tries to keep the peace, find them work, keep them in school. Runs a nonprofit auto body shop, where they can learn some skills. Joe wrote a column about him earlier this year."

"Very dedicated." I admired the *mestizo* features of a tough-looking usher as he passed. "So many bad boys in need of a spanking."

"Father Aragon seems sincere."

"And as queer as a three-dollar bill."

Templeton shot me a look. "Don't start, Justice. Please, not today."

The service began shortly after three. Father Aragon presided from behind an altar roughly hewn from oak that looked like it might have been with the church since its inception. The gold monstrance and two matching candlesticks shone brightly, but were surely gold plate, not solid.

The only luxurious touch in the modest church was an arched window of leaded glass, set in the south wall. The moment I saw it, I found myself riveted, while the strange sensation I'd experienced minutes earlier flooded through me again. The colored panes formed an image of a bearded Christ robed and kneeling at a rock, his hands folded in prayer, his eyes lifted to the heavens, while a shaft of light shone down from a fleecy cloud, bathing him in a soft glow. The window resembled one in the church I'd attended as a child back in Buffalo. I'd always been drawn to the soulful face of Jesus as the morning light streamed through, becoming lost in his image, in the sense of peace I found there. I'd wanted desperately to believe that with Christ as my Savior and God watching over me I was never alone, that with the promise of absolution and forgiveness, there was always hope. The Virgin Mother was a lovely and mysterious figure, but it was the image of Jesus that had always mesmerized me. I'd been especially fixated on scenes of the Crucifixion, the nearly naked Christ hanging in agony from the cross, his arms helplessly outstretched, his lean body torn and bleeding, his loins barely concealed by a snatch of cloth. My response had been so charged and visceral, so close to sexual, that I'd often forced myself to look away, ashamed of what I was feeling. For solace, I'd turned to the stained glass window, to see the fully robed and beatific Christ, kneeling in prayer. It had been my favorite moment on Sunday mornings, a blessed escape from conflict and confusion, until I'd inevitably felt the slap of my father's hand on the back of my head, commanding me back to the service, back to the droning voice of Fr. Stuart Blackley as he'd sermonized from the pulpit about sin.

Almost unconsciously, I reached into a jacket pocket, where I'd placed Sister Catherine Timothy's rosary before leaving home. The amber beads felt smooth and cool in my hand. Father Aragon began reciting a prayer requested by Joe's family that I recognized immediately as Anima Christi.

> *Soul of Christ, make me holy.*
> *Body of Christ, save me.*
> *Blood of Christ, fill me with love.*
> *Water from Christ's side, wash me.*
> *Passion of Christ, strengthen me.*
> *Good Jesus, hear me.*
> *Within your wounds, hide me.*
> *Never let me be parted from you.*
> *From the evil enemy, protect me.*
> *At the hour of my death, call me.*
> *And tell me to come to you.*
> *That with your saints I may praise you.*
> *Through all eternity. Amen.*

According to Joe's wishes, the memorial service was brief, simple and devoid of much ritual. Templeton broke down several times, weeping quietly. I took her hand and she allowed me to hold it until it was time to go.

As we filed out, I stole a final glance at the stained glass window. The sky beyond the colored panes had clouded over; the beautiful light was gone.

EIGHT

Templeton and I stepped from the church into a mob of mourners who seemed almost giddy with relief to be outside.

Many were *L.A. Times* staffers, presumably unaware of Templeton's close relationship with Joe, since they'd made a pointed effort to keep it out of the workplace and a secret to all but close friends and family. She exchanged words and hugs with a few, while I suffered curious or critical glances from others who milled about in bunches, darting their eyes in our direction. Father Aragon spent several minutes alone with Templeton, talking quietly off to the side, before disappearing back into the church. Finally, we were surrounded by Joe's sisters, four Rubenesque women in their forties and fifties who cried and laughed, fussing over Templeton like mother hens. They insisted that we come by the oldest sister's house for some food and beverage, and Templeton promised we would.

"My parents should have been here," Templeton said, when we were alone again. "I should have had the courage to call them, to tell them about Joe and me. What is it about our parents that keeps us so terrified of being ourselves?"

"Approval, I guess. Not something I wasted much time on."

"We do it in different ways, I think, sometimes completely unaware of what really drives us." I thought of my achievements as a high school wrestler, my youthful fascination with guns, my determination to become as hard a drinker as my father. Templeton laughed bitterly. "You spend your life trying to please them, and end up resenting them for it." Her lip quivered. "God, I miss Joe."

A few others came up, making awkward small talk. Templeton whispered to me that she'd like to get away from the crowd and stroll the church grounds in back. We were about to make our escape when an attractive, fiftyish woman in a navy business suit and short heels approached us. She stood stiffly erect, with impeccable makeup and hair, and a smile as brittle and transparent as fine crystal.

"Alexandra, I'm so glad you could make it." When she embraced Templeton, it was so brief the two women barely touched. "I know that you and Joe were good friends."

"I've known Joe for four years, Lindsay. Since the *Sun* folded and I joined the *Times*." Templeton extracted her hand. "Of course I made it to the service."

Lindsay St. John, I realized—the business-minded "editorial manager" I'd heard so much about.

"You've got three years on me then." St. John touched Templeton's wrist fleetingly. "I wish I could have known him longer."

"I'm sure you do." Templeton turned in my direction. "My friend, Benjamin Justice."

"Of course. I recognized Mr. Justice." St. John nodded perfunctorily and turned back to Templeton as if I'd vanished, or never been there at all. Her lips curled into a calculated smile. "It's my understanding that you and Joe may have been more than just friends."

Several seconds passed as Templeton absorbed and digested what she'd just heard. "How is that you came by that understanding, Lindsay?"

"You know, office scuttlebutt."

"I wasn't aware of any gossip like that."

"Isn't it the subject of the whispers who's always the last to know?"

"You don't strike me as the type who hangs out at the water cooler, Lindsay, trading office gossip. In fact, I can't remember the last time I saw you down on the third floor."

"I try to get down and mingle when I can. Not always easy, with my schedule."

"You're so much busier than the rest us, planning those big spreads on the new cathedral."

St. John cranked up her smile another notch, but with even less warmth. "And keeping an eye on you and Joe, so our coverage of the Church maintains some balance."

"You don't have Joe to worry about anymore, do you, Lindsay? Maybe we'll see more of you now, mingling and catching up on scuttlebutt."

"It's true isn't it? That you and Joe were—how shall I put it? Extremely close."

"It doesn't really matter any longer, does it?"

"On the contrary, dear. It occurred to me that you might need some time off. We'd be happy to give you a full week, with pay. Longer, if you need it."

"Time to grieve properly," Templeton said.

"Exactly."

"It's awfully kind, Lindsay. I'm overwhelmed. But I don't plan to miss a minute of work."

St. John's smile deflated by half. "You don't?"

"My intention is to pick up where Joe left off, chasing the Father Blackley story. It was Joe's final column, after all."

'Yes, but—"

"It cries out for resolution, don't you think?"

"This may not be the best time—"

"Are you suggesting we drop the story, Lindsay? Let it die?"

"Of course, not. I'm merely—"

"Good, then it's settled. I'll pick up the Father Blackley angle and run with it. I promise not to let it interfere with my regular assignments. If I have to, I'll work it on my own time. But I intend to wrap that story up the way Joe would have, to fulfill his promise to his readers. To cut through the lies and give them the truth."

St. John's smile held fast but the chill in her voice gave her away. "If you feel that's best, Alex."

"Joe deserves at least that much, don't you think?"

"Of course. He was a great journalist—irreplaceable. Still, Joe was a columnist and you're a reporter. You must be careful not to let your personal feelings cloud your professional judgment."

"Are you a religious person, Lindsay?"

"I'd say so, yes."

"Catholic?"

"Yes, as a matter of fact."

Templeton smiled benignly. "Now how did I know that?"

St. John flinched and her smile finally collapsed. Without turning her head, she shifted her eyes in my direction and slipped away, all in the same motion.

"She found out about Joe and me," Templeton said. "And I don't believe for a minute it was through the office grapevine."

We watched Lindsay St. John move gracefully among the mourners, anointing them with her starched smile, dispensing superficial hugs and handshakes like a skilled politician working a fresh crowd at election time.

"She mixes right in," I said, "although she seems to be alone."

"Lindsay St. John is always alone."

"Workaholic?"

Templeton nodded. "Driven by ambition. Determined to succeed."

"No private life?"

"None that she allows anyone to see." Templeton slipped her arm through mine. "Come on, let's take that walk."

Clouds hovered and the air nipped as Templeton and I made our way around the small church to the grounds behind. Gravel paths wound around and through a garden of cacti and succulents, framed at the edges by wooden benches under olive and eucalyptus trees. At the center sat a three-tiered, terra cotta fountain, splashing water. Statues stood here and there beside the path, copies of more famous originals—St. Francis of Assisi, St. Cecilia, St. Peter, one or two others. Three posted signs, shaped like arrows at a crossroads, pointed west, east, and southeast—back toward the church, and in the direction of two modest one-story buildings beyond the garden, newer but designed in faux adobe to blend in architecturally. The larger of the two, according to the second sign, served as the church office. The smaller, off by itself beyond a grove of trees, was the rectory. Covering the back wall of the church, facing east, was a faded mural by David Alfaro Siqueiros, dated 1932, depicting a Mexican peon crucified and dying in the shadow of an American eagle.

Templeton paused to look across the grounds. "Joe worked in this garden when he was a boy. Pulled weeds, kept the statues clean, that kind of thing. Some of these older plantings may have been his."

"A lot of history in this place, I guess."

"Yes, a lot of history." The wind kicked up and she pulled her shawl more snugly around her. "I can't believe he's gone. I haven't accepted it. I'm not sure I can."

"I know the feeling."

She glanced over. "Yes, of course you do." She smiled briefly, but it looked heartfelt. "I need to keep that in mind, don't I?"

As we moved on, she surprised me by taking my hand. I glanced up at the darkening sky, then over my shoulder. I'd sensed for the past minute or two that we were not alone. I saw no one immediately behind us, but I was certain someone lurked around one of the bends in the path. Every so often, I heard heavy footfalls crunching gravel.

I pulled up. "Could we sit a minute? I'm a little tired."

Templeton knew my routine with the meds, the way certain prescriptions induced mild nausea or sapped my energy. "We can go, if you need to."

"I'd like to get off my feet a moment, that's all." I glanced toward a side path that led to an alcove with a bench, partially hidden from the main trail.

"You go on," Templeton said. "I think I'll stay in Joe's garden for a bit."

I turned away toward the bench. When I was out of sight, I cut back among the trees, partially concealed by shadows. On the twisting trail, a large figure—male, dark suit, matching fedora—moved slowly in Templeton's direction, flattening gravel under his boat-sized wingtips. He stopped, bending to peer through the trunks of two towering saguaros. I circled widely around him, coming in from behind. From my vantage point, I could clearly see what had so captured his attention: Templeton, standing alone, looking contemplative but lovely, and completely vulnerable to his prying eyes. The stranger contorted his big body for a clearer view, fixed on her as if she were a rare specimen in his specialized field of study.

I moved closer, until only a few yards separated us. "Next time, you should bring field glasses."

The man rose and whirled in the same motion, surprisingly agile for someone so large. When he came around, I recognized the dark face and features.

"Lieutenant Claude DeWinter, LAPD homicide." I shook my head in mock wonderment. "What a coincidence, running into you like this."

"Dammit, Justice, you scared the stuffing out of me."

"Did you get an eyeful, Lieutenant, or do you need more time?"

"OK, you caught me. I feel like a jerk. Satisfied?" He turned to look at Templeton again, but she was gone. "What can I say? She's a beautiful woman. Worth looking at, even if I have to make a fool of myself."

"As I recall, you did plenty of that a few years ago, when we met you on the Reza Jafari case. I thought you got over her, Lieutenant, when you realized your romantic feelings were unrequited."

64

"I'm here on official business." He pulled out a pack of sugarless gum, unwrapped a stick, popped it into his mouth, tucked the empty wrapper away in a pocket. Same habit he'd had half a dozen years back, when Templeton and I had become entangled with him in a troubling investigation involving a plagiarized screenplay and murder. DeWinter worked his jaws against the gum. "I need to talk to Alexandra, ask her some questions."

"She's got a phone, Lieutenant, same as most people."

"I felt the best way to handle it was personally."

"I'll bet you did."

He shrugged sheepishly, holding his hands out, palms up. "I was hanging back out of respect, OK? Waiting until the time felt right. It involves Joe Soto. I wanted to give her a few minutes before I made my approach."

"Joe Soto died in a hit-and-run, Lieutenant. That's not your usual homicide assignment, is it?"

He sighed, looking pained. "It is now."

Templeton's voice came sharply. "Meaning what?"

We both turned as she stepped around the bend in the path, facing DeWinter. He removed his hat, revealing a short-cropped Afro; below that were large, heavily veined brown eyes; a broad, blunt nose; and a small mustache shaved to a thin line that ran along the ridge of his upper lip. He held the brim of his hat in his big paws, looking sheepish. Claude DeWinter was a huge man, standing a good three inches above my six feet and carrying close to three hundred pounds. His reputation as a skilled homicide investigator was solid. But in Templeton's presence, he could turn suddenly into a little boy, clumsy and tongue-tied.

"Alexandra—Miss Templeton. It's been awhile."

"You're handling Joe's case now?"

"It's been shifted over to me, yes. So—how are you?"

Templeton's voice was steely. "Why, Lieutenant?"

He nibbled his lip, looked at his big shoes. "There's been a development."

"Go on, Lieutenant. We're all adults here."

He looked up, speaking softly. "We've got some new evidence about Mr. Soto's death."

"Then by all means, tell us."

"It seems the driver waited in ambush and deliberately ran Mr. Soto down."

Templeton kept her poise, but her troubled eyes gave her away. "You're sure about this?"

"It seems likely."

"Details, please."

"We needn't go into that right now."

"You're here just to spy on me?"

"No, of course not."

Templeton's voice cut. "Then please, Lieutenant, tell me what you know."

"As Mr. Soto crossed the street, the driver sped around the corner, right at him, and never slowed down."

"I saw that with my own eyes. That's nothing new."

"The car was a Jeep Grand Cherokee."

"Yes, light gray. I reported that to the detective at the scene."

DeWinter studied the hat in his hands. "A witness noticed that the license plates were papered over."

Templeton blanched, and was silent for a moment. "I guess I missed that."

"We also know that the vehicle was parked around the corner for some time, until Mr. Soto stepped into the street. It appeared to be lying in wait."

"Lying in wait," Templeton said.

"Those were the words the witness used."

"The earmarks of an execution."

"We're considering that possibility. I'm sorry, Miss Templeton."

"So Joe *was* murdered." Templeton finally sagged a little. She surveyed the ground around us, saw a bench nearby and went to it. We followed, catching up as she sat. Her eyes roved the garden, as if searching but unseeing. I sat beside her. DeWinter remained standing. Templeton looked up at him as she spoke. "I suppose the first question is, 'Who would want Joe dead?' After that, why. My god, what awful questions."

"I have access to Mr. Soto's files," DeWinter said. "But between his home and his office at the newspaper, there must be a ton of notes and transcripts. I don't know quite where to start. I was hoping you might have some ideas in that regard."

"Joe didn't pull many punches," I said. "I'm sure he had enemies."

But DeWinter was focused on Templeton, who seemed distant from us both. "Are you OK, Miss Templeton?"

She looked up at him, slowly. "How did you happen to get this case?"

DeWinter shrugged. "The captain sent it my way. Remembered that we'd connected on that other case a few years ago. Thought I might be helpful."

"But how did you put me with Joe? We've kept our relationship pretty much to ourselves."

"The detective you spoke to at the crime scene, he put it in his report."

"Of course," Templeton said. "I'd forgotten. You must have gotten the case a day or two after that."

"Something like that, yes. When I learned the service was to be held here, I spoke with Father Aragon. He told me you and Mr. Soto had wedding plans."

Templeton nodded, looking as if her mind had already moved on. "I'll be happy to work with you, Lieutenant, help you any way I can."

"I'd be grateful."

"On one condition—that you share any information with me that doesn't compromise your investigation."

"We'll certainly keep you involved."

"I'm talking about information I'll need as a reporter."

DeWinter's eyes widened. "They assigned you to cover the death of your fiancé?"

"Not yet." Templeton half-smiled. "They will."

"OK," DeWinter said, sounding unconvinced.

"Maybe I'll start with the new details you just gave me. I can call the city desk before we stop at Joe's sister's house. It's breaking news. No point in putting it off. That is, if you're willing to go public with it this soon."

"I don't see the harm." DeWinter reached into an inside pocket of his jacket, pulled out a folded sheet of paper, handed it over. "Here's a copy of my report. If you have any questions—"

"As for where you should start," Templeton said, "I'd suggest you try Joe's recent column on Father Stuart Blackley, and work back from there."

I swung my head in her direction. "Blackley?"

"It was published the same day Joe was killed. The lieutenant has to begin somewhere. Why not there?"

My stomach did a somersault. "I guess I hadn't considered it."

"You're losing your edge, Justice."

I smiled weakly. "I've been trying."

DeWinter handed each of us a business card. "I'll leave you two alone now. I apologize for the intrusion." His smile was pained. "I'm sorry for your loss, Miss Templeton."

He put on his hat, turned, and lumbered back toward the church, leaving indentions in the gravel behind him.

Templeton looked over at me. "So someone decided to take Joe out."

"I'm sorry, Alex. That it turned out like this. That it wasn't an accident."

"He's dead either way, isn't he?" Her voice was chill, almost flippant. "Either way, one has to deal with it and move on."

"Murder makes a difference," I said. "You know that, as well as anyone."

She stood, drew her shawl around her, smiled grimly. "If I don't already, I imagine I will, soon enough. When it starts to sink in."

———

I was ready to get out of there, away from a place where religion and God mingled so uneasily in my consciousness with sex and death. But Templeton wanted to finish our walk, so we continued on. She stopped at the central fountain and each of us tossed in a coin. I made a private wish, she said a silent prayer. A minute after that, we reached the end of the meandering trail.

My eyes were drawn to the windows of the church office, which glowed in the early evening gloom. Inside, Fr. Ismael Aragon stood talking with a thin, bookish, elderly man dressed in a black suit and a parson brand collar. They couldn't have been more different—the handsome young priest, so dark and vibrant, and the older cleric, so parched and bloodless.

"Bishop Finatti," Templeton said. "I didn't expect to see *him* here."

Anthony Finatti was a smallish man, lean almost to gauntness, with wisps of gray hair drawn self-consciously across his pate to camouflage his baldness. Perched on his bony nose was a pair of moon-shaped, wire-rimmed spectacles. Despite his small stature, he projected a sense of inner strength, as if there was a formidable intelligence behind those old-fashioned spectacles and rheumy eyes. He seemed to be doing most of the talking, in an animated, forceful manner, while Father Aragon listened, looking slightly cowed.

"I wonder what brings the second-highest ranking official in the L.A. archdiocese to a little eastside church like this one," Templeton said. "Especially today."

"Maybe he attended the service."

"Joe was a constant thorn in Bishop Finatti's side."

"Still, out of respect."

"I didn't see him inside. Did you?"

I shrugged. "I wasn't really looking."

"Had your eye on that pretty stained glass window, didn't you?" She smiled, more pleasantly than before. "And probably on Father Aragon." She studied him for a long moment. "He is a fine looking man, isn't he? He seems to have a good soul. He was very kind, when we spoke just after the service."

"I don't trust any of them. Though I wouldn't mind taking him to bed."

"Why am I not surprised?" She glanced over. "You ready to go, Romeo?"

I nodded and we turned back. Immediately, we found our path blocked. Facing us was a coatless young man who stood casually as if he'd been there awhile, listening to our every word. He stood a couple of inches shorter than me, about Templeton's height, with a well-tanned, wiry body packed into snug jeans and a tight T-shirt that showed off his hard muscles. His straw-colored hair was buzz cut, his face narrow and angular, and stubbly along the jaw and upper lip. He might have been twenty-six or twenty-seven, taking into account a leathery look that suggested too much sun and decadence. His eyes were slightly buggy and the pupils huge; I figured he was on something.

"Keeping an eye on Bishop Finatti?" He laughed cryptically, with a self-satisfied smile, his piercing blue eyes moving from Templeton to me, where he let them stay. "You and your nice-looking boyfriend here."

"Just taking a walk." Templeton spoke carefully, the way you talk to a stranger who has an agenda or might even be unbalanced.

He cackled with amusement. "Right, just taking a walk."

I asked him off-handedly if he was a friend of Joe Soto.

"No, but I read his column about Father Blackley in Thursday's paper. I found it very interesting."

"Did you," Templeton said, perking up a little.

"Too bad, the way he died like that."

"Who," I asked, "Joe Soto or Father Blackley, eleven years ago?"

The young man shrugged. "Take your pick." He grinned insidiously, bringing something around from behind his back. He clutched it to his chest with both hands, glancing down like it was a treasured secret. "I brought Bishop Finatti a little present. Had it made especially for him. You want to see it?"

"Sure."

"Sure," Templeton echoed.

He held it up, face forward—a copy of Joe's final column, carefully clipped from the *Times* and laminated on a wooden plaque. "You think he'll like it?"

"I have no idea," Templeton said, sounding curious but troubled.

The young man laughed so biliously that I took her arm and whisked her around him. I figured she'd had enough for one day; I knew I had. As we made our way back to the church, his cackle followed us, and I worried that he might be coming after us for some reason. But as I glanced over my shoulder, his back was to us.

He stood with his legs spread and firmly planted, staring into the office in a way that he couldn't be missed. Inside, Bishop Finatti stepped away from Father Aragon to the window, peering out through his wire-rimmed spectacles. His sense of stature and authority had evaporated. He looked distracted now, even a bit unhinged, as if he were seeing an apparition that had risen from among the plaster saints in the garden, stepping forward in the twilight to haunt him.

TEN

I woke at dawn to a fact as stark and unshakable as the prover-
bial pink elephant that you dare yourself not to think about.

Joe Soto had been murdered.

It wasn't as if murder was all that rare in Los Angeles
County, where the homicide rate was climbing again, pushing
toward a thousand for the year. Gang activity alone had accounted for a dozen killings in a recent one-week period. Still,
when violent death strikes close, it's a seismic shock to one's
world for which there's no preparation or reparation, no matter
how efficiently the machinery of justice grinds. For someone—a
sibling, parent, child, lover, friend—every murder is unbearable,
yet every murder must somehow be borne.

*Joe Soto had been murdered. He was gone, erased from ex-
istence.*

My next thought was that Templeton was surely fixed on the
same truth as she came awake, if she'd even slept at all. I should
have called her, if not at that moment, then in the hours that
followed, to give her a sounding board, a shoulder for support.
I didn't. Instead, I looked for things to occupy me that had nothing to do with Joe Soto, or the manner of his death, or who
might have wanted him out of the picture.

By midmorning, in preparation for the writing of my book,

I was scanning articles I'd written for various newspapers and magazines, going back twenty years and more. During the lost years after Jacques's death, when I was drunk or sleeping in my car much of the time, I'd sold off most of my belongings or misplaced what remained. Fortunately, my landlords, Maurice and Fred, had looked after the important things—personal photographs, my published work, Jacques's poetry, vital documents, even my old appointment calendars. They'd sealed them away in boxes and stashed them in the garage without telling me, when I was off on binges. Without that rescued material, I'm not sure I could have put together the manuscript that was due on my editor's desk in eighteen months. It gave me a timeline, dates, and published articles that jogged my memory and provided a sense of structure for a life that had collapsed into a shapeless heap. So I had Maurice and Fred to thank, once again, for saving me from myself.

I was at the kitchen table, looking painfully through my earliest clips—the self-conscious, poorly crafted pieces I'd written in the years just out of college—when the phone rang. The caller was Bishop Anthony Finatti. He wondered if I could meet him downtown at church headquarters to discuss my interest in Fr. Stuart Blackley.

I felt the excitement rising. "You've reconsidered my letter?"

"You could put it that way, yes." Finatti's speech was businesslike and precise. "Might we meet this afternoon?"

"Yes, of course. What time?"

"Would two o'clock fit your schedule?"

I told him I'd be there.

"It's kind of you to come down on such short notice, Mr. Justice."

Bishop Finatti extended a palsied hand, steadying it enough to shake mine with a surprisingly firm grip. He was wearing a dark suit and cleric's collar, much like the one he'd worn the previous day, when Templeton and I had seen him in the office of The Church of the Virgin of Charity. With his wire-rimmed spectacles, wrinkles and kindly smile, he presented an image both scholarly and grandfatherly.

"Not at all, Bishop. I've been hoping for some response."

He offered me an upholstered chair facing him across a broad, spotless desk. His office was large and comfortably furnished, though hardly ostentatious. One wall held shelves laden with religious books and legal journals. On another were framed or laminated legal degrees and various citations, and perhaps two dozen framed photos of Finatti with notable public figures and a few celebrities. Behind him hung two portraits—the current pope and Cardinal Kendall Doyle—with a crucifix in between. A broad, plate glass window was set in the wall to my right, behind a standing statue of the Virgin and Christ Child. Across rooftops to the west, I could see St. Agnes rising on its construction site, with a busy freeway just beyond.

As I sat, Finatti took the chair behind his desk, folding his hands primly in front of him. When he spoke, his voice was firm; there was no sense of the frailty one saw in his thin frame. "From what I understand, Mr. Justice, you're a single man."

"For the past few months, since breaking up with a boyfriend. Before that, nearly ten years, following the death of my lover from AIDS."

"May God be with him."

"I'm sure he'd appreciate that."

"Was he Catholic, as you are?"

"*Was,* Bishop. I haven't worshiped for at least thirty years. Yes, Jacques was Catholic, though a questioner, like me."

"Questions can be valuable, if one's essential faith remains intact."

"I'll try to remember that as I'm asking questions about Father Blackley. That is why I'm here, isn't it? To finally get some answers?"

"We believe we can accommodate you, if we can find a middle ground."

"A middle ground."

Finatti asked me how informed I was about the Roman Catholic Archdiocese of Los Angeles. I knew it to be the largest in the country, I said, with over four million worshipers, mostly Hispanic, but not much more than that. He explained with some pride that the archdiocese encompassed three counties—Santa Barbara and Ventura, as well as Los Angeles—spread over 8,762 square miles. He rattled off other impressive figures: More than three-hundred parishes, more than sixteen-hundred priests, nearly three-thousand nuns, and a vast collection of hospitals, health care centers, day care centers, seminaries, colleges, and universities.

"Did you know, Mr. Justice, that we now administer more than fifty Catholic high schools and over two hundred Catholic elementary schools?"

"That's a lot of children, Bishop."

"That's a lot of important work, Mr. Justice." Finatti placed his fingers together under his pointy chin. "The importance of Southern California in Catholic affairs can hardly be overestimated. Almost routinely now the archbishop of Los Angeles rises to cardinal to, in effect, preside over the western United States. The position and influence of Cardinal Kendall Doyle is enormous. You must realize that?"

"To be frank, I'm more interested in Father Stuart Blackley."

Finatti lowered his small hands, folded them in his lap, studied them a moment, then looked up at me as if he had all his thoughts in order. "Father Blackley must be seen in the larger context of the archdiocese, the Catholic Church, even the Vatican itself."

"Why is that?"

"We are none of us mere individuals, Mr. Justice. We are all part of a greater whole. And, in the case of priests, even wayward priests, part of a greater good. We are, after all, speaking of one of the world's great religions." He smiled, looking mildly embarrassed. "In my view, of course, the *only* great religion, speaking purely in terms of spirituality and truth."

"With the Vatican its unquestioned center of authority."

"Of course, the Vatican is our—"

"An independent state within the city of Rome. A corporation of vast global wealth and influence, that operates in near secrecy, virtually above the law."

"The Vatican," Finatti said, forcing a smile, "is the historic residence of our popes. We are a Church, Mr. Justice, bringing the word of God and the hope of eternal salvation to the world."

I matched his manufactured smile. "Damn big, though."

He said nothing, keeping his smile propped up. I glanced at the portraits of the pontiff and Cardinal Kendall Doyle on the wall behind him. When I returned my gaze to the Bishop, I directed it straight through the lenses of his spectacles, finding his rheumy gray eyes. "You're not going to open Father Blackley's files to me, are you? You're not going to tell me much about him at all. The conversation so far is the prelude to an elaborate runaround, isn't it?"

"You've made certain claims, Mr. Justice. We take such charges with the utmost seriousness."

"I'm sure that you do, Bishop, given the press you've been getting, and the kind of hush money you've been paying out."

He ignored that and pressed on. "Whenever we are presented with evidence that a priest has done what you've suggested, our hearts go out to the victim."

"Before or after you've consulted with your battery of lawyers?"

He ignored that as well. "Unfortunately, the incidents you allege date back more than thirty years. The Buffalo diocese has no record of any complaints by you or your family in all that time. Perhaps, if someone could back you up—"

"My family's gone, Bishop. Father, mother, sister. I'm all that's left. I suspect you knew that. It's been written about, here and there, when the press has covered my various escapades."

"You do come with a past, Mr. Justice."

"We all do, Bishop."

"And something of a tarnished reputation. May I speak frankly?"

"It might save us some time."

"You're not a man whose word can be trusted. Fair to say?"

"Father Blackley and I had sex on a regular basis, starting a few months after my twelfth birthday and ending just after I turned fourteen. He did the same with other children back in Buffalo, girls as well as boys. I've got the documents to prove it. I suspect you know that too."

"We've seen nothing like that."

"But you surely read Joe Soto last week. You must have figured out from the letters I sent you previously that I'm the anonymous victim mentioned in his column. Or I wouldn't be sitting here, would I?"

"What exactly is it you want from us, Mr. Justice?"

"I'd like to know something about Stuart Blackley after he joined this archdiocese. Where he worked, how many times he was reassigned, and why. I'd like to know about your efforts to rehabilitate him, how well they succeeded, documentation to that effect. Parishioners who knew him especially well, with whom I might speak. Conversations he might have had with bishops or other priests, records of such if they exist. Anything that will help me form a more complete picture of the man, how he behaved after he left Buffalo, what made him tick."

Finatti raised his hands again, bringing his fingers together under his nose, while peering at me over the tips. "I must say, you're a very thorough fellow. You must have been an excellent reporter, before your—your problems."

"Stuart Blackley's going to be part of my book, Bishop, whether you like it or not. You can either assist me, or run the risk of looking like you're pulling yet another cover-up."

He studied me placidly for a long moment. Then: "We're prepared to make you a generous financial settlement for your suffering."

"I'm not asking for money."

"One million dollars." I gasped, in spite of myself. Finatti smiled confidently. "That's quite a lot for someone who hasn't worked much in recent years."

I sat back in my chair, collecting myself. "You've had me investigated?"

"One million dollars, Mr. Justice. We've already worked things out with the Buffalo diocese. They're picking up half the cost. Their liability coverage will cover most of their end. We're willing to make up the rest, as a matter of expediency." His smile broadened. "And, of course, because it's the right thing to do."

"I thought you didn't believe me, Bishop."

"It's not that we don't believe you. The point is, will others, given your unsavory history? You're very fortunate to be hearing this offer at all."

"Naturally, you'd want something in return."

"There would be certain stipulations, yes."

"Such as?"

"You'd give up the right to pursue any legal claims against the Church or any diocese in relation to Father Blackley or any other priest."

"No gag order? I could still write about him in my book?"

"As long as you limit your scope to Father Blackley when he was in Buffalo, and that you leave the Los Angeles archdiocese out of it, since his years with us have no appreciable connection to you or your family."

"Why are you so eager to pay for sins committed three thousand miles away by a priest in upstate New York? You haven't even had time to properly investigate my charges. It doesn't make sense."

"I'm going to be forthright, Mr. Justice. Your claims, along with your curiosity, come at a particularly sensitive time." Finatti rose, standing between the portraits of the pope and Cardinal Doyle. He glanced first at the painting on the left. "It's hardly a secret that the health of the pontiff is precarious. He alone has the choice to step down or to die in office. Whatever he decides, we're looking at a year or two, at the most, may God bless his soul." The Bishop crossed himself, then swung his eyes to the right, settling on the portrait of Cardinal Kendall Doyle. "Cardinal Doyle is almost certainly on the short list of possible replacements."

"You're saying that Cardinal Doyle could become the next pope."

"Yes!" Finatti became animated, placing the flat of his hands on his desk, leaning forward excitedly. "Do you know what that means? Cardinal Doyle has a chance to become the first American pope in history. It would be an achievement that would honor not just our archdiocese and the city of Los Angeles but the entire country."

"The larger context," I said.

"Yes, yes, yes! Precisely." He straightened, spreading his arms, his palms up. "We simply wish to avoid adverse publicity at such a precipitous time. I'm sure you can understand that. At the same time, we have the opportunity to compensate a victim with Christian charity. It's worth a million dollars for us to accomplish both."

"You and Buffalo."

"We have mutual interests in this." He folded his thin arms across his chest, looking pleased. "A million dollars. Not such a shabby sum, my boy."

"No, not shabby at all."

"We have an agreement then?"

I stood. "I'll think about it, get back to you."

Finatti came around the desk. "What is there to think about?"

I shrugged. "My conscience?"

A notepad next to his phone caught my eye; on the top sheet, he'd printed a reminder: *Lindsay, lunch, Thursday.* He placed a hand on my elbow, turned me away toward the door. "I wouldn't take too long, Mr. Justice. Offers like this can be withdrawn."

There was a knock at the door. Finatti opened it. A middle-aged woman in an inexpensive business suit stuck her head in, pointing at her wristwatch.

"Yes, yes," Finatti said. "Mr. Justice was just leaving."

I faced Finatti as she disappeared. "Tell me something, Bishop."

"If I can."

"You and Father Blackley were friends."

"Somewhat, yes."

"Did he ever talk to you about any of the children he was close to?"

Finatti's speech grew clipped, cautious. "He might have mentioned a particular child from time to time. It's been so long. I wouldn't remember exactly whom."

"I ask, because I'm curious if he cared about us, if he thought of as individuals, as human beings. Or if it was just an act, to get what he wanted from us."

The Bishop placed a spotted hand on my shoulder. When he looked up, finding my eyes, his own eyes reflected what looked like real compassion. "Is that what all this is about, my son? You want to know if Father Blackley had genuine affection for you?"

"It matters to me, yes." I felt my face flush, and swallowed with difficulty. "I wish it didn't but it does."

"I think I understand. I'm not sure I can tell you what you need to know." Finatti's voice had grown soft; he gently squeezed my shoulder. "Stuart Blackley was a troubled man, Mr. Justice. A man deeply conflicted by undesirable compulsions. But he's dead. Whatever he did was settled between him and God long ago. Perhaps you could find it in your heart to forgive him, so that both of you might have some peace."

Outside, in the anteroom, the woman reappeared, holding a briefcase and a pair of sunglasses like a butler seeing his master off to work.

I turned my attention back to Finatti. "Is that part of the million-dollar deal, Bishop? Forgive and forget."

He smiled with faint amusement, while removing his hand. "You have my number, Mr. Justice. Don't let our generous offer slip away."

TEN

It was a quarter past three by the time I left archdiocese head-quarters and pulled out on to Father Junipero Serra Boulevard. The first thing I noticed was Bishop Finatti at the curb, climbing into the back of a black Lincoln Town Car.

I drove west in something of a daze, mulling Finatti's unexpected proposal. As I neared the cathedral construction site, I found myself imagining what I might do with a million dollars. It seemed like a fantasy, akin to winning the lottery, or selling a screenplay that looked like a blockbuster to a producer with more dollars than sense. For somebody like me, a million bucks could change everything. Taxes and my agent's cut had whittled the first installment of my book advance—fifty thousand dol-lars—nearly in half. I wouldn't see another payment until the manuscript was done, well over a year away. The final payment would come many months after that, when acceptable revisions were complete. My HMO coverage—perhaps my most crucial asset, left over from a previous job—was draining six hundred bucks a month from my bank account. My monthly co-pay on the five prescriptions I took to stay healthy siphoned off another hundred. At the moment, a million dollars seemed like a fool's dream.

Then St. Agnes loomed into view, putting the sum into perspective. For Cardinal Kendall Doyle, I realized, a million bucks would barely cover the hundred fine tapestries being designed and woven to decorate his fabulous new church.

As I pulled over for a better look, I understood why the coverage in the *L.A. Times* had emphasized the sweep and grandeur of the cardinal's vision: St. Agnes spread out around and rose above me in monolithic proportions, merging architectural design both historic and futuristic, looming like a mountain of angles against the windswept sky. The church itself was twelve stories at the highest point of its roofline. Separated from it and rising thirty feet higher was a fifteen-story campanile, awaiting nearly three dozen bells. Much of the work was yet to be finished— doors, windows, tiles, paint, landscaping. But the walls were up and the roof was in place, making it clear that St. Agnes would surely take its place among the great cathedrals of the world.

Workers in hardhats swarmed over the site, sawing lumber, pounding nails, connecting wire, pouring concrete. Others transported endless objects, large and small, through the enormous opening that served as the front entrance, which would soon be fitted with two twenty-five-ton copper doors bearing sculpted images of the Virgin Mary. At least that's what the *L.A. Times* had reported, along with other impressive figures that rattled around in my head: nearly sixty thousand square feet in the church alone, seating for three thousand, underground parking for six hundred vehicles, and twelve hundred crypt spaces and four thousand niches for urns in the underground mausoleum. All of it had been designed with state-of-the-art materials and technology to withstand the worst anticipated earthquake, and achieve a life span of at least five hundred years.

I scanned the ground that would serve as a sprawling plaza out front, across several acres, until a human form closer to the street caught my eye—a shirtless construction worker, standing with his back to me perhaps fifty feet inside the chain link gates. In one hand, he held a water bottle that he twisted back and forth like a propeller in motion; the other hand was on his thigh, drumming on it like he couldn't keep his fingers still. He was the wiry type, his muscles corded and taut, his wide but knobby shoulders tapering to a narrow waist slung with a heavy tool belt. He tilted back his hardhat to guzzle from the water bottle, while a T-shirt dangled from a back pocket of his tight jeans and the afternoon sun warmed his freckled skin. By the way he stood in narcissistic repose, so obviously on display, I got the feeling he understood only too well the sensual impact of the male body.

He was worth looking at, that's for sure. I wondered if the face measured up to the rest of him. I climbed from the Mustang for a better look.

At that moment—half past three—the black Lincoln Town Car pulled up to the gates, which security guards scrambled to open. The shirtless worker turned to face the incoming vehicle, showing me a smooth chest that daily labor had left chiseled and hard. It wasn't the artificial gym look, all those overdeveloped bulges and calculated ripples that had turned so many men, gay and straight, into self-conscious clones. This was Michelangelo's David, just the way natural physical exertion had shaped him. Only this David came with a distinctly sinister feature: Tattooed across the taut chest was a black cross extending from breastbone down to navel, and across from nipple to nipple. Winding around the cross was a dark strand of menacing barbed wire.

As the worker turned a bit more, I got a better look at his face: Good cheekbones and a strong chin; narrow in between, with a long, shapely nose and blue eyes that blazed; not an exceptional face, not flawless and movie star striking, but handsome enough to make a nice match with the sharply cut body.

It was also a familiar face—I recognized the edgy young man with the unsettling laugh and grin, whom Templeton and I had encountered the previous evening at the Church of the Virgin of Charity—the mysterious figure with the laminated copy of Joe Soto's column, who'd gone out of his way to unnerve Bishop Anthony Finatti.

"Nick, get back, dammit! Let the car pass!"

85

So that was his name: Nick. The voice came from a middle-aged man in shirtsleeves and tie who emerged from a nearby mobile home, hollering at the worker with a familiarity that suggested a stronger connection than just boss and employee. Attached to the trailer were two signs, stenciled on metal sheeting:

CHARLES GASH CONSTRUCTION CO.

OFFICE

The older man scurried anxiously in the direction of the arriving car, clutching a clipboard under one arm while cinching up his tie. Nick stood aside to let the gleaming Town Car through, but not by much, keeping his workman's boots planted insolently on the rough ground. His hands were in motion again, rolling the empty water bottle between them, while his shoulders twitched like those of a hipster hearing an edgy bop tune in his head. The man with the clipboard stopped to stare at the tattoo with obvious disgust. Then he gave his bare-chested worker a tongue-lashing, ordering him to cover himself out of respect to Cardinal Doyle. Hardhats and security guards looked on bemused, as if they'd witnessed this kind of confrontation before. Nick threw back his head, while his sharp laugh cracked the air and the other man flushed and fumed.

"Cover yourself, dammit!"

Nick stared the other man down in silent defiance. His shirt stayed in his back pocket, untouched. They were almost nose to nose, and I saw that they shared the same intense blue eyes, and similar facial structure. Father and son, I thought, one still lean and strong from manual labor, the other going soft and thick from too many years behind a desk.

The older man lowered his voice, his jaw clenched. "We'll talk about this later."

"Whatever." Nick began beating the water bottle in a staccato rhythm against his empty hand. Some part of him always seemed to be moving.

His father—if that's who he was—turned furiously on his heel, making for the big car as it rolled to a stop. Two security guards pushed the gate closed from either side. The harried man with the clipboard opened a rear door. Cardinal Kendall Doyle stepped out, holding a book-sized box; his eyes rose instantly to the unfinished cathedral, while his broad, reddish face broke into a proud smile. He was a big, well-fed man with fleshy features and a healthy crop of thick white hair, dressed in clerical black; his wide face, heavy with jowls, was distinguished by sparkling green eyes, a round button nose, and a small, perfect mole in the middle of his deeply cleft chin.

"Your Eminence!" the man with the clipboard cried.

"Charles." The Cardinal's voice was warm and fulsome, as he turned, extending both hands, to greet the other man.

Charles Gash—again, my assumption—welcomed Cardinal Doyle almost worshipfully, all but kneeling to kiss his ring. Eventually, he fixed on the box in the Cardinal's hands. "This is it, then?"

Doyle regarded it with reverence. "The Bible that's been in my family for generations."

"May I?" Gash held out his hands tentatively.

"By all means." The Cardinal handed over the box, which Gash accepted as if it was a sacred object. "It's just an old Bible, Charles. But it means everything to me."

"Of course, Your Eminence. We've prepared a special place for it. You'll see."

Doyle beamed again, as his eyes went back to the cathedral that towered over everything. "Every day, I see something new, some small detail that reflects the everlasting glory of God."

"We're blessed to be able to do our small part, Cardinal."

As Charles Gash fawned and fussed, Bishop Finatti stepped from the other side of the car, shutting off his cell phone and coming around behind.

A few yards away, Nick stood his ground. For a moment, all his nervous tics and movements halted and he seemed to relax, to find focus. He tipped back his hardhat, giving Finatti the full benefit of his malevolent grin. Finatti reacted, clearly startled to see him again. Then Finatti's troubled stare descended to Nick's bare chest—the tattooed cross entangled in barbed wire. Nick let out one of his unearthly laughs, causing the Bishop to flinch and turn abruptly away. He hurried after Cardinal Doyle, who was striding off toward the cathedral as Charles Gash scurried along beside him, holding the small, rectangular box with great delicacy, as if it contained a live bomb.

A security guard stepped to the gate, looking me over. "We need to keep the driveway clear. Don't mind if you look in, but you got to step to the side."

I glanced again at the sign above the mobile home, then toward the receding figures. "That would be Charles Gash—the clipboard with the Cardinal?"

"That's the man. Been helping plan this thing for close to fifteen years, or so they tell me. In charge of construction for the last five."

"Quite a project to land."

"They don't come much bigger. You got business with Mr. Gash? Because he'll be tied up for awhile. Always is about this time, when the Cardinal stops by to check up on things."

"The Cardinal comes every day?"

"Right on schedule."

"The hardhat without the shirt—I guess that would be Mr. Gash's kid, Nick."

The guard glanced over. Nick stood with his back to us, staring after the scurrying figure of Bishop Finatti, twitching again like a man wired for electric current. The guard clucked. "Yeah, that's Nick, all right."

"He and the old man don't seem to get along too well."

"Mr. Gash has him learning the business, seems to want him involved. He tries hard. But there's something eating away at that kid. He's a strange one."

"Seems kind of jumpy."

"That's one way to put it." The guard seemed to realize he was talking more than he should. He nodded toward the sidewalk to my right. "Like I said, just step to the side and you'll be OK."

As the guard moved off, Nick Gash swung slowly around to face me, as if equipped with radar. Our eyes locked and held. He stepped over, until only the chain link fence and a few feet stood between us.

"Nice church, huh?" His grin broadened. "Amazing what you can get these days for two hundred million bucks."

"I don't see how you'll have it finished in six months."

"We'll have it finished. We're working round the clock now, except for holidays. Sometimes, I work thirty-six hours straight, without blinking an eye."

"Doesn't seem possible."

"I couldn't do it on my own, that's for sure." His voice took on a seductive hue. "You interested in architecture?"

"I might be. Why?"

"I got the blueprints to this place, you ever want to see 'em."

"Where would that be?"

"My place." He spread his legs and thrust his nervous hands into the pockets of his jeans, tugging them lower, showing off a washboard abdomen under a web of blond hair. "You like to party?"

"You're pretty forward."

"You're pretty sexy."

I was always amazed when a man as trim and good-looking as Nick Gash showed an interest in a more ordinary guy like me, but it still happened from time to time. It's like they say: There's no accounting for taste.

"What makes you think I'm interested, Nick?"

"The way you're looking at me." His right hand came out of its pocket to caress his hairless chest. Then his fingers slowly traced a path between his hardening nipples, along the arms of his unholy tattoo. I drew my eyes away with some difficulty, finding his face again. He hadn't shaved that day, maybe two, and the golden bristle of his beard glinted in the fading sunlight. He ran his tongue over his lips like a vamp in a bad B movie, then grinned with insinuation.

"Sorry," I said, "you got it wrong."

I turned away, before my eyes gave up my lie. The truth was that I felt powerfully attracted to Nick Gash, in spite of the fact that he looked like trouble, or maybe because of it. It was a dangerous feeling, one that I hadn't allowed myself in a long time. As I climbed behind the wheel of the Mustang, I stole a glance back. Nick had departed, but I could still see him standing there, lean and leering, radiating his special kind of heat. His image was seared into my brain, like fire on flesh.

ELEVEN

I arrived home at dusk to find Templeton sitting at the top of the steps outside my door, twisting a damp hankie with both hands. A large manila envelope, well stuffed, leaned against the gray skirt covering her thigh. When she raised her head at the sound of my footsteps, the lids of her eyes were swollen.

She rose, looking fragile. "Benjamin, I'm sorry."

"Bad day, huh?"

She nodded, fighting tears.

"Come on in," I said. "I'll make tea."

We stood in the kitchen, saying nothing, as the water boiled. When the tea had steeped, and the cups were full and steaming, Templeton said, "I guess things are catching up with me."

"It happens."

"I swore I wouldn't let it. I promised myself I'd tough it out."

She broke down, fell into my arms, and wept against my shoulder. I wanted to remind her that I wasn't very good at this. There were other things that came more easily—tracking people down, sifting through clues, punching somebody if it came to that. But every atom in me resisted getting this close to grief again.

Finally, her tears ebbed. She took a deep breath, wiped her eyes, blew her nose. "I brought something you might want to see." She picked up the bulky manila envelope, opened it, dumped the contents on the table. "Or maybe not. That's up to you."

"What is this?"

"Letters that came to the *Times* for Joe. They collected in his mail slot after he was—after what happened the other night."

"Photocopies?"

"I turned the originals over to Claude DeWinter."

"He should have thought to pick these up on his own."

"These came in before he was assigned the case—before they knew it was something more than just a hit-and-run. I shouldn't have taken them, since they're addressed to Joe. Violates the company rules. But I don't really give a damn."

"You looked through them?"

She nodded as we took chairs and sat. "Most of them were written by readers responding to his final column." She glanced at me cautiously. "Quite a few had some knowledge of Father Blackley."

I felt my gut tighten. "Not surprising, really. That's what we were hoping for, wasn't it?"

Her eyes went back to the piles of paper. The photocopied letters were separated into three groups, each bundle secured with a hinged paper clip and marked with a Post-it note. "I organized them by category." Templeton began laying them out, one by one. "This is the correspondence from readers responding to the column in general. Most of the letters are positive but there are about a dozen that take issue with Joe's viewpoint. Some of the dissenting letters are quite strong—consigning Joe to the devil, wishing that he burn in hell, that kind of thing." She paused, swallowed hard. "The two letters on top wish him dead. The way they read, it just sounds like talk, angry readers ranting. I don't think it means anything." She pushed the pile away, which left two.

I glanced at them. "And the others?"

Templeton sipped some tea, then set her cup aside. "This is from group of readers who knew Father Blackley personally, or had some contact with him, and wrote in his defense. They could be useful, I suppose, if I feel I need that point of view when I put my story together."

"Balance," I said.

"Right, balance." She picked up the final stack. "This is the other group." Her skittish eyes met mine, then skipped away. "The people who knew Father Blackley, and have a different view of him."

"A different view."

"There's no reason for you to look at them if you don't want to. Lieutenant DeWinter and I plan to follow up each one. He's retrieved all of Joe's phone messages and e-mails, and anything else that came in. If there are any good leads here, we'll find them."

"Then why bring them with you?"

"I felt you had a right to decide, Justice. About how much you need to know."

"Like I said, it's what I wanted—to fill in my background on Father Blackley."

"OK, if you're sure." She placed the pile of papers on the table. Without touching it, I read the top letter. It was a handwritten note in English, with a few errors of grammar and spelling. The writer was a woman called Bing Crisologo, a name which I recognized as Filipino, a common ethnicity in polyglot L.A. The handwriting was neat and precise, yet graceful.

Dear Mr. Soto,

I read your column this morning in the newspaper and my heart is breaking, the pain inside me is so big. I have always kept a belief in God and try my best to be a good Catholic and loyal to the church. But when I read your story I know I cannot keep my silent any longer, I must tell someone the truth. I know now that they hide behind God and Jesus with their lies. It is all so bad that I cry at night instead of sleep. He promised me he will name the church St. Lucy but now I know it was a lie and that he has been telling me other lies for all of these years. Maybe also about Father Blackley I think and what happened to my beautiful little girl. Please call me, Mr. Soto, and I will tell you my story if you wish me.

Sincerely,

Bing Crisologo

Bing Crisologo had printed her phone number neatly below her name. There was a staple in the upper left hand corner, attaching a second page. I glanced at it. Templeton had photocopied the envelope as well, which bore a return address in the San Fernando Valley.

"Why is this one on top?"

"I prioritized them subjectively," Templeton said. "This one seemed particularly interesting."

"The cryptic reference to St. Lucy?"

"That was part of it." She smiled self-critically. "I also figured Bing Crisologo might be useful. Not to stereotype, but Filipino women tend to be trusting and open, even submissive. Filipinos in general, for that matter. It's a gentle culture for the most part."

"Easily exploited," I said. "Look at the country's history. Could be a productive interview."

Templeton smiled painfully again. "We do what we have to do."

I glanced at the other pile, the letters in support of Father Blackley. "And this one? The letter on top?"

"From a couple named Jim and Cathy Quimby, praising Father Blackley to the skies. They describe him as a kind, caring, devoted priest. They can't believe that's he's molested anyone. They run a home for unwed mothers-to-be out in Redondo Beach."

"What's the tone of the letter?"

"They seem like nice people. Christian to the core, but without the sanctimony and hysteria. They questioned the credibility of Joe's anonymous victim, suggesting it might be an attempt to extort money from the Church."

I drew the pile closer, looking at the letter. It was typed flawlessly on a business letterhead: Hope Haven, a Non-Profit Sanctuary for Unwed Mothers. When I unclipped it, I found a color brochure attached that described the charity the Quimbys ran, a home where girls and young women could live while bringing their babies to term and giving birth, as an alternative to abortion. It ended with a pitch for a donation, and a P.O. box where money could be sent. There was also a photo of Jim and Cathy Quimby. They were a blond, blue-eyed, well-scrubbed couple, in their forties by the look of them. Their smiles bordered on the angelic.

"And why is this one on top?"

Templeton shrugged. "The Quimbys seem like a well-meaning couple. The letter's articulate and rational, with a strong sense of belief."

"Plus, they're photogenic."

"Doesn't hurt. We'll need pictures." I sipped my tea, while Templeton straightened the piles of letters. "We've got some real leads now, Justice. I expect we'll have more quite soon. I smell a good story developing."

I gestured at the bundles of paper. "You'll need these, then."

"I have my own copies." Our eyes met for a second of silence. "These are for you—if you want them."

I sat back, studying them again, weighing where I was willing to go. "Sure, leave them. It never hurts to have an extra set for safekeeping."

We both turned at the sound of light rapping from the landing. I opened the door to find Maurice outside, wearing his customary evening silk kimono and smelling of French cologne. Fred stood at the bottom of the stairs in a shapeless old sweat suit, one hand deep inside the waistband, scratching himself.

Maurice held out a tray with covered containers. "We had some leftovers. Nothing fancy, but everything's still warm." He peeked around the door, lowering his voice. "Fred saw Alexandra earlier, waiting for you on the steps. He was concerned. We figured you two could use some dinner."

"It's very kind, Maurice."

"Not at all. I'll pick up the Tupperware in the morning."

"I'll have it washed and waiting."

"I've heard that before!" Maurice waved me off, rolling his eyes. "You have some fine qualities, Benjamin, but housekeeping is not among them. Just enjoy your meal. I'll handle the cleaning up."

I gave Fred a nod of thanks as Maurice scurried down the steps, and he nodded in return. They made their way back across the patio with their arms around each other, two old men who'd been together nearly five decades and couldn't imagine being with anyone else. A beefy trucker and a more delicate dance instructor, both retired and strikingly unalike, who'd fallen in love as young men and felt their affection deepen through the decades, and whom only death could separate now. It was how I'd imagined Jacques and me one day, before he'd come down with a dry cough and then his first lesion, back when everything had still seemed possible.

I stood watching until Maurice and Fred were inside the house and the cats had dashed in after them, just before the door was closed.

Templeton and I cleared space at the table and ate our meal while catching up. She talked about Lindsay St. John, speculating on what kind of clamps the editorial manager might try to put on Templeton's Father Blackley investigation. I mentioned seeing Bishop Finatti and Cardinal Doyle at the cathedral site that afternoon, and told her about Finatti's financial offer.

Templeton's eyes opened wide. "A *million* dollars?"

"That's the figure he put out."

"You're going to take it, right?"

"I'm not sure. It comes with strings attached."

"For a million dollars, maybe you could live with a few strings."

"Maybe. Could you?"

"I've got a career, remember? You should at least think about it, Justice. You'd be crazy not to."

"Believe me, it's been difficult to think about anything else."

We grew silent as we finished our meal. As I was clearing the plates, she kept her eyes averted, busying herself with the stacks of photocopied correspondence. When I stopped what I was doing and stood over her, she failed to look up.

"You want to tell me what's on your mind?"

She gave up fussing with the papers, took a deep breath, raised her eyes. "I have a special favor to ask."

"OK."

"I was wondering if I could spend the night."

"Here?" She nodded slowly. I pulled out a chair and sat. "What's going on?"

"I came by because I don't think I can take another night alone."

"Maybe it's time you talk to your folks, tell them about Joe."

She shook her head resolutely. "I'm not ready yet. I don't want to deal with their judgment. That's not what I need right now."

"What do you need, Alex?"

She shrugged self-consciously. "Someone warm beside me. Someone who cares about me. A friend."

Years ago, when we'd first met, Templeton and I had faced some thorny issues involving her romantic feelings for me. She'd been a lot younger then, less sure of herself and still angry with me for the way I'd disgraced myself and the journalism trade in general. Her resentment had gotten mixed up with a cub reporter's crush, making for a tense relationship in the beginning. We'd worked through it, both grown up a little, and put it behind us. At least I thought we had.

"A friend? You're sure that's what you need?"

"That's all I'm asking, Justice. I'm not looking for anything more."

I glanced at the unmade bed. "Sure, we can try it." I laughed remotely. "I'm not the best sleeper, you know. I'm up and down a lot."

"I figured that."

"Your timing's good, though."

"How so?"

"Fresh sheets. I changed them just last week."

She fell asleep beside me sometime after midnight, facing away, the two of us apart but with our heads on the same pillow. When I heard her breathing grow deep and rhythmic, I withdrew as carefully as I could, slipping from the bed to the bathroom without flicking on a light. I took my late-night pill and peed without flushing, so as not to wake her.

A quarter moon was out, obscured by clouds. I stood at the window watching them drift and change shape, and separate every now and then to let some light through. After awhile, I became aware of a figure standing near the end of the drive, looking up at the apartment, obscured by the distance and insufficient light. It wasn't unknown in Boys Town for a man to stand outside another man's home like that, fixed on the occupant. Ex-lovers, spurned boyfriends, shy men with unspoken crushes, even stalkers—there were plenty of explanations. It wasn't commonplace, but it happened now and then in a neighborhood where the air was constantly alive with romantic possibilities. There had been a time, not all that many years ago, when I would have been down the stairs in a heartbeat—to see who the stranger was, if he belonged there or needed chasing off, or maybe an invitation up. That was then.

I quietly drew the shade, checked the lock on the door, then slipped back into bed beside Templeton, wondering if the stranger was still out there and what he wanted. I didn't sleep.

TWELVE

At half past six, Templeton woke to find me at the kitchen table, jotting down more notes for my book.

The section I was working on was to cover the night I met Jacques at a steamy disco on Santa Monica Boulevard, where I'd first glimpsed him whirling like a dervish to "Dancing Queen" under the rotating glitter ball. In some ways, it felt like it had happened yesterday, as vivid as the sweat glistening on his lithe frame as he leaped and twirled to the beat, seducing me with every move as I stood with a drink at the bar, unable to take my eyes off him. In other ways, it felt like a dream, a surreal image from a make believe time before his illness that never was.

"Busy on the book?"

Templeton stood over me from behind, her hands on my shoulders. I turned my yellow legal pad over, pushed it aside, smiled blandly. "Nothing important. Just notes."

I suggested breakfast down on the boulevard at Boy Meets Grill but she said she needed to get home, to make herself presentable for work. I walked her down to the street, telling her about the stranger I'd seen at the end of the drive, unrecognizable in the dark, only hours before.

"I don't know what it means," I said. "Just the same, you're the primary witness in Joe's death. Maybe you should reconsider St. John's suggestion to take some time off."

"Back off the story?"

"Let someone else handle it. People would understand."

"I never thought I'd hear that from you, Justice."

I shrugged haplessly. "People change, I guess."

She shook her head. "Sorry, not possible."

"Why not?"

"I have a duty to Joe. To finish the story, see it through."

"It's that simple?"

She nodded, then kissed me quickly. "Thanks for letting me stay over last night. It means a lot."

"At least be careful."

"You do the same."

"Me? I'm not involved like you are."

"*Au contraire.* You're the anonymous victim, Justice—the catalyst for all this."

I hadn't thought of it that way before, and it bothered me. "For Joe's death, you mean."

She put her fingers to my lips. "No. That's not what I meant."

"What then?"

"All I'm saying is if Joe's last column has any connection to his murder, then maybe you need to be careful too." She glanced at her watch. "I've got to go. You know me, Miss Punctuality."

Back in the apartment, I stirred boiling water into a spoonful of instant coffee and drank it standing up, while staring down at the stacks of letters on my kitchen table, the copies Templeton had brought with her last night. The letter I kept coming back to was from Bing Crisologo, the Filipino woman with the neat handwriting and plaintive voice, who'd written to Joe Soto expressing the need to talk.

After breakfast and a shower, I called the number she'd printed beneath her signature. An automated recording informed me the number had been disconnected.

A minute after that I was in the Mustang, on my way over

the hills and into the Valley to the address I'd copied from Bing Crisologo's envelope.

The street number belonged to a plain, two-story stucco apartment house in the working class community of Van Nuys, a few blocks from the busy intersection of the San Diego and Ventura freeways. I climbed to the second floor and rang the bell at number twenty-four. No one answered. After ringing again and getting no response, I pulled open the screen and pounded on the door. No one came.

A rectangular window with sliding sections and screens at either end faced the balcony. I found one section open a crack but the curtains drawn together, with a sliver where they didn't quite connect. I bent to peer in at the same moment an eye peered out. Inside, a startled scream was followed by two tiny fists snatching the curtains closed the rest of the way.

"Bing Crisologo? I'm a friend of Joe Soto, the newspaper writer. I have a few questions."

"Please, not now. Thank you." Her voice was small, frightened.

"In your letter, you told Mr. Soto that you needed to talk."

"Go away, please. I'm very busy."

"I've come all this way to see you. At least open the door and talk to me face to face. Please."

I'd never known a Filipino to act inhospitably, if it could be helped; during the regime of dictator Ferdinand Marcos, I'd interviewed corrupt cops and politicians in Manila who'd been unerringly cordial and polite, even the ones with blood on their hands. Bing Crisologo lived up to my expectations. I heard the door being unlatched, then the dead bolt being turned. As the door came open, I faced a small, brown woman with a round, pleasant face, dressed in a blue nurse's uniform. Behind her and to the side, luggage was stacked.

"I tried to call," I said. "Your phone's been disconnected."

"I must have forgotten to pay the bill. Please, I have things

I must do." She tried to close the door; I stopped it with my hand. Her eyes grew more frightened. "What is it you want, please?"

"I've come to talk about Father Blackley."

"I'm sorry, I do not know what you mean."

"You wrote a letter to Joe Soto. I've seen it."

"Please, go away now."

"Mr. Soto's death has you spooked, doesn't it?"

"I cannot talk about this. It was a mistake to write the letter. Please, I would like you to go."

"What did you mean, when you referred to St. Lucy in your letter?"

"You are from the newspaper?"

"I'm here as a friend of Joe Soto. My name's Benjamin Justice."

"You are not the police?"

"No."

"Then please, sir. Go away and leave me be."

With an apologetic look, she shut the door. When she had the door latched and bolted, she pulled the sliding window section tight and secured that as well. I retreated back down the stairs and across the street to the Mustang, where I climbed behind the wheel and waited.

Not quite twenty minutes later, a faded Toyota pulled out of the apartment house driveway. Bing Crisologo was behind the wheel, a white nursing cap pinned atop her wavy dark hair.

She turned right and I followed. She made another turn, reached Sepulveda Boulevard, then took an on-ramp that put her in the sluggish southbound lanes of the Ventura Freeway. When the Hollywood Freeway interchange came up, she veered off, into commuter traffic that was slowing to a crawl. Not quite fifteen minutes later, with the downtown skyscrapers looming a mile or two ahead, she made an exit on to surface streets that took us into the business and residential neighborhoods of Filipinotown.

Groceries and restaurants bore signs in both English and Tagalog, the principal Filipino language. But there were also Korean and Persian influences along the boulevard, as well as the occasional nod to soul food or Hispanic commerce that encompassed every culture south of the border from Mexico to Guatemala.

I kept my distance as Bing Crisologo glanced frequently into her rearview mirror. We were on First Street, heading toward the central city, when she turned off on to a wide street called Carondelet. Up and down each side were clean curbs and sidewalks, and vintage, single-story houses with neatly kept lawns and flowerbeds. Out front, spaced evenly along the street, towering palms stretched upward, skinny up the rough trunk and bushy with shaggy fronds at the top. Here and there, mothers were out with children too young for school, sometimes watching over a gaggle that probably combined the offspring of several families.

Midway down the long block, Bing Crisologo swung into a paved driveway beside an old California Craftsman with a broad front porch. A younger Filipina, slightly taller and quite pretty, emerged from the side of the house to pull open a detached garage in back. Bing Crisologo drove straight in, parked and got out. Together, the two women unloaded suitcases from the car, pulled the garage door down, and scurried into the house with the luggage. They moved quickly, their eyes darting toward the street, where I sat in the idling Mustang at the opposite curb.

The next thing I noticed were curtains being drawn, with unmistakable haste. Not just at one window, but every curtain in the house.

THIRTEEN

Back on First Street I made a right turn that pointed me east, toward Boyle Heights and the Church of the Virgin of Charity.

I picked up the route Templeton and I had taken the day of Joe Soto's memorial mass—past the *L.A. Times,* City Hall, and Parker Center, as police headquarters was officially known; through the few blocks comprising Little Tokyo; then across the Los Angeles River into the barrios of East L.A. I stopped at a corner stall hung with colorful piñatas to buy one for Maurice— he always had a party in his future—and ten minutes later I was parking across the street from La Iglesia de la Virgen de la Caridad.

The day was cloudless and sunlight slanted sharply across the garden behind the church. Among the cacti and succulents, an old man under a straw hat raked leaves. I followed the winding path past the statues of saints to the door of the church office, which was open to the crisp autumn air.

A young Hispanic woman in a wheelchair sat behind a desk handling phones and files, moving efficiently between her desk and a bank of short cabinets behind her. Several older women were busy in other rooms, chatting in a mix of Spanish and English. The rooms were small and minimally furnished, depending for decoration on potted plants near the windows and religious imagery on the walls. I asked the young woman behind the desk if Father Aragon was in. She called to the other rooms, but no one seemed sure exactly where the priest might be.

"If I had to guess," she said, "I'd say he was over at the body shop, checking on the boys."

"The one he operates to keep gang members out of trouble."

"Saving Grace Auto Body," she said, with a helpful smile. "That's the actual name. Father Aragon thought of it himself."

"Cute. Where would I find it?"

"Not far from here, on Whittier Boulevard. I could call over for you, if you'd like."

"I'd appreciate that."

"Your name?"

"Benjamin Justice."

While she dialed, I turned my attention to a set of bookshelves against a wall, crammed with all manner of well-thumbed volumes related to Catholicism. The books that caught my eye were several editions of *Who's Who in the Catholic Church,* not so much because of the title but because of their age. According to the years stamped on the spines, the directories spanned sporadically from 1965 through 1999, each one covering names worldwide. The books had been relegated to a lower shelf in the corner, as if they weren't terribly important. I reached down and pulled out one of the older volumes to see if Fr. Stuart Blackley might be listed, scanning the alphabetical index in back. Generally, the lowest rank among the clerics listed was bishop, except for a few monsignors and priests who'd distinguished themselves in some unusual way, warranting special attention. Father Blackley wasn't among them.

"I'm afraid we don't have a current copy," the young woman said, as she covered the phone with one hand. "We barely manage on our budget. Father Aragon doesn't place much priority on books like that, so all we have are the books that came with the church when Father Aragon arrived four years ago. Sorry."

She went back to her phone as someone came on the line. I turned in the index to the *D*s and found Kendall Doyle listed as a bishop, newly arrived to Los Angeles from the Chicago archdiocese. The brief biographical entry put his birth year at 1937, noting that he was the son of a working class Irish-American couple, who'd joined the seminary as a teenager shortly after his parents' death in a car accident. His only sibling, a sister named Agnes, had died from polio at age seven. He held advanced degrees in theology and philosophy from Notre Dame and Georgetown Universities, respectively. According to the entry, he'd made his mark as a tireless and resourceful fund-raiser for the Chicago archdiocese, and seemed well on his way up the ecumenical ladder. Neither Ismael Aragon nor Anthony Finatti were listed in the older directory, although I found Finatti in the 1999 volume. It mentioned his status as second in command to Cardinal Doyle, a law degree from St. Bonaventure, stints as a priest or monsignor in Cleveland, San Francisco, and Mexico, Spanish as his second language, and additional fluency in Italian. Finatti was well prepared, I thought, should he ever follow Cardinal Doyle to the Vatican.

"Mr. Justice?" I turned to find the receptionist hanging up the phone. "Just as I suspected," she said. "Father Aragon sneaked off to the body shop. He's always doing that."

"Keeping an eye on the boys, I guess."

"He does his best. We're very proud of him."

I placed the edition of *Who's Who in the Catholic Church* back on the shelf. "What about the volumes for the last few years? The ones that are missing. Would I find Father Aragon in any of those?"

She laughed. "Goodness, no. He's not important enough, assigned to this little church. Anyway, he'd be embarrassed if they ever put him in there, with all the bishops and cardinals. There'd be no end to the kidding we'd give him."

She jotted down the address of the Saving Grace Auto Body Shop on a notepad, tore off the slip of paper, and handed it across the desk. Printed above the address she'd scribbled was the hallowed image of Mary Magdalene and a snippet of common prayer: *From envy, hatred, and malice, and all uncharitableness, Good Lord, deliver us.*

I thanked her and made my way back through the garden, where a pesky wind whipped up the trees, causing leaves to fall faster than the old man could rake them up.

The Saving Grace Auto Body Shop operated out of a one-story building that partially framed an open courtyard clogged with vehicles in need of exterior repair.

The old stucco building had been painted white, with the name of the shop stenciled crudely in powder blue above the garages, facing the street. Below the name was a slogan—A Nonprofit Enterprise of La Iglesia de la Virgen de la Caridad—bordered at each end by a small cross of darker blue. Surrounding the lot was a chain link fence and front gate topped with razor-sharp concertina wire. The place was alive with labor—hammers clanging on metal, the hiss of hydraulic spray guns, paint fumes stinging the air—performed to an upbeat Los Lobos tune issuing from a boom box.

Heads turned as I rolled through the gate into the yard. A few years earlier, I'd restored my '65 Mustang convertible to cherry condition—fire engine red, with matching tuck-and-roll—and I wasn't surprised that it drew attention. Or maybe it wasn't the cool car at all. Maybe it was the balding white guy behind the wheel with the inquisitive look of a cop. Whatever the reason, I felt a dozen pair of youthful eyes on me as I stepped from the Mustang on to the oil-saturated asphalt.

Someone lowered the volume on the music as Father Aragon emerged from an office at one end of the building's shortest wing.

"Mr. Justice, what a pleasure to see you again."

I looked him over, taking my time. "The pleasure's all mine, Father."

He was wearing slacks and a black clergy vest and collar set, with the sleeves of his white shirt turned up to reveal slender forearms under a sheen of silky dark hairs. A recent trim and fresh shave made him look younger, almost pretty, accentuating the long lashes over his puppyish brown eyes.

The eyes flickered as mine held fast. "Your car looks immaculate," he said, forcing a smile. "So I assume you must be here on other business."

One by one, the young men who'd taken notice of my arrival turned back to their work, but a few kept me on their radar screen with sidelong glances.

"If we could," I said, "I'd prefer talking in your office."

"If you feel the need for privacy."

"I was thinking more of your needs, Father."

By the time we'd worked our way through the cars to his office door, he'd given me a profile of the business: employment for sixteen boys and young men, who earned minimum wage as they learned a trade, with a high school diploma or work toward a GED required to be in the program. Another requisite was that they renounce violence and promise to carry no weapons, at any time. Church attendance was voluntary, but encouraged. I asked if Saving Grace was paying its own way.

"Not yet, but soon. For now, we survive on donations and goodwill."

"Then how do you measure your success?"

"We've buried only one boy this year, and the year's nearly over. Last year, it was four. We count that as progress."

We stepped in and he shut the door behind us. The office was threadbare and musty, its surfaces gritty with dust. A central window that needed washing looked out on the yard and shops. A side panel was unlatched and open for air, allowing the clatter of labor and the beat of the music to drift in.

"Is this private enough, Mr. Justice?"

"Sure, this will do."

Father Aragon gestured toward a chair that was losing its stuffing. I settled into it while he took a rolling office chair behind a metal desk painted Army green. He folded his hands in front of him, squared his shoulders, lifted his chin.

"Does this have something to do with Mr. Soto's death?"

"Why would you think that, Father?"

"It's what brought us together in the first place, at the church. Our common ground, if you will."

"I suspect we have other common ground." I fixed him with my eyes again. "Worth plowing, from my perspective."

His gaze was steadfast, almost cool. "What is it you want, Mr. Justice?"

"To know what you're hiding, for one thing."

"I'm sorry?"

"You heard me, Father. You're concealing something—something involving Joe Soto, Alexandra Templeton, Bishop Finatti. I'd like to know what it is."

"I'm not sure I know what you mean."

"Let's try Lindsay St. John, for starters. How was it that she came to know about Templeton's relationship with Joe, after they were so careful to keep it quiet?"

"I've never spoken with Lindsay St. John, except briefly, after the service."

"That may be true. But St. John is a buddy of Finatti, who seems to be rather chummy with you. I saw her name on a notepad in his office, for a lunch date. I also saw you and Finatti together, talking rather urgently, after the service for Joe."

"Bishop Finatti takes an interest in each parish. It's quite natural that we talk from time to time."

"Last Thursday, right after Joe's service had ended? Odd time for Bishop Finatti to stop by for a chat, wouldn't you say?"

"Joe Soto was a notable man."

"Joe was a journalist on a mission to expose some of the truths the archdiocese would prefer to keep under wraps. To Finatti, he was a pest who wouldn't go away. To Cardinal Doyle as well, I imagine."

"They have a right, even a duty, to stand up for the Church." Father Aragon spoke quietly, but leveled his eyes accusingly on mine. "They know that the press can be irresponsible, careless with the facts, even reckless at times."

"You've been reporting to Finatti, haven't you, Father? Keeping an eye on Joe, milking him for useful information when he sought your counsel. From Joe to Bishop Finatti to Lindsay St. John. Connect the dots." I smiled a little. "You're finally looking me in the eye, Father. So tell me I've got it wrong."

He lost his resolve and turned away, without leaving his chair. For nearly a minute, he stared out the window at the young men working in the shops and yard. Finally, without looking at me, he said, "It's a complicated situation, Mr. Justice."

"Murder often is."

He swung back around. "What's murder got to do with this?"

"You've read the newspaper, Father. You know that Joe Soto didn't die accidentally."

"You can't possibly think—"

"Think what, Father?"

"That, that—"

"That any of the people I just mentioned could possibly be involved in Mr. Soto's death?" I shrugged nonchalantly. "Never crossed my mind."

"Because it's unthinkable."

"You thought of it, Father, just now."

He stared at me as if trying to foresee my next trick, the next hoop I might place in his path. "Lieutenant DeWinter contacted me. He asked me some questions I found offensive. I'm sure he's just doing his job, conducting a thorough investigation. But to think that any of the people we just spoke of could possibly be involved—it's ludicrous, out of the question."

"You sound like you're trying to convince yourself, Father. Like I said, it never crossed my mind."

He folded his arms across his chest. "Nor mine, Mr. Justice. So—what else can I do for you?" He looked out again as a tow truck dragged a wrecked car through the gate. "We're quite busy, as you can see."

"Undoing the damage?"

"We try."

"Or just giving it a cosmetic fix?"

"We salvage what we can. What is it, Mr. Justice?"

"Father Stuart Blackley," I said.

"What about him?"

"Did you know him?"

"No."

"But you've heard about him?"

"I read about him in Mr. Soto's column."

I rose to my feet, my hands on his desk, zeroing in on him. "That's all you know?"

He swallowed hard, his eyes on the move again. "I was at seminary college eleven years ago, about the time Stuart Blackley died." He backed his chair away, stood, turned away from me. "I'm aware of his death because my first assignment happened to be at the last church where he served as pastor."

"You didn't answer my question, Father." I stepped around his desk until I was in front of him, so close that I could see the tiny golden flecks in the brown of his irises. "Deception's a dangerous thing, isn't it? You start off thinking it will protect you. Before long, you find that it just keeps getting you in deeper and deeper. By then, you're in too deep to get out. The pretending becomes second nature. It rules your life in the end, it consumes you."

He made a half-hearted effort to meet my eyes. "I've tried to live my life honestly, in accordance with God's teaching and my holy vows."

"Answer me, Father."

"I know nothing more about Father Blackley than you do." He sighed wearily, painfully. "Considerably less, I imagine, if your claims are true."

"What claims would those be, Father?"

He suddenly found himself stuck in one of my hoops, looking squeezed. "You're quite good at this, aren't you, Mr. Justice?"

"Finatti filled you in, told you about my past with Father Blackley. It's the only way you could have known. I don't think Alexandra Templeton told you. Or Lieutenant DeWinter."

"Alright, yes, Bishop Finatti spoke to me about your allegations. He felt I should know."

"So you could be careful, if I came around asking questions."

"Like I said, there's nothing I can tell you."

"Why should I believe you, Father?"

"I give you my word. As a priest, as a man."

"As a man?"

"Yes."

I glanced past him to the swarm of younger men in the yard. It was a warm day, even with the breeze, and several were shirtless, bristling with body hair and flaunting their muscles in the generous sunlight.

"Tell me, Father, when you're counseling your homeboys, the handsome ones with the Valentino eyes, is their salvation the only thing on your mind?"

"That's enough." He tried to step past me.

I got in his way, leaning close, our faces inches apart. "Behind your pious smile, are you secretly lusting for them, thinking what it would be like to lure them into your rectory, to lie down with them, to touch them?"

"I—I think you should go now." He kept his head down, like a whipped cur. "Really, it would be best if you'd just leave."

"Or maybe it's me you're having fantasies about, Father. Is that why you're so uncomfortable? Into older men, are you? The scruffier type, with some belly and a receding hairline."

"Please, leave me alone." His head came up and his eyes were moving again, almost desperately. "I've done nothing to you. I've hurt no one. Have the decency to leave me be."

I studied his long lashes, his full lips, the dusky trace of beard along his nicely shaped jaw. "Are you aware of how desirable you are, Father?"

"Please!" He cried out, pushing me away with surprising force, raising his voice. "Get out! Leave me in peace! Let me do my work!"

Suddenly, he froze. I realized, as he must have, that the shop noise had abated. All I could hear was a Los Lobos tune thumping faintly in the background. His eyes went fearfully to the window. Out in the yard, a dozen of his acolytes stood bunched, staring in, their young faces etched with the anger of hardened men. Some of them gripped heavy tools like weapons in their grubby hands.

"You'll only cause trouble." Father Aragon's voice had lost its anxious pleading; his words came slowly now, as if weighted down by sadness. "Hasn't there been enough of that?"

Our eyes met, for the first time on what felt like even ground. He was a priest—one of *them*. I hated him for it. But I knew I could love him just as easily.

Behind me, the office door opened. I turned as four young men crowded in. One of them held a ball peen hammer. Another curled his fingers into fists. The one with the hammer asked Father Aragon if everything was OK. As the boy spoke, his eyes were on me.

The priest stepped toward the door, finding a weak smile. "Yes, thank you, Filiberto, everything's fine. Mr. Justice was about to go."

Father Aragon faced me, looking surprisingly composed. The young men stepped back, creating a gantlet, two on each side.

"Behave yourself, Father." I winked as I passed by. "Don't do anything I wouldn't do."

He reacted with a look of compassion, as if he understood me better than I understood myself, which made me hate him even more.

I was behind the wheel of the Mustang, about to back out, when the sight of another vehicle drew my attention to the paint shop. It was a Jeep Grand Cherokee, freshly sandblasted and given a coat of gray primer.

I shut off the ignition and crossed the yard for a closer inspection. Following whatever body work had been done, the windows and most of the chrome had been covered and taped. All that was left was the application of a new paint job. A skinny

kid of about seventeen with more tattoos than muscles was tap-
ing over the last of the grillwork.

"When did this one come in?"

He looked up, shrugged a little. "Few days ago, I guess."

"Front end damage?"

"How'd you know?"

"Just a hunch. What about the color?"

"We're painting it red."

"I meant before, when it came in."

The kid said gray. I asked who brought it in. "I don't know.
Father Aragon handled it."

"Does Father Aragon usually handle business like this?"

"Not usually. He did it special, for some friend."

"No kidding." A friend with a gray Jeep Cherokee, I thought,
with front end damage, sandblasted spic and span. How about
that.

"We put on a new grill and hood," the kid said. "You got
friends want their car done good, you send 'em here, OK?"

"I don't suppose the old hood and grill are still around?" I
was thinking blood and tissue evidence, as well as damage patterns that forensics might find useful.

"Naw, they're gone. Some old black dude, he took 'em for
scrap."

Long gone, I thought, the way I'd better be gone, unless I
wanted Father Aragon's thugs coming after me again with their
greasy tools. I thanked the kid but he didn't look up. Just kept
at his work, learning a trade, staying out of trouble.

I backed the Mustang out of Saving Grace Auto Body, while
Father Aragon watched from his office window and his home-
boys drifted back to their stations, following my exit with their
Valentino eyes.

FOURTEEN

The next morning, determined to make real progress on my book, I sat at the kitchen table jotting down possible chapter headings.

Over the next few hours, I delineated thirty-two chapters, starting with the Pulitzer scandal, then going back to my birth in Buffalo and working forward to Jacques's death and the scandal again, completing the circle. What I had, I realized, were the broad strokes of my early life—thirty-two years on an upward if uneven trajectory that suddenly went disastrously wrong, like a space shuttle exploding minutes before its triumphant return to earth, leaving the world to wonder about the fatal flaw imbedded in the wiring or the superstructure. My plan was to sum up the years since in a fast-paced epilogue: my raging bouts with alcohol and other self-destructive habits; the baffling murders I'd looked into with Templeton, as an unofficial freelance; my rape at the hands of a lethal ex-cop four years ago; and my sero-conversion to HIV a few months after that and the initial anguish it had caused. My search for Fr. Stuart Blackley was to have provided my dramatic ending, as I found and confronted him, bringing some meaning and closure to my personal saga. Such a neat device had always been in the back of my mind; I'd just never spoken it aloud or put it down on paper. But Stuart Blackley was dead, killed in a hiking accident and buried behind a Catholic church in Whittier. Just like that, my nifty conclusion had become wishful thinking.

I put a question mark after the word "epilogue," shoved my notebook aside, and got ready for another trip downtown with Templeton, to visit Lt. Claude DeWinter.

Templeton left her Thunderbird in the newspaper parking lot and we walked the three blocks to Parker Center. Downstairs, we passed through security and took an elevator up to face DeWinter across his messy desk. The room smelled of pizza and overcooked coffee, but it could have been worse. In the old days, when I'd worked the cop shop as a young reporter and before smoking was banned, the odor of stale cigarette smoke had always hung in the air, adding to the stink.

"On the phone," Templeton said, sitting upright and speaking crisply, "you told me you had new information on Joe's case."

"That's right." DeWinter worked on a fresh stick of sugarless gum, tossing the wrapper toward an overflowing trashcan, while doing his best not to look Templeton over. "We think we may have a lead on the suspect."

"I see."

Templeton sat and spoke as if she were held together with tautly stretched piano wire; one snip in the wrong place, I thought, and she might collapse into a hundred pieces. For our visit, she'd worked hard on her façade, dressed in shapely one-inch pumps and a well-cut business suit of dark green, with a thin gold chain at her throat. Her braids were loose and dangling down the back, beaded tastefully for adornment. Surrounded by the drab walls, dull linoleum floor, and pale fluorescent lighting of the detective's room, she was a woman of contrasts and contradictions, difficult to figure out. For a man like Claude De-Winter—divorced, lonely, well into his forties—she must have seemed as alluring but as unattainable as a Hollywood diva.

She certainly had his attention; the man acted as if there was no one else in the room.

"I wanted to give you the news personally, Miss Templeton. You know, before you heard it through some other source."

"I appreciate it, Lieutenant."

"Do you prefer Miss Templeton? Some women don't like the term Miss, do they? A few still prefer Ms., I guess." DeWinter laughed awkwardly. "It's hard to know what to call a single lady these days, unless one asks."

"Alexandra would be fine, Lieutenant."

He smiled as he chewed his gum. "Good, that's settled."

"About Joe," she said.

"Of course. We've been reviewing videotapes from security cameras in and around the area where the hit-and-run took place. More than a dozen cameras, just in a single block. Several of these video cams captured images of what we believe is the suspect's vehicle. Only one camera got a shot of the driver."

Templeton adjusted her skirt to better cover her knees. "I'm surprised it's taken this long to secure these tapes, and have them analyzed."

"We had possession of the tapes the morning after Mr. Soto was killed. I saw to that personally. The problem was the quality. Too many businesses reuse or forget to replace their videotape. In this case, the tape with the driver's face was in need of serious computer enhancement. Don't ask me to explain it technically. I'd need the dummy's manual for that." He laughed but Templeton didn't, which caused his weak grin to freeze uncomfortably on his broad, black face. Very quickly, he shifted his large bottom and swiveled on his chair, which groaned beneath his weight. Behind him was a VCR and television monitor on a wheeled cart. He pushed a button before facing us again. "That's the original image, captured by a video cam at a business across the street. Jeep Grand Cherokee, light gray, as you reported earlier. It was night, shot from about forty feet. Driver's hard to see."

"The window's open," I said. "You'd think he'd be more careful."

"Temperature was in the fifties that night. We figure the windows fogged up while he waited for Alexandra and Mr. Soto to come out of the restaurant. If this is our man the car was probably stolen. It's possible he didn't know how to work the defroster. It's one of the last things drivers figure out on an unfamiliar vehicle. Anyway, while he sat there, he lowered the window, kept it down for several minutes."

Templeton leaned forward on her chair. "You can't see much of his face. He's white, apparently, or possibly Asian or Hispanic. Dark hair. Beyond that—"

"Here comes the next sequence," DeWinter said. "This is what came back from the tech lab."

We watched a succession of images—frames blown up and digitally enhanced until a more recognizable face emerged on the screen. Long dark hair covering the ears, beaked nose that may have been broken, scraggly mustache and similar goatee not quite hiding what was probably a weak chin. The driver appeared to be neither young nor very old; late thirties to late forties would have been a good guess. It was hard to tell.

"It's difficult to see how an individual identification could be made from this," I said. "The sharpest image is grainy at best."

DeWinter's eyes bypassed me for Templeton. "We think we know who he is."

She sat back, stunned. "You have a name?"

DeWinter nodded. "General appearance fits. The scar's the giveaway." He turned to point at the driver's face on the screen, running his finger from the ear to the corner of the mouth.

"I don't see a scar," I said.

"It's faint, but if you look close, you can see it." DeWinter spoke to me dismissively, sounding annoyed. He rummaged among the papers on his desk, found a photo, handed it across to Templeton. "This was taken not quite thirty years ago. You can see the scar quite clearly. Jilted girlfriend did it to him with a broken bottle when he was nineteen. He killed the girl, sliced her up like a Thanksgiving turkey. It's the only known photograph ever taken of the suspect after he reached manhood."

Quietly, somberly, Templeton studied the photograph. "Who is he?"

DeWinter's chair squeaked as he leaned back, folding his big hands behind his head. "Pablo Zuniga. Nickname, *el Mutilador*. Mean anything to you?"

She shook her head, handed the photograph over to me.

"Pablo Zuniga made a name for himself in the eighties and nineties as an assassin for hire," DeWinter said, "working from Mexico all the way to Panama. He's laid low for a few years now." DeWinter slid his eyes purposefully in my direction, and kept them there. "But Mr. Justice knows who Pablo Zuniga is. Don't you, buddy?"

I looked up from the photograph. "Joe was planning to write a book about this guy."

DeWinter leveled his eyes on me. "You want to explain why I'm just hearing this from you now?"

"A book—Joe?" Templeton was glaring at me. "Why didn't I know about this?"

"Zuniga's a cold-blooded killer, Alex. Joe didn't want you to worry. He was waiting until the time was right to tell you."

"But he told *you?*"

"He asked me to read his outline, give him some feedback. This was going to be the book he was going to write after the two of you married and Joe put in for his pension."

"Joe was going to *retire?*"

I nodded. "So you could keep working at the *LAT*. Like I said, he was waiting for the right time to tell you. He asked me to keep it to myself."

"I asked you a question," DeWinter said, his eyes still on me.

"It never occurred to me to tell you, Lieutenant."

"Never occurred to you."

"I still have Joe's book proposal in my car. I guess I forgot about it."

"Your friend's writing a book about one of the most lethal

assassins ever to come out of Latin America, a guy with dozens of notches on his belt. The author investigating the bad guy gets murdered, execution style. And it doesn't occur to you that there might be a connection?"

"He wasn't writing a book about Zuniga," I said. "He was in the research phase."

"Don't bullshit me with semantics, Justice. I'm not in the mood."

"Fuck you, DeWinter. I forgot about it, that's all. A lot's been happening. I haven't been feeling very well."

"You look OK to me."

"He could be gone by now." Templeton's voice rose, her eyes on the move. "He could be out of the country. If the police had known—"

"We might have gotten him," DeWinter said, driving it home the way a master carpenter sets a nail. "We might have had him locked up and facing trial by now."

I saw something strange in DeWinter's eyes—a grim determination that looked more personal than professional. I pointed a finger at him. "How did you know I had the outline?"

"Mr. Soto kept a diary," DeWinter said. "I went through it yesterday. I found a notation referring to the proposal he'd asked you to read. I found a copy in his home office, read it myself. I'm no critic, but I bet it would have made a hell of a book."

I held his gaze a moment, trying to figure out what it was about him that had me spooked. Then I turned to Templeton again. "I'm sorry, Alex. I don't know what else to say. It never crossed my mind, that's all." I shrugged, feeling like a slug. "Like I said the other day, I'm losing my edge. I guess I've been losing it for a while now."

She stared at me for a moment, with a mix of outrage and disappointment. Then, abruptly, she pulled herself together, sitting up straight and facing DeWinter again.

"So what do we do now, Lieutenant?"

"How about I bring you up to date on this Pablo Zuniga character, and you get a story into tomorrow's paper? I'd like to get his photo out there, along with a sketch of what he might look like now. See if it turns over some rocks."

Templeton opened her handbag and pulled out her reporter's notebook without giving me another glance.

While they talked, and Templeton jotted notes, I used the time to study the photo of Pablo Zuniga more closely, comparing it to the frozen video image on the TV monitor. The resemblance was general at best. I couldn't even be sure that the driver on the videotape was scarred across the face. It might have been a bad shaving job against his sparse beard, or even part of the grain on the film. In the still, as a young man, Zuniga was clean-shaven, which made a match even more problematic.

"This is the only photograph of Zuniga you could get?"

DeWinter responded in a condescending voice. "Like I said, Justice, this is the only photo in existence of Zuniga as a man. He got the negatives from the photographer, then gouged out his eyes and cut his throat. Zuniga likes to use his victims to send messages, intimidate his enemies. It's said that no one ever dared take his picture again. After that photo was taken, he lost two fingers and an ear at different times, to different enemies. So we have that to go by, if we should run into the man."

"If this is the only photograph you've got of Zuniga," I said, "how can you be so sure he and the driver are the same guy?"

"I can't be sure, not yet. But there's a general likeness, and he's the best suspect we've got at the moment."

"You're naming him as a suspect?"

He glanced at Templeton's notepad. "Off the record. Officially, he's wanted for questioning."

"From what Joe told me," I said, "a lot of people want him for questioning."

"I guess I'll get in line then."

"All I'm saying is, this isn't a whole lot to go on."

DeWinter sighed with exasperation, then glanced at the TV monitor behind him. "The driver on the video was taped waiting around the corner from Pietro's, the restaurant where the crime went down. He was there for a full half hour before Mr. Soto and Alexandra finished their meal and came out. The time code on the video has the driver raising his window, starting the car, and taking off seconds before Mr. Soto was run down." De-Winter raised his hands in a supplicating gesture. "Is that good enough for you, Justice?"

"I'm just raising legitimate questions, Lieutenant."

"Drop it, Benjamin." Templeton's voice sliced like a shard of ice. "The lieutenant's in charge here, and he knows what he's doing."

"Would you prefer that I leave, Alex? So that you and the lieutenant can be alone?"

"I didn't say that. But we've got work to do, and you're not helping."

"Fine, do your work." I slid my eyes toward DeWinter. "You and the lieutenant."

DeWinter found a file on his desk and went through it, rattling off information about Pablo Zuniga, gleaned from various law enforcement sources, including Interpol. From time to time, he handed Templeton copies of reports and other documents he thought might help her with her story. "Pablo Zuniga's a complicated man—as cold-blooded and sadistic as you'll find, but also very religious. Raised in the Catholic Church, never misses Mass if he can help it, even known to quote scripture when he's torturing his victims."

"He would have been useful during the Inquisition," I said.

"What about M.O.?" Templeton looked up from her notebook. "Any trademarks?"

"Zuniga's been linked to at least two dozen political and drug-cartel murders, and suspected in twice that many. He likes to play with his victims before killing them, watching them suffer. It's part of his legend, one reason he's feared so much. Others say he does it simply because he enjoys it. Mutilation is one of his specialties. Hence the nickname, *el Mutilador*."

"Joe died instantly," I said.

DeWinter glanced over irritably. "I was about to say that every now and then, when he feels it's necessary, Zuniga kills quickly and cleanly. He's not stupid, or he wouldn't have survived this long." DeWinter raised his eyebrows for my benefit. "When he carries out a quick hit, his preferred M.O. is the hit-and-run, using a stolen vehicle. That's not my conclusion. It comes from Interpol. You got a problem with it, Justice, take it up with them."

"If it was stolen, why would he bother to paper over the plates? That would just call attention, wouldn't it? He'd only cover the plates if the car was his own, or borrowed for the job."

That one took DeWinter aback. He opened his mouth to speak, but nothing came out.

"I guess Joe was lucky then." Templeton had stopped writing. Her eyes had a faraway look. "I mean, in the sense that he didn't suffer."

"You could look at it that way, I guess." DeWinter's voice grew soft, sympathetic. "It could have been a whole lot worse."

"If Zuniga's your man," I said.

They ignored me, as DeWinter dispensed more details and Templeton resumed taking notes. "The authorities lost track of him years ago, although they suspect he may be here in L.A., where it's easier for him to blend in. They've had a few leads on him. He always slips away. He could be out there on the streets right now for all we know, hiding in plain sight. Or—like you said before—he could be out of the country by now."

"*Monster in the Shadows*," I said. Then, to Templeton: "It was the title Joe was thinking of using for his book." She wrote it down.

"I've made a copy of Mr. Soto's outline for you," DeWinter said.

"I can give her mine, Lieutenant."

He was already handing her the document. He also gave her a copy of the photo of Zuniga as a young man, and one that had been age-enhanced. "Today, he'd be getting close to fifty. Has eight or ten children by several women. Two of his kids have become priests, reportedly at their father's urging. He's donated cash to build churches in villages all over South and Central America, and as far north as Mexico City. He's something of a folk hero down there, which is one reason he never got caught."

"I'll write it up this afternoon," Templeton said, "and ask the desk to run both photos. Can you give me an exclusive on it until morning, when we hit the streets?"

"No problem." DeWinter laughed. "The local stations pick up half their news leads from the morning *Times,* anyway, don't they?"

Templeton managed a smile. "True enough. By tomorrow afternoon, you'll have it on every channel."

DeWinter dropped his eyes for a moment. "When you've filed your story, maybe we could get together, see if we can make some more headway on the case."

"Sure, I'd like that."

"Dinner, maybe?"

Templeton stood, slipping her notebook into her handbag. "Why not?" She stretched her hand across the desk as DeWinter lifted his huge body from his overworked chair. "As long as we keep it on a professional basis."

"I wouldn't have it any other way, Alexandra."

"I'll call you from the *Times,* let you know my schedule."

I got to my feet and we all started toward the door.

"There's one more thing." DeWinter laid his hand lightly on her shoulder. Two detectives passed, giving them the eye. "You could be in danger. You're an eyewitness to the crime, and now you're pursuing Zuniga as a reporter."

"A certain amount of risk comes with the job, Lieutenant."

"I doubt that you've ever faced a suspect like this."

"I'll be careful, Claude. I appreciate the advice."

"I gave you the same advice yesterday," I said.

They both ignored me while DeWinter found a business card and scribbled on the back of it. "Here's my home phone. My cell's on the other side. Call me anytime you need to. Don't take any chances, Alexandra. Not with a psycho like this."

He honed in on her as if she was the only person on the planet. It occurred to me that this was what he'd intended all along—just the two of them, working closely together, without outside interference. Templeton wasn't even calling him Lieutenant any more. Now, it was Claude.

FIFTEEN

Outside Parker Center, Templeton and I turned east, walking a block into Little Tokyo for an early lunch. Pedestrian traffic was thick along the sidewalks and in the small plazas, where hand-painted lanterns and paper fish hung in profusion and rubber sandals and colorful toys were piled high in bins outside the shops. The little neighborhood between San Pedro Street and Central Avenue had developed as a haven for Japanese around the turn of the twentieth century, burgeoning in 1907 with immigrants from the largest influx of Japanese in a single year. Most were produce farmers who sold what they raised, and the community had thrived as Los Angeles mushroomed from a general population of 102,000 in 1906 to more than a million by 1930. The number of Japanese in Little Tokyo had reached thirty thousand by early 1942, when the U.S. government had rounded them up for internment during World War II. Most had never returned, at least not to live. But a tiny Japanese business district had survived, along with the Japanese Union Church and a Buddhist temple, Higashi Honganji. In time, they'd become the core of the cultural and tourist center that Templeton and I were entering now.

We chose a quiet place on a side street where I'd sometimes eaten in the old days, when I was working at the *LAT*. The service was polite but no-nonsense and brisk. Templeton placed her order, then used her cell to phone the city desk. She prepared the city editor for a breaking story, giving him the basics and wrangling for a big enough hole to cover it adequately. After the food came—chicken teriyaki for me, tuna roll for Templeton—she went over her notes while she ate, giving me the silent treatment.

She was still at it as the waitress cleared away the empty bowls and plates. I counted out my pills and capsules, the ones requiring food to blunt their toxic bite, and washed them down with warm green tea.

"There was a time when you would have asked for my advice," I said.

She finally glanced up. "About what?"

"The angle, the lead, the order of the most important facts."

"Maybe you should write it instead." She pushed her notebook at me, held out her pen. "Go ahead. You write it, Justice. I'll phone it in."

"That's not what I'm suggesting."

"Then what's the problem?"

"You're shutting me out. The way you did earlier, in De-Winter's office."

"I got the impression in recent days that you didn't want to be that involved."

"I let you sleep in my bed. Does that count?"

She sighed and poured steaming tea into her little cup. "I'm not a cub reporter, Justice, fresh out of J school. I'm thirty-two, the same age you were when—" She caught herself. "I'm sorry. That came out wrong."

"The same age I was when my career came to a crashing halt. You might as well say it."

"The same age you were when you were doing your best work. Don't forget that." She glanced up as the waitress laid the check down between us. "I'm grateful for what you taught me, Justice. But I'm doing pretty well on my own."

"Yes you are." I pushed the check across the table at her. "Which is why I'm letting you take me to lunch."

We walked back to the newspaper's parking compound, where I intended to crawl into the rear seat of Templeton's T-Bird for a nap while she put her story together down the street in the newsroom. She was using her remote control to unlock the car doors when Lindsay St. John appeared, coming from the street as she rummaged in her handbag for keys. The moment she saw us, St. John lost a hitch in her stride. A second later, she'd regained her rhythm, while her glossy lips formed one of her pat smiles. Like Templeton, her hair and clothes were perfect, but without the personal flair, the self-expression. Hers was the cloned corporate look, suggesting that odd mix of obedience and authority—command and trepidation—characteristic of so many executives who try to project confidence to mask a constant fear of failure.

"Good morning, Alexandra." St. John's voice was cool, bordering on snippy. She glanced at the Bulgari on her wrist. "Actually, it's half past noon."

"I've been at Parker Center, working a story."

"Yes, I know—the Joe Soto matter. The desk informed me."

"Does the desk clear everything with you now, Lindsay?"

"Anything involving Joe has to be handled carefully, given his connection to the paper."

Templeton held up her notebook like a trophy. "We've got an exclusive. Someone wanted for questioning, linked to a vehicle that could be the one used in the hit-and-run."

"Sounds like a lot of ifs."

"I think it's worth page one, with a decent jump—at least thirty inches."

"He's wanted for questioning, you said. There's no official suspect?"

"It's still a good story, a great break for us." Templeton showed St. John the photos of Pablo Zuniga and summarized the information she'd gleaned from DeWinter.

"An assassin who hasn't been seen in years," St John said, "and who may or may not be involved—it hardly seems strong enough to warrant the front page. Not even in the California section."

"The Jeep Grand Cherokee in the video," Templeton said. "The same model linked to the hit-and-run."

"There must be thousands of those in Southern California." St. John laughed lightly, including me with a slight glance. "Tens of thousands, for all I know. It's a popular model, isn't it?"

"Joe was writing a book on Zuniga," Templeton said.

"On his own time, I hope."

Templeton gritted her teeth. "*Planning* on writing one."

"Ah—so he *wasn't* writing a book on Mr. Zuniga."

"The point is, Lindsay—"

"I think we should sit on this story for awhile, see how it develops."

"Sit on it? Are you crazy?"

St. John's smile and voice became gentler, but also patronizing. "What if the driver caught on the video turns out to be someone else, someone completely innocent? Surely, Alexandra, you realize the position that puts the paper in. The liability issues."

Templeton's voice quivered with emotion. "Publishing these photos could help us find Joe's killer."

"It's not our job to do the work of the police, Alexandra. It's to report the news. Facts, not speculation and conjecture."

"We publish photos of suspects all the time that lead to their arrests."

St. John handed back the photos. "Officially, he's not a suspect, is he?"

Templeton verged on tears. "I guess we should use the space for another puff piece on the new cathedral."

"You're worn out, Alexandra. You're not yourself."

"I've never been more motivated."

St. John laid a consoling hand on Templeton's arm. Templeton pulled away. "You're much too close to this story to be working on it," St. John said. "It was a mistake to allow it. A mistake, thankfully, that I've remedied."

"Meaning what?"

"A few minutes ago we pulled you off the story."

Templeton's eyes glistened with tears, which she blinked back. "You can't do that."

"Oh, but we can, dear. I called a meeting with the appropriate people and we discussed the issues involved. Particularly your fragile state of mind. The decision was to reassign the story to someone less emotionally involved."

Templeton clenched her jaw. "You bitch."

St. John flinched, as if slapped, then studied Templeton carefully. "I want you to take some time off, dear, and get some rest."

"No." Templeton shook her head forcefully. "Absolutely not."

"This is not a request, Alexandra."

"Say *what?*"

St. John looked my way. "Mr. Justice? Could you excuse us for a moment?"

"He stays," Templeton said. "Whatever you have to say, just say it."

St. John fixed Templeton with her cool, calculating eyes. "Not long after Joe's death, you were observed removing items from his mail slot. Surely, you know that violates regulations regarding employee privacy."

"Joe was dead. I was his fiancée. I think you know that too, don't you?"

"Another problem, I'm afraid. Your lack of objectivity."

"The letters were from his readers. They needed to be read."

"And you appointed yourself to do that?"

"Who better?"

"The bottom line, Alexandra, is that you pilfered private mail belonging to another employee. You could be fired." Her measured smile returned. "However, I'm going to take into account the tragic loss you'd just suffered."

Templeton's smile was grim. "Aren't you just the sweetest thing?"

"You have a choice, Alexandra. You can accept a paid, two-week leave of absence, or face a disciplinary suspension that could lead to dismissal." St. John's eyes slid in my direction for a moment. "I'd also suggest that you reconsider certain of your relationships outside the paper that seem to be influencing you in a negative way."

"What I do on my own time is none of your business, Lindsay. Any more than what you do in your private life is any of mine."

"You have such a bright future ahead of you, Alexandra. It's not easy in these days of downsizing to find another good newspaper job. Especially if you left your last one under the cloud of a disciplinary action."

"You'd really terminate me?"

"I think I've made myself quite clear. Your choice, dear."

Templeton dropped her head, her shoulders sagging, her voice barely audible. "I'll take the two weeks."

"I'm sorry, Alexandra. I didn't hear you."

Templeton looked up, her eyes molten. "I said I'd take the two weeks!"

St. John brightened. "Splendid! You'll realize later it's in the best interest of everyone. And while you're away, resting up, we'll begin the transition we have in mind for you—over to the style section."

"You're assigning me to features?"

"We think the change will do you a world of good."

"I'm a news reporter. I don't belong on the soft side of the paper."

"We think you do." St. John glanced again at her fancy wristwatch. "Forgive me, I'm running late."

"Off to lunch with Bishop Finatti?" I asked.

St. John whipped her head around, shooting daggers at me. For a moment, behind the anger, I thought I saw a flicker of unease. Then she turned and departed on shapely legs that tapered nicely into her three-inch heels. Templeton watched her go, biting her lip, wiping away tears. Seconds later, she was sliding behind the wheel of her T-Bird, firing up the ignition while I climbed in the other side.

As the motor idled, she sat staring out the windshield. "Drop the investigation into Joe's death. Give up hard news to write features. Be a good little girl for Lindsay St. John. Sure, I can do all that." She released her emergency brake and shifted into drive. "Just as soon as Palm Springs freezes over."

Then she was pulling out fast, her tires squealing, and shooting into midday traffic like a bat out of hell.

SIXTEEN

For nearly a week, I heard nothing from Templeton. Between the approach of Halloween and preparation for my book, it wasn't difficult staying occupied.

Halloween meant helping Maurice and Fred decorate the house, always a big deal at their place. Maurice was particularly fond of witches and goblins, spotted with light in the trees and along the rooftop. Years ago, he'd purchased a machine that could make them dance, to the delight of anyone passing on the street. But Fred was getting too heavy and both of them too old to climb safely onto the roof and into the oak, so I volunteered. We got out the ladder and I made the ascent, while Fred handed up the decorations and Maurice stood in the yard, dispensing instructions with the authority of a Broadway set designer.

Otherwise, I kept to my book project, working out a timetable balanced against my bank account. All told—with planning, research and final revisions—I figured on roughly two years of work. The one hundred and fifty thousand dollar advance was against royalties; that meant I was unlikely to see more money, unless the book became a blockbuster, which seemed improbable. After the government and my agent took their cuts, and I figured in my expenses, I'd end up with something less than half.

When I did the division, I found myself earning less than a trades-man's wage. Writing books, I realized, was not necessarily the route to riches some perceived it to be.

The month was almost over—time to write another check for next month's medical coverage, along with payments for the rent, car insurance and utility bills. The million-dollar settlement the archdiocese was offering looked more and more tempting. I reminded myself that knowing more about Father Blackley wasn't truly essential for the writing of my autobiography. Authors never got down every detail they wanted. We were all forced to take shortcuts, make compromises here and there. For hours, I paced alone in my apartment mulling the issues, while my reluctance to take Finatti's deal gradually waned. Then I got a notice in the mail informing me that my monthly HMO premium was about to be increased.

I dialed Bishop Finatti at his office and told him I was ready to sign. We made an appointment for a time and day to go over the exact wording of the contract and finalize things. I was about to be a millionaire and cease my inquiries about Father Blackley. Simple as that.

Templeton checked in on the morning of October thirty-first. I was in my apartment, fending off Maurice as he tried to outfit me as a giant bunny for the night's celebration, which I had no intention of joining. Templeton wondered if I might have dinner with her that evening, before the street festivities got into full swing. She added that Lt. Claude DeWinter would be joining us.

"It's Halloween, Templeton. The city's expecting more than two hundred thousand people to show up in Boys Town. Getting in and out of the neighborhood will be a nightmare."

"We can meet for sushi at that little place up on the Strip. The one with the twin waiters you think are so cute. You can walk up."

"We had Japanese two days ago, in Little Tokyo."

"Pizza, then, at the Rainbow Bar & Grill. Maybe we'll see some faded rock stars."

"You think it's a good idea, DeWinter and me sharing the same table?"

"He's promised to be civil. I'd like the same promise from you."

"I won't pretend to like him."

"God forbid that you should make such a sacrifice."

"What's so important that you need me there?"

She hesitated, adopting a more somber tone. "We've learned a bit more about Father Blackley."

"Father Blackley." I'd talked myself into forgetting him, or at least minimizing his role in my book. Now he was back. And Templeton and DeWinter had learned something about him that required me to hear it in person. "I don't suppose we can handle this over the phone?"

"Better if we do it face to face," Templeton said.

There were no rocks stars that night at the Rainbow Bar & Grill, not that I recognized, anyway.

Templeton and I shared the Rainbow special pizza with the works, while Claude DeWinter nibbled at a salad with fat-free dressing, mentioning pointedly that he was shedding some pounds. I noticed that he was wearing a new suit—the giveaway was the tag still on the cuff—and a stylish tie with a bold Italian design. We engaged in awkward small talk until I grew tired of it. As I helped myself to a second slice, I asked flat out what they'd discovered about Father Blackley that was worth the price of a twenty-two-dollar pizza.

DeWinter explained that he and Templeton had been following up on the correspondence generated by Joe Soto's final column—telephone messages, e-mails, snail mail, all of it. They'd come up with about three dozen individuals or couples in Southern California who had something to say about Father Blackley that seemed pertinent, valuable, and verifiable.

"What they told us helped us to chart Father Blackley's movements and activities," Templeton said, "over the nearly seventeen years before his death. There was a pattern of reassignments, ending when he died."

"Finatti told me that much in his letter."

Templeton dabbed at her mouth with a napkin, buying a little time. Then, looking directly at me, she said, "We've uncovered a trail of sexual abuse victims, Benjamin. Many more than in Buffalo."

I put my slice down, pushed my plate away, girding myself for the rest. "What else?"

"As in Buffalo, his victims tended to be slim, dark-haired girls and more sturdily-built boys, on the fair side. Again, the age range was ten to thirteen." Templeton unfolded a sheet of paper, pushing it at me. On it was a list of names, numbered from one to twenty-two. "So far, Claude and I have confirmed twenty-two victims. Most of them boys, but several girls as well."

"Twenty-two," I said.

"Those are just the ones we've come up with so far," DeWinter said. "Who knows how many more have moved away, or don't want to get involved."

"One can only guess." I reached for my water; my hand trembled, so I pulled it back and hid it in my lap.

"Father Blackley was obviously prolific." DeWinter drilled me with his eyes. "It's too bad someone didn't turn him in before all this happened."

"Someone like me, Lieutenant?"

He shrugged his huge shoulders. "If we'd known, a lot of kids would have been spared."

"That's not what's important now," Templeton said.

I smiled falsely. "Isn't it?"

"No, it's not. What's important is that we get to the truth, after all these years. That we expose the cover-up, so it doesn't happen again." She rattled off more details, a predictable litany that I heard distantly, as I withdrew into a more private place. In each case, she said, the parents of the children had settled quietly with the archdiocese for a substantial sum of money, assured that Father Blackley had undergone counseling and was rehabilitated. Bishop Anthony Finatti had personally handled each case.

"Why would these people suddenly start talking to you now, after all this time?"

"Joe's column," Templeton said. "Your personal story, Benjamin. They're coming forward because of you. Before, they'd figured theirs was an isolated case. That's what Finatti wanted them to believe, and they did."

"Better late than never, I guess."

She seized my hand. "Don't you understand? We've nailed Finatti and Doyle! I'll be able to finish what Joe started. And you've got some terrific material for your book." She stared at me, off my silence. "What is it, what's wrong?"

"You don't know?"

"I expected you to be ecstatic." She laughed a little. "OK, in your case, moderately enthused."

"You heard what DeWinter said. Nearly two dozen kids were molested because I didn't have the guts to turn Blackley in."

"You were a victim, too."

"I'm an accomplice, Templeton. I knew what he was capable of. I could have stopped him. All those years I knew. I didn't do squat."

"Victims of these crimes frequently internalize it, try to forget it ever happened. Shame, embarrassment, fear, all kinds of reasons. Pedophiles count on that." She swung her head toward DeWinter. "Isn't that right, Claude?"

He shrugged, without much conviction. "I suppose you could look at it that way."

Templeton leaned closer, finding my eyes. "You were a child, Benjamin. A twelve-year-old boy."

"In all due respect, Templeton, I haven't been a child for roughly thirty years. I've done plenty since that's a hell of a lot more shameful than sucking a priest's dick. My right to use shame and embarrassment as an excuse ran out a long time ago."

"Benjamin—"

"The bottom line is I could have saved those kids from being victimized. The excuses don't mean crap."

"Benjamin, please—"

I removed her hand, got to my feet, pulled out my wallet. My hands were trembling again and my head was reeling. "I'm afraid I've lost my appetite." I drank my warter, tossed a twenty on the table. "You've done some good work." I glanced at DeWinter. "Both of you. Congratulations."

Templeton stood, reaching for me as I stepped away. "Don't go, Benjamin. Please, stay and talk."

"Happy Halloween." My smile was tight. "Don't let the goblins get you."

She spoke my name again but I was already headed for the door. I dashed out past the parking valets and across Sunset Boulevard, causing horns to blast and tires to squeal. The sidewalks were already filling up with revelers, hundreds of straight kids, some in masks or costumes, most not. By midnight, there'd be thousands of them. Plenty would be getting into fistfights or puking their guts out, or groping and screwing each other in nearby residential streets and yards, if things went the way of most other nights on the Strip. That's where most of the trouble was in West Hollywood after midnight, not down the hill in the gay bars where the occasional drunk or druggie got tossed for rude behavior. I pushed through all the young breeders, forcing them aside, daring someone to push back or give me a hard time, any bit of hostility to draw off some of the rage I was feeling toward myself.

Then I was careening down the hill toward Boys Town, the place I'd fled to so often for comfort, desperate for something or someone that would take me away from the voice that was screaming at me inside. Screaming the number *twenty-two*. Screaming out my silence, my cowardice, my complicity.

SEVENTEEN

As I reached the heart of Boys Town, I found the side streets barricaded to keep out vehicles and a ten-block stretch of Santa Monica Boulevard closed from end to end. Tonight, the boulevard belonged to all manner of pedestrians—hundreds in drag, thousands more in fantastic costumes and makeup, adventurous parents out with toddlers, kinetic teenagers gawking at the endless spectacle, unprepared tourists looking like they'd stumbled by mistake into a sideshow from hell. Dozens of sheriff's deputies patrolled on foot and horseback, a few pausing to pose for snapshots with muscular, six-foot drag queens decked out in high heels and boas. Lesbians were less visible than gay men but they were still a presence, generally seen in friendly packs, like most of the gay Asian men. It was only half past nine, but the boulevard was jammed—block after block, sidewalk to sidewalk, shoulder to shoulder—and the energy was crackling like a hot power line.

I plunged headlong into the throng, with no purpose but escape. The momentum grabbed me and swept me along, past a group of bearish men in leather pants and suspenders, their corpulent torsos exposed to show off hairy chests and nipple rings. Stages for various events had been erected over several blocks, spaced out to spread the crowd, with dozens of concession stands in between. The air was a chaotic mix of distant dance music, the amplified voice of a comedian emceeing a nearby costume contest, and the wail of ambulance sirens, punctuated by frequent outbursts of laughter and cheers that signaled the latest sighting of a favored outfit. Martha Stewart and Osama bin Laden seemed to be the costumes of choice but there were thousands more. Bare chests and lean muscles were visible all around me, along with stunning faces impossible to ignore. The sight of so many fine-looking men in one place was startling, even after so many celebrations over so many years. Bodies touched, eyes flirted, fantasies flamed. If there was a night in which to get lost from oneself it was Halloween in Boys Town.

I'd been flowing with the crowd for more than an hour, jostled and elbowed along, lulled into an edgy euphoria, when I glanced back to see the Grim Reaper not far behind. He was costumed in a hooded cloak of deathly black, carrying the traditional scythe. Through the holes of his gnarly rubber mask a pair of shadowed eyes peered out. From my vantage point, those eyes seemed to be fixed on me. I lost sight of him as the West Hollywood Cheerleaders sashayed between us, shaking their colorful pom-poms. A crowd favorite, they showed up every Halloween—a horde of broad-shouldered, hairy men decked out in wigs, saddle shoes, cheerleading skirts, and fake breasts the size of watermelons. I faced forward and kept moving across the epicenter at San Vicente Boulevard.

A muscular black man passed on my right, smooth and dark in a shimmering gold thong, winking for my benefit. To my left, a group of cropped-hair dykes marched through in Doc Martens, clearing the crowd like Moses parting the Red Sea. Straight ahead, Alice and the Mad Hatter posed with a little girl dressed as Cinderella while her parents snapped a picture. I smelled burning cannabis, alcohol, cologne, sweat, the musty odor of costumes out of storage—all of it blending into its own intoxicating aroma. A cute kid, still in his teens, pinched my nipple as he moved past, never missing stride. I felt carried along by the swirl of sights and sounds, by so much dazzling flesh, so much unchecked sensuality; I was ready to surrender to the night, to be swept away.

I glanced again over my shoulder, looking for the Grim Reaper. The cheerleaders had veered off, to entertain another segment of the crowd. But Death was still there, keeping a steadfast distance, as if he might be following, as if he might be interested. I angled across Santa Monica Boulevard, wondering who he might be, what he might want—or if he was even following me at all. An old friend, maybe, wanting to say hello. But except for Maurice and Fred, I had no old friends now, not after the plague had taken so many and my self-destructive behavior had chased away the rest. No, I decided, the Grim Reaper must be a stranger. When I realized that, an undefined fear edged into the heady mix. I felt the tingle of adrenaline, the shiver up the back, the shriveling of the testicles that comes when the possibility of danger lurks but isn't necessarily unwelcome.

As I crossed the grassy median, then reached the other side, I stepped up on the curb, ostensibly to take another look. In truth, I wanted to give him a chance to catch up, make contact, maybe say something. I scanned the sea of masks and faces but couldn't pick him out. I surveyed the crowd again, feeling more urgency than made me comfortable. The Grim Reaper had disappeared, swallowed up by the mob. Or maybe he'd turned away, I thought, losing interest. Or maybe he'd never been interested at all. I'd been a fool to think otherwise, to raise my hopes. Suddenly, I felt disappointment and frustration settle heavily over me, weighing me down. I pushed on, like a man dragging chains, on the outside chance that my flight might attract him again, while hating myself for needing a stranger's attention so desperately. From time to time, I glanced back, but he was nowhere to be seen. No hooded cloak, no scythe, no keen eyes fixing me from behind the painted skull of his grinning mask. The danger was gone, and with it all the thrilling possibilities.

The comforting mass of humanity felt crushing now, suffocating. I needed space, to be away from the cacophony and the compression of bodies. I shoved my way through a narrow parking lot between a restaurant and a bar, toward the alley that ran between a block of businesses and the grassy fields of West Hollywood Park, like a man seeking refuge in a storm. When I finally reached the wooden steps that descended to the alley, the crowd thinned a bit and I felt like I could breathe again.

Everything seemed slower and quieter now, safer.

A scattered line of celebrants flowed toward me, coming from their distantly parked cars. Here and there, in the shadows, couples smoked joints or made out; a few men urinated against walls. A group of college types, looking ridiculously fresh-faced, passed laughing, without a glance my way from the bunch. My loneliness was disturbingly acute, almost like physical pain. Making it through the night seemed impossible now; it would take a fifth of tequila for that, or a hundred dollar hustler from the pickup bar down the street or, at the very least, a trip to Hollywood and a sex club dim enough for kindness toward a man my age. I'd use condoms and keep my mouth where it belonged. I'd feel the heat of another body, the mutual need. I'd cry out and clutch someone in the dark. In that moment, I'd feel alive. In that moment, I'd know I existed.

I realized how pathetic I must look, stumbling down the alley, alone. The eyes I'd sought out with such yearning only moments ago seemed threatening now, full of pity and ridicule. Laughter erupted from another group of young men and I was certain they were deriding me. Just ahead was a dark stretch that ran along the trees at the edge of the park, behind the hardware store. I hastened my steps and slipped into the deepest shadows with immense relief, shrinking under a stairwell where I could look out without being seen.

How many Halloweens had I experienced in Boys Town? I tried to remember but lost count. Once, when Jacques and I had been in love and he'd still been healthy, Halloween in West Hollywood had consisted of a couple of thousand gay men coming out of the bars at midnight to swarm the boulevard and defy the law, shutting down the street and celebrating on our own terms. Back then it had been a glorious, liberating night; the boulevard had belonged to us, if only for a few hours. We'd felt like one, laughing in the face of a world that judged and excluded us, that turned us into sexual outlaws and then condemned us for it. God, how Jacques and I had loved Halloween in Boys Town, how we'd rejoiced in its anarchy. Now it was a crass commercial enterprise, sanctioned and controlled by the city. Once a year, the breeders flooded into the neighborhood for the evening to spend their cash, gawk at the freaks, convince themselves they'd walked on the wild side, then sneak back to their safe, conventional lives for the next twelve months. Halloween in Boys Town had become a co-opted cultural artifact, clinging to the tatters of the past, and I was a ruined man of forty-five, trying to reclaim some small part of my old self. Trying to hang on—but to what? So much was gone, lost. Foolishly, hopelessly, I wanted Jacques back. I needed him, as intensely as I knew I'd never have him. So much was gone, Jacques most of all.

I'm not sure how long I'd stood there in the shadows, wrapped in my cocoon of longing and self-pity, when I became aware that I was not alone. It was just a feeling at first. The sense that someone might be sharing my space, observing me, while all the others paraded past on the narrow street. Slowly, I swung my eyes around, beyond the edge of the stairwell, sorting through shapes in the darkness.

The Grim Reaper: He was back.

He stood a few yards away, next to a Dumpster, studying me through the holes in his mask. Bony costume on a lanky frame, scythe at his side. The adrenaline coursed through my system again, quickening my heartbeat, shrinking my balls. I felt my saliva dry up as I took a tentative step from beneath the stairs.

"Who are you? What do you want?"

"Don't you know?" The voice was small, muffled. I shook my head. He moved slowly forward, closing the distance between us by half. "Death," he said, "coming to take you away." Then he laughed, and I had my answer.

"Nick Gash." I spoke his name as if amused, but my blood raced faster just the same.

"Next year," he said, "you should try a costume. You get to see everyone, but no one sees you. That way, you don't have to hide under stairwells."

"I'll try to remember that."

"Having fun?"

"Things could be better."

"Maybe I can help."

"How would you do that?"

"All kinds of ways." A second later he was on me, pushing me back into the shadows, up against a wall. His narrow fingers emerged from under the heavy cuff of his cloak, touching my face. "Halloween," he whispered playfully, "the most dangerous day of the year. The day Satanists and witches snatch children off the streets and sacrifice them in the name of the Devil." He placed a hand on my throat and his voice grew serious. "You were asking questions about me, at the construction site. Why?"

"You fascinate me, Nick."

"Do I?" He let go of me and pulled off his mask. The pupils of his blue eyes were huge. "You're Benjamin Justice. The famous reporter."

"Ex-reporter. Not so famous, really."

"Come on, I've read about you in the papers. Everybody has." One by one, he unfastened the top buttons of my shirt, playing with the thick hair at my collarbone. "You've done bad things. I like men who do bad things." He placed a hand behind my head, pulled me forward, kissed me on the mouth. His breath was coming faster now. "Maybe we should get out of here, go to my place."

"Why should we do that?"

"Because you want to."

"I'm HIV-positive. You need to know that up front."

"OK, so now I know."

"We have to be careful, Nick."

"I'm not the careful type."

"Maybe it's not such a good idea then." I swallowed with difficulty, heard the weakness in my voice. "Maybe we'd better skip it."

Nick Gash kissed me again, harder and longer this time. Then he scoured my rough beard with his mouth until his lips were raw. "Oh, it's a good idea alright."

He took my hand, pulled me from the shadows, then along the alley and around the corner. Leading me into familiar side streets, then others less familiar. Further and further away from the noise and the people. Deeper and deeper into a place I never should have gone.

EIGHTEEN

Nick Gash locked his apartment door behind us, keeping the lights off. Street light filtered through the windows, casting soft shadows. I could hear a clock ticking.

"You're in my world now," he whispered. "My rules." His face was inches from mine. "You have a problem with that?"

"Not yet."

Our mouths joined and I pulled him into me, kissing him fiercely, our bodies grinding. I'd neither kissed nor had my hands on a man since Oree Joffrien. Oree was a classy guy, a sleek, gorgeous black man with nice suits, nice manners, and a Ph.D., who made love intensely but always with a degree of control, respectful of his partner. Nick Gash was nothing like that. His needs were more primal, more voracious. He grabbed, growled, grunted, clawed. This sex was going to be hot and bruising, I thought, the kind that means nothing tomorrow but that you never forget.

I knelt down to grab the hem of his cloak, which I pulled up and off him as he raised his hands to assist me. Except for his construction boots, he stood before me naked, lean and well-muscled from head to toe. Still, I was disappointed that he wasn't hard. When I reached to touch his cock, he pulled away.

"First things first." He untied and kicked off his boots, then crossed the darkened living room on long, lanky legs to rummage in a lower drawer. "This'll take a couple of minutes. Look around if you want."

While he went about his business, I wandered through the apartment. It was a decent-sized two-bedroom on the second floor of an old building designed in the Spanish revival style, probably dating to the late 1920s. Windows looked out on arched doorways, wrought iron gates and colorful tiles bordering steps, and a courtyard of fern and philodendron with a bubbling fountain at the center. Separating the building from its quiet street was a path winding through heavy landscaping. Out by the street stood a row of jacarandas, shedding their pinnules and seed pods to the bumpy sidewalk below. Inside, a hallway ran between the two bedrooms, with a bathroom at the end. In one bedroom, a framed poster of the late rock star, Kurt Cobain, hung above a king-sized bed, his little boy eyes looking haunted and lost. Next to the bed, on a nightstand, a small lamp provided muted light. A drawer was partially open; inside, I could see the blue steel plating of a handgun.

I walked across the hall to the second bedroom. It was cluttered with all manner of construction tools, along with skis, roller blades, a mountain bike, boxing gear, and rock climbing equipment. A set of blueprints lay spread on a worktable—complete architectural diagrams of St. Agnes Cathedral. Nick's tool belt also lay on the table; next to it was a security clearance badge for the construction site, bearing his photo.

"Ready to party?"

I turned to find Nick standing in the doorway. He'd removed his boots and socks. In his hand was a small glass pipe—the kind used for smoking crack or methamphetamine. In the bowl was a generous pinch of granules that looked like crystal meth.

"Maybe partying isn't my thing."

"Then you're in the wrong place, dude." Nick strutted over, his cock swinging, and lay the pipe on the table. Silently, methodically, he undressed me. He lit the pipe, inhaled, then held it out to me. I shook my head no.

"Take it," he commanded.

I stared into his piercing blue eyes, then down at the cross and barbed wire tattooed on his hard, smooth chest. He took my hand, placed it on the apex of the cross. His skin was warm, slightly moist. With my fingers, I traced the pattern of the cross—from collarbone down to navel, and across from nipple to nipple. Then I followed the same path with my tongue, tasting his salt, gently biting, then less gently, leaving teeth marks in the meat of his pectorals while he hissed with pain and pleasure. His cock rose, quivering.

He thrust the pipe at me. "Take it."

"Why is it so important?"

"I need you with me."

He stroked my face, then my body, never taking his eyes off mine. He touched me in places and in ways that only the most liberated man dares to do, the man who comes to terms with himself and his desire and leaves less adventurous men behind. "The rule is," he said, "there are no rules. No rules, no boundaries, no past, no future. Just you and me, now." He knelt, ran his tongue along the inside of my thigh, and around my balls. I felt a tremor run through my body, craving more. He rose, eyeball to eyeball again. "It's what you wanted, when you hit the boulevard tonight." He grabbed a handful of my hair, made me look directly at him. "Tell me I'm wrong."

I took the pipe. He struck a match, torched the crystal. I inhaled.

"Deeply," he said, keeping the flame above the burning granules. "Deeply, deeply."

The first sensation I experienced was the rapid beating of my heart, then a prickly warmth, followed by a surge of power, not unlike the most potent adrenaline rush. It may have taken seconds or minutes, I couldn't be sure. But when the rush came, I felt fearless, invincible, insatiable. I wanted Nick Gash, all of him, every muscle, every hair, every inch of his flesh, right now. I handed him the pipe and he sucked down the smoke staring straight into my eyes. There was no turning back.

After that, we went crazy together.

For hours—on the floor, in the bed, against walls—it went on. Somewhere in the background, the musical wail of Nirvana issued forth, penetrating my brain, driving my sexual motion, taking me further and further into Nick's world. I have no idea how many hits I took from his pipe, how many times I was inside him, how many times my semen exploded out of me while I screamed and laughed and cried. There were no condoms, no antiseptic foam, no thought of anything except the craving that consumed us and the flailing and thrashing and pounding that carried us maddeningly toward a point of satisfaction we never quite reached.

Finally, around dawn, it ended.

I was still high, still charged with sexual energy. But I was also too sore and too spent to do more. Nick lay on the big bed, fingering his tattoo, while I stood at a window, looking down at the lushly green courtyard.

"Should I fire up the pipe again?"

I shook my head. "Have you been tested, Nick?"

"Doesn't interest me."

"You could be infected," I said. "I could drive you to the hospital. They can start you on post-exposure prophylaxis."

He laughed. "Them's big words."

"It's a big disease."

"I'll take my chances."

"Why?"

"Because I don't give a shit."

I turned to face him. "Maybe I do."

"That's your problem." He patted the bed beside him. "Come on, get next to me for awhile. Don't spoil things. I'm not getting no treatment for something I might not have."

I lay down beside him. He slipped an arm around my shoulders, pulled me closer. I longed to touch him again, anywhere he'd let me, but I couldn't bring myself to do it. It troubled me to think what might be happening beneath the surface at that moment, as my virus seized new ground inside him.

"My viral load is undetectable," I said.

"Then there's probably nothing to worry about."

"They don't know that for sure. It hasn't been confirmed."

"Like I said, it doesn't matter." He looked over, grinning. "I like to live dangerously. Makes life more interesting."

I reached over, pulled open the nightstand drawer, lifted out the pistol. It was a nine-millimeter Ruger, the brand clearly imprinted on the stock. When I hefted it, it felt surprisingly light in my hand. "Is it loaded?"

"Oh, yeah." He grabbed my balls, laughing. "Just like you."

Later, we showered together. While he was rinsing, I carried my towel down the hall and into his extra bedroom. I wanted to take something with me. Not a souvenir of the event, but of Nick. I saw his face looking at me from his construction-site security pass. A moment after that, the badge was in a pocket of my jeans.

I was slipping into them when he entered the bedroom, toweling off. We kissed but when he started after me again I told him I'd had enough.

He shrugged his damp shoulders. "I got to get to work, anyway." He opened a drawer, found fresh underwear. "My old man's a stickler for punching in on time."

"I stole your security badge, Nick."

He looked over, pulling on briefs. "Yeah?"

I nodded. "I wanted something to remember you by."

"You're weird, man." He pulled on a T-shirt. "Keep it. I'll tell them I lost it. They'll issue me a new one. Any other mementos you're hankering for?"

"You're hardhat's kind of cute."

He laughed. "Take it. I got another one."

"How long have you worked for Charles Gash Construction?"

"Too fucking long. But it's a paycheck, keeps me in crystal.

My old man figures I'll take over the company some day. No fucking way."

"So what's going on between you and the Bishop?"

He paused in the middle of buttoning up his Levis. "Finatti? Finatti and I go back a long way." He winked. "I like to keep tabs on him. Freak him out a little."

"Is that why you gave him that laminated copy of Joe Soto's column? To freak him out?"

Nick tucked his T-shirt in all around. "You ask a lot of questions, Justice."

"I'm the curious type."

He flashed his familiar grin. "And I'm the sly type." He sat on the bed, pulling on socks and construction boots. "Come back again, and maybe I'll tell you more."

"I don't think I should do this again. I shouldn't have done it the first time."

"That's too bad. I had a blast."

I rubbed the buzz cut barely covering his skull. "I like you, Nick."

He looked up from lacing his boots. "I'd grab some breakfast with you, man, but I'm running late. Don't want to get in trouble with dear old Dad."

"I'll find my own way out then."

I grabbed his hardhat across the hall and was almost to the front door when he called my name. When I turned, he said, "I've got something else for you."

He crossed the living room and handed me the copy of Joe Soto's last column, laminated on a plaque. "Finatti didn't want it. Maybe you'd like it."

"What makes you think that?"

"You're the guy in the column, aren't you? The kid Father Blackley got his hands on when he was back in Buffalo." He handed me the plaque. "I read somewhere that you were from Buffalo. I put two and two together."

"I'll find a special place for it."

He reached out, ran a hand through my thinning hair. "If I were you, Justice, I'd watch my back."

"Did you know Father Blackley, Nick?"

"Like I said—I'd watch my back."

I stood out on the sidewalk staring up at Nick's apartment, thinking about his last words to me, wondering what their connection might be to Joe Soto's murder, if any.

Then came a more troubling concern: What I may have done to Nick during our long night together. The fact that he'd given permission didn't matter, not to me, not any more than if I'd fired a bullet into the heart of some person of diminished capacity who was begging me to end his life. It left me feeling sick, horrified by what I'd done. Yet even as my weakness shamed me, I could feel it reasserting itself. Already, I missed Nick's body, his smell, the feel and taste of him, his wild heart. Most of all, I missed the faraway place where the smoke from his pipe had taken us.

NINETEEN

"You must have been out the whole night, Benjamin."

It was almost ten. Maurice placed a breakfast tray near the edge of the bed, where I'd lain awake for hours, still edgy and pumped up. He poured a cup of coffee from a small pot, handed it to me. "Fred saw you come in around sunup. He was up early, puttering around the kitchen." Maurice sought out my eyes. I glanced away, picked up the *L.A. Times* from the tray, scanned the front page. "While you were out carousing, did you manage to stay on schedule with your meds?"

I kept my eyes on the paper. "I may have missed a dose or two."

"Benjamin, for goodness' sake—"

"Not now, Maurice. OK?" I gave him the benefit of a glance, then sipped the coffee, grateful for the caffeine. "Like you said, it was a long night."

"At least you'll have a decent breakfast." He lifted lids, showing me his bowls. "There's fresh fruit, yogurt, and that granola you're so fond of. Nonfat milk in the little pitcher." He stood over me, fists planted on his narrow hips. "Then I want you back on schedule with your meds. Are you listening, Benjamin?"

"Do I have a choice?"

"Promise me."

"I promise." I tilted my head, indicating the tray. "Thanks for bringing it up."

"Breakfast? Or your naughty night out?" Our eyes met and we laughed uneasily. "We worry about you, that's all. You're like a son to us, you know that." He wiggled a finger at the tray. "I expect to see those bowls come back empty—every single bite."

"What would I do without you, Maurice? You and Fred."

"I'm not sure, Benjamin." His smile was pained. "Sometimes, I'm not sure at all."

When he was gone, I sipped my coffee and settled back with the newspaper, trying not to think about my night with Nick Gash and the methamphetamine still messing with my nervous system. I found nothing in the news pages on the Joe Soto case, but I did come across a city section brief that stopped me cold:

Hospital Plunge Kills Nurse

A nurse fell to her death last night from the rooftop of St. Anthony's Hospital in Echo Park in what police are calling a probable accident. Bing Crisologo, 41, of Van Nuys, was apparently smoking during a break shortly after 10 P.M. when she toppled seven stories to the pavement below. There were no witnesses and no indications of suicide or foul play, according to police. Following the incident, hospital officials put the rooftop off limits to unauthorized staff. A further investigation is pending.

Bing Crisologo, who'd sent the letter to Joe Soto, expressing a need to talk to him, before changing her mind. The same woman I'd followed to the house on Carondelet, where a younger woman had taken her in. Now Bing Crisologo was dead as well.

Maybe it was just a coincidence. Maybe.

I forced down my breakfast on the run, as I showered, shaved and dressed. After gulping a handful of meds, I jumped into the Mustang, heading for Filipinotown.

Vehicles lined the driveway of the house and more were parked along the curb out front. Brown-skinned neighbors, carrying covered pots and baking dishes, trooped from nearby houses and up the steps of the broad front porch. Small children tagged along, clutching bunches of fresh-cut flowers.

I followed them up the walk but lingered on the porch with a few others. The dialect of choice seemed to be Tagalog. Nearby, a young woman lapsed into English. When the opportunity came, I approached her, asking if I might meet with the owner of the house.

"Teresa?"

"I'm not sure who she is," I said. "Bing and I were barely acquainted."

"Teresa Sandoval," the young woman said, "Bing's married sister. She owns the house. Please, come in."

"I don't want to intrude, I just—"

"It's not an intrusion." She glanced at my ring finger. "You're single?" When I nodded, she smiled coyly. "There are several girls inside who are single. Very pretty girls." She winked. "Just to let you know."

Moments later, I was in a living room paneled in dark wood and decorated with colorful tapestries, native Filipino masks, and bubbling aquariums filled with exotic fish. Unfamiliar music was playing and, in the center of the room, children danced. Standing to the side, surrounded by friends and relatives, was Teresa Sandoval, the pretty young woman I'd seen helping Bing Crisologo into the house the day I'd tailed her from her Van Nuys apartment. She looked over as I approached, her eyes sparking with recognition.

"I read about Bing's death in the newspaper," I said, after introducing myself. "I'm very sorry."

Before I could say more, Teresa Sandoval was leading me to a buffet, insisting that I eat. I begged off, citing a late breakfast, but she handed me a plate just the same. I faced a long table laid out with Filipino dishes, heavy on the noodles, with bowls of peanut sauce on the side. She escorted me from dish to dish, making sure I sampled each one. After that, she introduced me to several young women while I picked at my plate. Their reaction ranged from shy to flirtatious, even brazen; I became aware of other eyes on me from around the room, most of them female.

Finally, I set my plate down and pulled Teresa aside. "I need to ask you a few questions about Bing."

"Would you like something to drink? More food?"

I shook my head. "Privately, if you don't mind."

She glanced around, suddenly uneasy. "This way." I followed her to a back bedroom, where she shut the door behind us. When she faced me, her eyes were fraught with apprehension. "I saw you when you drove up—your red convertible. You were here before, weren't you? When Bing came. You followed her."

I nodded. "I wanted to talk to her about a priest named Stuart Blackley."

"She told you at her apartment that she didn't want to talk."

"Bing wrote a letter to Joe Soto at the *Los Angeles Times*."

"That was a mistake. After she mailed it, she realized it might cause problems."

"Mr. Soto was a friend of mine. Now they're both dead."

Teresa Sandoval turned to a window that looked out on a vegetable garden going to seed. "This is a very bad situation, Mr. Justice. Very bad."

"You don't think Bing's death was accidental, do you?"

"What I think doesn't matter. I'm just a little person, Mr. Justice, like my sister. I need to bury Bing and forget about the rest."

"Do you feel you're also in danger, Teresa?"

"I have three children. I worry more about them, and my husband." She turned, her eyes brimming with tears. "Why do you come here with your questions? What good can it do?"

"You read Joe Soto's column? The one about Father Blackley?"

"Yes, I saw it."

"I'm the anonymous man Joe mentioned—I was that boy, back in Buffalo."

A breath escaped her like a groan; her large brown eyes ached. "This Father Blackley, he hurt so many people."

"Did he hurt Bing in some way?" She wrung her hands, chewed her lip, but remained silent. "Please, Teresa. If you know anything about him—"

"Is it so important to you, after all these years?"

"Maybe, if I had a family like yours, it wouldn't mean as much. But I don't."

She attempted a smile. "Maybe you should marry a nice Filipino girl, start a family of your own. You're a nice-looking man. You present yourself well. I can think of many girls who would be happy to be your wife."

"Did Bing marry an American? Is that how she became a citizen?"

"Bing found another way. Bishop Doyle helped her. He was very good to her."

"Kendall Doyle, the Cardinal?"

"He was a bishop when Bing arrived from Manila. She came when she was fifteen, on a tourist visa. The first in our family to come. Like so many, she stayed, to find work and send money home, to help our parents. Her great hope was to become a nurse."

"And how did Doyle figure into it?"

"Bing worked as a volunteer at the church headquarters. Bishop Doyle was her supervisor. He was a kind man. When she was confused about immigration matters, he counseled her. When she grew homesick, he consoled her." Teresa dropped her eyes. "When she was sixteen, she became pregnant. The father—it was impossible for him to marry Bing."

"She kept the baby?"

Teresa nodded. "Bishop Doyle urged Bing to give the baby up for adoption, but she could not do that. She was determined to raise Lucy, to give her a good life. The bishop made sure she got the best medical care possible. After Lucy was born, he used his influence to help Bing get a student visa, then a scholarship to nursing school. When she graduated, he helped her find a good job in a Catholic hospital—St. Anthony's, where she died last night."

"And Lucy—she must be grown by now."

"We lost Lucy, Mr. Justice, many years ago."

"I'm sorry. I didn't know."

"Lucy was a beautiful baby, a wonderful child." Mrs. Sandoval made the sign of the cross. "We thank God every day for the time she was with us." She began to weep. "And now I thank God for the time we had with my sister Bing."

"Perhaps I should come back, when you have some of this behind you."

"No, Mr. Justice. Please, do not return. No more questions. I've already said too much."

"Even if the answers might help explain Bing's death?"

"Perhaps some things are better left unexplained. Bing is in heaven now, with God and the angels. Nothing I say will bring her back. It would only cause more trouble."

"Why, Teresa? What are you so afraid of?"

She crossed the room to open the door. "Are you sure you won't have more to eat, Mr. Justice? We have so much. A big man like you, you need to eat."

I shook my head, apologized for intruding. She showed me back through the living room, where the young women again stole bashful glances or flirted. The last thing I saw before the door closed—just a glimpse—was a framed photo on a table, surrounded by flowers and burning candles: Bing Crisologo as a younger woman, with her arm around a pretty, dark-haired, light-skinned little girl, with bright green eyes, a button nose, and an endearing beauty mark in the dimple of her delicate chin.

"Bing named her after St. Lucy," Teresa said, following my eyes across the room to the picture.

"The patron saint of the blind," I said.

"You know the saints, Mr. Justice?"

"I studied them as a kid. Found them interesting. Martyr complex, I suppose."

"Our father was blind. That was why Bing chose St. Lucy." Teresa sighed deeply. "So many Saints, to protect us from so many things."

"Was Bing a devout Catholic, Teresa?"

"Oh, yes. She prayed every day. Her faith was very strong."

"Meaning no disrespect. But given what's happened, she must have been praying to the wrong saints."

Out front, a real estate broker was jamming a FOR SALE sign into Teresa Sandoval's front lawn.

I crossed the sidewalk, then the street, and slid behind the wheel of the Mustang. It was time to tell Lt. Claude DeWinter what I knew about Bing Crisologo, even if it wasn't much. I should have talked with him long before now, I realized. If I had, Bing Crisologo might still be alive.

I drove away from the Sandoval house thinking about that. About that, and about other things I should and should not have done, which were beginning to pile up like bad debts that could never be paid.

TWENTY

I called DeWinter from a pay phone outside LAPD headquarters but he was out. Not because it was Saturday but because he was in the field, piling up overtime. The female detective who picked up asked me what it was about. When I mentioned Bing Crisologo, the nurse who'd died in a fall from the roof of St. Anthony's, the detective asked me to wait where I was.

A minute later, a male detective approached, identifying himself as a sergeant investigating the Crisologo death. He was younger than DeWinter—no more than forty—with a nice suit, expensive haircut and cocky walk that prepared me for a dose of attitude. He recognized my name from my past exploits, and said so.

"DeWinter flagged the Crisologo case for us," he said, after I explained why I was there. "Gave us a copy of the letter she wrote to Joe Soto. So we've got it covered."

"I guess Lieutenant DeWinter's one step ahead of me."

"You got anything to add that we should know?"

I filled him in on what I'd learned about Bing Crisologo, including the fact that her sister seemed to be as frightened as Bing had been.

"What's your interest in this, anyway?"

"Joe Soto was a friend of mine," I said. "I'm also close to Alexandra Templeton, his fiancée."

"Alexandra Templeton." The detective spoke her name slowly, running his tongue across his lips. "Now there's one fine lady. That's a case I wouldn't mind being assigned. Of course, with DeWinter around, nobody else had a chance."

"How's that?"

"It's no secret that DeWinter's had a serious crush on the lady for years, going back to that homicide investigation in '97. You were involved in that one, weren't you, Justice? The 187, up in the Hollywood Hills."

I nodded. "But DeWinter hasn't been in contact with Alex since. Not until last week, when he showed up at the church after the service for Joe."

"Maybe not, but the man's still got a hard-on for the lady. Keeps a photo of her in his desk drawer, where he thinks we haven't seen it. Fat chance."

"Where would he get a photo of Templeton?"

"Shot it himself, probably, with a telephoto." The detective glanced around, lowered his voice. "When DeWinter found out your friend was dating Soto, he went into a serious depression. Dived into the cookies and ice cream. Gained at least a belt size."

I worked hard to sound nonchalant. "DeWinter knew about Templeton's relationship with Joe, before he was killed?"

"Oh, yeah, he knew." The cop's eyebrows went up, like it was funny—not funny ha-ha, funny weird. "DeWinter used to follow the two of them to restaurants and moon over her from across the room. I know, because my wife and I caught him one night, ducking his head at a corner table."

"The way I understood it, your captain *assigned* DeWinter the Soto homicide—because of DeWinter's connection to Templeton from that case six years ago."

"Is that how DeWinter tells it?" The detective winked broadly. "I guess that's how it happened then. Funny, though, how the file was on his desk the next morning, bright and early."

DeWinter had also ordered a check of all security cameras near the crime scene the morning after Joe had been killed—supposedly when it was still someone's else's case. DeWinter had let that slip himself, the day he'd spoken to Templeton and me at Parker Center. At the time, I hadn't realized the implications.

"Like I said," the detective went on, "the man's got a serious crush. Anything else I can do you for, buddy?"

"I was going to suggest DeWinter run a background check on someone."

"In connection with the Soto case?" I nodded. He poised his pen above his notebook. "Give me a name. I'll pass it along."

"Nick Gash." I gave him Nick's address and approximate age. "Son of Charles Gash, the guy who owns Gash Construction."

"The church guy?" I nodded. "Any special reason?"

"Nothing concrete. DeWinter can call me if he wants to know more."

"I'll see that he gets it." He pocketed the notebook and pen. "Miss Templeton, how's she holding up? After the death of her boyfriend and all."

"OK, I guess. You know how it is."

His grin turned catty. "I imagine DeWinter's doing his best to console her."

"I suppose so."

"Do me a favor? If DeWinter starts drooling around your foxy friend, wipe his chin for me, will you? I'd hate to see him embarrass the department."

Before turning away, he laughed and slapped me on the shoulder. I felt anger bubbling up inside me, like oil over a flame. It wasn't the departing sergeant I had a problem with; he was merely guilty of misogyny and crudeness. The rage I felt was for Lt. Claude DeWinter, a conniving sonofabitch who was using Joe Soto's death and Templeton's grief to worm his way back into her life.

Maybe it was even more sinister than that, I thought. Looking back at the way certain events had unfolded—the odd timing of things—maybe Claude DeWinter had more to answer for than just a cadged assignment to investigate a hit-and-run. A hit-and-run that, to me, was suddenly looking awfully convenient.

TWENTY-ONE

That Monday, as I did every three months, I visited my doctor for a checkup and got the results of lab tests run on samples of my blood. The blood panel measured how well my drug regimen was keeping my virus in check and also the damage its toxicity might be having on my vital organs. According to the lab numbers, my kidneys, liver and pancreas were all functioning normally, so that was good. But my T cell count had come down, a sign that my immune system was weakening, while my viral load had become detectable for the first time in a couple of years. My doctor advised me to follow the exact protocol for taking my meds, without missing a dose, and to avoid stressful situations. If the numbers didn't improve, he said, I'd have to switch to a new drug combination. That wouldn't be easy, because I carried a strain of the virus that was resistant to roughly a third of the drugs currently approved by the FDA for HIV suppression, which made finding the right combination a challenge. I listened dutifully to his lecture, and promised I'd do better.

Avoid stressful situations. My HMO policy covered the bulk of the tab, which ran to about fifteen thousand dollars a year, most of that for pharmaceuticals. There were all kinds of ways a guy like me could lose his coverage. It was something many of us with HIV thought about constantly, or tried not to—that anxious feeling that we were hanging on by threads, our lives measured by viral loads, T cell counts, and health insurance stubs, if we were lucky enough to have them. It was hard to complain, since most of the forty million HIV positives outside the U.S. had zip—not a single drug to ward off the virus, let alone a complete cocktail. On the African continent alone they were dying by the millions. Still, without my precious coverage, things could quickly get bleak.

Avoid stressful situations. I kept reminding myself of that as I handed over the fifteen bucks for my copayment and scheduled my next appointment.

Minutes later, I was in the Mustang on Interstate 10, on my way to a noon appointment with Bishop Anthony Finatti. This time I was thinking about how much stress might suddenly evaporate when I had a cool million in the bank.

"Mr. Justice! Please, come right in. All the papers are in order." Bishop Finatti rose from his chair, coming around his desk. "I can't tell you how pleased we are that we've come to a resolution."

"I still have a few questions."

"Of course, of course, my boy. Have a seat. May we get you something? Coffee, tea?"

I sat, facing his desk. "Just some answers, thanks."

Finatti sat across from me, folding his hands in front of him, looking cordial, almost ebullient. "You're concerned about the wording of the contract. You mentioned that on the phone the other day. Perfectly natural. Please, fire away."

"If I take this money, I agree to drop any further inquiry into Father Blackley's behavior after he left Buffalo. Those are the ground rules, correct?"

He nodded once. "One of them, yes."

"And the others?"

"That the Los Angeles archdiocese in no way be mentioned in your book, or in any other kind of writing that you might undertake. Also, nothing about anyone associated with the arch-diocese."

"Even parishioners, or past parishioners? Members of their families?"

Again, the small nod. "The wording in the contract covers that as well."

"Rather broad, isn't it?"

This time he raised his chin to show me a more thoughtful look, pushing his wire rims higher on his bony nose. "Not so restricting, really, for a million dollars. I believe if you were to research this aspect of our agreement, or consult an attorney of your own choosing—which you're certainly welcome to do—you'll find the wording to be almost standard for this kind of document."

"You mentioned writing about these people, Bishop. Any other restrictions in that area?"

His smile came quickly. "Just one small proviso." He opened a drawer with his palsied hand, removed a four-page contract with his good hand, and laid the document on the table. "We'd like you to cease and desist in any and all inquiries regarding church business here in Los Angeles, and any further contact you might be contemplating with anyone associated with the church."

"No contact whatsoever?"

"That's correct."

I glanced at the portrait of Cardinal Kendall Doyle on the wall behind the Bishop. "And what does the cardinal say about all this?"

Finatti's smile broadened and his voice grew slightly patronizing. "I can assure you, Mr. Justice, Cardinal Doyle has more important matters on his mind."

My eyes swung to the west-looking window. "The new cathedral?"

"Among other things, yes." The faintest impatience crept into Finatti's voice. "Let's stay focused on the matter at hand, shall we?"

He reached across the desk, placing a pen atop the document.

"Before I sign," I said, "I'd like to speak with Cardinal Doyle."

Finatti cocked his head quizzically to one side. "You wish to do what?"

"A few minutes of his time, that's all."

"Oh, my," Finatti said, laughing. "What on earth for?"

"I have some questions about a parishioner the Cardinal apparently knew quite well. Before I sign off on this, I need to tie up some loose ends, for my own peace of mind."

"What parishioner would that be, Mr. Justice?"

"Bing Crisolgo."

Finatti's stared keenly at me, then folded his hands again, so tightly this time I could see the knuckles turning white. His voice remained steady, unperturbed. Too steady, I thought. "You can imagine how busy Cardinal Doyle is, Mr. Justice. The new cathedral, the pontiff's declining health, so many matters of grave concern."

"You're aware that Bing Crisologo is dead?"

"We were informed, yes. But I don't see what this has to do with—"

"I believe Cardinal Doyle was once quite close to Miss Crisologo, when she first arrived here from the Philippines."

"Miss Crisologo was a longtime member of the church, a lovely woman. Her death is a great sadness for all of us." Finatti found his insipid smile again, adopting a softer, more conciliatory tone. "When she was younger, she had some problems. Cardinal Doyle was a great comfort to her."

"If I'm not mistaken, Father Blackley was her parish priest."

The bishop shrugged indifferently. "He might have been. I can't be sure."

"You don't recall?"

"It's been so many years—"

"You were close to Father Blackley, weren't you, Bishop?"

"Stuart Blackley and I grew up in the same neighborhood in

Buffalo. Naturally, after he was transferred here, we saw each other from time to time."

"You personally arranged for that transfer."

"We're getting off point again, aren't we?"

"You're right, we'd been discussing Cardinal Doyle. So—when can I meet with him?"

"I'm afraid that's impossible."

"Because of questions I might ask about Bing Crisologo?"

"Because the cardinal's an important man, with a very full schedule." Finatti glanced at the contract, then took a deep breath, as if replenishing his patience. "We're offering you a million dollars, Mr. Justice. I'm sure you've thought about the difference that kind of sum could make in your life."

"More than you'll ever know, Bishop."

"Then, please—I need an answer."

"I'm sure you're aware of how Miss Crisologo died."

He sighed, this time with undisguised exasperation. "According to the news report, she died in a fall."

"Presumably an accident," I said.

"That's my understanding, yes."

"Joe Soto died in a hit-and-run. Presumably an accident, although now it seems otherwise."

"What's your point, Mr. Justice?"

"Both of them had connections to Father Blackley, and to each other, through Joe's final column. Miss Crisologo wrote a letter to Joe, expressing the need to talk with him."

"A coincidence, I'm sure."

"Do you screen Cardinal Doyle's mail, Bishop?"

Finatti grabbed the document and thrust it at me. "We had an agreement, Mr. Justice. You asked for this appointment to go over the final details and to sign the contract. It's time to attend to business. Do you want the money or not?"

The question was obviously rhetorical. I took the contract and scanned its few pages, while Finatti followed my every move like a department store security guard watching a shoplifter. The wording was just as he'd described it, binding me from any inquiries regarding the archdiocese and gagging me from writing about it. The key monetary figure was there in black and white: *one million dollars.* The sight of it nearly took away my breath.

"I've marked the lines where you're signature is needed." Bishop Finatti held out the pen. "There are two copies, one for each of us. After you sign them, I'll add my signature. Then we need only process the check."

One million dollars. I accepted the pen, then studied the words again, gripping the pen so hard I was afraid I might break it. I touched the point to paper, about to scrawl my name.

"As for Bing Crisologo," Finatti said, with a tone of compassion, "the cardinal himself intends to conduct the funeral mass. If that's any consolation to you." His voice drew me away from the contract, and back to his sickly eyes. "He's reserved a space for Miss Crisologo at St. Agnes, in the mausoleum."

"Unless I'm mistaken," I said, "that's awfully pricey real estate."

"Ordinarily, yes. But Cardinal Doyle has the authority to make exceptions, based on need and special circumstances."

"What might those be?"

He nodded at the unsigned document. "The contract, Mr. Justice."

"What special circumstances, Bishop?"

His placid mask remained in place but his eyes shifted slightly. "Well, of course, Miss Crisologo has been such a good and loyal parishioner. Devoted to the Church, to her work. And her death was so sudden, so untimely."

"That must be true of many parishioners. Why the cardinal's special interest in this one?"

"I suppose you'd have to ask the cardinal that."

"I'd like to. You won't let me."

The phone buzzed and one of the buttons lighted up. Finatti ignored it, keeping his attention on me. "We need to finish up, Mr. Justice. Without further ado."

"I've missed something," I said, more to myself than to Finatti.

"I beg your pardon?"

"Or maybe I haven't been asking the right questions."

"Mr. Justice, please."

Finatti's voice drew me back from thought. I pushed the contract away, laid down the pen. "I already have enough trouble sleeping at night, Bishop."

His eyes widened. "You're rejecting our offer?"

"More like saving my soul, or what's left of it."

"Don't be an idiot." For the first time, I saw blood rise in Finatti's pallid face. "For God's sake, we're talking about a million dollars."

His phone buzzed again and once more he let it go. I stood, but didn't step away. The sheets of paper lying on the desk had their own special power, holding me transfixed. I'd made so many bad choices in my life. For all I knew, this might be one more. But which was the wrong choice, and which the right?

Finatti surely saw my uncertainty; hope rose like a warming barometer in his look and manner. He rose with it, eagerly, as if it was pulling him to his feet. "If you walk away now, Mr. Justice, this offer will not be proffered again. And you'll spend the rest of your life wondering what could have been, what you let slip through your fingers that might have changed everything." He came around the desk until we were so close that I could see finest details in the silver crucifix that hung from his withered neck. "Have you ever taken a good look at the homeless people who proliferate in this city, begging for handouts? Have you ever wondered how they got there? Considered how fine the line between solvency and destitution for individuals like yourself, who don't operate so easily within the constraints and demands of our pecuniary society?"

My voice was small, shaky. "Many times, actually."

The line of his mouth tightened to suggest the faintest smile. The flesh around his eyes crinkled. "Walk out that door without signing these papers and you won't be invited back. I promise you that, Mr. Justice, as God is my witness."

He fixed me with his gray eyes, which had fire in them now. I suddenly saw Anthony Finatti in a completely different light. Inside his frail figure, beneath his parched skin, behind his palsied hand, was the kind of strength and confidence that springs from cunning and knowledge, which trump physical power more times than not. Finatti was a formidable individual, the kind who knew more than most how the game was played, and always played to win. And he wasn't kidding, I was pretty sure of that. This *was* my final chance.

I picked up the pen again, bent over the desk, turned to the page where my signature was required. I was about to add my name when I heard a tap at the door. The door opened a crack and Finatti's assistant peeked in.

"Miss St. John is on line two, Bishop. She's quite insistent."

I glanced from the woman at the door to Finatti. The spark was gone from his eyes, which struck me more as conflicted than irritated, as one might have expected. His self-assured smile had also disappeared. Hearing Lindsay St. John's name in my presence troubled him. Her name also troubled me. I was reminded—starkly—of the way St. John had humiliated Templeton the last time the two women had met. Remembering Templeton reminded me that Joe Soto was dead.

That's what this was about, or should have been. Alexandra Templeton—the friend who'd stood by me through thick and thin, who'd put up with my arrogance and bullshit time after time, who still cared about me when she had every reason to turn away. She'd watched the man she loved get run down and killed in cold blood. This was about Templeton, not me. About Templeton, and Joe, and maybe Bing Crisologo as well. And maybe about a lot of kids who'd suffered while Finatti scrambled to cover things up and protect the image of the Church. This was about getting to the truth, for their sake. Because whatever it might cost me, it would never equal the price each of them had paid.

I tossed the pen down and turned toward the door. Finatti's assistant stepped back, giving me room. Finatti grabbed the contract and chased after me, trying to get in front of me, shaking it in my face. "For God sake, man, a million dollars!"

I pushed him aside without much effort. When I was out the door and through the reception office and striding down the hallway, I heard Finatti screeching behind me.

"Go! Write your book and make your spurious claims! You haven't a shred of credibility with anyone who matters. They'll laugh at you. They'll dredge up your despicable, rotten past and throw it in your face, as well they should."

I could still hear him carrying on as the elevator doors slid closed, showing me my reflection in the polished brass. Maybe I was a fool, I thought, who'd made another stupid choice. But at least I was a fool who could still look himself in the eye.

TWENTY-TWO

I grabbed lunch in Chinatown, eating in a basement café past the main tourist drag, where the bowls of soup were spicy and cheap and most of the table conversation was in Chinese. By the time I'd finished, I'd read Joe Soto's book proposal for *Monster in the Shadows*. After that, I spent a couple of hours at the downtown central library, searching various databases for more tidbits on Pablo Zuniga, the elusive assassin whom Lt. Claude DeWinter seemed awfully eager to finger for Joe's murder.

Much of what I found duplicated what I'd gleaned from Joe's outline, but with a few new wrinkles. Zuniga had been born and raised in a desperately poor barrio of Bogotá. His father, a man preoccupied with sin and salvation, had flailed his only son so many times as a child that his back and buttocks were permanently scarred. As a teenager, he'd lost an ear fighting in a bar and, later, two fingers on his left hand while being tortured by enemies. He'd started his career as a policeman, graduating from bribes and intimidation to the more rewarding work of hit man for hire. Since the late seventies, he'd been on the payrolls of dictators and drug cartels alike, so fearsome an assassin that many Spanish-speaking parents invoked his name to keep disobedient children in line: *Si no te portas vien, Pablo vendra i te llebara cuando estes dormido*— "If you do not behave, Pablo will come and get you while you sleep." His fondness for mutilation was well documented, hence the nickname, *el Mutilador*. On various Web sites, I saw photos of his victims with hands or feet missing, noses and ears hacked off, eyes gouged out, genitalia gone, messages of warning carved into chests and stomachs. Just as deep as his sadistic streak, according to the research, was his devotion to Catholicism; his love of church ritual was said to be rapturous and his generosity to the Church extraordinary.

The Web sites I visited were starting to have a similar feel, duplicating facts and folklore, when I punched into a five-year-old article in the *New York Times* index and came across this passage:

> *The last verified sighting of Zuniga was in Montevideo in 1997, when the region's most hunted criminal was on the run, with federal police and international agents closing in. A number of witnesses reported seeing Zuniga plunge from a rooftop to a certain death five stories below. According to these accounts, peasants made off with his body, returning it to his family for a secret burial and a handsome reward. According to a copy of a classified Interpol file obtained by the* Times, *a Mexican archbishop presided over the clandestine service, in exchange for funding for a new hospital in Culiacan. Authorities seem generally divided on Zuniga's fate. Some feel certain that he fled to the United States seeking refuge in a major city. The majority, however, seem to believe that Pablo Zuniga never got out of Uruguay alive.*

I returned to the beginning and ran through the section again, my suspicions about Lieutenant DeWinter growing deeper. Of all the background he'd given Templeton and me on Pablo Zuniga, he'd never mentioned that *el Mutilador* was probably dead.

By half past three, I'd found a parking spot across from the cathedral construction site on Father Junipero Serra Boulevard. Right on schedule, Cardinal Doyle's black Lincoln Town Car pulled up out front. Two smaller cars were just behind it. Security guards rushed to open the gates, and the three vehicles drove through.

I put on the hardhat Nick Gash had given me, grabbed a clipboard I'd brought along, climbed out and walked east and around the corner to the union workers' entrance. Before long, a herd of other hardhats appeared, coming from a vendor's truck with sodas and Styrofoam cups brimming with coffee. I slipped in among them, flashing Nick's security pass as we trooped by the guard, without drawing a second glance.

Across the open ground that was to serve as the sprawling plaza, I could see the tall, bulky, white-haired figure of Cardinal Doyle hurrying toward the cathedral, his cassock flowing at his sides. Charles Gash was on the cardinal's right, clutching his clipboard, pointing here and there, chattering nervously. On the cardinal's left was Bishop Finatti, scampering to keep up on his short, spindly legs. Keeping stride were several unfamiliar men and women, all dressed in conservative business attire.

I followed at a distance, pausing now and then to glance at my clipboard and check off imaginary items, hoping to blend in among the hundreds of workers scrambling over the twelve-acre site. As we approached the cathedral, Cardinal Doyle's booming voice made it clear that the group was there to plan an important photo shoot, to document the building's progress before its official opening on Easter Sunday, not quite six months away.

Doyle brought the group to a halt, pointing up at the fifteen-story campanile that rose several stories above the cathedral's soaring walls and rooftop, explaining that the first of its many bells would be arriving in the next few weeks for installation and testing. Then he turned toward the impressive cathedral itself, indicating its fourth floor, where a broad window, still without glass, looked down on the plaza from behind a stately balcony. It was here, the cardinal told the group, that the pope himself would step out and speak to the gathered masses on his first visit to St. Agnes.

"And what a glorious day that will be!"

With barely a pause, he marched on, leading the group up the steps and through the main entrance on the cathedral's north side, which still awaited the installation of its mammoth copper doors. Moments later, we were all inside. Deafening noise filled the enormous space—the clatter of hammers, whine of hydraulic drills, stutter of staple guns—while blinding sparks showered the concrete floor as workers bore down on structural joints with acetylene torches.

The cardinal set out along an entrance hall for access to the nave, stepping over and around workers and their tools. He grew more animated as he went, his hands fluttering, his jowls jiggling, color rising in his fleshy face, speaking with unabashed pride about various church features yet to be completed or installed: Spanish limestone floors; luminous alabaster windowpanes; dozens of fine sconces, designed as individual works of art; a hundred tapestries, each ten feet tall, portraying the saintly and the blessed, that would hang along the entranceway we were in now, as well as in the nave itself. As he reached the end of the long hall, he pointed out a glistening *retablo*—a gilded altarpiece—that could be glimpsed in the shadows ahead. A moment later, he flicked on the lights, showing off the immensity of the nave, and the lovely *retablo* in particular.

"Seventeenth century Spanish baroque," the cardinal said, sounding giddy, his green eyes sparkling. "I just had to have it."

I stayed behind, listening inconspicuously, while the others entered the cavernous room. The cardinal stopped to admire the baptismal font, shaped from white marble, then continued on, speaking of the fine cherrywood that was being used for the pews and kneelers, which were now being fashioned in Mexico. He strode across the empty floor to the front to show off the cathedra, the stately bishop's chair in which he'd sit during part of every Mass, carved from the wood of six continents.

Then he turned reverently to the nave's centerpiece, a magnificent altar on a round pedestal, carved of rare burgundy marble, polished smooth as glass. "The first thing we installed. The cathedral is literally rising up around it."

"The color," Bishop Finatti said. "It's stunning."

"Deep red," Cardinal Doyle said, "to symbolize the heart of Jesus." He tapped on the open notepad of a red-haired woman in a business suit. "Make a note. When we take our pictures, the light must be just right, or it will end up looking black." He picked up a placard that had fallen to the floor and placed it atop the altar. It was hand-lettered: *Photo Shoot Saturday.*

"I must show you one more thing, modest in size and monetary value, but just as precious." The cardinal turned, striding back across the nave toward the entranceway. I retreated, ducking into a small chapel, slipping into the shadows near a tabernacle that would hold the Eucharist and the wine for Communion. Outside, the cardinal breezed by in his cassock, back the way he'd come, his flock at his heels. I poked my head out and followed.

Just inside the main entrance, a stairwell led upward—bare wooden steps, waiting to be finished. The cardinal mounted the stairs, climbing at a good clip, with the others hurrying after him. I glanced around the corner to see a row of empty elevator shafts, rising to the upper floors or descending to the crypts and mausoleum underground. Each shaft was barricaded by two-by-fours nailed up to form an X, prohibiting entry. Someone had posted a warning sign:

DANGER!

OPEN SHAFT

As the group disappeared around the first landing, I mounted the stairs and started up. I followed the others to a second flight, then a third, and, finally, to level four.

We emerged into a long, narrow room with expansive, window-like openings on either side. The interior opening looked into the nave, with a choir loft just below, at the third story; the opening on the far side opened to the plaza, with its balcony just outside, from which the pope would one day greet the masses. Cardinal Doyle explained that this was a special prayer room, where prelates could come for private meditation. He strode to the south end of the room, drawing us with him. Set back in a shallow alcove was a glass case, spotted with gentle light from above, adding a celestial touch. Inside the glass was a tattered, leather-bound copy of the Bible, open to Psalms.

"The *pièce de résistance*." Doyle said. "My family's Bible, brought to this country by my grandparents. Before that, it was in the family for generations. My dear baby sister, Agnes, read from this holy book the day the Lord called her to heaven. There's nothing I treasure more." He swept a hand about him. "And it will remain here, in this great house of worship, for centuries to come."

"Close-ups," Finatti whispered to the woman with the note-pad, as she scribbled dutifully. "Be sure to get close-ups."

The cardinal strode back to the middle of the prayer room, spreading his hands toward the open windows at each side, east and west. "I deliberately placed this room between the interior of the cathedral and the outer world, to integrate them. A sense of community—this is what the cathedral must represent. The bringing together of the people." He led us to the window facing outward, pointing to a statue perhaps twenty feet high being erected in the middle of the plaza, facing its entrance. It depicted a young girl with long hair, cradling a lamb. "St. Agnes, welcoming the faithful."

From the back of the pack, I stepped closer. "St. Agnes," I said, "patron of the children of Mary. Protector of the innocent."

The cardinal turned to see who might be speaking, and the small group between us parted. "Yes," the cardinal said, "precisely. Patron saint of girls."

Bishop Finatti stared at me wide-eyed, his mouth agape.

Charles Gash looked merely confused. A moment later, Finatti was voicing his outrage at seeing me inside such a sacred place.

"This man is an enemy of the Church," Finatti said, fury transforming his wrinkled features. "His very presence here is blasphemy."

Charles Gash was immediately on his cell, alerting his security staff to a breach and ordering me removed. I ignored them both, keeping my focus on the Cardinal.

"St. Agnes was martyred at thirteen, around A.D. 300," I said, "for refusing to renounce her love of Jesus and marry a suitor. Tortured and beheaded, for refusing to give up her purity."

"Christ made my soul beautiful with the jewels of grace and virtue." Cardinal Doyle recited the words historically attributed to St. Agnes as she suffered before dying. "I belong to him who the angels serve."

Bishop Finatti leaned toward the cardinal, whispering. "Benjamin Justice—the one I told you about. The one making the wild claims."

Cardinal Doyle smiled warmly, placing an upraised finger in the deep cleft of his chin, obscuring the mole. "Ah, the young man with all the questions. Such persistence." He raised his chin, looking down his round nose to study me more closely. "And what do you think of St. Agnes, Mr. Justice, now that you've seen our great building both inside and out?"

"Quite impressive, Your Eminence. A worthy monument to your sister's memory."

Cardinal Doyle beamed. "I'm delighted you find it so."

"What a shame," I added, "that it's built on a cesspool of hypocrisy and lies."

The others gasped and stared at me, horrified. Cardinal Doyle barely paid them attention, keeping his eyes on me instead. He took on, if anything, a more kindly countenance. "Perhaps, Mr. Justice, if you worshipped with us, and gave yourself to God, you'd feel differently."

187

"I look for truth in other ways, Cardinal. More secular truths, if you will, right here on earth."

"Exactly which truths elude you, my son?"

"The ones hidden in the archdiocese records on Father Stuart Blackley."

Doyle cocked his head curiously, then looked at Finatti as if confused. "We offered him a settlement, didn't we? I thought it was all taken care of."

"He turned our offer down, Your Eminence."

"No offense," I said, "but I'd rather do business with the devil."

Finatti curled his lips smugly. "I believe you've already consorted with the devil more than once."

"If I did, Bishop, his name was Father Blackley."

Cardinal Doyle stepped forward, laying a hand on my shoulder. "I'm deeply sorry if you suffered, Mr. Justice. I abhor the abuse of children, more than anything. But I can't undo what was done. My zero tolerance policy for molesting priests has been in place for nearly a decade. My conscience on the matter is clear. Now, please, leave us to finish our labor in this sacred place. When we open the cathedral, bring your sins, and I'll personally take your confession."

I heard distant footsteps pounding up the stairwell. "Tell me about Bing Crisologo, Cardinal. You knew her well, didn't you?"

"That's why you're here? About Miss Crisologo?"

I nodded. "Tell me why someone would want her dead."

"Miss Crisologo died in a tragic fall, Mr. Justice."

"I don't think so, Cardinal. I doubt that you do, either."

Bishop Finatti closed his eyes and crossed himself. Two men in the group restrained Charles Gash as he started for me, looking outraged.

The cardinal removed his hand from my shoulder, the color rising from his throat into his jowls, though he never relinquished his compassionate smile. "We've been patient, Mr. Justice, and we've more than tried to be charitable." He glanced toward the stairway as several security guards emerged, nightsticks banging against their thighs. "Now, I think it's time for you to go. I'll pray for you, my son, with all my heart."

"Wait!" Charles Gash shook the others off. He stepped over, removed the security pass hanging from my neck. "How did you get this?"

"From your son, Mr. Gash. He had no idea I planned to misuse it." I turned to Finatti. "You remember Nick Gash, don't you, Bishop? He seems to remember you."

Finatti flushed, his nostrils flaring. His eyes slid uneasily toward Charles Gash. I felt one of the guards prod me from behind with his nightstick.

"Don't," I said, and gave him a look that backed him off.

I crossed to the stairwell and trotted down the exposed wooden steps, making the guards hurry to keep up. Outside, a playful wind kicked up dust across the unpaved plaza. I stopped to take a last look at the cathedral and the surrounding grounds. The twenty-foot statue of St. Agnes was upright, being cemented into position. High in the campanile, workers readied a cable system to hoist the big bells when they arrived. Out on the cathedral's fourth-floor balcony Cardinal Doyle stood looking out, perhaps rehearsing his future moment as the pontiff.

"Move," a guard said. They kept their hands off me while they walked me to the main gate, which they closed behind me, standing watch until I was gone.

When I reached the Mustang, Nick Gash was leaning against the front fender, his arms folded across his bare chest, his hardhat and tool belt on the hood.

"I warned you to watch yourself, Justice. You don't listen, do you?"

"Maybe I'm like you, Nick—the careless type."

He grinned. "Maybe you and me should hook up again, get careless together."

"I want to know what's going on between you and Bishop Finatti."

"OK." He smiled like a fox. "But not now."

"When?"

"Tonight. My place, at ten."

"What'll it cost me, Nick?"

He looked me over. "I wouldn't mind taking a turn on top this time."

I felt a flutter in my stomach and tasted the metallic tang of adrenaline on my tongue. "What do I get in return?"

"Besides a good time? Anything you want to know."

The late afternoon sun warmed his well-muscled torso; the playful breeze teased the blond tendrils around his nipples. My body's memory fired a blast of desire through me like a depth charge. "OK. But I don't want to get high this time."

Nick Gash grabbed his hardhat and tool belt, departing with a wink and a grin. "Sure you do."

TWENTY-THREE

Inside the Mustang, I tossed the hardhat on to the backseat and slipped *Birth of the Cool* into the CD player. By the time I'd skipped forward to "Moon Dreams" and switched on the ignition, Lt. Claude DeWinter was plopping his wide behind onto the seat beside me, uninvited.

"What a happy surprise, Lieutenant, running into you like this."

"You just got to get into it, don't you, Justice?" He glanced across Serra Boulevard, where the gates opened and Cardinal Doyle's Town Car rolled out. "Got to push the damn envelope until it comes apart at the seams."

"It beats rolling over and playing dead." I kept my eyes straight ahead, feeling my anger boil up again. "You keeping tabs on me now, DeWinter? The way you've been bird-dogging Templeton."

"I intend to stay close to Miss Templeton until this case is closed. It's my job now."

"You want to explain why you're sitting in my car?"

DeWinter unwrapped a stick of sugarless gum, folded it neatly by sections, popped it into his mouth. "I came around to talk to Nick Gash. Then the cardinal shows up. I see you go in after him, looking like the construction guy in the Village People, sans the shades. Knowing you, I figure you're in there doing one of your confrontation numbers, making some kind of scene."

"I find it effective on occasion, when other avenues are closed."

"You're a cocky bastard, Justice. Too cocky. It can get you in trouble."

"You said you came around to see Nick Gash. Why the sudden interest? You following up on my suggestion to check him out?"

"What's *your* interest? Maybe we should start there."

"Which part of his body should I begin with?"

"It's your business who you sleep with, Justice. But if I were you, I'd look for safer company."

"You ran that background check?"

DeWinter nodded. "Nick Gash started having problems when he was a kid, eleven, twelve years old. Shoplifting, stealing bikes, that kind of thing. By the time he was thirteen, he'd hot-wired a car and taken it for a joy ride. His old man packed him off to a juvie boot camp in Arizona. Gash hoped it might do little Nick some good. It didn't. The kid just got worse—theft, drugs, robbery, fights—a lot of fights."

"A lot of anger," I said.

"A lot of violence. He's stayed out of jail for a few years now, but he's still got a nasty rap sheet. Take my word on this one. He's bad news."

"He has a steady job, his own place. Could have turned out worse."

"The old man keeps him employed, and pays for the apartment. Did you see that tattoo on his chest?"

"Kissed every inch of it, Lieutenant."

"If you're trying to get a rise out of me, Justice, forget it. You broke me of that six years ago, on the last case we worked. Like I said, it's your business where you put your dick."

"But I didn't break you of your crush on Templeton, did I?"

"I admitted before, I have a thing for the lady. I imagine

that's the case with more than a few men." He smirked. "At least the heterosexual kind."

"I prefer the term homosexually challenged." He didn't smile, so I played my best card. "You still keep a picture of Templeton in your desk drawer, Lieutenant?"

He swung his eyes around, as if someone had slapped him. His jaw was clenched, his words squeezed. "How do you know about that?"

"I've got my sources."

"Goddamn you, Justice."

"I also know you've been tailing Templeton for years like a lovesick bloodhound, watching her every move."

He faced forward, dropped his eyes. He stewed in silence, working hard on the gum. Finally, in a small voice, he said, "OK, maybe I got carried away. My divorce, the long hours, the nights alone—you know how it is." He glanced irritably at the CD player. "You mind turning the music down?"

"It's a cut called 'Deception,' Lieutenant. Is that the problem?" He gave me a look, reached over, shut it off. "You lied to Templeton and me, DeWinter. Your captain didn't call you in and assign you to the Joe Soto case. You maneuvered yourself into position, making sure you got assigned to it, so you could get close to her again."

"If I did, it's because I care about the lady."

"Which makes Joe Soto your rival. At least until the night somebody knocked him off. Where were you that night, De-Winter?"

His eyes came back around, hard with fury. "You don't ask me questions like that."

"You *stalked* her, Lieutenant. Kept track of her movements, followed her when she went out, knew about her relationship with Joe when she was being discreet about it."

"OK, I was an idiot. But I kept my distance. It was strictly fantasy, nothing more."

"Maybe you followed her and Joe that night to Pietro's.

Waited in an SUV with tinted windows, knowing where Joe was parked. Hit the accelerator when he crossed the street."

"What about the videotape? The driver was light-skinned."

"Maybe you got lucky. Maybe that driver just happened to be there that night, caught on camera. Then you learned about Joe's book proposal on Pablo Zuniga and you put the two together—the photos of Zuniga and a face on the videotape that bore a general resemblance. Or maybe that videotape didn't come from that location at all. Who knows how far you'd go, given your obsession with Templeton."

"That's crazy talk."

"Joe's death went down too late to make the L.A. *Times* morning edition."

"So what?"

"So, you wouldn't have known about it that soon. But the file was on your desk that morning. Why?"

"I must have seen it on one of the morning news shows."

"You ordered security tapes checked in the vicinity of the hit-and-run about the same time. You were already behaving like it was your case."

"We pitch in where we can, if we think we can help."

"We could check with your captain, see if that's how it went down. Or maybe you went to him, begging and wheedling to be put on the case."

DeWinter glanced at me again, looking badly conflicted. Then he stared down at his gargantuan wingtips. "They had a window table—Alexandra and Mr. Soto. They'd been to the same place quite a few times before. It was one of their favorite joints."

"You were there, then."

He nodded miserably. "I watched from across the street. Until they finished the main course and started holding hands across the table and making eyes at each other. I couldn't take it any more, so I left. Went home, ate half a pecan pie, watched some CNN, hit the sack."

"That's what you say."

"I wish I'd stayed!" His eyes flashed with emotion I couldn't identify. Regret, maybe, or fury with himself or with me. Or maybe it was just an act. "If I'd hung around," he went on, "maybe Soto would still be alive, and I wouldn't have to see her grieving the way she is."

"You could lose your badge over this. You know that."

"Is that what you want? To see me off the force?"

"I want people to start dealing straight with me."

"I'm straight when I tell you Pablo Zuniga killed Joe Soto. It all points to him."

"And away from you?"

"I'm not involved in Soto's death. I may be an asshole when it comes to women, but I'm not a cold-blooded killer."

"You seem awfully eager to pin this murder on a mythical assassin who's probably been dead awhile."

"I don't think he's dead. I think he's good for Soto, and maybe for Bing Crisologo, too."

"Then where is he, Lieutenant? Where's your fabled killer, *el Mutilador?*"

DeWinter cast his eyes from one length of the windshield to the other, sweeping the city. "Out there, somewhere."

"The monster in the shadows."

"That's right. And if I were you, I'd watch my back."

"Funny, that's just what Nick Gash told me."

"If you had some sense, you'd listen to him, at least about that." DeWinter slumped his shoulders, hung his chin, kept his eyes down. "You gonna tell her? About how I've been acting like a jerk all these years, how I burrowed my way into this case to get close to her again?"

"No, Lieutenant. You are."

He swallowed hard, a huge man who looked like a little boy about to get a licking. "I know how you must feel about me, Justice. I got no excuses. But don't let my bad behavior get in the way of your good sense. I'm telling you, this Zuniga is one bad dude. You don't want to mess with him."

"Or Nick Gash, either."

"That's right."

I reached across, opened the passenger door. "Tell her, Lieutenant. All of it. Or I'll do it for you."

He nodded unhappily, hauled his big body from the Mustang. I switched the CD back on; Miles was just launching into "Boplicity," with J. J. Johnson on trombone and Gerry Mulligan on baritone sax. My head bobbed, picking up the beat.

Outside, the wind chased bits of litter down the wide street. I watched DeWinter shuffle to his unmarked car, his shoulders sagging, his hands thrust deep into the pockets of his size forty-four pants, a whipped man.

TWENTY-FOUR

"So tell me about you and Bishop Finatti, Nick."

"Where do you want me to start?"

It was a quarter past ten. Nick sat cross-legged on his big bed, barefoot and bare-chested in a pair of jeans, preparing a pipe with a dose of crystal meth.

I tried to keep my eyes off the pipe and on Nick, but its pull was powerful. "How about that column by Joe Soto that you had laminated and mounted as a gift for the Bishop."

Nick looked up, grinning. "Like I said before, he didn't want the damn thing. Can't really blame him. He doesn't need any more reminders of Father Blackley, does he?"

"He refused to accept it?"

"When he saw me staring at him through the window of the church office, he sent Father Aragon out to talk to me. Aragon convinced me to back off, leave it alone."

"You and Father Aragon close?"

"Not my type. Too pretty."

"What about you and Father Blackley? Did you know him?"

Nick flicked a lighter, fired up the crystal in the pipe, sucked on the mouthpiece, drawing in the smoke. I watched him close his eyes and keep them shut as the drug did its job. Then he clenched his jaw as if the euphoria was more than he could handle, shaking his head rapidly, baring his teeth, hissing.

"That's what Nick needed," he said.

"Father Blackley, Nick. Tell me about him."

He flicked the lighter again, got a flame, held the pipe out to me. I shook my head. He took the hit himself, sucking hard and deep.

"I'm guessing you're in your mid-twenties, Nick. Twenty-five, twenty-six."

He expelled the spent smoke. "Twenty-eight."

"You started getting into trouble sixteen, seventeen years ago, a few years before Father Blackley died."

He patted the bed. "Don't be a stranger."

I sat down beside him. "Was Father Blackley your parish priest?"

He placed fresh granules in the pipe, held it out to me again. Again, I shook my head. He caught my chin, held it steady. "Don't leave me alone, Ben." He stared into my eyes, his pupils expanding. "Come fly with me, man."

"Father Blackley, Nick."

"One hit. Then I'll tell you everything."

My eyes settled on the pipe. He fired it up, passed it over. I took a monster hit, holding down the smoke, waiting to be transformed. Half a minute later, exhaling, I felt myself turning into Superman.

"My family attended a church in Pasadena." Nick took the pipe, set it on the nightstand. "Father Blackley became the associate pastor when I was ten. He had a cabin up in the mountains above Lake Arrowhead. He liked to take kids up there for retreats and stuff."

"Your parents had no problem with that?"

"My parents were zombies, totally hooked by all the holy bullshit." Nick pushed me back on the pillows, began to work at the buttons on my shirt.

"You and Father Blackley went to his cabin alone?"

"Not at first. He'd take girls up sometimes, in one group. Then, other times, groups of boys. When I was eleven, I became his favorite." Nick got my shirt off, went to work on my pants. "It started out with foot massages. Blackley had gout, so that was the reason he gave."

"Blackley had bad feet?"

"He was lame, man. He could hardly walk."

I sat up. "You're sure about that?"

"I'm telling you, dude, he got around with a cane."

Nick pushed me back down, slipped off my shoes and socks, then pulled off my pants and shorts. As I lay there naked, he began kneading the souls of my feet, sending bolts of pleasure up through my legs, into my groin. "He had me massage his feet, just like this. Kept telling me how good it felt." Nick's hands moved to my legs, caressing, working the muscles. "Then it was other places. You know the routine."

"How'd you feel about that?"

"I was like a lot of guys—curious. Plus, I'd been turned on by other guys for a long time by then." His fingers were on my upper body now, crawling over my skin. "It wasn't like Blackley made me queer. It doesn't work that way. If it did, all the guys he messed with would be queer, wouldn't they?"

"At some point, he told you that you needed to learn more about your body. That God wanted you to know how beautiful you were."

"He fed you the same line?'

I nodded. Nick touched my stiff cock, feeling the texture and the shape, regarding it with a mix of curiosity and admiration. "After he got me comfortable being naked, he taught me about masturbation." I clamped my eyes shut as Nick stroked me, closing his fingers around the head just enough to make me want more. "Said all boys did it, that he needed to show me how. After that, we got into the oral phase." I opened my eyes to see Nick go down on me, taking me deep into his throat. Just when I started going crazy, he came up for air, leaving me panting and deflated. "By the time I was twelve, he figured I was ready to take the big plunge." Nick stripped off his pants and shorts, spread my legs, kneeled between them.

"Condom, Nick."

He ignored me, reached over to the nightstand, pulled open the drawer. He placed his nine-millimeter Ruger on the pillow next to my head, then spit into his hand and lubricated himself. "He kept after me, feeding me his bullshit lines, touching me, getting me all worked up." Nick raised my legs, positioned himself. He spit again, lubing me with his finger. "I didn't know what he was going to do exactly. I kinda had an idea, though. I told him not to."

"Condom, Nick."

"Blackley had all the power, you know?" Nick reached for the gun, placed the muzzle to my left temple, between my ear and my eye. His voice grew ugly, as if it belonged to someone else. "They talk about love but what it's really about for them is the power, the control."

"Take it easy, Nick."

He drew a line down my face with the muzzle of the gun, then forced it into my mouth. "He was a priest. The dude with the authority, all the answers. Plus, he was big and strong, you know? I was a scared little kid just starting to get hair on my dick."

"Condom, Nick."

"He didn't care about me, only about what he wanted."

All at once, Nick forced himself into me. I clenched my teeth, holding back my cry, letting him in. Moments later, lubricated with my own blood, I started to relax. The shock of pain began to ebb.

"You must have hated him," I said.

"I hated myself more." Nick transferred the gun's muzzle to his own mouth, while his finger found the trigger and his eyes glazed over, as if he were seeing something far off, or deep within. I reached up, gripped the blue steel barrel.

"You haven't finished your story, Nick." His lips moved hungrily down the muzzle, like a man sucking cock. "We have a deal, remember?" His faraway look faded and our eyes slowly connected. "You tell me everything I want to know. That was the deal, Nick." Gently, I worked his finger off the trigger, then withdrew the gun from his mouth. "Father Blackley, Nick." I pried the gun from his hand, tossed it across the bed. "It's time to tell the rest about Father Blackley."

"I don't want to talk about him anymore." He shook his head, while tears rimmed his eyes. "I don't want to!"

"Then tell me about you, Nick. Tell me what happened to you."

"I was so fucking ashamed." He began to weep. "My own priest fucked me, after I told him no." His tears splashed my face, dampened the hair on my chest. "Afterward, I had this huge secret I couldn't tell nobody. I wanted to kill myself, but I was too afraid. I wanted to kill him, but I couldn't do it."

"So you started doing other things. Stealing, drugs, hurting people."

He nodded, tears catching and bubbling on his lips. I wrapped my legs around his waist, grabbed his buttocks, drew him in deeper. "He fucked me all that year. Then he stopped. I guess it was time for somebody new."

"You never told anyone?"

"When I was fifteen." Nick choked back a sob. "I told my old man."

"What did he do?"

"Went to Bishop Finatti. My old man was doing construction work for the archdiocese, so they knew each other. Finatti told my father not to worry, that he'd take care of it. He convinced my parents not to go to the police. I wanted to, but my old man said no. He figured they might not believe me, because of the trouble I'd been getting into. Get this—Finatti said it would just bring shame on our family. That the best thing was to put it in God's hands."

Nick wiped his nose with the back of his hand. I grabbed his hips, helping him find his stroke again, wanting him as close to me as possible, wishing I could take his whole body inside me, wishing I could somehow make him part of me.

"So your father went along with it."

Nick nodded, sniffling. "He needed the church business. Cardinal Doyle got involved. He promised my father that if he didn't make a stink, he could have the contract to help build the new cathedral. Doyle convinced him that if he signed on, he'd be glorifying God, ensuring his place in heaven."

"Tough offer to turn down, for a believer."

Nick's laugh was bitter. "They gave my old man a great contract. It was the biggest break of his life."

"He traded you for the chance to help build the cathedral."

Nick shut his eyes, letting out a wail, convulsed in sobs again. I reached up and pulled his mouth to mine, arching up until our bodies joined. He rode me like that through the night, forging his pain into pleasure, his fury into a different kind of passion, his hate into something akin to love, while I rose up to meet him with my own.

I wasn't sure of the hour when I finally stumbled from Nick's apartment and down to the street. Three, four in the morning, something like that. I was coming down fast from the crystal. Anxiety crept over me like spiders crawling on my skin; I ached for more of the drug. I'd heard from users that it only took one encounter with crystal meth to get hooked. I'd never believed it. I'd figured it was a cop-out, a way of excusing their weakness for the high. Now, I believed.

At the end of the long block, I could make out the red Mustang parked at the curb, beneath one of the shedding jacarandas. As I stumbled down the sidewalk, fighting the craving, squirming to ward off the spiders, I could see shrivelled leaflets on the hood. The predawn quiet felt oddly unsettling to me now, accentuating my anxiousness, etching my isolation in bolder relief against the emptiness of the street. I scratched frantically at my arms and chest to chase away the spiders.

Suddenly, in the dimness between street lamps, I pulled up, sensing another presence in the shadows. I looked around but there was no one to be seen. It must have been the drug working at me, I thought, and laughed at myself for letting a chemical play with my head like that.

Just then, movement caught my eye. A few yards ahead, a white cat darted from under a parked car. It dashed between the bars of the wrought iron fence that bordered the grounds of Nick's apartment house to my left. Safe inside the barrier, the cat stopped abruptly, one eye on me as it calmly licked a paw.

I moved forward and knelt, making friendly noises, trying to entice it out. A few strokes through its fur, a few scratches on its head, the sound of its purr. That's all I wanted. Contact with something soft and warm, a receptive being. An antidote to the shiver of unease I was feeling, the craving that lapped like cold waves against my insides. The cat stopped licking its paw, perked its ears. It looked up startled, then dashed off into the heavy foliage. OK, I thought, it's not interested in the attention of a needy stranger, at least not at the moment. Cats could be like that. Life lived on their terms, according to their own needs, their own schedule.

I rose, headed more purposefully toward the Mustang. Get home, take a hot shower, crawl into bed. Put the long night behind me. Start a new day. Shake off the meth. Never touch the stuff again. That was the plan.

Up ahead, a mere few yards now, a seed pod dropped from a jacaranda and landed on the convertible top. I made a mental note: Pay a visit to the car wash, the cheap one where I could use my coupon and get the discount. Get back to the order and routine of life, the mundane things. The car wash. Laundry. The outline for my book. That was the answer.

I was reaching into my pocket for my keys when I sensed again that I was not alone. This time, it wasn't the drug messing with my mind.

The stranger assaulted me from behind, with practiced, efficient force. First, a sharp blow to the back of the neck, leaving me stunned; then his arm around my throat, tight in the crook, cutting off the blood to my brain. For the first few seconds, I resisted ferociously, but it was useless; unconsciousness came on quickly. My last, desperate act was to reach back, clawing for his eyes. Instead, my hand found the side of his head where an ear should have been, and felt only its scarred remnants.

A missing ear, lost in a bar fight in Bogotá.

My last thought, just before I blacked out, was that Lt. Claude DeWinter had been right all along. Pablo Zuniga was alive and well and living in Los Angeles.

TWENTY-FIVE

I was drawn back to consciousness by excruciating pain, followed by the shrillness of a scream. The scream, I quickly realized, was my own.

For a moment, muddled and confused, I had trouble making sense of the sound or connecting it to my body. It seemed to fly from my mouth and away from me, like a bird alighting briefly on my lips before exploding upward in fright. After that, my senses returned one by one and I began to focus on my condition and my surroundings. I was naked, face down on the grubby concrete floor of a cavernous space, what might have been an empty warehouse or an airplane hangar. Votive candles in tall, narrow glass jars—decaled with the image of the Virgin Mary—had been placed in a half-halo around my head, their flames casting jumpy light into the outlying darkness. A tape was playing, filling the air with a lovely Gregorian chant. Bats circled above, among dark rafters that reminded me of ribs hugging the belly of a dead whale floating on its back, overturned like a capsized boat. Maybe I was Jonah, I thought, swallowed by a leviathan that had perished, trapping me inside. Or maybe I'd descended to eternal damnation. Finally gone to hell, as Father Blackley had so often warned us back in Buffalo.

Father Blackley.

From out of nowhere, it occurred to me that he was at the crux of all this. Then I remembered Joe Soto and after that all the others—Bishop Finatti, Father Aragon, Cardinal Doyle, Lindsay St. John, Charles Gash, Nick Gash, Lt. Claude DeWinter. They swam into my murky consciousness like sea creatures in a dark aquarium, nosing up against the glass before darting away. I was about to turn my head, to see who was kneeling over me, when the pain returned. It was fixed somewhere in the flesh between my shoulder blades and lower back, that much I could tell. I gritted my teeth, holding in my cry. The pain seemed shaped as a clean slice, being traced slowly in the meat of my back, like someone making a conscious incision. The intensity increased as my tormentor retraced the line, deepening and widening the original wound. Again, blessedly, the pain stopped. I got my breath, praying that he was finished, while trying to figure out who he was and what he wanted, how I'd gotten here and why.

Then Nick Gash swam back into view, staring at me wall-eyed through the aquarium glass, and I remembered. I'd stumbled from Nick's place, still hyped up on speed but crashing fast. In the street, someone had grabbed me from behind. Someone possessed of tensile strength and impressive combative skills. Someone who knew how to render a bigger man helpless in half a minute. Someone who was missing an ear.

Pablo Zuniga. *El Mutilador,* the Monster in the Shadows.

I didn't try to move, not just yet. It wouldn't have mattered at any rate; leather cuffs bound my wrists and ankles, attached to chains that kept me spread-eagled to the cold concrete floor. I lifted my eyes, saw the bats circle and settle again up in the rafters. Only for a moment, though, before another cry escaped me as Zuniga dug his blade once more into my flesh. Seconds passed before the deepening pain eased. From the site of each incision he'd made, I felt a warm trickle. As the series of maddening sensations continued and abated, and the chorus of chanting male voices swelled with transcendent passion, it became clear to me that Zuniga was carving a message on my body. That gave me a degree of hope. Perhaps he intended me to live, allowing me to take his message back to the other world, using my body as his billboard. Then again, he may have intended to finish me off here, and let them see his message when they found me, bloody and lifeless. I needed to fix on something other than doom and the terrible pain he was inflicting. So I concentrated on the cutting itself, taking inventory.

As it proceeded, I counted eight marks in all—six short, straight lines, perpendicular, horizontal, or at angles; a rounded mark resembling a C, which was drawn more slowly in my flesh and brought the pain to an excruciating new level; followed by another, shorter line, horizontal again, near the lower opening of the C that had just been carved. As the pain faded to throbbing, I tried to make sense of the marks, to put them in order, figure out their meaning. Before I could, Zuniga grabbed the hair at the back of my head with his left hand. He seemed to have trouble getting a good hold. Of course. Hadn't Lieutenant DeWinter told me? Zuniga was missing two fingers on his left hand. I'd have to compliment DeWinter on his facts, if I ever had the displeasure of seeing him again.

Finally, securing his grip, Zuniga yanked my head back and up until I was looking directly into his face, as he stared down into mine. In his right hand, inches from my left eye, he gripped the handle of a penknife with a short blade that glistened with my blood.

False bravado seemed as good a tack as any. "Doing God's work, Zuniga?"

He spit into my face, near my mouth. "*Puta!*"

His countenance was terrifying. It wasn't the knife scar running across his unshaven face from his ear to the corner of his mouth, or even the lumpy orifice where his other ear should have been. It was the stark rage in the dark eyes, the hateful twist to the mouth, the spittle on the lips that reminded me of acid bubbling up.

"I am going to kill you, faggot. Slowly, so you feel every moment."

"You speak English. I like the accent."

"You make jokes. You the big, brave man, huh?"

"I wouldn't say that, no."

"You like what I do to you, *maricon?*"

"Not much."

His lips curled into a smile more fearsome than the sneer. "What you feel already is nothing like what I will do to you before I finish."

"Why, Zuniga? Why hurt me like this?"

"I punish you, for what you are, for what you do."

"Like your father punished you?"

His eyes flared and he tightened his grip on my hair. "My father believe in the Virgin Mary. He talk to God, he make a family. He is no *maricon,* like you, fucking other men."

"How would you know what I am, Zuniga?"

"Because I know, that's how."

"Someone's been telling you about me. Someone sent you after me, the way they sent you after Joe Soto. Because of all the questions we've been asking."

He laughed, showing broken teeth. "You want me to tell you, yes? You want to know why I hunt you down and kill you like a dog."

"If I'm going to die, why not?"

"Maybe you right, *Señor* Justice. Big gringo who ask too many fucking questions. Maybe I tell you, before I kill you. So what you want to know?"

"Who you work for—we could start there."

"Maybe I work *solo,* only for Pablo."

"Why would you do that?"

"Maybe I like to kill faggots like you who spread your disease all over the earth."

"There are plenty of other homosexuals you could kill. Why pick me?"

"You speak against God, against the Church."

"I want to uncover the truth, that's all."

"You shut up, you fucking gringo faggot!" He turned the blade of the knife toward my eye, leveling the tip with my pupil.

"I tell you what the truth is. You listen, OK?"

I blinked, focusing on the blade, measuring its distance. "Sure, Pablo, whatever you say."

"You talk too much. That *es verdad*." Zuniga's tone had changed, growing colder, as if he was moving toward an arctic zone inside himself where no humane instinct could possibly exist. "You hear too many things, you see too much. I cut out your eyes, you see no more. I cut off your ears, you hear nothing no more. I cut the tongue from your mouth, you say nothing bad against the Church no more." He ratcheted up my head another notch, until my scalp felt close to ripping. "Maybe I cut off your dick and your balls, so you no more do your dirty things with your faggot *amigos*. And I leave you like this, cut up like a filthy pig, for them to take pictures and write about."

The tip of the blade quivered, an inch from my eye, if that. I felt myself lose control; urine warmed the cold floor beneath me. "Why do all that to me, Pablo, if you're just going to kill me, anyway?"

"Why?" He said it grandly, rising to his big moment. "To show the others, this is what happen to motherfuckers like *Señor* Benjamin Justice. I show the world why Pablo Zuniga is the one they call *el Mutilador*."

He moved the blade almost imperceptibly, until the tip was a fraction of an inch from the surface of my eye. I found it impossible to swallow; my speech became a whisper; my words came from a cowering, terrified man who seemed like someone else.

"Please, don't."

My bowels, like my bladder, betrayed me; the stench reached my nostrils. I thought: *This must be the worst moment—the degradation, the abject humiliation, before the end.*

I was wrong.

The worst moment followed quickly, as he thrust the blade into my eye and twisted. My world was reduced to that focal point of indescribable pain, while a scream erupted out of me like a fireball, scorching my throat. It was a scream of the most pure physical agony, combined with the anguish of a lifetime, all of it drawn into one last cry of longing and despair, of immeasurable loss. As it faded, and Pablo Zuniga withdrew his blade, I prepared to die, hoping only that it wouldn't last too long.

Among the last things I heard before unconsciousness reclaimed me were a door being kicked open, the scuffle of footsteps, voices shouting warnings, shots being fired, the swelling of a Gregorian chant, and the clatter of glass breaking as Pablo Zuniga scrambled to flee, knocking over candles.

Flames sputtered and died, but I saw them with only one eye.

TWENTY-SIX

My next memory was of clean, crisp sheets, smelling freshly laundered, as I woke face down on a hospital bed.

There was the odor of antiseptic, the murmur of voices in the background. When I reached to touch my left eye, I felt a gauze bandage, taped by the corners to my face. Someone was dabbing at the wounds on my back, though the sensation was dull, painless; it felt like the pecking of a bird with a blunt beak. On my right, I became aware of a needle inserted into my arm and taped down, with a narrow, plastic line ascending to an IV drip.

"He's awake." Templeton's voice. "Benjamin? How are you doing?"

She came around to my right side, where the IV bag was hanging. I turned my head a little more to better see her, and asked where I was.

"UCLA Med." She touched my wrist. "They have two police officers posted outside the door. They'll be here until you're ready to go home. You're safe now."

"What about Zuniga?"

"You're sure that's who it was?"

"It was definitely Zuniga. DeWinter gets a gold star."

"I'm afraid Zuniga got away. They did find the van he abducted you in."

"Stolen?"

She nodded. "Maybe you shouldn't talk."

I lay my face back on the pillow. "You talk then. Fill me in."

"Zuniga took to you to an abandoned building in South L.A., in a warehouse district. An officer passing in his patrol car heard you scream."

"How bad did Zuniga hurt me?"

"All your vital signs are stable. They gave you a sedative for the pain." Templeton glanced at a nurse hovering over me, swabbing my back. "That's why you don't feel much."

I tried to find her eyes. "Templeton?"

She glanced away again. "The doctor should be back soon. She can talk to you."

"I want you to talk to me."

"I called Claude DeWinter. He's on his way."

"I don't want to see him."

"He came clean, Benjamin. Told me everything."

"From the beginning? The photograph in his desk, the stalking—"

"All of it."

"You sound like you've forgiven him."

"He used bad judgment, but he's still a good cop. He's working hard to close the case on Joe's murder. That's what matters most."

"Just the same, keep him away from me."

"If you'd listened to him in the first place—"

"I know." My smile was tight. "I wouldn't be in the mess I'm in. So how bad a mess is it, Templeton? I'm still waiting for an answer."

"You'll have some scars."

I laughed a little. "I don't imagine that was a valentine he was carving on me."

"The doctor said cosmetic surgery will help."

"You going to tell me, or do I make the nurse do it?"

Templeton shrugged halfheartedly. "It's only a word."

One word. I thought about the lines I'd counted, the angles and positions. Then about Zuniga—his epithets, his hatred, the teachings of his church.

"Fag?"

She nodded, then tried to smile. "All caps, no lower case. At least he didn't leave an exclamation mark."

"No, he saved that for my eye, didn't he?"

"He could have killed you, Benjamin."

"I'd like to get the name of the cops, thank them personally."

"I already have a list, with the ranks and the precinct. I gave it to the desk, for the morning paper."

"Must be frustrating, on your leave of absence, not being able to write it up yourself."

"That's not my concern right now."

"About my eye, Templeton."

She looked up, toward the doorway. "There's the doctor now."

A plump woman with pleasant features and a warm smile came into view, introducing herself as Dr. Sarkissian. She was dressed in surgical garb, and had dark-eyed, Armenian looks, which matched the name.

"You're a very lucky man, Mr. Justice."

"I've heard that part already, doctor. How about the other part?"

She leaned down, checked the bandage over my left eye. "There's a lot of damage, Mr. Justice. The eye is a fragile organ."

I swallowed hard. "So what can you do for me?"

Her false smile told me everything I needed to know. "I'm afraid you've lost the sight in your left eye. We can't save it."

"Blind in one eye, forever. That's what you're saying?"

"I'm afraid so."

I closed my eyes a moment, not to deal with the news but to push it away. Then, looking at her again, trying to sound tough: "So what now?"

"An excision, as soon as possible. There's a danger of infection. Whoever did this to you used a dirty knife. We can schedule you for surgery in the morning."

"Excision—a nice word for plucking out my eyeball."

"It's a fairly simple procedure."

"Easy for you to say."

She smiled again. "Easier for me than you, I guess."

The nurse finished bandaging my wounds, asked me to remain face down until told otherwise, and left us.

"Eye injuries are rather common," Dr. Sarkissian said. "This kind of surgery is done almost routinely now. After that comes a prosthesis."

"A glass eye?"

"Prosthetic eyes are made of plastic now. You'll find very few glass eyes being made any longer, if at all."

She asked Templeton to give her a minute, closed the curtains for privacy, and lifted the bandage over my eye. While she examined the wound, she gave me a brief history of the prosthetic eye. Until World War II, she said, most artificial eyes were made of glass, in Germany. During the war, when the supply was cut off to the U.S. and thousands of eyes were needed for returning combat victims, dentists were pressed into service to fill the void. By 1945, optometrists became involved, using the new wonder material, plastic, which proved safer and more durable than glass. Today, she said, a well-trained ocularist could provide a client like me with a flawless false eye, virtually identical in appearance to the original.

"Maybe I'll try a brown eye for variety," I said. "Yours are nice."

She laughed. "You could, if you wanted to. I know of a rather eccentric gentleman who had a diamond implanted in his pupil. Quite a conversation piece, if you like the attention."

"I prefer a low profile, though it doesn't always work out that way."

"You might want to stick with blue then." She pulled open the curtains, glanced at her watch. "I'll check back later, see how you're doing. Right now, you should try to get some rest. The sedative should help. We've got you on an IV drip, an antibiotic, to ward off infection. I understand you're HIV positive."

"I told her," Templeton said.

"How are your blood counts?" Dr. Sarkissian asked.

"Not bad but not great, either." I rattled off the relevant numbers.

"All the more reason to head off infection then, with your immune system compromised." She touched my shoulder. "You're going to be fine, Mr. Justice. We'll take good care of you."

When she was gone, Templeton pulled up a chair. "So now you know."

I propped up a smile. "Hey, it's just an eye."

"You've just lost half your sight, Justice. It's OK to feel bad. You don't have to pretend with me."

"Like you said, I'm lucky. Alive and breathing, right?"

She reached over, laid a hand on my wrist. "A psychopath bushwhacked you. That's all this is."

"Is it?"

"You didn't deserve this, Benjamin."

"Don't be so sure." I closed my right eye, eclipsing the light, shutting out her kindness, her sympathy. "Don't be so sure."

I heard the scrape of her chair as she rose. "I'll call Claude DeWinter on his cell, ask him not to come by. If that's the way you want it."

"I'll need my meds."

"Maurice is bringing them. He should be around soon."

I heard her footsteps as she left the room. I was alone in near silence. Almost immediately, I heard a Gregorian chant and saw Pablo Zuniga again, in the flickering light of votive candles. He yanked me by the hair, drove the blade of his knife into my left eye, twisted. I screamed, but this time the scream was inside, in my head, where I couldn't make it stop.

TWENTY-SEVEN

By the end of the day, Pablo Zuniga's face—as a young man, and age-enhanced—was featured in afternoon newspapers around the country, and broadcast widely on the evening news. Because of his assault on me, and details gleaned from De-Winter's investigation, Zuniga was now a prime suspect in Joe Soto's murder. My name and picture also got splashed across the media, which dredged up my scandalous past yet again. At least that's what Templeton told me that night when she came again to visit and I pressed her for an accounting of events.

The next morning, belatedly, Zuniga finally landed on the front page of the *Los Angeles Times*. Lindsay St. John made sure the coverage emphasized Joe's probe of Zuniga as the subject for a book; his fervent Catholicism was mentioned only in passing. The implication was that Joe had been eliminated because his research had drawn him too close to a dangerous assassin in hiding, while I'd been attacked for looking into Joe's murder. Templeton, still on her involuntary leave of absence and destined for style section features upon her return, was kept off the story. Instead, a veteran reporter with an eye on his pension and a reputation as a management patsy got the assignment, interviewing me by phone. According to office scuttlebutt, relayed to Templeton, he'd quoted me at length in the draft he'd filed, which the copy desk then whittled down to half its original length, under St. John's personal supervision. The desk eliminated all my quotes linking Zuniga to Joe's column about Father Blackley, as well as any mention of Bing Crisologo. A reporter with backbone like Templeton would have fought for the integrity of her piece, taking it all the way to the editor-in-chief if she had to. As it was, the guy who got the byline let it be emasculated without a whimper.

"Lindsay's determined to go as soft on the archdiocese as possible," Templeton said, sitting next to my bed with the morning edition of the *LAT* in her lap. "With its vested interest in downtown redevelopment, the *Times* brass seems more than willing to back her up. And it doesn't hurt that she's the publisher's niece."

"There's got to be another explanation. She's risking a lot, tampering with a hot story like this."

"We'll worry about Lindsay St. John later," Templeton said, "after you're home and on the mend. Anything I can get you now?"

"There's a nice-looking male nurse on the evening shift. Red hair, gold highlights, bedroom eyes. I was thinking a sponge bath was in order."

Her smile was brief. "Nice to see you feeling better, Justice."

The next morning, surgeons removed my mutilated eye. Hours later, as the anesthesia was wearing off, my room turned into Grand Central Station.

Templeton was back, along with Maurice and Fred, who'd brought books and flowers. Dr. Sarkissian was there, popping in for a minute, while a nurse adjusted my morphine drip. I was only supposed to be on morphine a short time, before easing off to Percocet and then to Empirin with codeine. Whatever they gave me, I was happy to have it, to take the edge off the pain that throbbed from the gaping hole where my eye had been.

"Let's take a look," Dr. Sarkissian said.

She drew the curtain closed, pulled the bandage back and studied that portion of my face with quiet concentration. "Very nice. They did an excellent job. Muscle, tissue, all of it cleanly excised, and everything cauterized."

"What exactly are you seeing?"

"When it's healed, you'll have a clean, pink socket. In a few weeks, you'll be fitted with a prosthetic. After a while, you'll hardly know the difference."

"And now?"

She replaced the bandage, taped it down. "At the moment, it's a mess—swelling, discoloration, raw tissue that needs time to heal."

"Doesn't sound too pretty."

"I wouldn't look at it just yet. It's not easy, seeing it for the first time, even when everything's healed." She placed a hand on my shoulder. "You might want to consider talking with someone first. They have a counseling program here in the hospital, if you feel the need. Spiritual or otherwise."

"Not my style, doc."

"Your friend Alexandra warned me you'd respond like that."

"She knows me pretty well."

"You truly are a lucky man, Mr. Justice."

"How so?"

She shrugged, as if I should already know the answer. "To have such good friends, who obviously care a great deal about you."

When the doctor was gone, Maurice fussed over me, while Fred stood around with his hands in his pockets, not quite sure what to say or do.

"We've given your apartment a good cleaning," Maurice said, plumping my pillows, "so it will be nice and fresh when you come home." He put a hand to each of his cheeks. "The dust and lint, Benjamin! Don't you ever clean under your bed?"

"What for? No one ever looks under there but you."

He rolled his eyes extravagantly. "We also brought you some reading material, to help you pass the time. Lots of choices." Fred handed him a bag from Dutton's, out of which Maurice pulled several mystery novels. "There's a Laurie R. King, a James Lee Burke, and a Val McDermid. And a fairly recent Walter Mosley, so you can catch up with Easy Rawlins." Maurice peered into the bag, pulling out a final book. "Oh, and this one, by a young man named Harlan Coben. I haven't actually read him, but I saw him interviewed on one of the morning shows and found him quite engaging." Maurice fanned himself, looking flushed. "Rather attractive too." He covered his mouth, lowering his voice. "Such big hands."

"I'll do my best, Maurice. Although they tell me reading with one eye may feel odd for a while."

"Oh, my—we didn't even think of that. Did we, Fred?"

I reached for the books. "Not a problem, Maurice. I'm happy to have them. They're just what I need."

Tears sprang to his eyes. "Oh, Benjamin, I can't tell you how troubling this has been for us." He bent to embrace me, mindful of my wounds. "Fred and I, we both do love you so. When will you ever stop getting yourself into these terrible situations?"

"I keep asking myself the same question, Maurice."

Templeton reached into a pocket. "And I brought you this." In her hand were Sister Catherine Timothy's amber rosary beads, with the carved wood crucifix attached. "I thought you might want it."

"Not really."

"I'll leave it just the same, in case you change your mind." She set the rosary on the tray next to the bed. Then, to the others: "Maybe we should let him get some rest."

"Yes, of course." Maurice made two fists, with the thumbs up. "Rest—that's what the lad needs now. In a few days, we'll get him home where he belongs."

I thanked them for dropping by, and for the books. When they were gone, I picked up a copy of *Bad Boy Brawly Brown*. I tried to read, but it was no use. All I could think about was the fact that my left eye was gone, that someone had taken it violently from me, leaving me forever half-blind.

I put the Mosley novel aside and reached almost unconsciously for the string of rosary beads, clutching them as I drifted off.

I woke late in the day to find the sunlight dimming beyond my window and a dark-clad figure facing me from a chair near the end of the bed. With only one eye, my depth perception was seriously impaired, and it took a moment to get him fully into focus. When I did, I saw that it was Bishop Anthony Finatti.

He sat stiff-backed, with one knee crossed over the other, peering at me through his wire rims down the bumpy ridge of his nose.

"I hope I'm not intruding, Mr. Justice."

"How did you get in?"

"They saw my cleric's collar. I showed them my identification. Told them we had business." He smiled mildly. "They saw no reason to keep me out."

"Say what you came to say and go."

"I came by to express our profound regrets about the misfortune that's befallen you. It's been a shock to all of us. Cardinal Doyle, in particular, asked me to extend his deepest sympathy. He's praying for your swift recovery, as I am."

"Get to the point, Finatti."

He reached for a briefcase beside his chair. He opened it on his lap and extracted a document similar to the contract I'd rejected a few days earlier. "I've been authorized to double our offer, Mr. Justice. Considering how you've suffered, we're willing to write a check for two million dollars."

"Why would the archdiocese want to do that?"

"What happened to you—it's absolutely reprehensible."

"I don't understand, Bishop."

"It's very simple. We want this to end."

"You came with the authorization of Cardinal Doyle?"

"At his express direction."

"The cardinal sees a connection between my interest in Father Blackley and the fact that an assassin-for-hire named Pablo Zuniga disfigured and nearly killed me?"

Finatti raised his chin. "I—I didn't say that."

"You're stammering, Bishop. My question troubles you."

"It's—it's just that—" He broke off, smiled weakly, tried again. "Why would you assume we'd made a connection between the two?"

"Your presence here, and this new offer, implies it."

Finatti looked away, toward the window, allowing his lenses to reflect the dying light. "Wouldn't it be best for everyone, Mr. Justice, if all this turmoil ended?" He turned back, leaning toward me, his confidential tone suggesting a special intimacy between us. "Wouldn't it be a positive step if you took the money, started a new life for yourself, and allowed Cardinal Doyle to get on with his important work?"

"Finish his cathedral and become the next pope, without any nasty scandals to slow him down?"

"We've made our mistakes. None of us, even the cardinal, is infallible. I realize that." The cadence of Finatti's speech sounded rehearsed, like litany. "There's nothing perfect in this world, except God's love. In more earthly matters, one must learn to accept imperfection, weighing the good against the bad, finding an acceptable balance."

"Your faith is stronger than mine, Bishop."

"Faith isn't relative, Mr. Justice, to be tossed aside and forgotten when one is faced with challenge. Faith is absolute. Without it, life would be intolerable, unlivable."

"How many children have suffered for your acceptable balance, Bishop?"

"How many more have been saved and committed to the Lord?"

"Not Pablo Zuniga, that's for sure."

"Perhaps he's been put among us as a test."

I reached up and tore the bandage from my eye, exposing

the empty socket, the messy surgical wound that I hadn't yet dared to look at. Finatti gasped, recoiling with revulsion.

"He certainly tested me, didn't he?"

Finatti swallowed with difficulty and stood, attempting to compose himself. He stepped closer, thrusting out the contract while keeping his eyes averted. "It's all here. Two million dollars, Mr. Justice. It only needs your signature."

I raised my head, spit on his contract. "Go to hell, Finatti."

"I repeat the cardinal's words—we've tried to be charitable." He grabbed a handful of tissues, swiped at my spittle with disgust. "I came here to reason with an unreasonable man." He dropped the tissues, shoved the contract into his briefcase, buckled it up. "Your mind's obviously been poisoned against the Church, Mr. Justice. We'll pray for you—for your recovery, and for your soul."

"While you're at it, say a prayer for Nick Gash, will you? And all the other kids you tossed on the scrap heap."

Finatti froze for a moment, daring to look in my direction. Then he turned and made a hurried exit.

I sank back on to the pillow, staring at the ceiling with my good eye. Rejecting Finatti's money, telling him off, should have felt good. It didn't. Nothing would feel good again until I had the answers I was after. And that might never happen at all, I thought, since the questions changed every time I turned another corner.

I pressed a button to signal a nurse for more morphine, then fell back to wait, realizing I was starting to like the stuff.

TWENTY-EIGHT

Early the next week I was home, settling back into a refurbished apartment that felt like it belonged to a stranger.

Maurice and Fred had installed their old PC on a computer table in a corner of the room, with all the cables hooked up and the modem plugging me into the world of the Internet. On the wall above the monitor, for inspiration, they'd hung the plaque laminated with Joe Soto's last column. They'd also stocked the refrigerator, laundered and folded my clothes, put a fresh coat of paint on the walls, and left a bouquet of long-stemmed sunflowers on the kitchen table, next to the window. The panes of the window were clean and sparkling, looking out on a flower box newly planted with colorful impatiens.

The place was cheery as hell but I didn't feel the same. I was off the most potent painkillers, without anything to take their place. The craving for crystal meth was miraculously gone—too closely associated, I surmised, with what Pablo Zuniga had done to me—which pretty much left booze as the drug of choice. I'd thought more than once in recent days about how easy a pint of Cuervo Gold would go down, how nice it would be to sink again into an alcoholic haze. Then I'd recall what would surely come after—the rage, the binge, the deep black hole sucking me down until I was lost again.

So I drank coffee and clung tenaciously to my rosary beads and shaky discipline.

On my second day home, I was standing at the front window, listening to Eric Dolphy work his alto sax on *Far Cry*, when I spotted Fr. Ismael Aragon coming up the drive. He'd dispensed with his usual clerical garb, dressing less formally in neatly pressed jeans, a polo shirt and walking shoes. As he approached, speckled sunlight through the eucalyptus trees played alluringly off his fine, dark features. I'd known some beautiful men in my life, and slept with my share, but I couldn't remember a single one who'd tempted me more than Father Aragon.

As he mounted the stairs, I was waiting at the top. When he saw me, he stopped halfway.

"Have I come at a bad time?"

"Depends on why you're here, Father."

"To talk, if you're willing."

I stepped back and held open the door, allowing him to pass, and taking a closer look at him from behind. While I turned down the volume on the jazz, he made a quick survey of my room, settling on a photograph of Elizabeth Jane, when she was eleven. Next to it was a picture of Jacques. There were no others.

"My little sister," I said, "at her eleventh birthday party. I was seventeen when that was taken."

"That was the same year that—"

"Yes."

His eyes moved to the other photograph. "And the young man?"

"My lover, Jacques, a year before he died."

"He looks so healthy."

"AIDS hit hard and fast in those days. I knew people who died within two weeks of their diagnosis. Thousands went like that. They were the lucky ones."

Father Aragon turned to face me. "He was Latino?"

"Mixed. His father was white."

"He was the one you wrote about, the two of you—the stories that won the Pulitzer."

"He was the one whose death I idealized in the articles I fabricated, along with our relationship."

"How much was the truth?"

"That I loved him and that he died. Most of the rest I sugarcoated, so I could live with the guilt of not having loved him more, or better."

"Not the worst sin," Father Aragon said.

"I was a journalist, Father. I gave us different names, ages, looks—created an imaginary couple, living an imaginary life. Then I offered my fantasy to the public as the truth. I had the misfortune of winning a Pulitzer for it. I got caught and punished, which I deserved." Then, sharply: "What do you want? You didn't come here to rehash my history or supplement what you've obviously read in the magazines."

He glanced at my bandaged eye. "I wanted to know if you were OK, after what you've been through."

"You could have called."

"I did. You never returned my messages."

My voice became a purr. "You wanted to see me that badly, Father?"

"I wanted to know how you were doing."

"I've been ignoring my voice mail, avoiding reporters."

"I'm not a reporter, Benjamin."

"What are you, Father, exactly?"

"A priest, a human being. A friend, if you'd allow me to be that."

"Just a friend, Father?" I moved close to him, until our bodies almost touched. "Or maybe something more?"

He stood like a deer caught in the headlights. A light film of perspiration appeared on his forehead, faintly glistening. "You don't have many friends, do you, Benjamin?"

"I prefer friends who tell the truth, not who evade."

"Maybe you expect too much of people. Perhaps you judge too harshly. Not just others, but yourself as well."

"Maybe."

"Or maybe it's just an excuse—a reason to keep people at a distance, never letting them get too close."

"I like being close to you, Father."

He stepped away, found a handkerchief in a pocket, used it to pat his brow. "I came to check up on you. That's why I'm here, Benjamin, to see how you're feeling."

"You really want to know?"

He tucked the hankie away, looking earnest. "Yes, I do."

I began circling him, making him follow me with his eyes. "When I was twelve, a priest seduced me, then tossed me aside like yesterday's garbage. At seventeen, I caught my father molesting my littler sister and shot him dead. I lost my lover to AIDS, back in '90, then destroyed my career with scandal. Now I'm HIV-positive and blind in one eye. Other than that, Father, things are just swell." I stopped to bear down on him, unblinking. "Oh, and one more thing—I screwed a man the other night without using protection, exposing him to the virus. I'm feeling real good about that."

"Is it better, getting it out like this?"

I laughed. "Ah, I get it—the call to the confessional."

"It might not be the worst idea—a return to the Church."

"You should have been a comedian, not a priest."

"You might be surprised by the solace you'll find, bringing God back into your life. If you'd learn to count your blessings, instead of your losses—"

"Seeing you again is all the blessing I need, Father. In fact, I'm undressing you in my mind right now—thinking about what I'd do with you, if you'd let me." I grinned, enjoying his discomfort. "And what I'd do if you wouldn't."

"I understand your anger, Benjamin, your need to lash back. I'm also deeply angered by what's happened—by what certain priests have done to innocent children. But you need to understand that they comprise a tiny minority within our clergy. Not all of us are like that."

"Hundreds, Father. The ones we know about, anyway. A sizable fraction, I'd say."

"Do you know what it's done to certain priests who have become the scapegoats? How certain priests are being tarred with the same brush, men who've never touched a child improperly in their lives?"

"Gay priests. Is that what you mean, Father?"

"Men who may have entered the priesthood with certain feelings and desires that they've willingly subjugated to serve God. Who have taken a vow of chastity and celibacy and never wavered. They're suffering in all this as well."

I took three steps until I was back in his face again. "I'm supposed to feel sorry for gay priests who support a church that demonizes us? Gay priests, innocent though they may be of molestation, who knew or suspected that children were suffering and did nothing to stop it?" His eyes shifted uneasily; I spit my words through clenched teeth. "How much did you know, Father? And when you found out, or suspected, what did you do to protect the children? My guess is you looked the other way and kept quiet, like all the others, gay or straight, to preserve your precious position and career. You're as guilty as any of them."

"You sound as if you might be speaking of yourself."

"Maybe I am!"

He flinched in the face of my fury. "One heard things." His voice was small, weak. "But that's not enough to accuse."

"Go back to your Church, Father. Make your confession. Ask for absolution. That's how it works, isn't it? Slip into the booth, confess your sins, and sleep peacefully at night, with your conscience clear." I stepped away, turning my back. "Get out of here. Stay away from me. You make me sick."

"If it helps," he said, "I haven't slept peacefully for a long time."

I clenched my right fist. "I told you to leave, Father."

"God loves you, Benjamin. I love you, as a priest who feels your pain, as a friend who understands your loneliness."

I whirled, striking him hard on the jaw, knocking him to the floor. "Father Blackley used words like that, when I was twelve years old back in Buffalo."

Father Aragon put a hand to his jaw, testing it and wincing. Yet I saw no sign of fear in his eyes. "This is my fault." He rose slowly, glancing at me with apologetic eyes. "I was foolish to come here, to bother you like this. I thought I might be of some good, that's all." We faced each other in the middle of the room, two men who understood each other so well it felt dangerous. "I won't bother you again. Good-bye, Benjamin."

He started out. I stuck out an arm, blocking his way. "Wait—I just remembered something. A Jeep Grand Cherokee, light gray, with front end damage. You had your boys at Saving Grace Auto Body give it a makeover."

"What about it?"

"Who's the friend who brought it in, Father? The friend who needed some special body work done."

"I'm not sure that's any of your business."

I grabbed his shirt front and slammed him against the wall, hard enough to put some fear in his eyes. "You know how Joe Soto was killed, don't you?"

"I didn't read all the details. A hit-and-run, I know that much. Now, please, let me go."

He struggled but I held him firmly in place. "It was an execution, Father, carried out by a killer driving a Jeep Grand Cherokee, light gray. He struck Joe head-on, most surely damaging the vehicle's front end."

Father Aragon relaxed under my grip, regarding me with something stronger than curiosity. "Is that true?"

I nodded. "Who's your friend who owns the Jeep, Father?"

"You don't think that—?"

I reached for his neck, gripping tight. "Your friend, Father—I want a name!"

"The car belongs to the archdiocese." His eyes were wide, his voice a mix of surrender and consternation. "Bishop Finatti brought it in."

"And you had it fixed up, without any questions?"

"He told me one of the nuns had gotten into an accident while she was learning to drive. Said she was embarrassed. Asked me to handle it quietly, for her sake."

"And you believed him?"

"Of course. Why wouldn't I?"

I let go and backed off. "I'll let you think about that one, Father. That and a lot of other matters you need to give some thought to, if you give a damn about the truth."

"You can't possibly be suggesting—"

"Then I'll let you decide what your next move is. To do the right thing for a change, or circle the wagons with Cardinal Doyle and the others." His eyes were on the move, as if a thousand questions and maybe a few troubling answers were suddenly flying around inside his beautiful head. "Now get out, Father, before I really lose it and toss you down the stairs."

He stared at me a long moment, his passionate eyes alert and searching, like those of a man whose bedrock of belief is suddenly crumbling.

Then, without another word between us, he was gone.

I stood before the bathroom mirror, pulled the chain for light, studied myself in the glass. I'd allowed my beard to grow while I was hospitalized and decided to keep it, at least for now. I measured my receding hairline, saw how dark the blond along the sides was getting, noticed some gray, and new wrinkles at the corners of my eyes. I didn't mind growing older, leaving behind the confusion and carelessness of youth, not to mention a past I'd been trying to escape for as long as I could remember. So the changes I saw seemed natural, even welcome. But I'd never anticipated becoming a Cyclops, a man with only one eye.

The bandage was taped down at four corners. I tugged at one piece of tape, then another, hesitating a moment before I lifted back the gauze. When I did, it was just as Dr. Sarkissian had predicted: a gaping pink hole like a shallow cave, moist, with a smooth, flat wall of flesh across the back. Eyeball, muscle and connecting tissue gone, with the socket and lids intact, cleaner than a good butcher's cut.

How easily blindness can come, I thought, and how final when it does.

TWENTY-NINE

Day by day I healed, while plodding forward with my book. That is, when I wasn't distracted by troubling daydreams and exhausted by terrifying nightmares in which Pablo Zuniga took various shapes and forms.

He was still at large, and every passing figure down on the street or unexpected footstep on the stairwell had the alarm bells going off inside my head. Fred offered to find me a gun for protection, but I turned him down. I'd killed my father because a gun was close and handy. Given my volcanic nature, it didn't seem prudent to put myself in that position again. Maybe I should have split town, like the cops had suggested, or at least laid low in a motel somewhere beyond the county limits. Law enforcement didn't automatically provide protection for people like me, round-the-clock surveillance with a nice-looking detective stationed outside your door or watching in his car from the street, the way they like to show it in the movies. There isn't the time, money or manpower to watch every victim or every witness to every serious violent crime, not in an urban jungle like L.A. So people like me are pretty much on our own. Lay low, split town, that's how it usually works.

But that didn't seem like an option now. I was on to something big that I was part of, with my own responsibility to account for. It was like Templeton had said, I was the catalyst for everything that had happened, I'd set the balls in motion. It was time to see it through to the end, come what may. So I stayed inside with the curtains drawn, lying alone for long hours each night, trying not to listen for creaking boards on the steps outside.

At week's end, I arranged for a first sitting to have a new eye shaped and painted. My appointment was scheduled in the afternoon, as the hour struck four and the sunlight waned. It was my first day venturing out alone since my return from the hospital.

The eye man I'd been referred to was Dr. Nathan Levy, a former optometrist who now specialized in restoring the appearance of people like me, who worked out of an office in unfashionable south Beverly Hills. He was a short, slender, bald man, on the far side of seventy, sprouting white hair from his nose and ears. Given his age, he moved quite nimbly, with toes pointed outward in a duck's waddle.

"I read about you in the paper," Dr. Levy said, as I followed him down a narrow hallway and into a room the size of a large closet. He spoke with the trace of an accent I couldn't quite place. "Not a pleasant way to lose an eye. Although I don't suppose there is a pleasant way, is there?"

I wasn't in the mood to talk, so I didn't. He sat me in the natural light of a window that looked down on the stream of traffic along Olympic Boulevard. Dr. Levy perched himself on a stool across from me, alternately peering into my right eye and mixing colors on a sketchpad. Between us was a small table holding an array of brushes and a palette of oils. Back and forth he went, intently studying my eye, then dabbing with his brush, until he said we were finished for the day.

"We'll do this maybe five or six times until I have the colors right, down to the tiniest flecks. That's the frustrating part of the craft, trying to reproduce exactly what you see. The other trick is knowing when you've got it, when to stop. Kind of like writing, I guess."

I reached for my jacket, feigning a smile. "I'm sure you'll do your best."

As I slipped the jacket on, he regarded me thoughtfully. "You have a minute, Ben? I'd like to show you something." He led me back down the hall, talking as he went. "We make several hundred new eyes every year. I've got clients as young as a year, and one who's nearly a hundred. From time to time, as they outgrow their eye, or the eye shows wear, they come in for a new one. It's nice to keep track, see how they're getting on with their lives." We reached the end of the hallway, where he opened a door. "After you."

I stepped into a spacious room cluttered with long tables and cabinets. Several female technicians sat at the tables, working meticulously without looking up. All around us were partitioned trays holding hundreds of plastic eyes, variously sized and colored. "We produce the iris separately," Dr. Levy said, "sizing and scoring it, and painting both sides. The bottom layer is opaque, followed by two translucent layers. We surround the finished iris with white Lucite, adding veins and other natural coloration. Then we laminate the whole thing with clear plastic and polish it on converted dental equipment. Getting the fit right is a matter of grinding and polishing, similar to capping a tooth." Dr. Levy grinned impishly. "We've made eyes for racehorses, show dogs, even ET, in the movie. And a few famous people you'd never know had one. That's the goal—to make an eye so perfect, no one notices."

I surveyed the room, humbled by what I saw. My voice grew quiet. "It must be satisfying, doing what you do."

"I saw a lot of GIs who lost their eyes in World War Two. That's where I got the idea to do this one day."

"You were old enough to fight back then?"

"I was just a kid. My family was German. I spent my early teenage years at Auschwitz." He clapped a hand on my shoulder; on the wrist, I saw small numbers tattooed in blue. "You're not alone, Ben. There are at least a quarter million people in this country with prosthetic eyes, probably more. You just don't know they're there." He winked. "Not if the craftsmanship is good."

He saw me back down the hallway and to his office door, his hand still on my shoulder, his smile like salve. It felt like a blessing washing over me. "Don't worry," he said. "We'll have you feeling whole again in no time."

Driving home, I threaded my way though side streets down to Wilshire, where I became trapped in the crawl of rush hour traffic. I checked the locks on my car doors for the third time, then flicked on my headlights. It was late November and Christmas decorations festooned the boulevard, lending their glitter to the posh boutiques and department stores overflowing with the season's fashions. The windows glowed, replete with Santas, elves, reindeer, snowflakes and packages bound up with big bows of colorful ribbon. All of it was frozen in a tableau of fake cheer designed to sell merchandise that I found utterly depressing.

I punched on the radio, tuning in NPR for the news, while I sat at an intersection through three light changes without getting across. After listening to a review of bloody world conflict that sounded bleakly familiar, I shut the radio off. The light changed again and I inched forward, while horns blasted from side streets and pedestrians weaved among the cars like robots on their way home, controlled by paychecks and clocks. I hadn't had coffee since morning and I suddenly felt the need for caffeine. Then I thought about how good a real drink would feel, just a shot or two of alcohol to warm the basement, so I turned on the radio again for diversion.

Up ahead, a familiar woman appeared on the sidewalk, coming out of a store. I recognized the business as one of the better clothiers for men, leaning toward more conservative and classic tailoring. As usual, she was hatless, trim and attractive, in heels and a nicely cut business suit. Weighted down with all her packages, she looked to be in wonderful spirits, buoyant and upbeat, quite different than I'd ever seen her.

Lindsay St. John was apparently holiday shopping for someone special.

She turned east, looking loose and relaxed, completely without affectation. The car ahead was immobile now, lodged in gridlock. I watched St. John stop at the corner, waiting for the light. The light changed, she walked across, but the vehicular traffic hardly budged. I craned to see her until she was across the street, out of sight, then sat back and drummed my fingers on the steering wheel in frustration. It was a rare opportunity to spy on Lindsay St. John away from work, to see her in a different setting and a different light. Private moments—that's what reporters often looked for in their subjects, the good ones who cared enough to dig beneath the surface. I'd hate to miss my chance with Lindsay St. John because of bad traffic.

A minute later I made it through the intersection, just in time to see her reach the next corner and turn into a residential side street. Suddenly, the right-hand lane opened up as a tow truck dragged a Mercedes away from a meter, beneath a sign forbidding parking between 4:00 and 6:00 P.M. I swung the wheel and hit the gas, shooting into the open lane and along the curb all the way to the corner, where the light turned red. I ran it, hanging a right, then quickly slowed as I found myself on one of the tree-lined, residential streets in the flats of Beverly Hills. Just ahead, Lindsay St. John was loading her bags into the trunk of a shiny black Lexus parallel parked in a two-hour zone. She closed the trunk, unlocked the car, and climbed behind the wheel. I stopped two car lengths back, as if waiting for the space. St. John started the car, pulled out, drove off. I waited a discreet half-minute, keeping an eye on her taillights, then followed.

She talked on her cell phone as she drove, looking animated and engaged, throwing back her head once or twice and laughing with obvious, unfettered delight. Not like a high-powered executive, I thought, rejoicing in a successful power play or shrewd business deal. More like someone in love.

St. John maneuvered skillfully through traffic, cutting down side streets and taking alternate routes to avoid the worst of it. I tailed her up to Sunset Plaza, where she parked behind Chin Chin and went in alone to pick up some Szechuan takeout. After that, she made her way south along Sunset Boulevard before angling up Doheny Road, then took a steeper street up into Trousdale Estates. Near the top of the hill, she made a left, then a right into a short, steep cul-de-sac with a house on each side and one at the far end. The three houses were situated on large parcels with walls all around, and plenty of trees for added privacy. The street was empty, not so much as a parked car or a housekeeper on her way to the bus stop a half mile down.

I pulled over, cut my ignition and lights, and set my brake. St. John drove on to the end of the cul-de-sac and up the short drive of a one-story Modernist house with elegant detailing and a three-million-dollar view. She got out, collected her bags and started up the front walk. The door opened and a little dog scampered out, leaping and yelping, its tail in a frenzy. A man emerged a moment later, framed in the light of the doorway. He was short and slightly built, with thinning hair and wire-rimmed glasses, bundled up in wool slacks and a bulky sweater instead of his usual clerical attire.

Bishop Anthony Finatti.

St. John scooped up the dog as Finatti descended the steps. She greeted him with unabashed affection, a warm hug, a lingering kiss on the lips. They both nuzzled the excited dog, then kissed again, the kind of serious lip lock you see in the movies but never with anyone old enough to have grandchildren, like these two. As they started toward the house, their arms around each other's waists, they talked and laughed with their heads close.

How touching, I thought. How nice for them both, to be joined in such sweet domestic bliss. And how convenient for Anthony Finatti, in so many ways.

I sat at a distance with my lights off, watching from the shadows, until they were inside their hideaway and the door was closed.

THIRTY

I parked on Norma Place, checked the street to see if it was safe, and crossed to the house. As I hit the sidewalk and started up the drive, my eyes were drawn to the living room, where the curtains were open and the lights were on.

Maurice and Fred sat on the couch, leaning forward, listening intently to a visitor who sat nearby in an easy chair—Fr. Ismael Aragon. Maurice glanced out, saw me, and got to his feet. I tried to escape, but he caught me as I reached the corner of the garage, about to take the steps to my apartment.

"Benjamin!"

"What is it, Maurice?"

"You have a visitor."

"No, *you* have a visitor."

"He's been waiting some time to talk to you."

"Tell him I'm not interested."

"It must be important, Benjamin, or he wouldn't be here. You could at least hear what he has to say."

No, I thought. No more of Father Aragon's anguish and guilt. No more of his offers of friendship and solace. No more of his excuses for a Church that demanded confession from its parishioners but spewed out denial and rationalization for egregious sins that ranged historically through the ages. No more of Father Aragon's sorrowful eyes regarding me from his heart-breaking face, tempting me to grab him and show him what kind of man he really was, whether he consented or not. How many chances should a Church get to finally face its own truth? How many chances for a man? If Father Aragon needed to live a lie, let him look for support elsewhere, let him find someone else to help assuage his shame. I had enough of my own needing for-giveness.

"Tell him to take it to the confessional, Maurice." I mounted the steps and started up.

"Benjamin!" I stopped and reluctantly faced him. He stood at the bottom step, a tight fist on each hip. "Could you stop behaving like a petulant teenager for five minutes? I realize you've had a rough time of it, but that's no reason to treat people with rudeness and disrespect." He thrust a finger toward the ground. "Get down here this minute! You're going to come inside and at least hear what he came to say."

"I punched him the last time, you know."

"Yes, he told us. If you try something like that in my house, I'll personally take a broomstick to you."

"Five minutes." I started down. "Not a moment more."

I followed Maurice through the back door and the kitchen and into the kitsch-filled living room. When he saw us, Father Aragon rose quickly from his chair. I stopped in the shadows just beyond the ring of light from a table lamp, keeping some dis-tance.

"Make it short, Father."

"First, I wanted you to know that I called Lieutenant DeWinter. Told him about the SUV, the gray one we repaired and painted red."

"The Jeep Cherokee that Bishop Finatti brought in to your shop."

He nodded unhappily. "I understand the police have confis-cated it. That they intend to check it for any evidence that might have survived the work we did on it."

"Is that it, Father? Came all this way to brag about your good deed?"

"No, there's something else."

"Get to it, then."

"I've thought a lot about what you said week before last, when I was up in your apartment. That perhaps I haven't been willing to see certain things, or to see them clearly."

"Or looked the other way," I said.

He dropped his eyes a moment, wringing his hands. "I've meditated in particular on the matter of my silence. What I might have done differently, to help the children."

"Sorry doesn't matter, Father. It's too late for that."

"Benjamin," Maurice said sharply.

"That's not why I'm here—to apologize." Father Aragon searched my face, his eyes anguished. "It's about Father Blackley."

The name caught my attention like a barbed hook in the mouth. "You said you never met him."

"I've heard things."

I took a step forward, closer to the light. "What kind of things?"

"I remembered something. It may not be significant."

"Try me."

"I'm acquainted with a couple, Jim and Cathy Quimby. They run a home for pregnant girls—unwed young women. It's out in Redondo Beach."

I recalled the letter and pamphlet atop the pile of correspondence sent to Joe Soto, still sitting on my kitchen table. It included a photo of the blond and photogenic couple, smiling like angels. "Hope Haven, I think they call it."

"Yes, that's it," Father Aragon said. "You've heard of it?"

"The Quimbys wrote to Joe after his column appeared, taking Father Blackley's side. What about the Quimbys, Father?"

"I've helped raise money for them. They do fine work, save a lot of unborn children."

"Get to the point."

"Years ago, before he died, Father Blackley was their parish priest. They spoke fondly of him a number of times. It seems he was particularly close to the family."

Close to the family. Deep inside, I felt myself go sick with anticipation what might be coming. "Go on."

"It may be nothing. It troubles me to bring it up. But—"

"For God's sake, Father, spit it out."

"What bothers me is what happened to the Quimby's daughter, Kimberly."

"Happened when?"

"A year or two before Father Blackley died."

Twenty-two. The number came back at me again. *Twenty-two.* I heard the voice inside saying: *Not twenty-three. Please, not twenty-three.*

I looked at Father Aragon evenly, trying to keep the dread from my voice. "She was molested?"

"I don't know about that. I suppose it's possible."

"Jesus, Father, what *do* you know?"

"One day, when she was eleven, Kimberly failed to come home from school."

"Failed to come home."

He nodded, looking stricken. The way he kept his eyes on me, never blinking, I sensed his compassion was as much for me as for the Quimbys.

"Kimberly Quimby disappeared, Benjamin. Without a trace."

THIRTY-ONE

Redondo Beach is an unpretentious seaside community roughly twenty miles southwest of downtown Los Angeles, where surfing had been introduced to California in 1907. There's a yacht harbor, a commercial pier, and a nice stretch of beach on the north end but not much else of particular distinction.

That night, I found Hope Haven on a residential street not quite a mile east of Pacific Coast Highway. Jim and Cathy Quimby ran it out of a large, two-story stucco they'd spruced up with blooming flower beds, porch swings and gingerbread shutters. The other houses on the block were well kept but plainer, suggesting working-class. Except for the damp ocean air, the neighborhood might have been in Bakersfield.

I sat out front in the Mustang for a minute or two, studying the Quimby's brochure: *Hope Haven, a Nonprofit Sanctuary for Unwed Mothers.* Then I climbed out clutching a stack of papers and trudged up the walk, part of me excited that I might have stumbled on to something important, while another part of me hoped I hadn't.

"Mr. Justice, please, come in."

Cathy Quimby opened the front door, looking exactly like

her brochure photo: blond, blue-eyed, blemish free and annoyingly perky. Jim Quimby, who appeared beside her, fit the image of her male clone. Their forty-something faces were youthful and unassuming, their upbeat smiles implacable, as if they'd been sutured permanently into place. They were also on the tall side, both of them. Father Blackley had preferred small, slim, darker girls. It seemed unlikely there would be a sexual connection between Blackley and their daughter, which afforded me a glimmer of optimism.

We shared herbal tea in the living room—caffeine was banned from the house, along with alcohol, tobacco, and illicit drugs—while innocuous pop music could be heard coming from down the hall. The Quimbys sat next to each other on a sofa piled with pillows embroidered with Scripture and such inspirational slogans as "Smile and God Smiles with You" and "Remember, You Always Have a Friend in Jesus." A portrait of the Virgin Mary hung above the fireplace, where small gas flames warmed the room. Now and then, I saw teenage girls in various stages of pregnancy moving between the stairway, dining room and kitchen.

"When you called," Cathy Quimby said, "you mentioned that you first learned of us through our letter to Mr. Soto."

"I happened to see a copy, a few days after his death."

"Our intent," Jim Quimby said, "was merely to offer another point of view. We knew Father Blackley quite well. He was almost like a member of the family."

Cathy Quimby cocked her head pertly, speaking softly. "There's simply no way he could be involved with children in the manner Mr. Soto described. We wanted Mr. Soto to know that. We aren't confrontational people, but we also believe strongly in making our point of view heard."

"In all due respect, Mrs. Quimby, I can assure you that Father Blackley was an active pedophile."

She glanced with distress at her hands, folded in her lap. "You have proof of this? Because that's a terrible accusation to make."

I handed over my photocopies of the documents from Buffalo. "At least six families settled with the Buffalo diocese, where Father Blackley was assigned before coming to Los Angeles."

She looked them over, before passing them to her husband. "Many people have taken advantage of the Church, Mr. Justice. These are merely claims—not actions that have been proven or corroborated. It's tragic, what's being done to the Church."

"Are you suggesting that the hundreds of cases across the country that have been settled, and hundreds more that are pending and being investigated, are fabrications?"

Jim Quimby handed back the papers. "We're not denying that there have been problems with a few priests, Mr. Justice, especially the homosexuals. But Father Blackley—no, that's just not possible."

"I'm the anonymous victim mentioned in Joe Soto's column," I said.

"You?" Mrs. Quimby sat up taller, tensing, as if she'd just discovered an evil force in the room. She pursed her lips critically, while her voice lost a degree of warmth. "And I imagine you have a lawsuit pending, don't you?"

"The Church came to me with an offer of two million dollars."

"Just as I suspected."

"It was intended to shut me up."

"That would be your interpretation, wouldn't it?"

"I turned it down, Mrs. Quimby."

She raised her narrow eyebrows. "You want *more?*"

"I want the truth, Mrs. Quimby." I sipped some tea, smiled ruefully. "I won't pretend their offer wasn't tempting. I'm sure everyone has his price."

Her smile faded, and she grew troubled. "You're saying that you're not after the money at all? That you won't take it?"

"I guess God never intended me to be rich."

She glanced at her husband, looking confused. "Jim, did you hear what he said?" He slipped an arm around her, his voice wary. "Yes, sweetheart, I heard."

"A police detective," I said, "working with a newspaper reporter, has traced Father Blackley to twenty-two molestation victims in Los Angeles County. All of them were children from families in the parishes where Father Blackley was assigned."

"We haven't read anything like that," she said.

"It hasn't been made public yet. At some point, I'm sure it will be."

"Twenty-two." Jim Quimby spoke as if the number were incomprehensible.

"I'm sorry," his wife said, pulling herself together, putting the resolve back into her voice. "But we knew Stuart Blackley as a friend. He was a wonderful man. Particularly after Kimberly—" She broke off abruptly, staring at her hands again, as if unwilling to confront the thought that had just popped into her head.

"Father Aragon told me that Kimberly disappeared," I said.

"Twelve years ago." Jim Quimby shot a troubled glance at his wife. "But Father Blackley had nothing to do with that. He was investigated, like anyone else who was close to our daughter at that time. The police even questioned us."

"Did they know at the time that Father Blackley was molesting other children? That he had a history of abusing both girls and boys going back at least twenty years, to Buffalo?"

"No." Jim Quimby shook his head, looking stunned. "None of us knew that." His voice became earnest, almost pleading. "But—but Father Blackley had an alibi for the day Kimberly disappeared."

"Bishop Finatti?" I asked.

Cathy Quimby stared at me wide-eyed. "How did you know that?"

"It follows a pattern. Finatti and Blackley were longtime friends. Finatti's a lawyer. He's handled the settlements, orchestrated the cover-ups."

She sat rigid, her face growing strained. Then she shook her head, staring in the direction of the fireplace. "No, it isn't possible. We let him into our home, we let him take her on trips, on retreats."

"To his mountain cabin?" She nodded, her eyes growing more conflicted. I set aside my cup and saucer, leaned forward, studied them closely. "When I came here, I assumed Kimberly was fair, like you and your husband."

"Why would that matter?" Jim Quimby asked.

"Father Blackley had a preference for blond boys and slim, dark girls."

Mrs. Quimby put a hand to her mouth, and tears welled up. "Oh, my God."

Jim Quimby held his wife close for a moment. Then he separated gently from her, rose and crossed to a bookshelf, and came back with a family album. He opened it to a school picture of a pretty girl of about ten, slim, with dark hair and eyes.

"Kimberly was Salvadoran." He sounded devastated. "She was adopted."

"When Kimberly disappeared, there were so many others," Cathy Quimby said, making her explanation sound like an apology, a plea for understanding. "So many children from broken homes, on drugs, runaways. Their faces were on milk cartons, billboards, telephone poles. There were so many. And our Kimberly became one more. After a few years, when we couldn't find her, we just assumed—"

"I don't want to upset you, Mrs. Quimby. It's possible someone else took her. It's possible it wasn't Father Blackley at all."

"But you don't really believe that," Jim Quimby said.

"I wish I could."

"If we'd known about him," Cathy Quimby said, "if the police had known—"

"We never would have let him into our home," her husband said. "We never would have let him near our child."

"You didn't know," I said, "because the Church didn't want you or anyone else to know. It's been going on for a long, long time."

She collapsed against her husband, sobbing. He held her, staring blankly toward the fireplace, as she had a moment ago, watching the gas-fed flames rise evenly from under artificial logs.

"Perhaps we could be alone now, Mr. Justice."

I was nearly to the car when I heard Jim Quimby behind me, calling from the porch. I stopped and he came down the steps to meet me.

"There was another girl," he said, "in the same parish, who disappeared about a year after Kimberly. It was a large parish, so it didn't occur to us that there might be some connection. But now—"

"Do you recall the girl's name, Mr. Quimby?"

"Lucy, I think. Yes, Lucy Crisologo. A little Filipino girl."

When we lost Lucy. Those had been Teresa Sandoval's exact words. I'd assumed she'd been referring to the girl's death, from accident or illness, not her abduction. *Assume nothing, check everything.* It's a fundamental rule of reporting. I hadn't been a reporter for a long time.

I asked Mr. Quimby if I could use a phone. He led me back inside, where I called Lt. Claude DeWinter, reaching him on his cell. I told him where I was calling from, and reminded him who the Quimbys were.

"I advised you to drop out of sight for awhile," he said. "It's still a good idea."

"I have some new information." I closed my eyes, as the possibilities began to take shape. "About a couple of kids Father Blackley had contact with."

"Let me grab a pen. OK, shoot."

"When you and Templeton charted Father Blackley's movements from parish to parish, you were looking for victims of sexual abuse. You might want to retrace your steps, Lieutenant. This time, I think you need to look for missing children."

THIRTY-TWO

I left Hope Haven and drove west, across PCH to the beach. It was nearly ten, blustery and cold. The beach was empty, the way I'd hoped to find it.

I sat on the dampish sand, listening to the waves and staring out at the lights of passing freighters, but seeing the face of Kimberly Quimby instead. When I'd been a reporter, stumbling across a twist like this would have been cause for celebration— at the very least, a few drinks at the Redwood Inn on Second Street with Joe Soto or some other *Times* staffer who was using the Redwood's long bar to take the edge off the job. Now, I prayed that my promising lead would go nowhere, that it would hit some frustrating dead end, that Father Blackley had never touched Kimberly Quimby at all. It wasn't a selfless wish, for the sake of her parents. It was for me.

I sat there for fifteen or twenty minutes, hunched over with my arms on my knees, trying to digest what I'd just learned, trying to figure out how I was going to live with it if it led where it seemed to be going. It wasn't just twenty-two kids any longer, I reminded myself, and molestation might not have been the worst of Father Blackley's crimes. It sounds melodramatic, I know, but all kinds of crimes flashed through my brain, down through time—the Inquisition, slavery, the massacre of the American Indian, Hitler's Holocaust, Stalin's purges and horrific famine, Mao's systematic slaughter, the genocide in Armenia, the killing fields of Cambodia, the horrors of Bosnia and Rwanda, it went on and on. All kinds of incomprehensible crimes that required all manner of complicity and silence, from which we never seemed to learn the right lessons.

I felt twisted up inside, sick with trepidation, thinking about where the truth might take me, wondering if I really wanted to get to the truth about Father Blackley at all anymore. *Be careful what you wish for.* Wasn't that the old saying? Suddenly, the bile rose up, and I puked between my legs on to the cold sand.

It was then, as I wiped my mouth with the back of my hand, that I realized someone else was sharing my stretch of beach, watching me.

The dark figure stood at a distance to my left, to the south. He'd approached on my blind side; I'd never noticed. I put him at a hundred yards, but it might have been less, in the darkness and with my depth perception mostly gone.

Beyond him was the outline of the distant Palos Verdes Peninsula, descending like a reptile slinking down into the water, house lights twinkling like jewels along the ridge of its bumpy back. To my right—north—more lights shone from the businesses crowded along the horseshoe-shaped pier, perhaps a mile away. In between, except for lifeguard towers, was nothing but wide, empty beach, nearly pitch black under a sliver of moon. Not a bad place to cut someone's throat, or put a bullet in him, and get away with it, if you were so inclined.

I rose slowly, brushing myself off, as if unconcerned. I sauntered north, in the direction of the big pier, measuring a dozen strides before I glanced over my shoulder. He was following. I walked on, half a dozen strides this time. When I looked back again, he was coming after me, at a run. I turned up the beach, toward the street, where the Mustang was parked. He veered off his course, angling toward me, gaining speed.

I ran, as hard and fast as I could, which wasn't nearly enough. My shoes filled with sand and I struggled to get my breath and keep my knees pumping. He came on like a light-footed animal, swift and sure, his feet seeming to barely brush the surface of the beach. Between us, halfway to the steep embankment that led up to the street was a wooden lifeguard tower. I knew that reaching the street was impossible. He'd catch me at the foot of the embankment, if not sooner, dragging me down like a predator running its slower and weaker prey to ground. I made for the kiosk, my lungs on fire, my legs turning rubbery beneath me. As I reached the tower's ramp, he was almost on me; I could hear the hiss of his breath, the grunts that issued between his clenched teeth, as he bore down. My goal now was modest and immediate: to reach the top of the ramp and somehow fend him off while I screamed for help to anyone who might be within hearing. It was a small hope, but it was something.

Just as I reached the top, he caught me. I felt his arms encircle my legs, felt myself going down, face first on to the sandy surface of the wood floor. Getting caught like that—literally in his clutches—was like a signal to end my struggle. I was surprised by how little fight I had in me, how little I seemed to care what he did with me now. It was as if I was giving permission for him to end things between us, to deliver my final punishment. Having him on me like that, while I submitted so completely to him, gave myself to him, felt almost sexual.

His breath was hot against my ear. "Ben, don't run away from me. Please, don't run."

"Nick?"

He loosened his grip as I rolled to my side and he crawled up next to me. His face was gaunt, deathly white, coated with sweat; his pupils were huge, expanded to fill most of the irises; he looked as if he hadn't eaten in days. The pores of his emaciated body gave off that sharp, sweet smell peculiar to speed freaks.

I reached over, took his head in my hands, leveled his wild

eyes. "Jesus, Nick, you scared the shit out of me. What are you doing?"

"I was watching you, to be sure you were OK. I followed you from your place. I warned you, man, you got to watch your back." He continually picked at his face, as if imaginary bugs were crawling on him. "When you came out on the beach, I could see you needed to be alone. Then you took off. I was afraid you were running away from me. I had to talk to you one last time." His words came at me fast and loose, tumbling out, piling up like a freeway wreck in the fog. His wild eyes scanned the beach. "They're everywhere, you know? And nowhere. You can't tell where they are. That's why you got to watch them all the time. If you don't, they'll get you."

"Calm down, Nick. Take it easy."

"I told you, didn't I? Didn't I tell you to watch your back?"

"You've been tweaking, haven't you?"

"Four days without sleep. Or maybe it's five, I don't know. No food, no sleep. Just me and my crystal, man."

"Smoking?"

He showed me needle tracks on the inside of one arm. "Shooting up, man. Works faster, lasts longer. It's like a blast from heaven when it hits. I could use some right now, you know?" He reached up, his hand trembling, and touched the patch on my eye. "This is my fault, what happened to you. I should have been watching out for you. Jesus, I'm so fucked up." The more he talked, the more he came unglued. Eventually, his words turned to gibberish and he was weeping, snot running from his nose, at turns remorseful and enraged, sputtering out something about how he should have taken care of things a long time ago. "I fucked up, man. I've been fucking up for so long. My life is shit, you know?"

"Let's get you home, get you cleaned up. You'll eat something. We'll talk."

"It's too late!" He reached into his waistband, pulled out his Ruger, shook it in my face. "Don't worry, Ben. Nobody's going to hurt you again. I'll see to it they don't. Go home, hide out.

Don't answer your door, don't answer your phone. I'll take care of everything."

"Nick, if you know something—"

"Finatti, man. I should never have let the fucker out of my sight. I should have watched him every minute, followed him, like I planned. But I got careless. It's the crystal, man. It's stronger than I am. It's so fucking strong!" He touched my face, my lips. "I let you down, Ben. But I'm going to make it right, you'll see."

"I know how that feels, Nick, to let people down. Let's go someplace and talk about it, OK? We'll find a way out of this, you and me."

He shook his head, sobbing. "I'm fucked, man. I want it to be over." Suddenly, he stood, staring at the Ruger. "At least I can do one good thing with my fucked up life."

He turned, stepped to the top of the railing, and leaped. I saw him land feet first in the sand, then take off up the beach. I called after him, but heard no response. Nick Gash ran pell-mell into the darkness, never looking back.

THIRTY-THREE

It was half past eleven when I got back to the house and parked out front, hanging my parking permit from the rear view mirror. The lights were out inside the house, which meant that Maurice and Fred were already snuggled down for the night in their big bed, the blankets pulled up to their chins and the cats curled up around them in furry balls. I was halfway up the drive when I heard footsteps behind me.

I glanced back, saw a figure in the deepest shadows. Someone moving toward me, hands in pockets. Dark pants, plaid jacket—that was about all I could make out. My heartbeat quickened and I felt my saliva dry up.

"Nick?"

Alexandra Templeton emerged, dressed like she was stepping out of a high-end catalog of outdoor winter fashions. "Just me. Disappointed?" She pulled up, studying my face. "You OK? You look a little spooked."

"It's been an eventful night." I glanced at my watch. "What are you doing here at this hour?"

"I dropped by earlier but you were out. Fell asleep in the car, waiting for you."

"How are you doing? About Joe, I mean. I haven't asked in awhile."

"Better. Thanks for asking." She shivered. "It's cold out here. Could we go upstairs and talk?"

I flicked on a light, locked the door, pulled the curtains closed. Templeton opened my closet and began rummaging around. "Where's your suitcase?"

"Don't have one."

She paused, giving me one of her looks. "No suitcase?"

"I had a gym bag once. Never used it. It might still be in there. Why?"

She dived back into the closet. "We're taking a little trip, up to the mountains."

"Since when?"

"Since about two hours ago." She found an old gym bag filled with worn running shoes, dumped them on the bed. "We'll use this. Grab your toothbrush, your meds, and a change of clothes. We'll probably be back tomorrow night, but we might stay longer."

I planted my feet, crossed my arms across my chest. "Not until you tell me what's going on."

She bit her lip, glanced at the bed. "Why don't you sit down?"

"I don't want to sit down. I want you to tell me what's going on."

"After you called Claude from the Quimby place, he ran a database check. He keyed in missing children cases for the seventeen years Blackley served as a priest before he died, going back almost thirty years, using Southern California as the general search area."

I sat on the edge of the bed. "He found something."

"Five other kids, in addition to the Quimby and the Crisologo girls. Four males, one female. All within the age range and physical type of Blackley's preferences when they disappeared."

I stared at the floor. "Seven."

She sat beside me, took my hand. "It's better that we know. For the families, if nothing else."

Half a minute passed in silence, while I tried to absorb it. "You mentioned the mountains."

"Claude called the Quimbys," Templeton said. "They had a location on Blackley's cabin, the one where he took kids on retreats. It's just outside Pine Hollow, about fifteen miles beyond Lake Arrowhead."

"I know that area. Lots of trails, decent fishing, good lakes for swimming." I shuddered. "I'll bet the kids couldn't wait to go up there with him."

"Claude thinks we should get out of town, anyway. At least until they get a bead on Pablo Zuniga. He's been pushing me pretty hard to talk you into it."

"Nice to know he cares."

Templeton stood, thrusting the empty bag at me. "Grab some warm clothes. The cabin's above six thousand feet and we're into late November. You have mittens, a nice wool scarf?" I gave her a look. "Never mind," she said, "we can buy some when we get there, if we need to."

I stared at the floor, feeling paralyzed. She took my bearded chin, made me look up at her. "We don't know anything for sure at this point. We haven't definitely tied Blackley to those missing kids. Maybe we won't find anything on his property."

"Not anything," I said. "Bodies. Why don't you just say it?"

"At least wait until we have something solid before you flake out on me."

I suddenly felt cold, and so empty inside that I could almost hear the wind whistling. "I'm sorry. I don't want to go up there."

"What about the truth, Justice?"

I hugged myself, feeling small, cowardly. "I don't care about the truth anymore."

She sat down beside me again. "Then what about Joe?" I looked over, saw angry tears in her eyes. "This might answer some questions about why he was killed. Do you care about that?"

She kept her eyes on mine, the way she had so many times in recent years, when she'd talked me into doing the right thing. Usually for my sake, not hers.

I got heavily to my feet. "I'll get my meds."

"And a toothbrush."

"And a toothbrush."

Minutes later, we were in Templeton's T-Bird, with the heater on. I was quiet as we started out of the city, still trying to absorb what was happening, or might be. As we sped out Interstate 10, leaving Los Angeles behind, I asked her to tell me the names of the seven children, if she could remember them.

"Just the first names would be OK," I said, "even a few."

She recited the names, in the order they'd disappeared, which she'd already committed to memory. It was just like Templeton to do that; it was the way she approached every crime story, much more humanely than I ever had. "The Crisologo girl was the last to disappear," she said. "Her mother reported her missing a few weeks before Father Blackley died."

"They never found any sign of her?"

"No."

"Lucy." I spoke her name softly, with great care, trying to make her more tangible, more real. "Lucy Crisologo."

I didn't talk again after that, not for a couple of hours, until we were in the mountains. Templeton concentrated on her driving, kind enough to leave it that way.

THIRTY-FOUR

We reached Pine Hollow in the early morning hours, well before dawn. The little town was closed up for the night, but vacancy signs were plentiful. We turned in at a rustic-looking motel off the main road, down by a small lake. A sleepy-eyed Korean man answered the night buzzer and checked us in. We asked for a room away from the road, with some privacy. He gave us our keys, instructed us to leave our car parked in the lot, and told us to take the trail along the lake until it reached the last cabin on the left.

A bitter wind came off the water as we hauled our luggage past a row of dark, quiet cabins. A forest thick with pine was all around.

"I'll bet we see some deer," Templeton said.

The cabin came equipped with a fireplace, a kitchenette, and two queen-sized beds. I tossed my bag of clothes into a corner while Templeton neatly placed her belongings in the drawers of a knotty pine dresser, arranging her socks by color. Then she sat on one of the beds and asked if there was anything I wanted to talk about.

I shook my head. "No."

She smiled halfheartedly. "Probably better to get some sleep, anyway."

When she was in her pajamas and I'd stripped down to my shorts and undershirt, we climbed into our separate beds and she switched off the lamp. "I didn't tell you," she said. "I like the beard. Looks good on you."

"I'll keep it for awhile then."

Before long, I heard her shallow, rhythmic breathing, and knew she was asleep. I lay on my side, eyes open, going over everything in my head, all the jagged little pieces, until I saw the dawn light insinuate itself though a crack in the heavy curtains. I got up, took a pill, and made coffee.

We ate breakfast at a diner in town and were on the road before nine.

Templeton drove up the winding highway while I followed a map she'd given me and we both looked for road signs. We were almost to six thousand feet when she spotted the turnoff we were looking for. We made the turn and a minute later passed a sign announcing a lake, with an arrow pointing down a side road, and another further on alerting drivers to a Girl Scout camp. Several minutes after that, we turned off again, on to a badly paved road that climbed into dense forest. Now and then, we passed a cabin set against the edge of the woods, but we saw them less and less often.

"It's almost deserted up here," Templeton said.

"Fishing season's over, skiing hasn't started."

"No, I mean the cabins. They're few and far between."

"I guess Father Blackley liked his privacy."

The road narrowed and lost its paving. We continued to climb, spitting gravel and leaving dust behind us. Suddenly, she pulled up.

Ahead, a two-story log cabin sat on a rise, with a commanding view of the forest below. A creek ran between the property and road; it was nearly dry, but deep enough to require a bridge for access to the unpaved drive going up. "This has to be it." Before I could offer an opinion, Templeton snatched the map from my hands, ran her finger along the roads we'd traveled, then glanced out the window at the number on a mailbox near a gate. "Definitely, this is the place."

"You notice anything different about it?"

"Other than the creek out front? Not really. Just more remote."

"It's fenced, for one thing."

She took a closer look. A chain-link fence surrounded the property—I guessed half an acre or more—connected in front by a padlocked gate. "You're right—locked up tight."

"You notice anything else?"

She studied the cabin, then the sloping land out front. "There's something about the landscaping. The other places we passed—"

"Had natural landscaping. This looks arranged."

Templeton shrugged, trying to make it seem unimportant. "Maybe Father Blackley had a green thumb, liked to move rocks around."

"Yeah, maybe that was it."

She shrugged again, trying harder. "Or maybe it was the new owner who did it."

She parked off the road and we got out for a better look. There were no vehicles in sight and no people. She hollered across the fence at the cabin, to no avail. We climbed an embankment to our left, up into the trees that ran along one side of the property. Within a few minutes, we'd made our way around the back, looking down on the cabin and its view of the road and valley below.

"You can pretty much see everybody coming or going," I said. "Not a place where anyone could surprise you. Not with that bridge and gate."

"He must have loved the outdoors," Templeton said, "to come all the way up here."

"Blackley was an active guy back in Buffalo, I remember that about him." I glanced around at the pines, thick with needles; a couple of hawks soared overhead, gliding slowly, while a squirrel chattered angrily at us from a nearby branch. "He liked to take us for hikes in upstate New York, the mountain inlets, places like this where he had us all to himself."

She studied my face closely. "You OK, Justice?"

"Yeah, I'm all right."

"Ready to go back?"

I nodded and we started down.

As we came around the property nearing the road, we saw a U.S. Forest Service truck pulled up behind Templeton's T-Bird. A ranger—lean, suntanned, graying, in uniform—was peering into the car. He straightened and turned as we clambered down the embankment to the gravelly surface.

"Hello, folks." He tipped his hat as we approached. A badge on his shirt had a number and he had a name tag: Chuck Aswell. "This your vehicle?"

Templeton told him it belonged to her. He said he was just checking, since he didn't see all that many "city cars" up this way this time of year.

"We were checking out the cabin," I said. "The fence had us intrigued."

"That fence," he said, looking past us at it. "I'm not too happy about that, if you want to know the truth. Most of the land around here is public, Forest Service property. Fences aren't too popular."

Templeton opened her big bag, pulled out a notebook and pen. "Been working up here a long time?"

"Nearly thirty years, since right after college." He glanced at Templeton's pen as she jotted notes. "Lousy pay but I wouldn't trade it for a city job."

Templeton showed him her *L.A. Times* photo ID, identified herself as a reporter. "I'm gathering some information about Father Stuart Blackley, the priest who owned this property until his death back in '92." She tipped her head toward me. "This gentleman was acquainted with Father Blackley. He's assisting me."

"Was the priest famous or something?"

"He led a fascinating life that few people are aware of," Templeton said. "We think it might make a good story."

"Did you happen to know Father Blackley?" I asked.

The ranger stroked his chin, narrowing his clear blue eyes. "Can't say that I ever met the man. Saw him quite a bit twenty, twenty-five years ago, when I first started working up here. He'd be out hiking with some kids from his church, or down at the lake, taking them swimming. I'd wave, he'd wave, that was about it. Otherwise, he kept pretty much to himself. I don't think anybody around here knew him too well."

"You never saw him in his later years," I asked, "just before he died?"

"Not out hiking or anything like that. I might see him up on the porch when I drove past. Or behind the wheel of his backhoe, digging around in the dirt. That was about it."

"He had a backhoe," I said.

"Oh, yeah, he had one, all right." The ranger threw his hand out toward the property, like he was tossing seeds. "That's how he did all this, rearranging nature. God, I hate to see a man up in the seat of a digging machine like that, working the gears and moving dirt around. They get a taste of it, it's hard to stop them." The ranger crossed the road and we followed, peering with him through the fence. "You see how scarred the earth is? And look at the vegetation. We hate to see non-native plant life take root up here. He even moved boulders around and grouped them together, like he was decorating a house, for God sake." He glanced at the two of us, shaking his head. "Now why would somebody need to do that, in a place that God already made perfect?"

"Why, indeed," Templeton said, offering me a fleeting glance. Then, to the ranger: "From what I understand, Father Blackley died in a hiking accident."

The ranger nodded his head once. "I was on the search and rescue team that brought him out. Old guy like that shouldn't have gone out hiking alone. Nobody should, for that matter. Or at least let someone know when you're due back."

"What can you tell us?"

The ranger stepped into the road, pointing northeast. "Trailhead's right up there, just around that turn in the road. Some backpackers found him about a half-mile up. He'd apparently tried to go off trail and take a shortcut by climbing over a ridge. Rock hit him from above, best we could figure. His head was crushed, top of the skull. A lot of folks think that most climbers who get killed die from falls. Actually, it's falling rocks that cause most of the fatalities."

Templeton lifted pen to notebook. "What kind of investigation was done?"

"Not much to speak of. Looked like an accident to us. We put his body over the back of a mule, brought him out."

"No autopsy?"

"You'd have to talk to the sheriff's department about that. They've got jurisdiction up this way. We just go in, find them, and bring them out alive when we can." He glanced toward the sun, which was moving south. "You folks have any more questions? Because I've got some campgrounds to check before noon."

Templeton got his phone number and exact job title, and thanked him for his help. As he drove off, I walked back across the road, hanging my fingers like claws in the chain link fence.

"He was right," I said. "You can see by looking at them that the boulders have been moved around, maybe even transported from off the property." I took a deep breath, trying to settle myself. " 'Now why would somebody need to do that?' Those were his exact words. I hope you wrote them down."

Templeton held up her notebook. "Right in here." She laid a hand on my back, rotating gently. "I think I'd better call Claude DeWinter. He'd want to know about this."

"I think there's something else he needs to know. You too."

We crossed the road back to her car. "What's that, Justice?"

"Father Blackley didn't die in a hiking accident."

She pulled up in the middle of the road. "What makes you say that?"

"Blackley used a cane the last years of his life. Had a severe case of gout. Nick Gash told me about it."

"Then he wouldn't have been out hiking," Templeton said.

"And a loose rock wouldn't have fallen on his head."

"You're saying somebody killed him and hauled his body up the mountain to make it look like an accident."

"I'm saying he had gout and used a cane. I'll leave the rest for Claude DeWinter to figure out."

I moved around the car and got in the passenger side. When Templeton was behind the wheel, she asked me how long I'd known what I'd just told her.

"Awhile."

"Why didn't you tell us before?"

"I was preoccupied."

"Not much of an excuse."

"It'll have to do." I glanced at the cabin and its surrounding grounds, wondering if I was looking at an unmarked graveyard. "Let's get out of here, OK?"

THIRTY-FIVE

After calling the LAPD from a pay phone, Templeton dropped me off at the motel and drove on, saying she had errands to run. I was too exhausted and too wrapped up in myself to ask what they were, so I didn't.

It was early afternoon when I crawled into bed with the curtains drawn. I rested badly, chased in my sleep by something that had no face or shape, while I stumbled frantically on, just a step out of reach. I woke abruptly, bathed in sweat, crying out one word: *Dad.* I hadn't used that word for my father since my early teens, when I'd started to resent his drinking and violence, even as I became more like him. Hearing it come from my mouth, unbidden and disconnected to anything but a feverish dream, left me shaken and more unsettled than ever. I washed my face at the sink and carried coffee in a thermal cup out to the porch to watch the lake. Clouds had moved in from the north, massing darkly. The water was slate gray, rippled with wind-driven whitecaps.

I saw Templeton coming down the trail, bundled up against the cold, her big purse hanging from one shoulder.

"Let's go down by the lake," she said, as she reached the steps. "Before the storm moves in."

I asked her to wait while I grabbed my coat.

We sat at the end of an empty dock, our feet dangling, while I sipped my coffee and Templeton told me about her day.

Her call to Lieutenant DeWinter had set him in motion, she said. He'd notified the sheriff's department that had jurisdiction over Pine Hollow, alerting them to a possible crime scene. Templeton figured there were deputies up there now, keeping watch. Meanwhile, DeWinter was working with various prosecutors and judges, coordinating between the two counties involved, seeking a court order giving permission to start digging.

"Things are happening fast," I said. "Did you call your news desk?"

Templeton shook her head. "Too soon, under the circumstances. I'll wait to see if anything turns up."

"Maybe there's nothing up there."

"That's what I was thinking." It sounded false, and we both knew it. Quickly, Templeton added, "Anyway, I'm still on leave, and off the news beat. If I go to the desk with something, I'd better have it nailed down pretty tight." We heard a cry and looked across the lake to see a flock of ducks flying in formation, heading south. Templeton's eyes followed them until they were specks against the darkening sky. "I drove down the mountain, Justice. To the county records building."

"You've been busy."

"I searched the file on Stuart Blackley's old property." She glanced over. "Care to guess who owns the property now?"

"What do I get if I'm right?"

"I'll buy dinner tonight."

"How many guesses do I get?"

"One. So think about it first."

I didn't have to. "Anthony Finatti."

"Care to guess when he purchased the place?"

"Double or nothing?"

"OK."

"The moment probate closed."

"Two for two," she said. "The property never went on the market."

We sat there weighing what it meant, or might. "Finatti and Blackley were friends," I said. "Maybe the place had sentimental value for him."

"That's possible, I guess."

"What else did you find?"

Templeton pulled out her notebook, flipping pages. "It was Finatti who put up the fence. He had to apply for a special permit. A copy of the application was in the property file."

"I didn't see a backhoe when we were snooping around."

"Neither did I."

I sagged from the accumulating weight. "Finatti must have gotten rid of it."

Templeton put an arm around me. "Whatever they might find up there, Justice, it has nothing to do with you. Don't go putting this on yourself."

Out on the lake, a solitary man paddled his kayak through the water, fighting the chop. He'd stroke a few times, deep and hard, making a little headway; then the wind would push the nose of his kayak back around, and he'd have to start over again, just to stay even.

"I killed my father when I was seventeen, Templeton."

"I know all about that. Lots of people know."

"You think you know."

She separated from me a little, her eyes keen. "You were defending your little sister. You ran into another room, grabbed your father's gun, came back and shot him. It was ruled justifiable homicide."

"That's what they ruled, yes." I turned my head until our eyes met. "In the second before I pulled the trigger, I thought about what I was doing."

"Maybe you shouldn't be telling me this."

"I could have kept the gun on him while my mother called

the PD. We could have testified against him, probably put him in jail, made sure he never came near Elizabeth again. I had that choice. It was very clear to me."

"Justice—"

"But in that second before I squeezed the trigger I made a different choice. A conscious choice."

"You were young, under incredible pressure."

"I wanted him dead, Templeton. Forget about Betsy. I wanted him gone, out of our lives. I had the opportunity, I took it."

"It was a long time ago. You've changed. You're different now."

"Am I?" I faced forward, looking across the frothing white-caps, where the man in the kayak redoubled his efforts, struggling against the headwind. Even on a small lake like this, I thought, a Kayaker could perish in a situation like this. Capsize, go under, die from drowning or exposure. It could easily happen. "I'm not so sure. Faced with a similar choice, I wonder what I'd do this time."

"You think about things too much, Benjamin. Things that may not happen, things you can't change."

We stared out together, quiet for several minutes. The man finally reached a dock down the shore, where he dragged his kayak from the water and went on his way, seemingly unperturbed. The whitecaps were coming in one behind the other now, riding the crests of small waves driven by a wind that was building fast.

"Looks like we're in for some weather," Templeton said.

THIRTY-SIX

We had dinner in town and got back to the motel as clouds were roiling and thunder rumbled distantly across the mountains to the north.

Templeton stretched out on her bed and pored over her notes, looking for holes and inconsistencies going all the way back to the day Joe Soto was murdered. I sat in a corner chair with my nose in *The Portable Graham Greene*, pretending to read. In truth, I was privately sorting through my own set of questions that still needed asking and answering.

Sometime after midnight, I looked over to see Templeton asleep, fully dressed with her notes piled around her. I was restless, so I covered her with an extra blanket, pulled on my jacket, grabbed a flashlight, and slipped quietly out the door for a stroll around the lake. I'd always appreciated the solitude of a mountain lake late at night—even this one, marred by motels and campgrounds hugging the edges. Alone, in the dark, I saw and heard the lake in a different way; I felt closer to it and farther from the fragmented and discordant world back in the city that you never really leave behind, not if you've lived there too long. There were stars here, bright when the nights were cloudless, and clean, piney smells and the rush of wind down through mountain passes and valleys that were here millennia before humans trod the earth and would be here long after we'd extinguished our-selves in our quest to control and our compulsion to destroy. There was no ego here. No illusions, delusions or lies. Time here might not purify a man, but at least it was a breath of fresh air.

I stopped for a moment, letting the raw wind scour my face, listening for its whispered message, wishing for a moment that Jacques were along to hear it with me. Thinking about crema-tion, about being turned to ash and scattered on the wind like Joe Soto, and how that wouldn't be so bad. Then I moved on.

I was circling the lake's south end, several hundred yards from the cabin, when I sensed movement in the woods to my left. I stopped, listening more keenly. I heard the crackle of twigs and leaves underfoot—then there was silence, save for the lap-ping of the water and the rumble of thunder far off across the peaks behind me. There was no doubt that there was someone or something out there. I considered running. But if it was dan-ger, and I ran for the cabin, I'd be drawing the trouble toward Templeton. If I went the other way, I'd be leaving the sanctuary of the motel behind, heading for empty campgrounds and cabins that were dark and probably boarded up for the season.

I stepped off the trail, aiming the flashlight into the blackness shrouding the trees, trying to make out some shape other than the rough poles of the pines. My left hand went unconsciously to the bandage over my eye, and the image of Pablo Zuniga flashed in my brain. I heard the shuffle of steps again, followed, as before, by silence. I gripped the flashlight tighter, raising it like a weapon. Behind me, the sky rumbled again. Seconds later, lightning flashed. Then raindrops began to fall.

Suddenly, a flurry of motion erupted in the woods. Someone or something was coming at me. I brought the beam of the flash-light down, straight ahead. A body came crashing through the foliage, while the light found a furry muzzle and a pair of large brown eyes. The speckled fawn veered off on its nimble legs, as the pounding in my heart subsided. I watched her bound away, back up the trail in the direction of the motel. Then I laughed out loud, thankful no one had been around to witness my encounter with the pretty deer Templeton had hoped to see. But as the fleeing animal drew my eyes toward the cabin, my laughter quickly died.

Lightning briefly illuminated the ground between the cabin and the lake. Someone was creeping about, peering in windows. As I watched, engulfed by a new wave of panic, the intruder began mounting the steps.

I started running, directing the flashlight ahead of me. A root caught my toe and I went down, banging the flashlight on the hard trail, cracking the filament in the bulb, losing the beam. I got up and sprinted on in darkness. As I rounded the lake at the southeast end, I lost sight of the cabin for maybe half a minute. When I glimpsed it again, closing in, I saw that the steps and porch were empty. The front door was wide open but the stranger was nowhere to be seen. I left the trail as it straightened out, angling across the open ground for the steps.

"Alexandra!"

I screamed her name two or three times and was up the steps in one leap. I raced through the open door, raising the flashlight, ready for combat. Templeton emerged from the kitchen, looking at me bewildered. Behind her was Lt. Claude DeWinter, dressed in a ridiculous red sweater covered with green holly and white snowflakes, carrying a saucer and cup in his big paws.

She stared at the flashlight gripped in my fist. "Was that you hollering?"

I bent at the waist, gasping for air. "I saw someone sneaking around, looking in. Then the door—"

"We left it open for you." Templeton repressed a smile. "Claude saw you down the trail, shining your flashlight. Said you had an encounter with a squirrel or something."

"It was a deer," I said. "It briefly charged me, if you must know."

"They can be very scary," Templeton said, keeping a straight face. "It's a miracle you came through it alive. Maybe you should sit down."

"I'll be fine, as soon as I get my breath."

"I saw a light on in the cabin," DeWinter explained. "I thought somebody might still be up." He hooked a thumb in the direction of the motel office. "I'm in the next cabin over. Just checked in."

"You could have called," I said.

"It was late."

"Not too late to sneak around and scare the crap out of us." I set the flashlight aside, brushed myself off, closed and locked the door behind me.

"What's the big deal?" Templeton said. "I was up, Claude knocked, I let him in."

"You have a habit of doing that, don't you?"

"Don't get pissy, Justice." She dropped her eyes a moment. "He's got a good reason to be here."

"Doesn't he always?" I turned to DeWinter. "So what is it?"

He set his coffee on the table, picked up a document, held it out. I took it, reacting uneasily to the Superior Court stamp at the top of the first page.

"You got your search warrant," I said.

DeWinter nodded. "We start digging in the morning."

THIRTY-SEVEN

The digging began at dawn, in a steady downpour. When Templeton and I reached the cabin, sheriff's department vehicles lined the far side of the road. Someone had sawed through the padlock and opened the gate, allowing a bulldozer on to the property. Inside the fence, a dozen deputies worked with picks and shovels or supervised, while another manned the bulldozer. The heavy machine lurched and groaned as the operator shifted through the gears, while the big scoop rose and came down, lifting and moving the waist-high boulders. Now and then, a deputy paused for hot coffee or a smoke. Mostly, though, they just kept steadily at their labor, scraping away the soil, sometimes on their knees using hand trowels. As the work continued, slowly and tediously, the rain rattled off the leaves littering the ground and caused a ghostly mist to rise.

Templeton and I stood outside the fence, draped in yellow slickers that DeWinter had brought with him from Los Angeles. For hours, we watched the deputies work, eating donuts and sipping lukewarm coffee, until DeWinter asked me if I wanted to go down the road with him for a pee. We found a game trail not far from the cabin and hiked off the shoulder, just out of sight, where we stood relieving ourselves into a bed of pine needles turning gray on their way to mulch.

"We've got a lead on Pablo Zuniga," DeWinter said. "Someone saw his picture on the eleven o'clock news and called our tip line. He's still around L.A., from the look of it."

"When was this?"

"The tip came in two nights ago."

"You could have told me last night."

"I figured you had enough on your mind without being reminded that he was still in the vicinity. I didn't see why it couldn't wait."

I zipped up. "That's it?"

"I was wondering if you've seen Nick Gash lately."

While he continued relieving himself, I told him about my encounter with Nick on the beach. When he'd finished, we started back up to the road.

"He's stopped showing up at the job site," DeWinter said. "His old man's worried about him. I thought you might know something."

"He's a mess, Lieutenant. His old man should have worried a long time before now."

"You know something I don't?"

I told him about the tradeoff Charles Gash had made with the archdiocese—exchanging his silence about Father Blackley for a chance to help build St. Agnes Cathedral. "So maybe I have a different perspective on Nick than you do, Lieutenant. Maybe I understand him a little better."

"That doesn't make him any less dangerous."

I stopped in the middle of the road. "What do you want from me?"

"If he contacts you, or you get a bead on him, let me know."

"I'll consider it. Anything else?"

He fidgeted a moment as he faced me. "About me and Alexandra. I'm not trying to jump her bones. That's not why I'm up here."

"Fine."

"I don't expect you to like me, either."

"Is this the part where you tell me I should be nice to you, for her sake?"

"It wouldn't hurt if you eased up a little. You forget—the lady lost someone she loved. She's still dealing with that."

"I forget nothing, DeWinter." I poked him in the chest. "And I sure don't need a lecture from you about what I should remember."

He glared at me, nostrils flaring. "Get your damn finger out of my chest."

I poked him again, harder. "As for Templeton, you're in no position to offer advice in that department, unless it's tips on how to stalk pretty women." Breath came like dragon's steam from his wide nostrils. He stepped forward, moving me back. His fists were clenched at his sides, the size of softballs. "Go ahead, DeWinter. Take your best shot. When you're finished pounding on me, Templeton can drive me down the hill and tend to my wounds, while you explain to your supervisor what it was we were arguing about."

"It'd be worth it, you sorry motherfucker." His neck and shoulders tensed and he cocked his big fist like he was about to launch it.

"Lieutenant!" The shout came from behind us.

I turned to see a young deputy running along the road in our direction. DeWinter brushed me aside with one hand, striding to meet him.

"We've found something," the deputy said. "I think you'd better have a look."

THIRTY-EIGHT

DeWinter followed the deputy across the bridge and on to the property, while I stayed behind at the gate with Templeton. I kept kidding myself that I was prepared for what was coming. You don't prepare for something like that, unless you're a veteran reporter on assignment who knows how to detach and compartmentalize. Even then it's tricky, more so when kids are involved.

They stopped at an excavation site under a tent that had been erected to keep out the rain. DeWinter knelt with two other officers, a sergeant and a commander, while the commander talked. DeWinter nodded from time to time, looking solemn. When he rose, I heard the commander order someone to call for a photographer and a coroner's team.

DeWinter trudged down the drive and across the bridge. He directed his words to Templeton, as if I wasn't there. "It's a skeleton. A child, judging by the size and thickness of the bones. That's about all we can tell at this point."

I asked if Bishop Finatti was going to be arrested, or at least detained as a material witness, since he owned the property.

"I'll question Finatti when I get back to L.A." DeWinter continued to show me his profile, facing Templeton. "It's not a crime to buy a piece of property from the estate of an old friend. Even with what we've found, we've got nothing to hold him on."

"What about the Jeep Cherokee—the one he got repaired and repainted at Saving Grace Auto Body?"

DeWinter finally showed me his mug, smirking. "Came up clean as a whistle."

"Sure, after all that work he had done on it."

"Maybe if somebody had tipped us to it sooner, forensics would have found something."

"Would you two please stop it," Templeton said.

I ignored her, honing in on DeWinter. "You could keep Finatti under surveillance, make sure he doesn't disappear."

"I doubt that Bishop Finatti's going anywhere soon. A man in his position."

"He's got ties to Mexico, where Zuniga's tight with the Church. Finatti spent time down there as a priest. Speaks fluent Spanish."

"How do you know that, big shot?"

"*Who's Who in the Catholic Church.* Research 101. You mean they didn't they teach you that at detective school?"

DeWinter clenched his jaw, kept his voice extra steady. "Like I said, I'll be speaking with the man when I get back to the city."

He turned back to Templeton, asking her to sit on the story for a while, to avoid a media horde stampeding up the mountain. She promised to keep the lid on as long as she could.

The rain let up around noon, and the digging proceeded more quickly.

One by one, through the day, more bodies were discovered—three children, DeWinter said, probably preteen like the first one. He pointed out that less than half the property had been searched, mostly ground where boulders had been moved away. There was also a basement in the house, with a concrete floor showing sections that didn't match the rest. None of this information was directed to me. I heard it as a bystander, while DeWinter spoke to Templeton, who took copious notes.

By late afternoon, trucks appeared coming up the road, hauling in portable generators and lights so the deputies could continue the search through the night. Templeton told DeWinter she needed to tip the news desk and dictate a story in the next hour or two. If she waited much longer, she said, she might risk losing the break altogether; the TV people would descend like vultures, presenting the story that night as if they'd uncovered it on their own, which they were prone to do.

"I need to get down to a land line," Templeton said. "Cell reception gets iffy up here."

"Sure, go ahead," DeWinter said. "I think I've told you everything I can."

"Not quite—there's still the matter of Father Blackley's death."

He glanced grimly at the search going on behind us. "First things first."

"Still, on the drive up here," Templeton said, "you must have given it some thought. The fact that a lame old man couldn't have been out hiking in the mountains, the way it supposedly went down."

"Believe me, Alexandra, I appreciate the information you relayed. I'll pass it along to the sheriff. I'm sure they'll take another look."

"Actually, it was Justice who tipped me. Maybe you should thank him."

So that was it, I thought—a peacemaking ploy.

"Sure." DeWinter tossed me a token glance. "Thanks for the information, pal."

"The original source was Nick Gash, Lieutenant. Maybe you should thank him."

"Thank him?" DeWinter's smile was razor thin. "Or bring him in for questioning?"

"You're looking at Nick as a suspect in Blackley's death?"

"Makes sense to me to me, given everything I've heard."

"If Nick killed Father Blackley, Lieutenant, I'm pretty sure he would have told me that night, when he revealed the rest of it. If you'd seen the state he was in, you'd understand."

"The man's a meth head, with a nasty rap sheet. Not someone I put much faith in."

"If not Nick Gash for a suspect," Templeton asked me, "then who?"

"Think about it a little, Templeton."

"I've thought about it a *lot,* Justice. I agree with Claude. Nick had the motive, probably the opportunity. And we know he's violent."

I smiled tightly. "I guess Nick's your prime suspect then. Case closed."

I turned away. DeWinter grabbed me by the sleeve and hauled me back. "Suppose you share your theory with us, anyway, professor."

I stared at his hand until he removed it. "How about the archdiocese?"

Templeton looked at me like I was crazy. "The archdiocese?"

"Or high officials therein. Who else had a better reason to want Father Blackley out of the picture?"

DeWinter guffawed, shaking his head. "You're so full of shit, Justice."

I ignored him, keying on Templeton. "We know that among serial molesters, a fraction will also be serial murderers. Correct?"

"A tiny fraction, yes."

"For seventeen years, the top officials of the archdiocese knew they had a serial molester on staff—Father Blackley—among numerous others. What would they do if they suddenly discovered that he was also killing some of his young victims?"

Templeton arched her brows. "Good question."

"Would they run to the authorities to turn him in, after protecting him for so long, knowing the scandal that would unleash? Not to mention the financial liability and the legal repercussions for those at the top. They'd have to stop him themselves—eliminate him, before he killed again, or implicated the church."

"A victim's parent might have done it," DeWinter said. "You can't discount a parent."

"I'm not so sure," I said. "A parent would likely go straight to the police. They'd want the whole, tragic mess out in the open, as quickly as possible."

"Likely doesn't cover everybody." DeWinter narrowed his eyes. "And let's not rule out the purest vengeance—retribution from a surviving victim. If not Nick Gash, then someone else."

I smiled, amused. "Why are you looking at me when you say that, Lieutenant?"

"You seem to know an awful lot about Father Blackley."

"Claude," Templeton said.

DeWinter pressed on. "You had a motive, and you said yourself you spent time up here years ago, that you knew the area. That equals opportunity."

"Justice has been *searching* for Father Blackley," Templeton said. "He even went to Joe for help, making it public. You know that."

"Could be an elaborate smokescreen. I've seen it before. Besides, his life is littered with the wreckage from his violence and bad judgment."

"And if I had killed him, Lieutenant, would you blame me?"

"Murder's murder. The law's the law."

"It's that cut and dried?"

"For me, it is."

"So what's the law on stalking, Lieutenant?" I watched his eyes get active as I tightened the noose. "What are the department rules about a horny investigator using his position of authority to get close to the object of his affection?"

DeWinter chomped hard on his gum, while I watched him squirm.

"It seems to me," Templeton said, speaking sharply, "that there are two key questions here. Who discovered that Father Blackley was abducting and killing children, and when. That should point to the best suspect in Blackley's murder."

"One more question," I said. "How did they find out? Let's not forget the how."

"No," DeWinter said, pinning me with his eyes, "let's not."

THIRTY-NINE

"He doesn't seriously consider you a suspect," Templeton said. "He's just posturing. You have to know that."

She turned off the side road on to the main highway, and down toward town.

"He's an arrogant S.O.B.," I said. "That much I know."

"And you're a model of maturity and civility."

"Let's just get to a phone, so you can file your story."

Templeton rolled her eyes. "I swear, when I'm with you two, I feel like I'm babysitting in testosterone hell. When all this is over, you both have some jealousy issues to work out."

I looked over. "Jealousy?"

Templeton drove with her eyes up the road. "There's a pay phone. This may take awhile. First, I've got to work my way past Lindsay St. John."

"I may be able to help you with that."

"Do me a favor, will you, Justice? Go inside, get yourself a nice cup of coffee, relax, and let me deal with St. John."

She pulled in at a small market and made a collect call, which Lindsay St. John accepted. I went inside for coffee and an oatmeal raisin cookie if they had one, which they did. When I came back out, Templeton and St. John were jousting again. It was clear from Templeton's end of the conversation that St. John was trying to take the story away from her and assign it to another reporter, arguing that Templeton was still on leave and off the news beat. The sun was moving around the mountains, it was getting cold, and I got tired of listening to Templeton go round and round. I gulped what was left of my coffee, tossed the cookie to a very happy squirrel, and grabbed the phone from Templeton's hand.

"Lindsay, this is Benjamin Justice. I want you to listen very carefully." Templeton, first startled, then furious, tried to get the phone back. I gave her a stiff arm, keeping her at bay. "Here's the deal. You're reinstating Templeton immediately, back in her old news slot. Her name goes on the story, nobody else's. If that doesn't happen, Templeton's next call is to the editor-in-chief."

"I beg your pardon?" At the other end, St. John's voice teetered somewhere between bafflement and outrage.

"You heard me, Lindsay. Templeton phones the big chief, who learns all about your relationship with Bishop Finatti. Even your uncle, the publisher, won't be able to save your ass on this one."

Templeton's jaw dropped and she stopped fighting for the phone. A moment of silence passed at the other end of the line.

Then, stiffly, St. John said, "Anthony Finatti and I are acquainted, through some fundraising work that I did before I came to the *Times*. There's nothing improper in that."

"You and Finatti are more than acquainted, Lindsay."

"We're friends, yes." She sounded like a woman who suddenly found herself on the high wire, trying not to look down. "Anthony is a fine man. Devoted to his faith, as I am. I respect him enormously."

"What did you buy him for Christmas, Lindsay?"

"Excuse me?"

"Slippers, a nice sweater, silk pajamas for those cold nights when the two of you slip into bed together?"

"How dare you!"

"You and Bishop Finatti are lovers, Lindsay. Have been for quite some time, by the look of things."

"This conversation is over, Mr. Justice." St. John's voice faltered badly. "Put Alexandra back on the line, immediately."

Instead, I rattled off some damning details—the name of the store where she'd done her Christmas shopping, the Chinese takeout for two, the street and house number where she and Finatti kept their secret love nest. "What's the name of the little dog, Lindsay? That's about all I don't know."

This time, the silence was longer. I could only imagine what Lindsay St. John was going through at the other end, how fast her mind must be working, how quickly so many of her hopes and ambitions were imploding. Not to mention her concern for the fallout her beloved was certain to suffer if any of this became public knowledge.

"Trixie." She spoke more staunchly now, mustering what dignity she could. "She's a Yorkie, and her name is Trixie."

"Your gift to the Bishop?"

"As a matter of fact, Anthony gave Trixie to me."

"I'm sure it was a Hallmark moment."

"Anthony Finatti is a kind and loving man." Her voice took on a different timber, proud, even reverential. "A brilliant man. Perhaps the most brilliant man I've ever known."

"Or screwed," I said.

"I don't expect you to understand. Not someone like you." Her voice lost some of its haughtiness, conceding more ground. "So, what now, Mr. Justice?"

"If this got out, it would pretty much finish your career, given the way you've been managing the news at the paper. As for the good Bishop—"

"What's your point?"

"I assume you'll be resigning."

"That would seem a fait accompli, wouldn't it?"

"Would tomorrow morning be convenient?"

"That's awfully soon."

"If you're gone by tomorrow, Lindsay, I'll keep what I know to myself." I glanced at Templeton, whose mouth was still agape. "I think Templeton would be willing to do the same." She nodded rapidly. A moment passed, with no response. "Lindsay? Are you there?"

"Yes, I'm here."

"Do we have a deal?"

"Yes, we have a deal."

"I'll sign off then, and let Templeton get her work done."

"You really are quite the amateur detective, aren't you?" St. John made the words sound like a lament for us both. "Imagine what you might have accomplished, Mr. Justice, if you'd been able to continue working as a reporter."

"Believe me, I have." I motioned Templeton to the phone. "I'm putting Alex back on. You can patch her through to the desk. Meanwhile, someone needs to put a hold on the front page, lead story, with plenty of jump. You can do that, can't you, Lindsay? Your final act, before leaving the paper."

"You're enjoying this, aren't you?"

"Less than you might think."

I handed the phone to Templeton, who got down to business. Roughly an hour later we were driving back up the mountain, while Templeton chattered excitedly about the stunning turn of events. I wasn't really listening. I was staring out the window, thinking about the makeshift graveyard up the road, and the little skeletons resting there in the cold earth.

As we neared the cabin, we saw DeWinter standing in the middle of the road, his cell phone to his ear. He finished the call as we pulled over and reached the T-Bird before either of us was out. He made a small, tight rolling motion with one hand. Templeton lowered her window.

DeWinter leaned in. "I just got off with a watch commander, down in L.A. We need to get back. There's been more trouble. Bishop Finatti's dead."

"Finatti?" Templeton was pulling out her notebook.

"Ambushed in his car behind a Mexican restaurant, not quite

an hour ago. Looks like an act of pure rage—whoever killed him pumped eight or nine slugs into him."

"Lindsay St. John is probably learning about it right now," I said. To my surprise, I felt sympathy for the lady. "Gotta be tough, losing your career and your sweetheart all in one day."

Templeton, however, was all business. "What else," she said to DeWinter, while scribbling furiously in her notebook.

"There was cash all over Finatti's car, large denominations. A passenger escaped, although he may have been wounded. Hispanic male, forty to fifty."

"Pablo Zuniga," I speculated, "getting a payoff."

"Fits Zuniga's description," DeWinter said, "right down to the missing ear and fingers. Witnesses saw him running off, bleeding around the belly. We're checking the hospitals but I don't figure him to run that risk. He's probably dressing his own wound and looking for a way out of town, now that the heat's been turned up. We've alerted the border patrol down south."

"What about the shooter?" Templeton asked, without looking up.

"No one saw the shooter."

She raised her eyes. "No description at all?"

DeWinter shook his head. "But they found nine-millimeter shell casings near the crime scene. Not that it tells us a whole lot."

Across the road, deputies adjusted the positions of the portable lights. Inside the fence, Father Blackley's old property had become an island of illumination in the encroaching darkness. Under the bright beams, several criminalists knelt at the graves, scraping and bagging evidence, doing their meticulous work.

Templeton had the story of her life. Once, I'd lived for moments like this. Now, I'd give just about anything not to be involved, not to know what I knew. One thing I knew was that

Nick Gash kept a gun, a nine-millimeter Ruger, and harbored the kind of rage toward Anthony Finatti that could make him want to empty a gun into a man the way I'd once done.

I didn't tell DeWinter that. I wanted to find Nick on my own, if I could, and convince him to turn himself in. Because if DeWinter and his fellow cops caught up with Nick before I did, someone else was likely to die, and that didn't appeal to me at the moment. It wasn't that I loved Nick Gash with all my heart, that I'd do anything for the chance to walk away with him one day hand and hand into the sunset, with violins playing. It wasn't like that at all.

It was this: I felt a deep and abiding kinship with Nick, as if our souls were fused by a unique kind of pain and longing. We were members of a special brotherhood, admitted as boys and anointed by Fr. Stuart Blackley, whose ghost hovered over our lives, whispering in the dark, haunting our dreams. I'd gone in search of Father Blackley and come up empty-handed. Now I had Nick Gash, as if Father Blackley had delivered him into my hands like a long-lost brother.

I couldn't abandon Nick now, any more than I could cut off my arm or gouge out my remaining eye. My fate and Nick's were intertwined to the end, whatever that might be. Maybe Nick was even meant to provide the conclusion to my autobiography, messier than my editor and readers might have hoped for, but some kind of coda just the same. Given all that had happened, and how fast things were moving, I sensed that the end wasn't far off and awaited us both back in Los Angeles, the City of Angels.

DeWinter was right—it was time to go back. Time to put the ghost to rest.

FORTY

While Lieutenant DeWinter investigated yet another murder, and Templeton reported on the unfolding events, I left several messages for Nick Gash that went unanswered. During that week, I also returned for my final sittings with Dr. Nathan Levy, watching him become more pleased and excited each time, until my moment arrived to be fitted with a new eye.

It was the last Wednesday in November, at half past three. I followed Dr. Levy down the hallway to the little room with the soft window light. He washed his hands in a small sink, dried them, then sat down next to me with the small table between us. On a tissue was a plastic eye with a blue iris, as hard and smooth as a finely polished gemstone. Dr. Levy picked it up and showed it to me in the palm of his hand—the domed front, the concave back, the edges rounded and buffed so they wouldn't cut. My new eye weighed about half an ounce, he said, and, with proper care, would last for many years.

"You ready?"

I nodded and he peeled off my bandage. He stuck a rubber suction device with a half inch nub to the dark blue pupil, dipped the eye in a sterile solution, then gently pried wide the lids of my left eye socket. Pinching the nub of the suction cup, he inserted the prosthetic eye, bottom edge first, then worked the rest of it in under the lids until it was snug. It felt odd but not uncomfortable as he adjusted the eye into place. He turned my face to the window, studying both eyes intently, scanning from one to the other.

He sat back, grinning. "Not bad work for an old man. How does it feel?"

"Big."

"They always feel that way at first. Your original eye was soft and flexible. If it still feels uncomfortable in a week or two, we'll cut it down a little." He reached for a hand mirror. "By the way, the tear duct is intact. You've got no problem there."

"I've never been the weepy kind."

He winked. "Always nice to have it just in case."

He handed me a mirror. The eye was a flawless match, right down to the finest veins and the tiniest silver flecks in the iris.

"I can't tell the difference. What can I say? It's beautiful."

Dr. Levy patted my knee, beaming. "If you're happy, Benjamin, I've done my job."

I stepped into the hallway and across to the elevators, and punched the down button. While I waited, I examined my new eye in a mirror on the nearest wall, both pleased and amazed. I was still admiring it as the elevator doors rolled open behind me, and a diminutive, dark-haired woman stepped out. A first I couldn't place the pretty face. Without seeing me, she turned away, toward Dr. Levy's office door.

I spun, calling after her. "Mrs. Sandoval? Teresa?"

She stopped and faced me, looking just as frightened as the last time I'd seen her at the house on Carondelet. "Mr. Justice, I'm sorry to bother you like this. I called Miss Templeton at the newspaper. She told me I might find you here."

"It must be urgent."

"The police phoned us this morning. They used Lucy's dental records to identify one of the children up in the mountains. Lucy was the third child they found."

"I'm sorry."

She shook her head. "No, it's better this way. At least we know." Then, more insistently, she said, "There are things I need to say, Mr. Justice. Things I should have told someone a long time ago."

"Why now?"

"My husband and I are flying back to the Philippines tonight. Taking the children. It's not safe here."

"There's a coffee shop downstairs." I punched the down button again. "Let's talk there."

Teresa Sandoval sat across from me in a corner booth away from the windows, where we both felt safer. I ordered a slice of pie with coffee, but she said she wanted nothing, while insisting on paying.

Until my order came, she talked about Lucy, what a blessing the little girl had been to the family, how she could rest beside her mother now in the family burial plot, while their souls lived with the angels. I'd never bought into the notion of eternal salvation but I kept my mouth shut and let her talk. If Teresa Sandoval felt better, imagining a heavenly afterlife, I wasn't about to spoil it for her.

Finally, as I sipped my coffee and ate my pie, she worked up her courage and addressed more earthly matters. "Before, when you came to our house, I told you about how good Bishop Doyle was to my sister Bing when she first came to this country."

"How he helped her with her pregnancy, got her into nursing school, assisted her with her immigration papers, helped her get a job. Yes, I remember."

"He was like a saint to Bing," Teresa went on. "She worshiped him. After he became a cardinal, she had less contact with him, of course. But she always sent him a small gift at Christmas and on his birthday, something nice that she could afford, and he always sent a thank you note in return. He was very decent to her. And Bing was very proud to be acknowledged by such a great man."

Teresa broke off as the waitress stopped to warm my coffee. "When Lucy disappeared—eleven years ago now—Bing was in great distress, as you can imagine. The police promised to investigate, but there were so many cases of missing children. We knew we needed to do more. Bing went to see Cardinal Doyle, to ask if he might use his position in some way to help find Lucy."

I put my fork down, paying close attention. "She went to the cardinal?"

"Bing told us that he was very upset by what had happened. Cardinal Doyle asked Bing many questions. He wanted to know if anyone had seemed unusually interested in Lucy—you know, in a way that didn't seem normal."

"Someone from outside the family."

"Bing could think of only one person. Our pastor, the priest at our church."

"Stuart Blackley," I said.

Teresa nodded. "Father Blackley had taken Lucy on outings, to his cabin in the mountains, also to other places."

"Alone?"

"Sometimes."

"How could a parent—?"

"Bing's faith was very deep, Mr. Justice. Her trust in the church was unshakable. The idea that a priest would do something to a child—it was unthinkable."

"And what did Cardinal Doyle do, when he learned of Father Blackley's interest in Lucy?"

"He told Bing that he would personally investigate. The next day, he came to our house and told us that Father Blackley could not have done something like that. He assured us that Father Blackley had been away at a retreat with Bishop Finatti the day Lucy was taken."

"And you never told the police about Father Blackley?"

"Why would we, Mr. Justice? Cardinal Doyle himself had

assured us that Father Blackley was not involved. He also warned us that if we mentioned anything like that to the police, or to anyone else, the enemies of the church would use it against us. He came to my house, to meet personally with Bing and me. The cardinal! Can you imagine?"

"It must have been very persuasive."

"That same day, he promised Bing that if a tragedy had befallen Lucy, that if we lost her, he would name the new cathedral in her memory. St. Lucy's, that was to be the name. Bing was so happy, Mr. Justice. She cried and fell to her knees and kissed his hand. It helped make losing Lucy just a little more bearable."

"Not too long after that," I said, "Father Blackley retired from the Church. Then he died in an accident, hiking in the mountains. At least that's the way it looked."

She nodded. "After Lucy was taken from us, Bing rededicated herself to God and the Church. She even considered joining a convent, becoming a nun. In the end, she decided that nursing the sick was her calling, her way of serving the Lord. We kept hoping we'd find Lucy, or that she'd come back to us. We spent all the money we had to find her, so much time, but we never did."

"Then, a few weeks ago," I said, "Bing read Joe Soto's column in the *L.A. Times*. After all these years, and with hundreds of priests exposed as pedophiles, she saw Father Blackley in a different light. Is that what happened, Teresa?"

Again, she nodded. "Bing showed me the column. Like my sister, I was shocked, horrified. We realized that Father Blackley may have taken Lucy after all."

"And that Cardinal Doyle must have known about Father Blackley, and covered for him."

"Bing was shattered, Mr. Justice. You can imagine. Then she became angry. I'd never seen her like that."

"Did she try to contact the cardinal?"

"By then, she knew it was pointless. You see, he'd already announced that the cathedral was to be named St. Agnes, long before Mr. Soto wrote his column. Bing had tried to reach the cardinal, to remind him of his promise to name the church St. Lucy's. But Cardinal Doyle had never responded. It was as if he'd shut Bing completely out of his life."

"Finatti probably had a hand in that. I doubt that Bing's letters ever reached the cardinal."

"When Bing saw Mr. Soto's column, she wrote directly to him, and sent a copy to Cardinal Doyle. Like I said, she was very angry with him."

"Then she learned of Joe Soto's death, and got scared."

"Both of us were scared, Mr. Justice. I'm still scared."

"You believe that Bing was pushed from that hospital roof, don't you? To keep her quiet about Father Blackley."

"About that, and other things."

"What other things, Teresa?"

She glanced at her watch. "I should go. We're flying out in the morning."

She started to rise. I put out a hand to gently stop her. "Bishop Finnati's dead, Teresa. Pablo Zuniga's a hunted man. If you went to the police—"

Her eyes flickered fearfully. "It's not so simple, Mr. Justice."

I took her hand, which was trembling. "What other things, Teresa?"

"When you were in my home, you saw a picture of Lucy?"

"Briefly, from across the room. I was on my way out."

Teresa Sandoval dug into her handbag, pulled out a wallet, opened it. She flipped through a set of family photos, found the one she was looking for, and displayed it to me. It was a school photo of a beautiful little girl in uniform. This time, I took a minute to study the face more closely, seeing more clearly the features I'd only glimpsed before.

"May I keep this, Teresa?"

She nodded, and I slipped the photo into my shirt pocket. She placed a few small bills on the check, smiled briefly, and hurried out, into the early dusk.

FORTY-ONE

I followed Teresa Sandoval home, made sure she was safely inside, then swung over to Santa Monica Boulevard and drove west into the glare of headlights. Not quite twenty minutes later, I crossed the West Hollywood city limits and turned left into the neighborhood where Nick Gash lived.

It was a typical early evening for this part of West Hollywood—men and women arriving home from work, couples out walking their dogs, senior citizens trudging back from their Early Bird discount dinners. It all looked so ordinary and hospitable. Yet I still felt tremulous as I parked the Mustang under a jacaranda not fifty feet from where Pablo Zuniga had grabbed me the night he'd carved me up. I kept my head swiveling, surveying the street and sidewalks, as I hurried to Nick's building and through the creaking front gate.

Several times, I pressed the buzzer to his unit but got no answer. Twice, residents passed through, on their way in. I asked them if they'd seen Nick Gash in recent days. One said she hadn't; the other said he didn't know who Nick Gash was. Neither would let me in when I tried to enter with them.

"Just to see if he's in and not answering," I pleaded. "To make sure he's OK."

"Sorry," the man said. "No exceptions."

I pressed the buzzer yet again. Still no answer. The chill got to me and I zipped up my jacket. Then I held the buzzer down long enough to annoy Nick if he was inside. As I let up, I decided I was wasting my time, that Nick was probably long gone by now after what he'd done, maybe even out of the country. I was turning to go when I heard the gate creak behind me. I swung around expectantly, hoping it might be Nick. But it wasn't Nick at all.

It was Pablo Zuniga, coming up the walkway toward me, no more than forty feet away. He was moving with his head down and his hands in his pockets, with his collar up and a knit cap pulled low for added concealment. But his wasn't a face I was likely to miss or to forget. He looked up, saw the fear in mine, and grinned.

We both ran toward each other at the same moment. I hit him hard, slamming him back into the gate, then took off down a brick walkway to my left as he bounced off the gate to the pavement in a heap. The bricks led me through ferns and ficus trees, dormant azaleas and beds of colorful impatiens. My heart pounded and my feet flew. I dashed across open grass, feeling vulnerable and unprotected but with nowhere else to go. At the far end of the property, I plunged into dense foliage, surrounded by meandering philodendron under a canopy of Japanese maples dropping their delicate, reddish leaves. I knelt down behind a spreading azalea bush to see Zuniga coming across the lawn. He paused halfway, pulling off his cap to listen, his eyes equally alert. His right hand—the one with all its fingers—disappeared into a pocket and came out with a slender object the size of a small cigar. I heard a click, saw a blade appear, catching just enough light to show me its edge and send a tremor through me.

My mind seized on a mantra, a silent prayer. *Don't come, don't come, don't come.*

His eyes scanned the shadowy landscape around me. I made the mistake of ducking lower. His eyes caught the movement, then settled on my location like radar locking in. It was as if all his other senses were at work, pointing him to where I was.

Trained police dogs often hunt down concealed fugitives by sniffing out the special scent triggered in the human body by extreme fear. That was what Pablo Zuniga was like at that moment. He'd sniffed me out like a human K-9.

His lips stretched wide—the taunting, ridiculing grin.

Then he was moving forward, directly toward me, waving the knife in front of him as if he was warming up his carving hand. I saw blood on the left side of his shirt, around the soft part of his belly between navel and hip. Where Nick must have hit him with a stray bullet, I thought, while he emptied his Ruger into Anthony Finatti, or winged Zuniga as he fled the car.

Don't come, don't come, don't come.

When he was close enough that I could see the scar that ran from ear to mouth, I rose and bounded away. I made for the street, tromping through shrubbery, flailing my arms through low-hanging branches, anything to put some distance between us. My foot struck a tree stump on my blind side and I went crashing down. The fetid smell of damp soil and leaf rot filled my nostrils. I was up a second later, staggering on, hearing him thrash through the growth behind me, as he gained ground.

Within seconds, I found myself facing the wrought-iron fence that bordered the property. It stood a foot above me, at seven feet. I grabbed the spikes at the top, struggled frantically to pull myself up. I was nearly over when I felt his hand on my ankle, pulling me down. I fought him maniacally, scratching and kicking, trying to get a piece of him, something to grab so that I might use an old wrestling move and maybe gain an advantage or at least throw him off. But it was useless; he was more skilled at this than I, quicker and just as strong. In short order, he threw me on to my back and straddled me, pinning my throat with one hand while he thrust the point of his knife at my good eye. I caught his wrist with my left hand, gripped it, kept the knife away, but barely. All of it happened fast, a flurry of frantic movements, not a second wasted, every motion fraught with terrible possibilities. Yet it also felt like time had slowed to a deathly crawl, everything a blur, the sounds muffled, the colors muted, the violence and panic blending into a slow motion ballet.

"So they gave the *puta* a pretty new eye." Zuniga's mouth curled to show his broken teeth. "Now, I cut out the other one. Except this time, you don't need no new eye, because this time, you be dead, *pinche cabron*. You get away from *el Mutilador* one time, but not two time."

I jammed my right hand between his legs, grabbed as much of him as I could, and squeezed with every ounce of strength I had. His grin turned to a grimace and a groan issued forth that told me he was in serious pain. While I crushed his gonads, and his groan rose to a keening, he held fast to my throat and kept the blade level with my eye. I turned my head, thrashing and screaming, figuring someone on the street had to hear. The tip of the blade was an inch away, maybe two. I squeezed harder between his legs, twisting his testicles, trying to rip them from his body. His face contorted but still he pressed forward with the knife. All I had was my death grip—one hand on his wrist, one on his balls—and nothing else to stop him. My arms and shoulders ached from fighting him; the muscles grew tight, weary. Somewhere inside the mania with which I resisted, I sensed myself weakening. The knife moved forward, an almost infinitesimal thrust. Zuniga grinned through his pain, knowing he was winning. Then I remembered the blood on his shirt, on the left side of his stomach.

I let go of his balls and thrust my hand into his wound. My fingers found the opening and I drove them in, ripping his flesh, feeling the gush of warm blood and tissue. He screamed horribly, let go of my throat, grabbed at the hand that was now inside him, ripping him apart. In the same moment I threw him off, scrambling on my hands and knees, trying to find my feet. But the second I was up, I went down. He had me again, by an ankle, and this time I knew I was finished.

I twisted enough to see him atop me again and the knife coming down. I threw up my hands in one last, feeble attempt to ward off the blade.

Then I heard three gunshots—*pop, pop, pop*—in rapid succession. Zuniga's eyes widened and he stiffened, rising up off me while still astraddle. Two more pops sounded. Zuniga jerked like a puppet, his arms flapping like broken wings. I saw blood spurt from his neck and chest, heard him gasp. He fell away from me onto his back into a bed of moldy leaves, struggling for air, wrenched with convulsions. His last voluntary act was to reach for the crucifix hanging from his neck and mumble words in Spanish I didn't understand. Then his mouth opened in a final grimace, expelling his last breath, while his eyes rolled upward. He didn't move again.

I stayed down, afraid more shots might come, hearing footsteps getting closer. Enormous relief engulfed me while I tried to shake off the shock of the last few minutes. I felt close to heaving but nothing came up. Time continued to unwind in slow motion, but gradually regained its natural momentum, the sense of seconds ticking by in their regular cadence. I looked over to see Claude DeWinter, crouching as he came, gripping his Beretta in both hands, keeping it pointed at Zuniga.

My teeth were rattling, so I attempted a little humor. "Nice shooting, Lieutenant. All that time on the practice range finally paid off."

"Shut up, Justice."

DeWinter knelt, checked for a pulse in Zuniga's neck, found none. He flipped Zuniga on his stomach and put him in handcuffs, anyway. Then he barked into a radio, stating he had a code four on an officer-involved shooting, giving his location and position. I saw sweat on his face and noticed he was shaking almost as badly as I was.

Finally, he looked my way. "You hurt?"

"Only my self-respect."

"You can say that again. Get up, turn your ass around."

When I was on my feet, he took me by one arm and led me roughly back to the open patch of lawn, where a younger detective came running. In the distance, sirens wailed.

"In there," DeWinter said to the other plainclothes, pointing back the way we'd come. "We'll probably have a crowd soon. You know the drill."

The other detective nodded and kept moving. I brushed myself off.

"Talk," DeWinter said.

"Up in the mountains, you mentioned nine-millimeter shell casings found near the crime scene where Bishop Finatti was shot. Nick Gash owns a nine-millimeter Ruger. The last time I saw him, he promised me he'd take care of some unfinished business."

"You decided to play cop, find Nick on your own."

"I thought I might do some good, get him to turn himself in. Mentally, he's on a pretty tight wire."

"Another good reason to leave it to us."

"So he can end up on a slab, like Zuniga?"

"I just saved your life, you fucking ingrate. In case you didn't notice."

"I'll send flowers and candy, Lieutenant." More cops were coming down the walk, pouring on to the property. "I take it you had this place staked out."

DeWinter nodded. "Nick's father called us, told us about the gun. He also mentioned that some accelerants and explosives are missing from the company warehouse. In the words of Charles Gash, 'Enough to destroy half the Vatican, if the thief had a mind to.' Nick had access, plus a key."

"Accelerants and explosives?"

"That mean something to you?"

"The cathedral," I said.

"What about it?"

"It stands for everything Nick hates, for all the suffering he's been put through."

"Tomorrow's Thanksgiving. Nick and the other workers ended their shifts early today. They won't be back until Friday."

"Exactly. Nick has the place all to himself."

"Shit." DeWinter pulled out his radio.

"We've got to get over there, Lieutenant."

"You're staying put. So am I. I'm up to my butt in an officer-involved shooting, with a fatality. We go nowhere until the O.I.S. team clears us to go."

Out on the street, sirens were screaming like banshees, while cops swarmed the property, their eyes alert and the veins in their necks pumping. Residents appeared on balconies to gawk while others crowded the lawn, where uniformed officers kept them back. DeWinter stepped aside to talk to a captain, his voice low, huddling so that I was behind him. I edged away, toward the onlookers.

I stopped at a spigot to wash my bloody hand and gulp water. Then I slipped inconspicuously into the crowd, back to the front gate and out to the sidewalk. The last thing I heard through the foliage and trees as I ran to the Mustang was Lieutenant DeWinter, bellowing my name at the top of his sizable lungs.

FORTY-TWO

I was still several blocks away when I saw flames rising from St. Agnes Cathedral, searing the night sky. Helicopters circled overhead, while converging fire vehicles jammed the streets, their sirens creating a spine-jarring wall of sound. I parked three blocks south of Serra Boulevard, figuring I wouldn't get much closer. Officers had used their patrol cars to barricade the streets, but the curious streamed through on foot, many of them Hispanics from poor neighborhoods nearby, making the sign of the cross, tears flowing down their faces. There were too many for the police to hold back, and they were too determined. It wasn't difficult to slip in among them and be swept along, toward the flames.

When we reached Serra Boulevard, pandemonium prevailed. A patrol car had skidded out of control, knocking down a section of fence along the north side of the construction site. Hundreds of civilians poured through, widening the gap as they went. The clamor and hysteria was expanding exponentially, feeding from within, like the fire itself. I went with them, pushing past helpless cops and fire officials who were shoved aside or knocked to the ground. There was no sense of mob violence, not the kind one saw in riots, when thousands of men and women ran amuck, in a frenzy of looting and destruction. This crowd was different, drawn forward in quiet religious fervor and a growing sense of horror, toward the spectacular conflagration that consumed the symbol of their most fervent hopes and dreams. For many of these people, who had so little, their faith was everything, embodied in St. Agnes Cathedral.

Within minutes, I found myself out on the plaza, staring up with all the others, awestruck. Large sections of the cathedral were in flames, which crackled like gunfire and cast their illumination widely, while sending up plumes of thick black smoke. Water rained down on all sides from hoses on the ground and from water cannons atop tanker trucks. The plaza—paved since my last visit—was filled with the faithful, weeping, shrieking, or falling to their knees in mumbled prayer. I saw a mother clutch her little boy, burying his face against her to keep him from seeing, while she looked upward with an expression of disbelief. I followed her eyes to the cathedral's pinnacle, the towering campanile.

That's when I saw Nick.

He stood in the campanile's empty bell tower, in the glare of police searchlights. The flames, climbing from below, had reached to within fifteen or twenty feet of him. From a distance, firefighters trained steady streams of water on him, in a futile effort to keep the voracious flames at bay. Out on the plaza, Charles Gash was on his knees, his hands clasped and raised above him, pleading with his son to come down while there was still time. Firefighters tried to drag the older man to a safer distance but he fought them off, keeping his attention fixed on Nick. Standing behind Gash was a middle-aged woman, thin and pale, who I took to be Nick's mother. As I looked on, she bowed her head and crossed herself, then allowed herself to be led away by a policewoman, glancing back as if imprinting in her memory a final, grotesque vision of her doomed son.

Nick showed no response to any of it. He stared out across the plaza, across the elevated freeway and the west side of the city, as if he'd finally risen above it—as if nothing could touch him now, as if no one could ever hurt him again. The spotlights struck him with their blinding glare but he didn't appear to even blink.

His face was as rigid as a mask, and strangely calm.

"Justice!"

Templeton pushed her way through the crowd. I gave her a quick rundown of the Pablo Zuniga shooting, which she'd already heard about. While she took notes, I told her pointedly that DeWinter had saved my life, and asked her to write it up that way.

"He must be furious with you, just the same."

I shrugged. "The usual."

She suddenly stopped scribbling, studying my face. "Your eye," she said. "You got your new eye."

"Forget about my eye. Tell me what's going on."

We watched the flames inch up the campanile. "Nick Gash wired explosives throughout the building," she explained. "At least that's what he told firefighters when they arrived. He convinced them that he's got the entire cathedral booby-trapped; that if the firefighters go in, the loss of life will be extreme."

"They're going to let it burn?"

"The chief's keeping his firefighters back. Says the risk is too great, without victims inside. For now, they're fighting the fire from a distance."

"Nick's going out in style," I said.

"Maybe you could talk to him. Through a bullhorn. Maybe you could convince him to come down, if that's still possible."

I shook my head. "No. Nick's on his own now."

I felt tears rise up, but fought them off, the way I always did, the way I'd learned to do early in life, when my father had laid his belt across my bare butt until the welts rose, while I refused to give him the satisfaction of seeing me cry. I forced the tears down, the way I'd done when Father Blackley had turned away from me and I'd realized, without really understanding at that young age, that his love had been hollow, a sham. I'd sensed—

without being able to put words to it—that he'd used me for his peculiar needs and pleasure, that I'd been nothing but a lovely object to him, whose innocence was the very thing that spurred his craving and compulsion. I'd wanted to cry but I wouldn't talk like that. Now I needed to cry but I couldn't. Not for Nick, not for myself. Maybe I'd forgotten how, or never learned.

"There's no turning back for Nick," I said. "He has to see it through. I'd probably do the same, if I were him."

"You're scaring me, Justice. I wish you wouldn't talk like that."

I offered her the briefest smile, trying to be kinder. "I understand him, that's all." I drew my eyes away from Templeton and up to Nick again. "He's finally in control. They can't muzzle him now, or buy his silence, or crush him with their power."

"He's about to die, for God sake."

"Yes, but on his own terms."

A nearby commotion drew our attention away from the bell tower. Cardinal Kendall Doyle, dressed in red robes, forced his way through the crowd. Several police officers and firefighters beseeched him to stay back. Doyle pushed past them, sweeping his eyes across the immensity of the burning structure.

"For the love of God, save my beautiful church!" He made the sign of the cross, then spread his hands plaintively. "I beg you, do something to save it!"

Photographers and camera crews pressed forward, capturing the image of the impassioned Cardinal framed by the hellish flames. Templeton opened her notebook and jotted down what she was seeing. While she scribbled in her reporter's shorthand, I reminded her that Pablo Zuniga and Bishop Finatti were both dead. "Only Cardinal Doyle can answer certain questions now. Only Doyle can tell us who ordered and paid for three murders—Joe, Bing Crisologo, Father Blackley."

"It had to be Finatti," Templeton said.

"Did it?"

"He spent time in Mexico, where he must have connected with Zuniga. Handled all the lawsuits. Personally covered up for Father Blackley all those years. And he was with Zuniga when he was killed, making what was surely some kind of payment."

"Sure, he could be the only one."

"You're not suggesting Cardinal Doyle was behind it?"

"Or someone higher in the chain of authority."

She arched her brows in disbelief. "The Vatican?"

"We'll never know, will we?" I shrugged. "It's not a story anyone could ever prove, or would ever dare to print."

Cardinal Doyle was on the move again, striding past the statue of St. Agnes. Templeton and I followed with the rest of the pack. Doyle pulled up as his eyes fell on the kneeling figure of Charles Gash. Gash was sobbing, his head raised, calling to Nick but getting no reaction. For a moment, Doyle looked confused. Then he spotted Nick, standing impassively fifteen stories up, only a few feet above the encroaching flames.

"The boy." Cardinal Doyle sounded astonished, disbelieving. "The boy did all this?" His eyes dropped to the fourth floor window of the prayer room. "The Bible—we've got to save my Bible!"

Just then, the crowd let out a collective cry as the campanile gave way. In a matter of seconds, it collapsed in a cascade of sparks and embers. I watched Nick get sucked into its flaming vortex, and instinctively crossed myself. I swallowed hard but threw up a wall against my tears, banished them. As the fiery debris came down, with Nick somewhere inside, Charles Gash rose to his feet with a wail. He ran toward the flaming pyre consuming his son as cops and firefighters went after him, drawing the attention of the crowd.

"The Bible!" Cardinal Doyle screamed at them as if they were idiots, wasting their time on a distraught father when his precious family Bible needed rescuing. "This way! To the prayer room! For the love of God, save the book!"

But no one was listening. Like the cops and firefighters, the cameras—always on the hunt for cinematic action—had followed Charles Gash as he raced toward the heap of flames and sparks. The crowd had moved with them. Cardinal Doyle watched for a moment, incredulous. Then he dashed off, in the direction of the cathedral's main entrance. He hesitated, a hand at his face, staring at the gaping opening that still awaited its ornate copper doors, as if confronting the jaws of hell.

A moment later, grabbing the folds of his robe, Cardinal Doyle ascended the steps. As he disappeared inside, I sprinted after him.

"Justice, don't!"

Templeton was calling after me, hollering "Come back!" and "Don't be a fool!" But something beyond reason propelled me now, a terrible fury that had been driving me most of my life, demanding to be heard. For me, as for Nick Gash, turning back was not an option.

FORTY-THREE

My immediate impression upon entering the burning building was how relatively little heat and smoke I encountered, how little fire was directly around me.

Then I realized that much of the roof above had burned through, allowing smoke to escape and water from the hoses to pour down, into an area that was mostly concrete and tile. Within seconds, I was drenched, and grateful for it. To my left, I saw the empty elevator bank engulfed in flames, which rose from the mausoleum floor and interior walls upward through the shafts. The fire had not yet reached the stairwell, so I started up for the prayer room. The smoke became heavier as I climbed, but as I reached the third landing and looked up, I was able to glimpse the cardinal's red robes as he disappeared around the banister to the next level.

I emerged from the stairwell feeling a blast of heat from the fourth floor elevator openings, which glowed from the fire raging below. Each opening was barred by two-by-fours nailed across as a barricade, as they'd been before, although the barriers on the first three floors had ignited and were charred. I turned the other way, crossing from the elevators through the smoke, until I found an open doorway. I stepped through, into the prayer room where I'd confronted Cardinal Doyle a few weeks before.

To my left, I could see the nave fully engulfed, billowing with smoke as the flames devoured the beautiful tapestries and cherrywood pews and anything else that was pervious to fire. Surely, I thought, the floor beneath my feet was just as vulnerable. It was only a matter of time before it too became engulfed. I'd imagined my death more times than I could count, particularly when I'd first been infected with the virus and the future had seemed so uncertain. But the absurd notion of being burned alive while trapped in a house of God had never occurred in my most dire imaginings. The thought of being incinerated terrified me, almost enough to drive me back, to make me turn and flee. But not quite, because at that moment Cardinal Doyle was almost within my grasp.

Just ahead, he staggered across the prayer room, spinning in confusion, lost in the thickening smoke, searching frantically for his cherished book. He was coughing harshly, his eyes red and weeping. Finally, he stumbled almost accidentally into the far wall, then felt his way along its surface until he reached the alcove where the Bible rested behind glass. Placing a hand against the wall, he bent to remove a shoe, then began striking the heel against the panels of the case. Five, six, seven times he struck, but failed to shatter the glass. I could see him growing weak, gasping for air, on the verge of collapse. I picked up a charred chunk of tile from the floor and crossed to the alcove, where Doyle was stooped and gagging.

"May I help, Cardinal?"

He looked up, startled, first at my face, then at the tile I raised to show him.

"God must have sent you!"

"That must be it, Your Eminence."

"Yes, yes! Please, break the glass. We must hurry!"

"Step back then."

With one good strike, I smashed the glass. I reached in, snatched the Bible, and held it out to him. When he grabbed for it, I drew it back.

"First some questions, Cardinal."

"Now? What kind of questions?"

"Pablo Zuniga's dead. Did you know that?"

Doyle coughed violently, waved a hand in front of his face. "Quickly, we must go." He stretched out his hands. "Please, the Bible. It means nothing to you. But to me—"

"Didn't you hear me, Cardinal? Zuniga—he's dead."

His weepy eyes regarded me as if I was mad. "Why are you telling me this? Of what concern is this to me?"

"Bishop Finatti's also dead. So is Nick Gash. It's just you and me now, Cardinal, with some matters left unsettled."

There was a rumble and crash behind him, from the nave. Flaming timbers fell from the rafters. Water cascaded in, the only thing keeping us alive.

"We must get out of here." Doyle stretched out his hands plaintively. "Please, let me have it and we'll go. You'll be rewarded, I promise you."

"The way you rewarded Zuniga to kill Joe Soto and Bing Crisologo, and Stuart Blackley all those years ago?"

"For God sake, man—"

"Who gave the order, Cardinal?"

"I wouldn't know anything about it!" He cried out as more timbers fell. "Do you want to die like this? Do you care so little for your own life?"

Before I could reply, flames billowed from the nave, sucked in by the air of the prayer room and the open window on the other side. They singed my beard and the hair on my hands and arms. As I ducked away, Cardinal Doyle snatched the Bible with one hand while pushing me to the floor with the other. Within moments, as he dashed back the way he'd come, I lost sight of him in the smoke. I stayed on my hands and knees, below the worst of it, crawling after him until I reached the door. Outside, on the fourth-floor landing, I caught sight of him again floundering in the choking smoke, somewhere between the stairwell and the elevators. I stood and moved directly behind him. When he turned, suddenly facing me, he cried out, clutching the Bible to his chest.

"Tell me what you know, Cardinal."

"Nothing! I know nothing! I'm a man of God, not a murderer!"

I moved forward, backing him up. "I don't believe you, Cardinal."

"I've answered you, now let me go!"

I pointed at the Bible in his hands. "Swear it on that Bible, Cardinal." I stepped closer, my eyes on his. "Swear it on the soul of your little sister." His eyes grew jumpy, conflicted. I pressed closer still, until only inches separated us. "Swear it before the Holy Trinity."

All around us, flames were roaring, smoke was billowing, burning debris was tumbling down. I was wrenched with coughing now myself, and felt seriously lightheaded.

"If we don't go now," Doyle shouted, "we're going to die here!"

"It's time to face our judgment then. Are you ready for that, Cardinal? Your moment of judgment?"

His chin trembled and his eyes grew deathly afraid. Suddenly, he whirled and ran blindly through the smoke. A moment later, I heard a clatter and a scream. I staggered through the smoke to the bank of elevators, where I found the barricade across the middle shaft broken, the planks splintered where the Cardinal had crashed through. Inside the shaft, he hung suspended, clutching a loop of steel cable, his feet dangling inches above the flames. The Bible lay on the floor, near the edge of the open shaft.

"I beg you." He reached for me with one hand. "Don't let me die."

"The truth, Your Eminence."

He cried out, drawing up his feet as the flames reached them. "I'm helpless before you. Please, be merciful."

"Kimberly Quimby was helpless, Cardinal. Lucy Crisologo was helpless. How many more do you have on your conscience?"

The flames touched the hem of his crimson cassock, igniting it. "For God's sake, don't let me burn!"

"Who gave Pablo Zuniga his orders, Cardinal?"

He screamed hideously as the length of his robe caught fire.

I reached out for him. Our fingers nearly touched as he stretched desperately for my hand. I withdrew it, reaching instead for the photo of Lucy Crisologo in my breast pocket. I held it out, forcing him to see it.

"Remember Lucy, Cardinal?" He stared, shocked, at the photo. "Remember her mother, Bing, when she was only fifteen, so innocent and submissive?"

He nodded pathetically. "Yes, I remember."

"Remember your promise, to name this church in memory of Lucy?"

"Yes, yes." He moaned as the flames rose up, engulfing him. Then he clamped his eyes shut, crossing himself with his free hand. "Almighty Father, forgive me."

He dropped away, into the flames. I watched them leap and spit, fed by the fuel of his garments. Then the heat became too much and I rose, turning for the stairs.

Claude DeWinter blocked my way. He stood towering over me halfway to the stairwell entrance, covering his mouth with a wet handkerchief. He lowered it, just enough to speak.

"I saw you try to save him," DeWinter said. "You tried to grab him but he fell. That's what I saw, and that's what you say when you give a statement. Got it?"

I nodded.

He stepped past me, picked up the Bible from the floor, then faced me again "You tell Alexandra the same thing." He coughed, put the handkerchief to his mouth for a moment to get some air. "She's a fine woman who doesn't need to be carrying around any more weight on her shoulders, particularly where you're concerned. So you just tell her the same story, so she can write it up that way and maybe sleep tonight. You hear me?"

Again, I nodded.

DeWinter jerked his head toward the stairwell. "Now get out of here."

I found my way back through the smoke, down the stairs, and out into the plaza. The crowd stood in stunned silence, watching the fire reduce the cathedral to a blackened skeleton of concrete and steel. Firefighters and cops immediately converged, but I sent them toward the cathedral, to assist DeWinter. Templeton spotted me from a distance, cried out my name and came running.

Already, I was seeing the tributes to Cardinal Kendall Doyle in my head, hearing the eulogies. He'd be remembered as a man of courage and sacrifice, devoted to God. The media would transform him into a martyr—a great religious figure, who'd given his life trying to save his beloved place of worship. The Vatican would conceal his transgressions, counting on other well-established institutions to go along, and the flock to blindly follow. Down the road, I figured, the Church might even make Cardinal Doyle a saint, naming one or two cathedrals after him.

It didn't really trouble me that much. That's the way the world was, that was how things worked. Most people probably didn't want it any other way, preferring the comfortable illusion to the enormity of the truth, in this and all things.

Anyway, I wasn't so sure I was all that different from Cardinal Doyle, when you got right down to it. We'd both lied, hurt people—even murdered—each in our own way. I knew I'd done things that were wrong, and that bothered me; my shame was deep, palpable, like a wound that would always gape inside me, aching, festering, infecting my system. Maybe that was the difference, I thought—that I had trouble living with what I'd done. The problem was it didn't seem enough.

Templeton reached me, throwing her arms around me, asking if I was OK. I told her I was, then that Cardinal Doyle was dead.

"My God. What happened?"

"You can read it in the police report. Better if you just used that."

"But—"

"DeWinter can give you a quote. He saw the whole thing."

Our eyes connected, and I saw the deep conflict in hers, the friend at odds with the reporter. "OK," she said, "if that's the only statement you're willing want to make."

"About Cardinal Doyle—something you should know. Off the record."

"Why off the record?"

"Because you'll never get it into the paper, anyway, even with Lindsay St. John out of your way. The suits upstairs will just call it wild speculation. They won't want to risk offending and losing massive numbers of readers. Besides, it involves Bing Crisologo—something that happened long ago that she kept a secret and wouldn't want people to know about, even now that she's gone."

Templeton tucked away her pen and notebook. I showed her the photo of Lucy Crisologo. "It's Bing's daughter. Take a good look."

She studied the headshot of the little girl—dark-haired but lighter skinned than her mother, with sparkling green eyes, a button nose, and a solitary mole in the middle of her dimpled chin.

"The resemblance," Templeton said. "If you look closely—"

"Father Blackley couldn't have known he was abducting the Cardinal's child," I said. "It was a grotesque coincidence."

"And a fatal mistake." Templeton glanced from the photo to me, her eyes keen. "Doyle seduced Bing, when she was just a teenager."

"Seduction's a nice word, isn't it?"

"What are you saying, Justice?"

"How much do you know about the Catholic saints, Templeton?"

"Not much. I was raised a Baptist."

"Have you thought about the name Cardinal Doyle chose for his cathedral?"

"It's in memory of his little sister, Agnes. That's no secret."

"There may be another reason, one that not even Doyle himself was aware of. It's said that the guilty mind sometimes works that way, subconsciously."

"This is no time for riddles, Justice. I'm on deadline."

"St. Agnes is the saint who watches over little girls."

"Yes, I read that."

I glanced across the plaza, to the comforting statue of the young girl holding a lamb in her arms, standing tall in the flickering light. "Like many of the saints, St. Agnes has another role. She's also the patron saint for virgins who have suffered rape."

FORTY-FOUR

I stuck to my story, just the way Lieutenant DeWinter had laid it out. He backed me up and things went smoothly enough. Around dawn, the cops cut me loose.

The city was as hushed as a cemetery as I drove across the river into East L.A. All around, ash drifted down like a fine mist. In my rear view mirror, I saw the first light strike the tallest buildings downtown, turning their windows gold. Beyond, smoke continued to rise from the remains of St. Agnes Cathedral, while news choppers careened above like buzzards at the feast.

I found Fr. Ismael Aragon at La Iglesia de la Virgen de la Caridad, kneeling in the garden, busy with a cloth. He rose to meet me as I wound my way along the gravel path. His hair was mussed and he hadn't shaved, so I assumed he'd been up through the night, as I had. As I approached, his face was a mix of emotions, impossible to sort out.

"I wanted to thank you, Father."

"For what?"

"For telling me about the Quimbys, about their missing daughter. It was the pivotal point in the case, the information that helped us turn the corner."

"I wish I'd thought of it sooner. Perhaps you wouldn't have

been injured the way you were." He smiled a little. "I see you have your new eye. They did a good job."

I glanced at the spot where he'd been kneeling. Just off the path, across from a bench, was a modest bronze plaque, set in stone.

IN LOVING MEMORY OF JOSEPH SOTO,
WHO TENDED THIS GARDEN AS A CHILD

"Someone made a donation?"

"Miss Templeton's parents wanted to do something. I suggested this. They also made a generous financial contribution to the church. We can begin restoring the mural now, and do some other things we've needed."

"Her parents? I didn't think they knew about Joe, let alone approved."

"I asked Alexandra if I might speak with them. It seemed important that they know, for Alexandra's sake. She gave her permission."

"Still, the thought of Alex and Joe as a couple—her folks aren't exactly open-minded on that issue."

"You'd be surprised what some people are capable of, if you give them half a chance." He glanced again at the modest memorial. "I was just cleaning it up, wiping away the ash. The church will be busy today, full of people. Especially after what happened last night."

"You'll have your homeboys to help you."

He smiled. "Yes, they'll be here."

I studied him closely for a long moment. "Have you ever molested a child, Father?"

"No." His voice was calm, untroubled.

"Ever thought about it?"

He shook his head, without the slightest hesitation.

"Ever been with a man, Father, in the carnal sense?"

This time he paused, swallowing hard. "No, never. Nor with a woman."

320

"You knew I'd come back to see you, didn't you? Sooner or later."

"It occurred to me that you might."

I reached out, touched his face. He closed his eyes, shuddering, as if no one had touched him that way in all the years he'd been waiting as a grown man—never the blessed physical contact that every human being needs, from birth to death, as much as food or water or oxygen. I stroked his rough beard with the back of my hand, ran my fingertips over the contours of his mouth, touched the lids of his eyes.

"We could be good together, Father." I laid a hand on the slope of his neck, which was warm and moist, even in the cool morning air.

His eyes remained closed. "My relationship is with Jesus Christ, Benjamin. It's absolute, inviolable, as are my vows."

"Other priests have made vows they've broken. Lots of them."

"I intend to honor mine, all the days of my life."

I cupped his neck, leaned close, kissed him on the lips. He kept his eyes shut, as if savoring the moment. "That can't be healthy, Father, denying yourself that way. It's not natural."

"It is for me, Benjamin." When he opened his eyes, they were clear, his gaze unwavering. "It's what I need, more than any other kind of love." His smile was implacable, serene. "I don't expect everyone to support my position, only to allow me my choice. Surely, you of all people can understand that."

The sunlight came over the office rooftop, warming us.

I swallowed with difficulty. "I've done some bad things, Father."

"We all have, Benjamin."

"Terrible things."

"Do you feel like talking now?"

"It's been a long time since my last confession."

"All the more reason. Perhaps we should sit." We stepped over to the bench. As we sat, I dug into my pocket, pulling out

Sister Catherine Timothy's rosary. "Start where you feel most comfortable."

I found myself paralyzed, unable to speak. Father Aragon took my hand in his. "You're with a friend, Benjamin. Someone who loves you. Someone you can trust."

I crossed myself, and pressed the crucifix to my lips. The tears came suddenly, spilling over, hot on my face.

"Bless me, Father," I said, "for I have sinned."